MARKED BY SHADOWS

A SIMPLY CRAFTY PARANORMAL MYSTERY

LISSA KASEY

Marked By Shadows

1st Edition

Copyright © 2020 Lissa Kasey

All rights reserved

Cover Art by Danielle Doolittle

Edited by Indie Pride, LLC

Published by Lissa Kasey

http://www.lissakasey.com

CHAPTER 1

S ilence can be defined in several ways. Sometimes it means late nights indoors with nothing but the sound of a sleeping pet or partner. Sometimes it is a relaxing bath covered in thick bubbles and warm water. Sometimes silence is more the tuning out of noise, like reading in a public place, or hiking down an active trail through the woods on a bright and sunny day.

Rarely is silence the complete absence of sound.

That had been my first mistake.

I had a handful of excuses: a morning fight with Tim; the chill in the air that whipped through my jacket; the vague memory of something someone said on our drive up to the park; and the annoying squawk of some kind of unidentified bird that no one else seemed to hear.

Preoccupied. Not paying attention. My fault.

Those thoughts echoed in my brain often enough as I recalled that day. Parts of it blurry, like the memory of morning sex which led to a fight and me not eating or having coffee before the hike *his* friends insisted on. I hadn't wanted to come at all. Nature was not my thing. I liked cities, technology, and being near people even if I didn't always want to talk to them.

The first part of the hike had been mostly uneventful. Teasing from his friends who weren't supposed to know about the videos we did. I found myself embarrassed, not for the first time, and slowed my step until I was at the back of the group. I'd been planning on leaving sex work, moving on to other things, including a fun craft shop which would give me time to expand my hobbies into a full-time career. Tim pushed back, not wanting the change. My age, always a factor, had become a constant battle point. I was too young to make those decisions, he claimed. Not too young to have sex on camera, but too young to know what I wanted to do with the rest of my life. His gaze strayed to younger men often enough for me to know his interest in me was waning.

Another squawk made me pause and look up, searching the trees for a source of the sound. Never heard a bird like that before, almost like a monkey, or an unusual parrot. Having lived in a half dozen countries in my life, I expected to have seen and heard just about everything. Whatever made that noise, I had never experienced before. A chill raced up my spine and the hint of a cold sweat touched my brow. My gut ached, not from something I ate, but anxiety. Last time it hurt this bad I had been in a classroom in the middle of nowhere China, when men had entered the room with guns and pointed them at my mother who was teaching.

No one had been hurt that day, but fear had taken up solid residence in my stomach and left a lasting impression. I remembered being on my knees outside the building, surrounded by pigeons, thousands of them. Yet despite their numbers, they were silent, mostly still, staring with those dark and eerie eyes. The world had turned motionless, lasted forever, though probably was only a half an hour or so, then the men re-emerged from the school. The birds took off all at once. A terrifying flap of wings as though they would descend on us any second and rip us apart like the gruesome horror movies of old.

Some memories ingrained themselves inside your soul that way. The taint of emotion making them unforgettable. Like that odd squawking. Or the feeling of being watched, which I'd tried to ignore all morning, and brush off as the others looking at me.

High up in the trees, nothing moved that I could tell. No one else seemed to notice, adding to my irritation. I continued up the trail, thankful that it was a wide dirt path, unmistakable through the towering trees and scattered rocks.

I sighed, brain back on high volume as once again I was reminded why I had agreed to this stupid trip. Tim. Our relationship began as a spark. I knew it was a spark. That hot burning attraction, the need to taste him, and wrap my body around him. I had hoped it would blossom into more. It hadn't. Why did I stay?

It came down to comfort, money, and control of course. Not a surprise really. He'd helped me a lot in getting settled in the USA with an income to support myself. The rest I'd done. Saved, built outlines and plans for things I wanted to happen in my life. None of them involved sex on camera. The fact that Tim wanted to film us this morning meant our conversation on the way up had fallen on deaf ears. Sex on camera was tedious. A show or an act. Turn this way, face the camera... not the intimacy I'd wanted with a partner. I often felt like a sex doll beneath him rather than a person. Used instead of cherished.

My mother had taught me to respect myself better. Love, she often reminded me, was a partnership. More than attraction or lust, it meant being comfortable with each other as only true friends could be. Despite how often she and my father argued; they were very different, him with his traditional Japanese values, and her a fiercely independent Irish woman. I could see their adoration for each other. Their affection made me long for something similar, a best friend as well as a lover, a partner and husband.

I gnawed on my lower lip as I followed the group up the trail, my pace a little slower than theirs, more out of my annoyance with them than my inability to keep up. My thoughts strayed back to the argument this morning. They'd wanted to know if we would have sex in front of them, put on a show. Tim's response? *Maybe.*

More like *not a chance*. If I'd had cell reception, I'd have called for a ride home. But I could grin and bear it for a few days. No big deal. Change didn't frighten me like it did a lot of people. Too many years of moving around with my parents, experiencing other countries, struggling to learn other languages. The subtle comfort of very little change that Americans seemed to think was their 'God-given' right, didn't really appeal to me. I had no desire to live in misery just to avoid a little discomfort of change.

I didn't look forward to the upcoming fight about me leaving. And maybe it wouldn't come to that. Perhaps Tim would change his mind. Or I would.

I questioned us a lot lately. Did I love him? Did he love me? Was it a relationship of convenience? Why stay? Why go?

The noise came again. So close I nearly leapt back thinking it was in front of me. Except again I saw nothing. Not even the other guys. Though I suspected they pushed ahead of my slow ass, likely annoyed that I wasn't putting up with their teasing like the good little boy toy Tim claimed I was.

Gooseflesh broke out on my skin. An eerie sense of something watching me arched down my spine. For a minute blood pulsed in my ears. My own heartbeat and labored breathing echoing in my head. I made myself move, rushing to try to catch up, racing into the distance while trying to catch a glimpse of the guys. How far ahead could they have gotten? They wouldn't have left me, would they?

I tripped, stumbling several feet. Not falling, but having to slow myself.

A prickling sensation danced over my skin. Not painful at first, a bit like walking through a spiderweb perhaps. I flailed, focused on it for a moment, fearing I had staggered into something. A thousand scenarios of deadly arachnids raced through my mind as the feeling intensified to the point of pain.

I didn't notice the silence that overtook the trail. Unlike a silence of bugs and birds gone quiet because a predator was nearby, but complete absence of sound. No wind. No crunch of my feet on the dirt path. Not even the sound of my own breath, heavy from walking at a slightly inclined angle for an hour.

I don't remember how I came to realize the silence wasn't natural or that the rest of the group had vanished. Somehow I knew something was wrong, that they were gone and I was alone. I sucked in a deep breath, trying to calm the panic of some unknown bug crawling on me and collect myself. Not much frightened me. Why an uneasy feeling curled around me in that moment, I couldn't begin to understand at the time. A bit like a rising panic attack, a sudden wave of anxiety flowing through me. The past few weeks had echoed the same feeling off and on. An odd sense of something on the verge of happening. Almost premonition-like, though instead of the vague deja vu, this was more of a horror movie something-is-going-to-leap-out-at-me feeling.

The sensation of being watched added to the prickling wriggle on my skin. Air didn't seem to reach my lungs and my mind screamed for oxygen. I stood on the path, stopped, frozen almost, staring into the distance, straining for the sound of life, my skin on fire with prickling pain.

Fans of paranormal fiction sometimes asked if I'd seen or felt a change. Wavers in the road, or smelled a distinct scent. Anything to indicate a shift in dimension.

Big concept. Leaving one dimension for another.

That day I'd seen only the dancing waver of heat on the trail in front of me. I didn't think anything of it at the time. Despite being cold enough to huddle in a winter coat, and walking on a dirt trail through towering trees, neither of which was conducive to heat waves from pavement. Had that been the change? Had I stumbled through some otherworld portal? Or had it happened when I first heard that terrifying monkey-bird cry no one else seemed to notice?

Perhaps it had been the pin pricks of dancing ants across my skin which had been the actual change. I'd spent far too many hours thinking about it, had endless nightmares about the feeling of being watched and sensing oncoming doom. Fears about what I'd missed, months vanished both from my life and my memory, echoes of running through woods and snow while something unseen chased me. Memories or simply things my mind conjured up to scare me?

"Micah?"

I glanced up, blinking away the brooding, to find Lukas towering over me, holding out a cup of coffee. The noise of the police precinct rushed back around me in a blanket of sound, voices, computer keys, doors, life in general arose around me. I took the cup.

Handsome, polished, and now clean shaven, hair trimmed, Lukas had pulled himself together in the last few hours. I hoped Skylar had helped.

"You okay?" he asked.

"Any news on Alex?" I replied, deflecting the question.

He shook his head. "They are still questioning him."

"Did he do something?" I knew Alex hadn't. Much like my own disappearance, Alex had vanished for a month, returning with no memory of the time passed. Unlike my event, traces of him had been found. Bits of video of him around the country, at least that was what I'd been able to deduce from the conversations around me. The idea that something had taken over Alex's body for a month, used it to travel around the country and perhaps do things that might be dangerous or illegal, seemed to be coming to fruition.

Lukas, as Alex's twin brother, really appeared bothered by the idea, though he'd been the first to bring it up. I wasn't sure how to feel about it yet. Relieved that he was back? Worried he'd be taken again? Grateful someone else had experienced something similar to me? Mostly I felt numb, which sent my mind into a spiral of questions into my relationship with Alex. Did we have one? Had his time away changed him? Or me? We barely knew each other before he'd vanished, so did that mean we should start over, or continue on with what we'd begun?

Lukas sat down beside me. I sipped the coffee, which was disgustingly dark and thick, but I needed the caffeine. He said nothing for a few minutes, leaving me to think and overthink. I should have brought something to work on. My hands ached with the need to move even if it was only to slow my brain down. Overanalyzing was one of my best skills, and bad habits.

"It wouldn't have been him," Lukas finally said.

"No," I agreed.

"I don't know what they have, don't have, or are even thinking." Because him being a police detective didn't mean he got access to everything. Lukas ran his career by the book. Likely why he had no complaints issued against him, and had one of the best solve rates in the city for the homicides he investigated. People talked to him, could relate, and feel comfortable around him since he didn't come across as a total douche. Most of the time at least.

He had overprotective big brother down to a science. The past month of Alex missing brought him down hard, demanding answers I didn't have and blaming me for things I couldn't possibly control. Unreasonable, but understandable. I worked hard not to be angry with him. The car ride across the country to retrieve Alex from a hospital in Georgia had been brutal, Lukas brooding the entire time. He gave off waves of anger, irritation, and terror. If I never had to be trapped in a car with him again, it would be too soon.

He ran his hands through his short hair. "I don't know what to do."

"About?"

He turned to glare at me. "This thing that took Alex."

I sighed. "What is there *to* do?"

"I'm supposed to just accept this as fact? Something took him, took control of his body and used it to do what?"

I did not have answers to that. Wasn't sure anyone really did, not even Alex. And honestly, it's what everyone expected of me. When I'd returned, everyone had thought I'd pick up life again where I'd left off, like it hadn't changed me. And I tried, but couldn't help always looking over my shoulder, or thinking about what might happen if it came for me again.

"You haven't been taken again," he said softly.

"Not because of anything I've done or haven't done."

"You haven't gone back into the woods."

Not the same one, no, but it wasn't like I hid from trees or never left my house.

"Maybe if he doesn't go on the cemetery tour with you?"

"He vanished from my garden," I pointed out.

"Fuck," Lukas swore and jumped from the seat to resume his pacing. He paused and looked at me, his gaze intense. "I have some money put away. I could help you find a new place. Help you move."

Instead of replying I raised a brow, waiting for him to come up with his own answers. Running changed nothing. Moving led to more of the same; I had tried it a dozen times. Even on the rare occasion I went home to visit my parents or another relative, the odd night noises followed.

I liked my place. Felt safe inside. Especially when Alex stayed over. Funny how short of a time I've actually known him and yet I felt so comfortable being with him. Maybe because I already knew and trusted Lukas for so long? Perhaps it didn't relate to Lukas at all. Alex had his own personal charisma that he kept locked away until someone knew him a little. A lot like his snark, which reared its head when you least expected it. He made me laugh, smile, and relax. I loved that about him. Huh. Love…

A month gone, after having only known him a few days and I still thought about him relentlessly.

"Stupid idea, I know. None of this makes any sense."

It didn't, but sometimes that was the way of things.

We coexisted in silence for a few minutes. Him pacing, me sitting and wishing I had something to do with my hands while a million things raced through my head.

"I hate when you're quiet like this…"

"Sorry," I said immediately. Everyone hated it. Well Alex hadn't commented on it, but maybe he hadn't experienced it yet. "I'm thinking."

Lukas let out a long sigh. "Anything you want to share?"

"I wish I'd brought something to work on," I confessed. My brain needed the focus.

"You're not worried about Alex?"

"What would worrying change?" Of course, I was worried. But dwelling on it got us nowhere.

"Have you told him you're leaving yet?" Lukas asked, making it sound like I was abandoning everything and returning to Japan or something. Currently my parents were in Ireland taking care of my mother's family, but they would be returning home soon. I had no intention of going anywhere.

"It's a week in Houston. Five hours by car. I'm not even that far away."

"He'll have to stay with me. I can see if I can take more time off."

Alex would not like that. He didn't want his brother to spend all his time worrying about him. And Lukas was one of the moodiest bastards I'd ever met. Funny, since he came across very polished to people who didn't know him. Maybe it was me who brought out his inner bastard. Well, me and Alex.

"He could come with me," I said bracing for the argument, but letting out the one thing I'd been thinking of since I'd walked into his hospital room. I didn't want to let him out of my sight again.

The argument never came. Lukas sat down in the chair beside me, collapsing like the air had been let out of a balloon.

"I planned this over a year ago," I reminded him.

"And Sky is looking after your place."

Ah, so that was part of it too. Lukas would be alone. "You can stay with her at my place. Jet likes you. You enjoy gardening. Maybe put in a new planter or two. It will give you a reason to leave work on time."

Lukas didn't look at me, instead staring intently at his lap. After a few minutes of silence, he said, "Sky told me this morning you'd take Alex with you."

She had probably read some cards. Her knack for determining immediately pending events was uncanny, though a little unnerving. On long term stuff her skills still lacked a lot of clarity. "Yeah?"

"She got very grim..."

Not all sunshine and rainbows, that, too, was normal for Skylar's readings. I pulled out my phone and sent her a text. *Convention with Alex?*

S: *Yes...*

But?

S: *I don't know.*

Skylar often answered exactly that way when the cards gave her negative readings she couldn't quite articulate.

Is he safe? I wrote back.

S: *Yes. Discovers new hobby.*

I thought about that for a moment, then wrote: *Good or bad?*

S: *Good.*

Of course there were a thousand meanings for good in this context. Good he found a new hobby. Good he had something to excite him. Or it could mean he found someone or something better than me. The thought had crossed my mind a hundred times or so since he'd returned. Would he be different? Would I? Time did strange things to people. Either way, I didn't press her for more answers. Later, while I packed for the week away, I would grill her for details.

"He'll be fine," I told Lukas.

Lukas' lips tightened into a thin grimace. Fine was a word he hated.

"Sky says he discovers a new hobby. He could use the focus," I said. Lukas often talked about how Alex needed focus. Before meeting him, I had thought Alex might have ADHD, but his ability to focus was fine. He had simply been in the military too long, and had yet to find things to occupy him instead.

"I've put away every dime he's given me of his military money. It's in an account for him. Earning interest. I'll give you the card so if there is something he needs..."

The far door opened and the detective led a tired looking Alex out. His long hair an afro of frizz I'd need to massage with some special conditioner to untangle. Like his brother, he ran his hands through his hair a lot when stressed. While Alex's hair was blond, it looked more like a bleached blond, though I knew it wasn't. And it was one of the only things that indicated he had an African American father. His dark molten chocolate eyes were ringed in shadows indicating he needed sleep and hydration. The overgrowth of his beard, though trimmed back, could use some major shaping. And while his skin still appeared tan, I knew it was more his natural color than sun exposure. Once I got him home, I'd put him in the bath, slather him with lotion again, and clean up the rest of that beard overgrowth.

Home. Hm. Was my home his already? Or was it just him?

Both Lukas and I got to our feet. I opened my arms for Alex when he approached us unfettered. The detective held out a hand for Lukas. Alex fell into my embrace, hugging me tightly and resting his weight on me.

"Can we go?" I asked. "Alex should eat." He was far too thin.

"Dying for a banana," Alex grumbled in my arms. "Or peanut butter cookies."

Lukas accepted the detective's hand, shaking it. "What's going on? What do you know?"

"Nothing for now," the detective said. Apparently he wasn't telling us anything. He looked at Alex. "Call if you remember anything."

Alex nodded a bit grimly.

"He's free to go?" Lukas clarified. We'd discussed the possibility of needing a lawyer, even instructing Alex to request one the second he felt the direction of his questioning was heading towards trouble. Either it hadn't come to that or there was a whole lot not being said.

"Yes," the detective agreed. "We'll be in touch if more questions arise."

I took that at face value and tugged Alex toward the door, ready to go home and be away from all the noise and the feeling of eyes on us. Alex stepped away, but took my hand, squeezing it before following me to the parking lot. Wasting an entire day at the police station had not been on my radar of fun things to do. At least we'd be taking him home with us rather than scrambling to find some kind of criminal attorney to get bail set for him.

Lukas lasted only until we got into his car, and had left the station, slowly navigating around traffic. "What did they ask? What do they know?" He demanded.

Alex and I sat in the backseat. He blinked, turning from staring out the window to look at his brother who sat behind the wheel. "Stuff I didn't know. There were a couple FBI guys. They showed me pictures of a few places they thought I'd been. The airport is the only one that actually looks like me. Asked me about people I've never met before."

"What about?" Lukas persisted.

"If I knew them or had seen anything." Alex shrugged. "I got the impression they thought I knew something about these guys, could point them in the right direction."

"Like drug dealers or something?" Lukas wanted to know.

"Right, 'cause me and drugs of any kind mix?" Alex asked. He turned my way and ran his fingers along my face. "How are you doing? You look tired."

"A little. Head is loud. The coffee sucked."

"Nothing is as good as that stuff you have," Alex said. "I'm an official coffee snob now."

The rest of the short drive Lukas fumed, though said nothing, and Alex took turns looking out the window and smiling at me. At least he was in good spirits.

CHAPTER 2

I almost expected Lukas to take us to his apartment, but we parked outside the gate to my place. Skylar greeted us as we walked up the path, her gaze darting back and forth between the brothers. I shook my head and made my way past her into the house. Jet met us at the door, greeting everyone with a full body rub along their legs. I had sort of been hoping to get home and curl up alone with Alex, but apparently that wasn't an option.

Alex made his way to the coffee pot and began to put together a pot. I needed a bigger brewer. The two of us drank too much to share from one small four cup machine. A fruit basket full of fresh bananas, apples, and oranges decorated the counter near the brewer. Skylar must have added it. She had been keeping my kitchen stocked in the past month while she stayed with me. I suspected she would rather have stayed with Lukas, but until Alex's return, he'd refused to do more than yell at either one of us. His calm, confident exterior had more than cracked, it had crumbled. Falling apart hadn't been pretty on Lukas, but necessary. I really hoped he let Skylar help put him back together.

Once Alex had the coffee going, he dove into the bananas, eating two in less than a minute. Lukas paced. Skylar rang her hands. The

13

two were an odd contrast. Lukas tall, polished, looking almost like a businessman in that moment despite wearing jeans and a simple polo, and Sky in a flirty top, and full circle skirt, her long gorgeous hair pulled into a loose ponytail. She was one of the prettiest girls I had ever met, and seeing her stare up at Lukas with longing made me think again of Alex and wonder if we had the same thing budding or if I were hoping for things that wouldn't manifest. Life had made me cynical, wary, and knowing all that, sad.

If the two of them could get their heads out of their asses, I knew Lukas and Skylar could be the real thing. It was almost a visible tension between the two of them. The need, a play of string or yarn aching to stitch them up into some elaborate duo. Sadly, I'd never been able to see or sense the same sorts of things for myself. Though as my gaze landed back on Alex, who swayed a little at the counter watching the coffee drip, I couldn't help but feel drawn to him. If we'd been alone, I would have gone to him and wrapped my arms around him, sank into his embrace and just breathed him in for a while.

Instead I went to the closet to find something to keep my hands busy, dug out the container of crochet roses I'd been working on for almost a year, and brought it to the kitchen table. My place didn't usually feel small, but with four adults, two of them somewhat flustered, claustrophobia began to tug at me. I sucked in a deep breath and focused on creating a new rose. As the pattern wasn't muscle memory, I ended up tugging the first few rows out and restarting twice before Alex set a mug of coffee in front of me. He and Lukas had been arguing about something, though I couldn't recall what. I sipped at the coffee, marveling at how he knew how to mix it for me with a bit of almond creamer and a lot of stevia.

The rose finally began to come to life in my hands. Someday I'd finish the elaborate design and send it to my mother. I only needed something like four hundred of the roses.

"You okay?" Alex asked.

I blinked up at him, mind finally clear enough to multitask. "Yes?"

He tilted his head toward me. "Was that a question or an answer?"

"Yes?" I glanced at Skylar sitting on the futon and Lukas who continued to pace. "Everything okay?"

"Lukas says we're going somewhere?"

Oh. I had wanted to talk to Alex about that myself once Lukas and Skylar were gone, though it didn't appear like they were leaving any time soon. "There's a textile convention coming up in Houston. I've been planning on going for a while. I'm hoping to get a few lines to carry in the shop. Plus," I flushed, "I am sort of meeting up with some old cosplay friends." While Alex had been missing I'd debated on changing plans, or even canceling the trip. But as time had stretched and he hadn't returned I decided I would go anyway. Before he had vanished, we had both agreed to live moving forward instead of constantly trying to decipher the past. I was trying to live my life. That meant doing things rather than hiding out at home. If he hadn't returned, I would have tried to bury myself in the commonality of the group, excitement of the new fabric lines, and perhaps find a new project, even if feeling that much would have cut like a knife. Now that he was back, I was looking forward to showing him new things.

"Sounds like fun. I've never heard of a textile convention before."

"You don't have to come if you don't want to," I assured him. "I understand if you'd rather stay here and rest." He looked exhausted, stressed, and gaunt. Should I make him stay home? Or bring him with so I could make him eat every two hours? I gnawed on my lip in thought.

"I have no idea what a textile convention is, and it's been years since I cosplayed, but I can't say I'm not intrigued. What about the shop and your tours?"

"No tours scheduled while I'm gone. And Skylar, Tim, and Brad are minding the shop," I said.

"I'll be helping out too," Lukas said. "When I'm not at work."

I wasn't sure he was ready to be back at work in homicide. Not with Alex freshly home, and Lukas still raw over his disappearance, but it wasn't my decision to make. I suspected that he and Skylar would be arguing over that a lot in the future. If Lukas was as smart as I suspected he was, he would let her take care of him, lean on her a little instead of constantly having to be the guy in charge. Thankfully, while Alex had his own fair share of white knight syndrome, he was much better at asking for help.

"The convention is a gathering of trends in fabric. Some non-fabric stuff too, but mostly fabric. Everything from quilt cotton to cosplay apparel options, sewing machines, trim, and the latest in design software. There's even a runway thing they do, days' worth of classes, and a couple 'Iron Design' type contests. The group I'm meeting up with... we've all rented at the same B&B, taking it over with our sewing machines and cosplay pieces. A few are really good with photography too, so there will be a studio space set up."

"Freya is going to be there," Skylar said with reverie.

"Who's Freya?" Alex asked. "Other than a Norse Goddess?"

"A real Goddess," Skylar assured him. Lukas looked at Skylar, jealousy clear on his face. Skylar did not like women that way any more than I did. Lukas had nothing to worry about. If Sky could be Freya, she would.

"She runs a patron group, her own website exclusively, like I used to," I said. "Boudoir cosplay. She also owns the B&B we'll be at. Freya is a legend at cosplay. You can find pictures of her all over the world as some of the best in cosplay. Designs and makes everything herself. She does a lot of online tutorials now, and events like this."

"Will you get her autograph for me?" Skylar asked.

"Sure," I said and focused on the next rose. Counting stitches, practicing putting aside all the noise in my head. Single crochet, V-stitch, repeat, turn, seven doubles, single, I repeated to myself as the petals came to life, then carefully stitched the winding strand into a circle. "She helped me get started. I didn't know there would be a place for me as a guy in sexy cosplay. I was seventeen when I reached out to her for advice with my idea. She's super nice. Has always been a big supporter of anyone in the trade." Freya hadn't liked my change from cosplay modeling to sex on the screen. A loss of talent she claimed. She'd been thrilled when I reached out to her about getting back into the hobby.

"Someday I'm going to be as beautiful as her," Skylar gushed, making me smile.

Freya was very much the giant blonde goddess of her namesake. Her assets were hereditary. Perfection as only a rare few had the luck to be born with. Skylar, being male to female trans, had to work for those same things as she was rail thin and didn't seem to be growing the curves she longed for even with added hormones. Time, I often reminded her, she'd only been on hormones for a year. Some of her features had softened, but even eating a ton didn't add to her figure. Her metabolism ran daily marathons. A lot of women would have been thrilled to have to work so hard to put on weight and gain curves, not Skylar. She wanted hips and boobs to fill out her wide collection of flirty dresses.

"You're already beautiful," I assured Skylar.

"Gorgeous," Alex agreed. "First time I saw you, I thought wow! That girl is amazing. You have hair like those TV models, and when you wore that Ice Queen dress Micah made you, I thought everyone in town was going to bow down and start worshiping you."

Skylar laughed, a throaty sound filled with joy, and threw herself at Alex for a tight hug. He let out an "oof," sound as she squeezed him tight.

I smiled down into my work, thrilled that Alex got along so well with Skylar. Not only because she was my best friend, but also because Lukas was crazy about her. Lukas had gone silent. I could almost feel his brooding from across the room. When he first told me about his brother, damaged from a never-ending war, plagued with memories of things everyone denied, Lukas led me to believe his brother was the serious one of them.

Alex could sit in silent vigil to his thoughts, and sometimes got lost in self-doubt, but his sense of humor, sarcasm, and quick wit left most smiling rather than worried. In reality he was a warmer, more open person than Lukas had ever been. Though with his façade cracked, Lukas began to feel more human and approachable every day. I'd thought of him as a friend for a long time, not realizing he'd never really returned the sentiment. He was protective, not friendly, as I'd pointed out before to Alex. Lukas was a cop at heart. Always. Not in a bad way, but in that 'I'm in charge and the world's problems are mine' sort of way. Lukas and I had never sparked, for that reason. I didn't want a protector. I wanted a partner and a friend.

Alex squirmed under Skylar's fierce hug. "Damn, girl. Your hugs are lethal. You should hire yourself out," Alex teased. "Hug torture, right up there below water boarding."

"Jerk!" Skylar said, no venom in her voice and still squeezing him hard. "Revel in my embrace, worthless worm!"

Alex's laughter filled the room with warmth and eased something that had frozen in my gut. I was tempted to glance up and see how jealous Lukas might be with us fawning over Sky, but forced myself to focus. Too much in my head. Worries. Lists of things to get done before I left. And now I'd lost another day since we'd been at the police station. I had to admit having Alex back calmed something I hadn't realized had been raging inside me. Some kind of vibrating noise of unease had taken residence at the base of my spine while he was gone. Strong enough that I felt it all the time, and had to work to tune it out. Only now was it gone, still, silent, but not in a scary way.

I counted through a bunch more rows, winding up roses and whispering the numbers of each stitch. The focus helped clear away the constant buzz of tension.

Alex kissed me on the cheek. I blinked up at him again. We were alone. Both Lukas and Sky gone. When had that happened? I really must have zoned out, but I'd also finished four roses without really realizing it.

"Where'd they go?"

"Home to Lukas's place. He was blazing with a need to claim her after our teasing." Alex grinned. "I thought we could use some quiet. I ordered food. It will be here in a bit. Do we need to go to the shop?"

"Brad is handling it today. He's been working a lot of hours."

"Time I was supposed to, yeah?" Alex said.

"Yes, but it's okay. I think he's trying to earn his independence."

"From Tim?"

"More general independence. He's very young." Brad had not traveled the world like I had. He came from small town Louisiana and hadn't gotten far. He wanted to see the world, and meet people, which I didn't think meant good things for Tim. "Not everything is sex work or small-town life. Even if his town is the Big Easy."

"Alien impregnators have ruined him for everyone else," Alex said with a completely straight face. "Narwal Dickmaster strikes again."

I couldn't help but laugh, thinking back to the shock on his face the first time he'd ever seen them, heard of the elaborate dildo, or that I had an adult section in the back of my shop. "Perhaps. Though new worlds featuring males with giant dragon dicks are an unlikely prospect."

"Dragon dicks..." Alex said. "We have the weirdest conversations."

And that was okay. It felt normal, natural, like maybe things hadn't really changed? I worked through two more roses thinking about a half dozen scenarios of Alex and I working out or breaking up. It was too much.

Alex waved at all the stuff I had laid out at the table. "How about we curl up on the futon? Might be more comfortable."

I studied him. "Are you mad at me?"

"No. Why would I be mad?"

Because a lot of people hated my silence. Even if it wasn't a true silence. Part of the way I was raised, to be seen and not heard. Respect and honor were very important to my father. Some parts of the world were the same. Even some parts of the United States, but I didn't really want to spend a lot of time explaining. So I opted for simple instead. "My head is loud."

"Is that my fault? Is it loud about me? Do you want me to go?" Alex asked.

"No." A little tick of anxiety raced through me at the thought of him leaving.

"Okay. Can I help somehow? Make your head less loud?"

"I don't know," I answered honestly. "Do you really want to go to the convention?"

"If you don't mind me being there, I think it would be fun. I'd like to meet your friends. You can teach me all about fabric." He said nothing for another minute and then, "Can I hold you? I'd like to hold you if that's okay."

"Okay," I agreed.

He got up and made his way to the futon. "Show me how you do that."

"What?" I asked, looking down at the mess in my lap, but gathering it up to find a place curled up in his lap. Settling back against his chest, feeling his heartbeat at my back, the anxiety eased almost instantly.

"The magic of how you take string and turn it into a rose."

"It's yarn, but okay." I dug through the bag to find another hook, I only had a thousand of the stupid things laying around, and a spare ball of yarn. "It's only four rows, and pretty basic, chain stitch, single, V-stitch, double."

"Sounds like a foreign language. Good thing I excel at languages." Alex took the hook and yarn, copying how I held things and mimicking until he seemed to get the chain stitch down. It was more about rhythm than skill. "We need fifty-six of these little stitches," I told him as I got up to answer the door and retrieve the food he'd ordered. It smelled like burgers.

By the time I got back to him he had his chain done, waiting. "Food first?"

"Sure," I held out the food. We ate spread out on the futon, sharing half of each burger, one beef with a giant stack of toppings, and the other a spicy chicken thing, that was fantastic. We had fries and onion rings, plus a handful of fried random veggies. By the time I washed my hands after cleaning up the food remnants to get back to the crochet work, I realized Alex and I had barely talked the entire meal. He hadn't pushed either. There was no taint of awkwardness in the air like with most people. It made me examine him to try to read his mood, but he focused on his own little slip of yarn, having made a giant tail of single crochets in practice. My silence didn't bother him at all.

"What did you and Lukas fight about?"

Alex blinked and looked up. "His job. He wants to bother some of his co-workers for more details. What they might know about what happened to me, but I'd rather he didn't lose his job over that."

"Even if it got answers?"

"What would it change? It won't erase the month I lost. I want to move forward," he paused, gaze intense, "with you, hopefully."

I smiled, feeling my anxiety ease a bit more. "Even if it's getting to know me and my weird cosplay friends?"

"Even if," he said, then glanced toward the door. "What if we hear something?"

Like a middle of the night monster. Years of being plagued by that odd squawking monkey thing, though it sometimes sounded like cats or other not quite benign things, left me more than a little raw. A month of brutal silence while praying for a sign of Alex's return had worn at me. I slept hard when I finally slept, but never peacefully. The fact that Alex heard it too, experienced the same things, gave us one more thing to bond over. I hated that it would stalk him too, but finally felt like I wasn't alone for the first time in years. I was not naïve enough to think it was gone forever. Even if I wasn't hearing it right now.

I closed my eyes for a moment and sucked in a breath, steadying myself as the internal noise descended again. So much in my head. Alex's lips touched mine in a soft kiss, and I opened my eyes to look at him. He pulled away with a little smile.

"I didn't mean to upset you," he said.

"Not upset." A thought occurred to me then. "Did you hear it last night?"

Alex glanced down as though considering for a half a second whether or not to lie. "Yes."

I leaned forward and rewarded him with a small kiss. "Thank you for not lying. As for the noise... It follows wherever I go. Sometimes it will go quiet for a while, and I'll think it's finally over, then it returns." I shrugged, refusing to focus on something I didn't seem to have the power to change. "The place we are staying has six rooms in the main house and three small cottages a few feet from the back door. We are staying in one of the cottages."

Better to not subject everyone to the weirdness of my reality. Noises in the night, shadows dogging my footsteps, and occasionally the feeling of fire beneath my skin did not need to be shared with anyone. Except maybe Alex, who never looked at me with pity or disbelief in his eyes. "The main house is supposed to be haunted, but I've been there twice and never experienced anything."

"Like the thrift shop you sent me to?" Alex wanted to know, reminding me of the ghost who had helped him shop for clothing.

"I've been by there a half dozen times in the past month..."

"No seventies ghost girl hanging out?"

I shook my head. He appeared thoughtful. Was he wallowing in his own anxiety about whatever had been awakened inside of him? Perhaps he'd always seen things and written them off as normal until presented with something that couldn't fit the narrative.

While I didn't know all the details about what he'd seen in the deserts of Afghanistan, Alex compared it to the djinn of Islamic legend. Djinn were mortal creatures, though longer lived than humans. They were also made up of fire and tended to take over people a lot like a demonic possession might. Whatever it had been had killed his teammates and somehow spared Alex, leaving him with memories everyone denied were possible. When he'd vanished, I vaguely recalled a dream of him, fire glowing beneath his skin as he was sucked into a grave. Terrifying, and yet I'd only been an observing party to it. I suspected he remembered a lot more than I did of the event.

Of course remembering it made my heart race and my skin prickle with fear. I set aside the crochet work, wanting more to bask in him for a little while. He was home. We'd have to take that for what it was—a blessing.

"How about we get in the bath and you let me rub you down with some lotion?" Sex was easy, a good distraction. Most men took sex as intimacy, letting the physical relationship sustain a relationship. Alex never let me get away with it. He wanted more than just my body. Which while thrilling, was also terrifying. Were there enough interesting things about me to keep him around? Would that have changed in the short time he was away? Maybe he would let me take care of him for a while, and that was okay too.

"Bath sounds good. My skin still feels tight," Alex agreed. "As long as you show me how to finish this later?" He held up the yarn string.

"Sure." I promised and held out a hand. He took it, his grip warm in mine and we headed to the bathroom. There was time for worrying later.

CHAPTER 3

A few days of normalcy went a long way in restoring my faith in life. Alex and I prepared for the trip, I made him eat at least three times a day, feeding him as many avocados and bananas as he could manage to eat since they were full of potassium. And we both worked the shop with an edge of lighthearted humor. While he was a horrible dancer, mostly because it kicked his hip out of place, he swayed with me on slow evenings. I enjoyed his laughter and smile, and the way he never hesitated to touch me in public. Alex seemed unchanged by the stolen time. Wary sometimes, but he'd had that before. His easy affection, and interest in learning everything there was to know about me, the shop, the tours, and even the city I called home, made my anxiety relax, and heart squeeze with happiness I hadn't felt in a long time.

He had returned to his brother's place once for a night, which ended up being a fitful night of sleep for me, and the first time I'd heard the noise outside in a long time. I'd ended up texting him in the middle of the night, when a rare panic attack had taken over my brain. While he hadn't come running to my house because I insisted he stay home, he did text me back until sleep finally took over and shut my brain down.

I felt bad for using him to stave off the terror though he didn't mind at all. Having him in my space helped quiet my mind even when it raged in insane circles of logic. He'd also become quite a master at crochet roses, completing dozens of the things while he practiced. My anxiety over the trip increased even though I'd planned it to death, although Alex's childlike excitement renewed my own.

I rented a smaller SUV for the trip, mostly to fit my sewing stuff. Two machines, a couple of boxes of fabric, several zippered garment bags of current projects or completed works, a suitcase of regular clothes, and I was about as ready as I was going to get. Alex arrived with a duffle bag full of what little he owned—I'd have to remedy that —and eyed the contents of the car.

"I guess this explains why we're driving?"

"It's a bit of a sewing retreat. The convention doesn't start until Thursday. Runs through Sunday, but we are there through the following Wednesday." Since it was Sunday and the shop was closed, it gave me more time to think. We weren't doing an early morning drive, my intent instead to arrive in time for dinner tonight. "It's a little over five hours, six if we have a lot of stops on the way."

I loaded a small cooler full of food behind the passenger seat. The bed and breakfast offered two meals a day, but I needed to make sure Alex kept eating, and hated the idea of shoving fast food into him. He wasn't a picky eater at all, for which I was thankful. So the chest full of sandwich supplies, fresh fruit and veggies, and a couple of bento boxes would hopefully get us through the drive. The cottage had a small kitchen not unlike my own. Which meant I planned to stop at a grocery store near the hotel.

The hardest part of the day was getting Alex to leave Jet. He spent a ridiculous amount of time with the cat in his lap while he crocheted roses. He didn't have the sewing it into a round flower part down, but could race through the four rows and cast off like a pro. He liked to have his hands busy. And unlike most guys or people I'd ever known, he didn't need to fill the silence with chatter. Alex rolled back and forth from petting the cat to crocheting roses while I ran around preparing things from lists. His calm presence was enough to keep me from pulling my hair out.

"Where is the convention again? Houston?" Alex asked as he got in the car with his faux leather bag filled with crochet hooks and random yarn balls. I'd found a tutorial online this morning to teach him how to make an amigurumi dragon. It was a bit on the cutesy side, more a child's toy version than something an ex-soldier might covet, but Alex had been fascinated and already completed the round section of the body. Nothing about this trip stressed him out. When asked, he said it was because he trusted me and knew I'd point him in the right direction. While that was more stress, it was also comforting to know he had faith in me.

"We're staying north of the city, near Conroe, not far from the Sam Houston National Forest."

That made Alex stop and look at me. He frowned. "National Forest?"

"Yeah, you know, where trees grow?" I half joked. "Did you know the planet is covered in like 700 million acres of forest?"

"We are not camping," Alex clarified. I didn't think he had an issue with camping, more a concern I might vanish again.

"No. We're in town. Though the hotel backs up to an area of trees, it's not officially part of the National Forest. That's a couple miles away. Our group didn't want to stay in the city, and a lot of area outside Houston is oil rigs and fracking. Freya's place specializes in crafters. She does a lot of quilting retreats, and the like. So she's close to the city, without being on top of it."

"Sounds... interesting?" Alex finished, obviously less than enthused with the idea we wouldn't be staying close to the city.

"You don't have to go. I can drop you off at Lukas's."

Alex narrowed his eyes at me. "I'd like to go. Didn't realize this thing was so expensive. Maybe we can work out a way for me to pay you back on the drive?" He got comfortable in his seat and shut the door. I checked over the contents of the back again, then double checked to make sure the door to my place was locked. Sky would be over later to install herself as guardian of my cat.

When I got in the driver's seat and adjusted it until it was comfortable, Alex was working on his dragon.

"Cost?" He prodded me again as I turned the car on and guided us out toward I-10 which would take us out of the state and directly into Houston. We would have to divert north once we got into Texas, but that was a few hours away.

"This was already planned, so you coming along is not costing me any more than it already did." Except the ticket to the convention.

"Convention?" Of course Alex had looked up the cost.

I sighed. "I'll take crochet roses in exchange for the ticket cost. Technically, since you'll be learning about stuff that helps Simply Crafty, I should be paying you for your time."

Alex scoffed. "Paying me to have fun?"

I couldn't help smiling. He really did enjoy the job. Loved all the weird little nuances that made up Simply Crafty as a shop, and a lot of its customers. He also seemed genuinely interested in crafts and fabric. He enjoyed the history of the tours, but was less enthusiastic about the haunted aspect of it, for which I didn't blame him. Sometimes we saw or felt things that sparked more questions than answers, and Alex seemed to be really good at capturing something unexplained on camera. His photos had gone viral, even being featured in major television station commentary.

"There will probably be a lot of boring sewing chatter," I told him.

"I may not understand it, but I find your sewing stuff fascinating. I've watched a few quilt videos. They make it look easy, cutting squares into other shapes, but I'm sure there's more to it."

"It's a bit like the game Tetris," I said.

"I can see that. Maybe I'll see if I can take a class when we get back. Teach me some basics. Videos are okay, but I need some hands on to really start." He waved his hands at the crochet project in his lap. "Wouldn't have known what half of this meant if you hadn't showed me."

"Crochet is really about getting your hand placement correct."

"Lots of things are about getting your hand placement correct," Alex teased, making it sound somewhat suggestive.

I smiled at his ease. He continued to focus on his crochet work.

"Let me know if you need your space," Alex said. "We don't have to be stuck together at the hip. You are not obligated to show me a good time. I love being with you, but that doesn't mean I can't exist if you need a few hours to yourself. If you meet some hot guy at the convention, however..."

"Ask you to join in?" I teased.

Alex's face turned pink with that telltale flush of his. It was sort of empowering, how small things I did turned him on.

"Really?" I teased him.

"I can't help that I spring boners every time you bring up sex. Note that it is not the idea of you and some random other guy. It's you and me. I'm glad we're in this cabin thing. I don't like the thought of everyone else listening to us."

"Planning to sex me up regularly?" Our sex life had been a slow exploration. Alex was not the kind of guy to throw me up against the wall and take what he wanted. Not yet. His bedroom shyness made him adorable and sweet. It was also something else I could teach him, since my own experience surpassed his. "Maybe more like this morning?" I'd started with lotion, massaging it into his skin until he melted into jelly beneath me, then I'd teased his prostate until he'd been screaming for release. I had never been with a guy who lasted as long as Alex. I could probably edge him for days and bask in his sweet heat.

Alex's moan was almost sexual. "Can we not talk about that while driving?" He shifted in his seat. "I seriously feel like my ass is throbbing for your fucking fingers. How is that normal?"

I smiled. "I have so much to teach you."

"Oh my God, stop. We've barely left home. I think pulling over on the side of the road to rub off is likely to get us arrested."

"Focus on your crochet," I reminded him of the project in his lap instead of his hard-on. "I can't wait to see what it's like when you're done." He had chosen a variegated green and teal yarn with silver accents to it. So far, the color change in the body was really looking like scales.

Alex took a couple shaky breaths then went back to work on the dragon. I turned up the radio and focused on the drive and the subtle calm of the road. We both sang along to the radio. Alex had a great voice, untrained, but pleasant. He didn't know all the Top 40 songs like I did, mostly because he'd been out of the world so long, first in the military, and then from being taken.

Taken. Fuck I hated that thought. I pushed it aside and tried to focus on the road.

"What sort of haunting does the B&B have?" Alex inquired as he stitched the little tubes that would make up the dragon's feet. We had been on the road an hour or so.

"Former owner sort of thing. I think everything in Texas is haunted. I read somewhere that it has the most haunted roads of the entire nation."

Alex put the crochet down and turned to look at me. "How does a road get haunted?"

"Same way anything else does, I suspect." Though a lot of the stories didn't actually feature ghosts, more creatures lurking on the side of the road. "People die or go missing."

Now Alex was less than happy.

"You did know car accidents kill a lot of people?" I asked him.

"Yes," Alex agreed. "Do you want me to drive?"

"No." Alex's PTSD could trigger him and render him completely incoherent. As far as I knew, he was not allowed to drive, though Lukas had said something about Alex being able to test to get his license back. In New Orleans, he didn't need to drive. In Houston, I'd be doing all the driving. Which reminded me, "You've been sleeping okay?"

"Yes," Alex said, focused back on his dragon. Whether he heard the noise at night or not, he didn't let on. I'd been keeping him busy

29

enough during the day that when we got into bed at night, after a round of sex, we both slept hard.

"You'll let me know if something bothers you, right?" I knew his triggers. Sometimes changing location could send him into an episode. Lukas had given me a dozen things to avoid before I'd ever met Alex. Most of those things were not on my daily schedule. No war zones or guns pointed our way. Though Houston, being a big city full of gun crazed Americans, meant we might encounter some of Alex's triggers. I knew gunfire and fireworks could set off a lot of soldiers, and hoped that staying far enough outside the city would minimize that.

"Sure," Alex said absently. "I've been okay though. Haven't had an episode since the cemetery." That event had been caused by a shadow figure attacking us and a fellow tour guide being murdered.

"If your anxiety kicks in, tell me, okay? The convention will be pretty packed."

"Can you promise the same?" Alex threw back. He was not as oblivious to my anxiety as everyone else seemed to be. Or perhaps everyone else noticed and didn't care.

"Yes," I vowed. "I can do that."

"Good." Alex threw me a smile, then put his crochet work away to pull out his new phone. "I'm going to research Texas ghosts."

"Stories of the skunk ape, aka Bigfoot, are more common," I told him.

Alex slowly panned to me. "Say what?"

"You know, Bigfoot. Sasquatch? Lots of stories of ape like creatures in the USA. Even in Texas. Louisiana is known for them too, in the bayou."

"Skunk ape…" Alex muttered.

"Supposed to smell like a skunk."

"Now I'm going to be looking for giant apes every time I smell a skunk."

I reached out and patted his knee. It was unlikely we'd encounter a Bigfoot, or whatever the stories came from. Though knowing our luck and Alex's paranormal magnetism, maybe we'd see something. "We'll be fine. You're an ex-Army Ranger."

"Which does shit all against ghosts and random forest apes."

I couldn't help but laugh at his indignant tone. He joined in, shaking his head, and insisting on continuing his research.

CHAPTER 4

The sun was beginning to set as we pulled down the last road, which was more of a gravel path, toward the B&B. Alex had dozed in the car after our last break in which I insisted on feeding him again, but now he was wide awake and looking warily at the rush of trees surrounding us.

"Not in the forest?" He prodded as we pulled up to the house which looked like an old Southern mansion with a giant wraparound porch. It wasn't quite as big as a lot of the plantations in Louisiana, but had the same vibe with a tree-lined drive, the house white and pristine amidst the greenery.

"Nope," I said pulling into the small lot in front of the house. The lot was little more than dirt and gravel, but there was plenty of room for the SUV to park or even turn around if necessary. "It's not like it's hidden in the woods," I pointed out. The area surrounding the house was a wide wash of green grass for probably a couple dozen meters before the wall of trees met the edge of the lawn. We were less than ten minutes from a small grocery store, which we'd already stopped at to refill the cooler, and gas station. And not twenty minutes from a Walmart. "This is not the middle of nowhere."

Alex was quiet, tension tightening his shoulders as we got out. I reached for his hand, and he took mine, squeezing it, his palm a little sweaty.

"I'm not going anywhere," I promised him.

The door to the main house opened and out came the goddess herself. Freya was dressed in jeans and a T-shirt, simple enough, though her blonde hair pulled up on the crown of her head looked a bit like some elaborate anime design with multiple ponytails and strategic curls. Her smile was wide as she tromped across the space to greet us, arms open for a hug.

I accepted her embrace, thankful for the warmth of having a mentor and friend like her. "Hey, Freya," I said, squeezing her for a moment before pulling away to introduce Alex. "This is Alex."

Freya offered her hand to him. "Nice to meet you, Alex," she said. "Micah said you used to cosplay."

Freya actually knew a lot more about Alex than that, as I'd filled her in on the past month's adventures. She collected knowledge about everything, crafts, TV and book genres, and people. I knew she would be careful with Alex, not only what I'd told her, but his PTSD. She had even kyboshed a few cosplay norms for this group adventure. There would be no weapon making tutorials and combat related costumes were off limits. If the group had protested, I had been spared their irritation at the last-minute change. But I'd rather have Alex calm and happy than anxious and lost in some memory.

"Yes, ma'am," Alex said taking her hand and shaking it. "Nothing as amazing as Micah does, but I did enjoy it. He's sort of a wizard when it comes to crafting. Can do anything."

"That is the way of things in cosplay," Freya agreed. "It's a bit of an eclectic hobby. Not all sewing, sometimes it's working with EVA foam or even clay, painting, or beading. Micah's skill is vision. He can recreate a costume from scratch, no pattern necessary, or even take a simple pattern and reconstruct something completely different and phenomenal."

While the praise was nice, it made me uncomfortable. "Thanks," I said.

She smiled warmly at me, and I noticed for the first time the tiny display of crow's feet on the edge of her warm eyes. It was a quick reminder that Freya was close to fifty, and while she was gorgeous, she still got a lot of pushback from new influencers trying to steal her thunder. I'd heard her called 'old school' enough to cringe myself every time someone said it.

"I'm nothing compared to your skill," I assured her. "I wouldn't even know where to start if you hadn't helped me out."

Freya reached out to squeeze my arm, but still spoke to Alex. "I'm thrilled Micah is looking to return to the hobby. Losing his talent to other pursuits was a tragedy for the community."

I scoffed. "Seeing me in tight hot pants is not going to save the world."

"No," Freya agreed. "But it gives many a few minutes of escape."

"I'm on board with that," Alex said. "Tight hot pants, I mean. Have you seen his ass? It's divine. The way it fits in my hands..." Alex's eyes widened as if he just realized what he said. "Shit... filter broken. Sorry, TMI." He looked at me. "I don't know if they know? Are supposed to know? Fuck, I'm messing this up by getting lost in the thought of cupping your ass and kissing..." He clapped his hands over his mouth.

Heat rushed into my cheeks. Odd since I wasn't used to being embarrassed by compliments. Though the way Alex talked about me, *looked* at me, often made me wonder if he saw something no one else did. He was an all-in sort of guy, jumping in feet first, and had taken the idea of being with me to full woke levels. Him not being shy about his interest in me was both startling, and refreshing.

"Stop," I grumbled at both of them, but took one of Alex's hands firmly in mine and squeezed it. "Freya knows. I don't care what anyone else thinks. We're sleeping together. We are a thing."

"More than a spark," Alex proclaimed like some sort of strutting cock wandering a yard of excited hens.

"Yes," I agreed. And I hoped it stayed that way.

Alex leaned over to kiss me on the cheek, his beard tickling my face. I reached up to stroke along his jaw, loving the softness of the texture of his trimmed beard. He spent time on it because he knew I liked it. Had in fact adopted an entire routine that helped his hair and skin. Sometimes I caught him running his hands through his hair, or over his beard, marveling how they could feel so decadent. And decadent was the word Alex used when I'd asked him about it, like a fine wine or dessert. I'd told him he could be my dessert. Which made him blush.

"You're adorable. Both of you."

"Is it dinner time yet?" I smelled something amazing, and hoped it was dinner. "Alex needs to eat."

"Almost," Freya said. "Let me help you guys get your stuff to the cabin and by then it should be done. After dinner I'll give you a quick reminder tour of the house, then you guys can get some rest for the night. I'm sure you're tired from the drive."

Unloading the car became a group effort when Chad appeared, grinning beside us with MaryAnn at his heels. Chad was a bear of a guy, built more like a linebacker, square-jawed, hair buzzed short. His hair had a touch of red-gold fire to it, and his eyes were large and brown. MaryAnn had long dark hair, and more curves than the media thought girls should have. While MaryAnn was pretty, she wasn't—at least without intense makeup—the sort of stop traffic beauty that everyone seemed to prefer these days. But she was a chameleon, able to transform herself into things with a bit of makeup and costume, that seemed scientifically impossible. She knew how to work a costume to best suit her body and features, and had done more than her fair share of sexy cosplay. I'd known them both for a handful of years.

"Hey guys," I greeted them. "Good to see you." I introduced them both to Alex as everyone grabbed something out of the car and then we all followed the little stone walkway around the house and to the cabins.

They weren't true cabins in the form of traditional thinking. They ran more along the line of tiny houses, complete with solar panels.

Instead of expanding the house and changing the charming old country layout, Freya had chosen to add the grouping of tiny houses behind the space, offering more privacy as well as more rooms. It had been my first inkling that a smaller place would work for me, and had helped fuel the ideas that went into designing my own space.

"You guys are on the end. The middle one is still a photography studio. I have the key if you want to do a shoot in there," Freya said as she walked us to our door, unlocked it, and handed me the key. "Breakfast is at eight, dinner at seven."

Having used this cabin before, the layout was familiar, though with Alex in the space it would be a little tight. The group left our stuff on the tiny porch outside the house, giving Alex and I a chance to set up our stuff.

"Dinner is in twenty minutes," Freya told us, and left us to get settled.

Alex stepped inside, looking around. "Okay, I thought your place was small."

The cabin was around 200 square feet with a loft overhead. The main part of the cabin was one room, starting with the living area, which had a small couch that could be converted into a bed, and tables that folded up or down off the walls. The kitchen in galley style ran the rest of the length until the small bathroom. A narrow set of stairs arched up the side to the loft, which had a queen-sized bed, and windows surrounding it, but not enough room to stand up.

"My place is around 400 square feet, not counting the loft," I said. "More than double the size of this."

"This brings new meaning to tiny home," Alex said as he set his bag down in one of the cubes that made up the stairs. He walked from the front to the tiny bathroom, then back and carefully up the stairs. "At least your stairs have a railing. Where should we put all our stuff?"

My stuff, since all he had was his little bag. I turned and opened a few of the doors beside the kitchen. There wasn't much storage, but what there was worked fine for most crafters on temporary holiday. I put the small fold-out kitchen table up, and set both of my machines on it, then hung the garment bags in the closet near the bathroom and left my rolling suitcase tucked neatly off to the side. The cooler was more complicated. It took a few minutes of unloading to get everything in the tiny fridge or the two tight cupboards. We had to take the empty cooler back to the car as there just wasn't enough room to fit it in the house.

"Still good?" I asked Alex as we headed toward the house, hand in hand.

"Yep," he agreed. "Not thrilled about the windows beside the bed," he said after a few minutes when we got to the porch of the main house. The big loft area had enough space to sit up, but the mattress stretched edge to edge of the space with windows on two sides to help the space feel a little less claustrophobic.

"We'll shut the curtains," I promised. We were both used to being more enclosed, mostly, I think, to get away from the sounds that scared us. "The breeze is nice this time of year. The house has air conditioning," and a ceiling fan that helped circulate the air in the small place. "But the temperature is nice enough that we shouldn't need it. Overnight and early morning should be in the fifties." I'd packed Alex's quilt for exactly that reason.

"I searched for ghost pictures online of this place and came up with nothing," Alex said, sounding relieved. "No stories online either. Nothing on the website or official that I could find."

"Some people use the stories as a way to attract customers," I reminded him. Though since Freya didn't advertise her place that way, I figured whatever happened on site was either mild, or didn't bother her. "Our cabin is new. Less than five years old. Nothing in there but us."

Alex grunted, obviously not convinced. I squeezed his hand and opened the main door to let us inside. The interior of the house, like the outside, had a lot of the same old-world type charm. The entry opened to a giant stairway, which had a railed landing above. There were curved doorways on two sides and a double door on the end, which was open to the giant kitchen. The door on the right led to what used to be a sitting room and den, but had been opened up and combined into a huge crafting area. The space on the left was a large formal dining room. The upstairs was all bedrooms, and the corner behind the craft room, beside the kitchen was Freya's private space.

"It smells amazing in here," Alex said. "Any idea what's for dinner?" He frowned as he glanced at me. "Does she know you can't do dairy?"

"Tonight is a taco bar," Chad said as he came through the doorway from the kitchen. "Chicken, beef, and pork, even some vegan options of beans if you all want." He grinned. "I love taco night. We don't get this sort of stuff in Michigan. Spices are not quite the same."

"You're from Michigan?" Alex asked him, headed his way. I followed, listening to the two of them banter about the quality of Mexican-American food. Freya had a Latina woman who made amazing tamales and real authentic Mexican food. Though when the B&B was full, it was easier to make blander, more universal dishes that might appeal to more picky palates. Which meant this trip would be filled with taco bars, pancakes and eggs, and some sort of meat and potatoes type dinners. As long as I got Alex to eat, the rest didn't matter.

"Yeah, Detroit. Not looking forward to the winter, man. I hate the cold. Been thinking about moving south. Lots of conventions down here. I wish I could make cosplay a full-time gig."

"I'm not sure how that works," Alex admitted as we entered the kitchen and found the taco bar set up off to the side on a wide stretch of counter leading to the dining room. "Is there a market for it? I didn't know sexy cosplay was a thing until recently. Do people travel around and make cosplay for a living?"

"Some people can," Chad said. "Freya does. MaryAnn does a lot, so do a few others. Some make costumes as their income. I'm not great at making things for other people. Sex sells anything, and people are into anime a lot of the time because it's sexy. Everyone wants the illusion of being with some favorite character. Sexy cosplay is huge. A very private community, but there are a lot of diehard fans. People get really well known for certain characters. Sometimes there are crossover shoots between favorites. Those always get buzz."

Chad picked up a plate and Alex mimicked him, getting ready to dish up food. I kept an eye on him, but said hello to the handful of other group members who were filling their plates too. "Not sure anyone would care to see my giant, hairy ass in sexy cosplay, so that's not really an option for me. But for them," Chad waved at me and the girls, "everyone loves that. Small and cute pings everyone's radar."

Alex squinted at him. "You do know bears are a thing, right? I mean, as long as you're okay with gay men fantasizing about you."

I couldn't help but grin at the somewhat comically startled look that appeared on Chad's face. While I knew he was on the Ace spectrum, he was also a white, cis, hetero-romantic male.

"You mean, like gay men would pay to see me sexy cosplay beefy guys?" Chad clarified, as though his brain had trouble processing the thought. His cosplay specialty did really translate to either big guys like Hellboy, or villains like Thanos from the Avengers, which had become his new obsession.

"You would probably have an easier time finding subscribers to that, than I do," I said. If I had a dollar for every time I'd been told I give gay men a bad name because I could look and act very feminine, I wouldn't need to run my own business. Yet those same men watched my videos in droves. My audience also ran to a lot of women who loved the idea of gay men, but that one man had to be smaller and submissive. Perpetuated by manga and boy-love anime, there was a lot of that genre that had migrated to America and been reshaped by its giant culture of romance readers.

It was a stereotype. I couldn't change how I looked, other than to maybe cut my hair. Bulking up wasn't of interest to me, and I would always be short. And honestly, I wasn't all that unhappy with my body. Feeling okay in my own skin had been necessary while I'd done porn. I'd lost a little of that confidence when I'd given it up, but could see how brushing off the negative helped. Something else Alex had given me in the short time knowing him, a faith in myself.

When it came to relationship dynamics, Alex and I reversed the typical roles. He was more submissive and shy, mostly due to lack of experience. I preferred being in control and admitted enjoying sex enough to be a bit aggressive about it. Teaching Alex to break free from societal norms of sex shaming was part of making us a couple. Together, just the two of us, he easily cast off the Southern Christian upbringing of sex for reproduction instead of pleasure. In time I hoped I wouldn't have to prod him for sex and he would take the initiative. The 'throw me against the wall' sort of thing. But he wasn't there yet, too worried about hurting me. However, when it came to seeing other people and their skewed world views, Alex was a pro.

"I don't know a lot of gay men," Alex said. "At least not out ones, 'cause you know, military," he waved his hand. "But the handful I knew were all over either the older guy kink, beard, graying hair, or bears, big hairy men." He looked at me, his eyes softening as they always did when turned in my direction. "Saves the pretty ones for me," Alex said.

"I've seen a lot of Thanos and Hellboy fan art that is sexy," MaryAnn pointed out. "Would be easy to translate it into cosplay."

"I could imagine that," Freya said, coming up behind us and putting a hand on Chad's arm. "There are a handful of women who would love that as well. Washboard abs are a thing in media, but there's a market for the real thing too."

Alex held out an empty plate for me. "You need to eat too," he told me.

I took the plate and followed his lead, filling it up with meat and veggies rather than carbs and chips. Chad and Freya were locked in intense conversation when Alex and I made our way to the dining room and the huge table. We found two seats together and sat down, Alex diving in right away. At least feeding him was easy.

"This is fantastic," Alex told me after a moment of chewing, marveling over the spices on the meat, and the authentic blends in the salsa.

I filled a lettuce leaf with meat and fresh salsa, creating a sort of taco. "Grace is an amazing cook. She has degrees and everything, but didn't like the high stress life of working in a restaurant. Here she has full control of the meals."

Nicole and Julie sat across from us, both waving my way. Both were blonde and pretty, in their late twenties. They could have been twins for how similar they were, and often cosplayed as a duo.

Byrony and Melissa took the opposite end of the table. While I didn't know either of them all that well, I pointed each of them out to Alex. Byrony with her red-gold mane, and startling blue eyes, not all that unlike mine, and Melissa, another brunet who was thin as a rail, but with cropped short hair and wide shoulders. I knew Melissa did a lot of cross-gender cosplays like myself, able to straddle the line enough to go either way. Byrony's skill ran similar to Freya's, sexy, curvy cosplay that was so spot on people begged for her time. Byrony was lucky enough to not have the typical freckles of being a redhead, meanwhile I'd been stuck with them my whole life, despite having only traces of red in my hair thanks to my Irish mother.

While I admired her skill, I had never been a fan of her holier-than-thou attitude. She had always said a guy had no place in sexy cosplay, all while sharing pictures of her favorite guys in costumes. Of course the difference was the men she shared were all the 'manly' men type with endless abs and bulging necks. She had not been supportive of my return to cosplay. I had planned to avoid her most of this trip.

Jonah patted my back as he passed to sit beside Byrony. Like me, Jonah was on the small and pretty side, and the only other male, beside Chad, in our group. He had actually been shifting into full modeling work. Someone had caught a glimpse of his delicate features perfectly carved into that burnt sienna skin of his, and his bedroom eyes, and decided he had to be seen everywhere. I was a little surprised he'd taken the time to join this retreat.

It was interesting to note that I was the only Asian person in the group, though being only half Asian, did that count? Back home in Japan, entire sections of big cities were devoted to cosplay. It was either an all-in hobby, or nonexistent, but everyone knew what it was. In Ireland, it was completely the opposite, not really a thing, or even well known, but there were a handful of people with the interest. The USA had pockets of fans, and a large enough comic book industry to support a vast growth of cosplay, but the average American had either never heard of it, or only vaguely had an idea of what it was. Jonah was the only African-American guy I knew who cosplayed, though I had seen others. No one matched Jonah's intensity. He was only a year older than me, but already making a name for himself. He had bigger aspirations than I ever did.

"Hey Jonah," I said. "I heard a rumor you were going to be on Next Top Model."

"Maybe," Jonah said, sashaying his hips. "They know a good thing when they see one. And so do I. Micah, sugar, your man is fine," he said looking over Alex.

Alex's cheeks immediately reddened and he almost choked on a mouthful of food. I patted his thigh and encouraged him to keep eating. "Alex isn't used to the praise, but I agree."

Now that dark shadows no longer hollowed out his face, and he had several days of sleep and food, Alex was beginning to look healthy again. He would need more time to really put back on the weight he'd lost, but he was still a beautiful man. A mix of ethnicities that gave him fine cheekbones and skin a shade or two beyond tan, not quite sepia, but close. Alex's hair, which could be described as an afro prior to the care he showed it now, gave away his own African American father, while still having that odd bleach blond edge to it, though it was completely natural in color. Alex was a fine mix of races, which fascinated me in a lot of ways. Like the way his skin looked against mine, or how plump his lips were when I kissed them, and his hair. I fucking loved his hair, even in its natural state, the body and life to it that I would never have in my own, and those intense deep brown eyes. Nothing seemed to change the way he looked at me. It was never a passing glance or sweep of casual acknowledgment. When that warm gaze fell on me it was filled with adoration, interest, and intensity.

Alex stopped to stare at me. Heat flushed up his cheeks. "Um…"

I gave him a sexy smile, leaning over to kiss the tip of his nose and run my hand over his beard.

"No fair," Alex grumbled. "Eating. You can't look at me like you're sexing me up while we're eating."

"Later," I promised him, patting his thigh and going back to my food. I was going to be all over him later.

"Much better than that giant dick Tim," Melissa said.

"Tim is Tim," I defended my ex. He had gone with me once to a cosplay thing, but found it 'childish' and a 'look-at-me-fest' that meant he hadn't understood the concept at all. Cosplay was about being *seen*. Not for who we were, but who we could become. It was more magic than simply putting on a costume and striking a pose. The work required was a whole level of crafting and acting, that most people would never understand.

Jonah waved his hand dismissing the whole tangent of conversation. "We are going to be ghost hunting tonight. Looking for the white lady," he said. "Will you join us?"

Alex tensed beside me, his gaze flicking up and darting around the room like he was looking for someone who wasn't there. He had been more than thrilled about having a few days off from ghost tours.

"We're pretty tired from the drive," I began, hoping for a chance to drag Alex off to the cabin without prancing around the dark trying to awaken things no one really understood.

"But you know how to do this sort of thing. Call spirits and all that, right?" Julie prompted.

"He does lockdowns a couple times a year," Nicole said. "I've seen the videos. You often catch some scary stuff."

"On video sometimes." Visual disturbances weren't something I experienced, never had been. I was all audio or physical sensation. Alex, however, got full unexplained visuals. "I didn't bring any equipment for that."

"We have digital recorders," Jonah said. "And our phones." He continued to study Alex, resting his face on his palm, elbow on the table, instead of eating. "Hey are you the Alex that posted those pictures in Micah's group? The ones of the ghosts from the tour? Man, that one in the French Market was crazy clear."

"Yeah, those are mine," Alex said. He had not been checking the group for comments, but a handful of technically inclined fans of the paranormal had enhanced his pictures. The one he'd taken from the French Market, showed what appeared to be a person, edges of a face visible, and the entire body defined until reaching the lower legs. The form appeared to be floating from the knee up. That picture had actually gone viral while Alex was away, featured on cable news shows about the paranormal, and dozens of YouTube vlogs. I had no answers, and knew Alex didn't either.

"Will you investigate with us?" Byrony asked.

Freya joined the group, sitting at the head of the table and smiling at the group. "Micah and Alex had a long drive. I'm going to run them through a short tour of the house after dinner, and then they probably need some rest. Tomorrow is a busy day."

"Riding around going to quilt shops. That's not busy," Melissa pointed out. "I'd rather go ghost hunting. There's a trail not far from here that has some scary stories. Make-out-point sort of bullshit. I'd love to see that."

Alex swallowed hard, and I took his hand.

"You don't have to go with the group tomorrow," Freya told Melissa smoothly. "But I know Micah and Alex will want to go."

"I'm all in for quilt shop tours," Alex piped up, grasping the conversation right away. "No forests or spooky trails."

"Seems silly for a couple of ghost tour guides to be afraid of the paranormal," Byrony said.

"I'm just a guard," Alex said. "To keep the human creeps away."

"And we are not working this week," I added. "We are on holiday." I put my foot down firmly on the idea of involving Alex or myself in anything paranormal. He'd been taken for an entire month. Home only a few days. I was not about to get aboard that train again.

"Everyone eat," Freya instructed. "Jonah, tell us about your upcoming reality TV debut."

And just that easily she turned the conversation away from us, for which I was grateful.

CHAPTER 5

A fter dinner Freya showed us around the house. The craft area
being the most detailed overview. A giant table doubled as a
cutting area, as well as a place to iron. Alex marveled over the handmade ironing boards since they were small, lightweight, and portable.
"This is nice."

"Thank you," Freya told him. "Easy enough to make with a few
yards of fabric, batting, and a board from Home Depot."

"Cool," Alex said, running his hand along the board.

"I know you know how to use the long arm, Micah, so I won't go
into a lecture about it," she said as we went through the layout of the
craft space and pointed out the machine. Most people didn't know
what a long arm machine was. Freya's was on the smaller end, having
two rods to separate out the quilt as it stitched them together. I had
seen machines that were fifteen feet wide. I was more interested in
playing with the two mid-arms she had set up as I'd been eyeing
getting one myself. Mid-arms looked more like wider sewing
machines, often with a lot of stitch options and a very long neck. A
lot of the newer versions had embroidery capabilities, which had
always sort of annoyed me since I didn't like the tight look of a

machine embroidered piece and often did my own. Preference from childhood mostly.

I was not in any way a pro at free motion quilting, though I'd had a few classes. Ruler quilting was easy enough, but needed a larger machine than what I had, and I had to go pretty slow with the stitching. The two machines I had were an everyday machine, which I used for anything cotton, and a heavy-duty machine, which was more for heavier fabrics like denim, vinyl, and leather. A better machine might give me more reason to practice, but it was a big investment. I gave Alex a quilting overview on what they did before we moved on to the rest of the space.

The long tables and comfortable chairs in the bright room, even with the sunset outside, made me itch to work on something. "I do ask that no one use any of the machines after ten p.m.," Freya continued. "Though you could probably work in your cabin later."

"Micah will be sleeping," Alex said. "We'll both be sleeping regular hours while here."

I hoped that was the case, but didn't try to correct him. Sometimes a retreat like this turned into late night sessions of costuming, or idea slinging. And if I couldn't sleep, I would find something in our cabin to do, to stay close to Alex.

The upstairs tour was fast. A hall of bedrooms and bathrooms, with a small sitting area. The house didn't have a TV, but had Wi-Fi if someone needed to watch a movie on their computer.

Twice Alex looked behind us as we moved around, a few times at his feet, and I wondered if he saw something. Perhaps even the 'white lady', but he said nothing, nor did his expression change. He was not alarmed, which I took to be good news. His sensitivity to the unseen was downright scary sometimes.

"Can I get your measurements?" Freya asked me as we were wrapping up near her space and the back door which led to a path out to our cabin. The others were gathered in the entry, all talking in hushed chatter about their ghost hunting plan. "I have something I've been working on for you."

"Wow, really?" I asked. Freya's costumes were legendary. I couldn't imagine her taking the time to make something for me.

"When you said you might be coming back to the trade, I thought, well I had an idea." She smiled warmly at us.

"Sure," Alex answered for me. "What do you need from Micah?"

Freya led us into her space and dug through a drawer until she found her tape measure and a pad of paper. "A few numbers to update. I have the old stuff, but I didn't want to finalize anything until I knew if there was a change."

I stood with my arms spread out as she took measurements, and watched Alex. He was starting to droop. He might come across as having endless energy, but he was still recovering from severe malnutrition. Feeding him wasn't enough. He needed rest. It was one of the reasons I'd wanted to bring him along on this trip, as we would spend a lot of days working on sewing projects or exploring shops instead of running around the city of New Orleans with a bunch of tourists, seeking ghosts.

"Your cat is beautiful," Alex said.

Freya glanced up, and then spotted the picture of her cat, Precious, on the wall. "Yeah, Precious the princess."

I had never met Precious as she had crossed the Rainbow Bridge before I'd met Freya, but I knew the cat had spent almost twenty years as Freya's partner in crime. There were even a handful of cosplays which Precious had ridden along, adding to the mythology of Freya's namesake.

"You've lost some weight," Freya said to me.

"We're working on that," Alex told her. I actually hadn't realized he'd noticed, but of course he had. He always seemed to pick up on those little things no one else did.

The month he'd been gone had been a struggle in a lot of ways. Keeping busy meant no time for food. Or at least no motivation for it. "I eat when Alex eats."

She patted my shoulder, knowing a lot more secrets about me than most anyone I knew.

"I'm fine, I promise," I said. I had not relapsed, and having Alex close helped with that internal thrum of anxiety that always had me on edge. "I'm looking forward to a few easy days of sewing and fabric shopping."

"He is a bit of a hoarder," Alex pointed out like he was divulging top secret information. "For fabric, mostly." His face scrunched up in thought for a few seconds before he added, "And crafts."

"Sounds like everything is normal then." Freya finished up my measurements. "Escape while you can. The longer you stay, the more they will bug you to join in." I could hear the group moving around the house asking the white lady questions. They had turned the lights off upstairs as soon as we'd left that floor.

"Is there a white lady?" Alex asked.

Freya held out her arms. "I'm a white lady, aren't I?"

I laughed. "Yes, but not a ghost."

"Nope," Freya assured us. "There is no confirmed history of any mishaps in the house. I've been here almost ten years. The house is old, so there could be something off record, but nothing I have seen or can point to in history. We are not a 'haunted hotel,' just a crafter's paradise."

"Well that's good news," Alex said.

I reached for his hand and tugged him out of Freya's space and toward the backdoor. "We'll see you in the morning," I told Freya. "Alex and I need some rest." And I was hoping to sex him up a little before calling it a night. Or at least wrap myself in him.

"Don't forget breakfast at eight. The bus will leave at 9 for the shop tour."

"We'll be ready," Alex assured her. "There's a bus?" He asked me.

"We are part of a tour. There will be other people on the bus, not here at the hotel, but it's easier if we travel with the group to all the Houston shops. Then there's no parking to worry about, or navigating an unfamiliar city." Though I knew Houston pretty well. "It's actually very relaxing. The shops all have different lines of fabric.

We'll likely see most of it at the convention, but I do like to support the small local stuff."

Alex nodded, deep in thought. Hopefully he wasn't going to be bored out of his mind during this trip. I dragged him toward the cabin. The dark path illuminated by solar lights helped ease some of my anxiety. Alex, however, vibrated with tension walking across the lawn.

"My yard is more closed in than this," I reminded him.

"And surrounded in lots of talismans to ward off scary stuff," he threw back, intent on keeping our feet on the path.

"Which helped when something took you?" He had vanished from the bench in my garden, sitting beneath the giant willow.

"Fuck," Alex muttered, gripping my hand tighter.

We got to our cabin. I was happy to get inside and turn the lights on. The distant trees and wide-open space before them felt a little unnerving, even if I knew whatever stories about the house the others might be seeking were probably false. My anxiety rose mostly because of Alex's unease. Although the sounds of the early evening were normal enough with birds and crickets singing. Alex relaxed a little when we got inside. He kicked off his shoes and the light coat I'd picked up for him for the chilly evenings.

"Weird that she has a cat and runs a craft hotel. What if people are allergic?" Alex said as he locked the door behind us and pulled the curtains shut for privacy. He double checked the lock on the door. "And all the cat hair on projects. Jet leaves his hair everywhere. I bet a white cat is insane for prints and dark fabrics."

I blinked at him, trying to catch up to his thought process. "Precious has been gone for almost a decade. She passed pretty quickly from cancer. That was before Freya began doing retreats."

Alex frowned, brows narrowing and deep thought coming to his face. I did not like that expression because it meant he was adding up things that didn't make sense to most people.

"You saw something," I said, instantly recognizing where his cogs were going and remembering the way he'd looked around as we had toured the house. "Did you see a ghost cat?"

"I saw a cat," Alex corrected.

"The one that was in the picture with Freya."

"Yeah, white fluffy, not quite Persian, since the face wasn't flat, but yeah." He stared at me, looking a little worried. "It was in the dining room with us during dinner, then a few other places wandering around as we got the tour." He paused. "No one else acknowledged it, but I thought maybe they were just ignoring it? I felt it rub against my leg like Jet does…"

I couldn't help but marvel at Alex. When he saw something like this, so clear he couldn't decipher reality from the paranormal, I wondered if it was something he'd been born with and never realized, or had been birthed from his encounter in the Afghanistan desert. That night, and the following terror filled days had awakened him, if not spiritually, then at least cognitively. We didn't discuss what he saw, not in any real context, though I knew he'd been researching the idea of djinn, which were a sort of demon-like mortal creature in Islam and a few other Middle Eastern beliefs. They lived mortal lives, like humans, but did not have a corporeal form other than fire and smoke. They could also possess people, make them do things. That part scared me.

Until Alex had been taken and showed up on camera feed in some far away airport looking liking a zombie, I would never have believed it possible. Now I wasn't sure.

Even this, such a small thing as a ghost cat or whatever. It scared him. Not seeing a cat, or even a shop girl long murdered, but the fact that he saw things other people didn't. Seeing things others couldn't made him vibrate with unease. He didn't like being different, and months of being told it was all in his head, that he was crazy, made him question his sanity. Was he crazy? He asked me that sometimes in a small childlike voice, worrying over the answer. He walked that line between believing he really did see stuff, and thinking we were all humoring him.

"Did you feel anything?" he asked. "Like skin prickles or anything?"

"No," I said because I hadn't. And didn't always, even when he saw stuff as plain as day.

He frowned at me, worry tightening his lips to almost a grimace.

"Hey," I said, pulling him into my arms, and wrapping him in a hug. He looked down to meet my eyes and accept a kiss. "It's okay."

"You really didn't feel anything?" he asked again.

No prickles on my skin, or anxiety filling my gut. Did those things come from darker presences? I had no idea. "No. But a ghost cat isn't all that scary, right? Did it do anything scary? Morph or glow with darkness or anything?"

He shrugged. "Seemed like a normal cat to me. I felt her..."

"How about you feel me right now?" I prompted him, dragging him toward the loft. It was almost nine, early for bed, but not too early to wrap myself up in Alex's affection.

Of course the suggestion made Alex gasp, his body going hard against mine. It took so little to turn him on, at least when it came to me. When we'd met, he admitted he'd been having trouble getting an erection. Something about me awakened that damaged part of his brain, turned him on like no one else ever had. That little fact made me feel powerful and careful all at once. I did not ever want to hurt him.

"Okay," he admitted quietly, his focus on me. He paused, but I could feel his heart pounding in his chest, anxiety not at all quieted. Distraction and sex did not mesh all that well with Alex. "Maybe I could hold you for a while?" He sucked in air like he couldn't get enough. He leaned forward, giving me most of his weight, and resting his forehead on my shoulder. He hated admitting he was tired, but I could tell in the way every bone in his body relaxed against me, that he needed sleep.

I pulled the curtains closed and stripped him down to just his boxers and a T-shirt. He shivered despite the room being comfortable. The idea of seeing things we couldn't was more unsettling than being in an unfamiliar place.

"You like Jet," I said.

"He's not here," Alex replied fast, like it was only common sense that he adore my very alive and moody cat rather than the ghost cat he'd seen wandering the hotel. "I thought maybe the scary stuff would stay at home."

Only that wasn't how it worked. Not even for him. He'd seen something in the desert across the world, and it had taken him right from my front yard. I'd been hearing noises in the night for years no matter where I moved, and so I understood. It was a childish hope that the things under our beds weren't real. Denial was a big part of being human. So was fear.

Having spent a lot of the last two years trying to figure out how to move forward myself, I knew acceptance was the key. Not only of what had happened, but of myself, and how big everything was, unchangeable, even as things shifted all around us.

I opened the comforter I'd brought, the one I made for Alex, a mix of green and brown, not all that unlike camo from a distance. The design was leaves and a few little dragons mixed with some grunge print. We'd been using it nonstop since his return, the only comforter large enough to cover us both. I flung it around my shoulders, and then wrapped myself and it around Alex, curling us up in the bed.

"How about we focus on us?" I prodded him gently, carefully brushing his hair back from his face. It was escaping the ponytail holder, so I tugged it free and set the band aside.

"What if you find me too weird and don't want to be with me anymore?"

"Because you see ghost cats?"

"And black-eyed children, and djinn, and who knows what."

Black-eyed children? I would need to prod him about that during daylight hours. My memory pinged back to something I'd seen in a video, but instead of lingering on it, I kissed the tip of his nose. His overthinking mirrored mine a lot of ways. "How about you think of things you'd like to find at the quilt shops tomorrow. I can make you another quilt. We could use another big one. I'll have to send it off to be long armed again, but we can aim for a king size blanket."

"I'd like to learn how," Alex said after a minute. "Seems to calm you."

"Keeping my hands busy calms me."

"Sometimes," Alex said, squinting. He knew it didn't always help. I quilted when I needed to think, and made costumes when my brain was too loud and needed to be shut up.

"Did the crochet roses help you?"

"A little." He had grown frustrated with something on the dragon I had yet to figure out, and couldn't go any further. Right this minute he looked too tired to do much of anything, his breath deepening as sleep tugged him down.

I wondered if I should have made him stay home. Left him with Jet to cat-sit and rest. Was it selfish of me to want him with? To enjoy seeing him find delight in things I normally did? To show him things that brought me happiness and find out he felt the same way? It was an odd emotion, the need to share my enthusiasm with him. I'd never had that before. Tim had no interest in my crafting, neither had either of my parents. The cosplay group was probably the closest thing, only all of our tastes were very different. Most of the group, other than Freya, did not quilt or crochet, they made costumes or apparel. A limited scope to my broad one, which had made me lonely.

"I'm glad you came," I told Alex quietly.

"Me too." Alex's eyes opened and closed a few times, exhaustion forcing his body to relax. "Sorry," he grumbled. "I don't know why I'm so tired. If I were more awake, I'd be all over you."

I ran my fingers over his face, enjoying the shape of it in the pale light of the room. "Nothing to be sorry for."

"It's not late and I'm already crapping out."

"You're recovering."

"From being possessed," Alex muttered bitterly.

"Maybe," I agreed. "Is that what worries you?"

"If I fall asleep, I might have an episode," he admitted. A PTSD episode. As far as I knew, he hadn't developed PSTD until that night in the desert. Or perhaps it was the following day in which his team was slaughtered by something he still couldn't explain. Either way, sometimes Alex woke up not remembering where or when he was.

"I'm here." And while I wasn't a psychologist, I'd had training in handling PTSD. Alex wasn't armed, and he was bigger than me, but he was also malnourished. He had combat training, but didn't seem to want to hurt me. His last attack, triggered by stumbling across a murder scene in a cemetery, had turned him back in time, and I'd become someone he had to protect. Hopefully this time there would be no police aiming guns his way since we also wouldn't have his twin to stand between us and death by cop.

"We'll be fine," I assured him. "I'm here. You'll protect me, right?"

Alex was quiet for a few minutes. I thought he'd fallen asleep, even though I could see his eyes open a tiny slit. Then he said, "Don't go into the woods without me."

"I won't," I promised, and that was the truth. We were here to craft, sew, cosplay, and socialize, not camp or discover some ghost in an old house. I wrapped my arms around him, tugging the blanket up until we were both beneath the subtle weight of it, and closed my eyes, willing myself to relax to the sound of his breathing.

I don't know when exactly I fell asleep, but knew I had been when the screaming started.

CHAPTER 6

After experiencing years' worth of unexplained night noises, the screaming shouldn't have been anything to react to. I'd grown used to tuning out noise, or even having it worked into my dreams sometimes. However, this shrieking did not sound like an animal of any kind, more like a person being murdered.

I reacted on instinct, and so did Alex. He bolted up, half falling down the stairs, me hot on his heels. Him in boxers and a snug T-shirt, and me in bikinis and an oversized T-shirt, neither of us were dressed for the chilly night air that blasted us when we stepped outside.

The sound, a female scream, unlike anything I'd ever heard outside my house at night, came from the main house. Alex paused, blinking into the distance as we stumbled down the path, his eyes trying to focus as he'd been startled from sleep. Was he seeing the here and now? Or some terrifying desert night?

Another scream echoed across the open lawn. I passed him, running up the back stairs, I vaguely remembered the house would be locked this late at night. We had no way to get in, so I paused, trying to think, would the key from the cabin work? Should we call the police? Was someone hurt? Alex moved, falling into step behind me, clutching the back of my shirt.

We reached the door just as it burst open and out came a rush of people. Alex caught me, pulling me into a tight embrace as they bolted down the stairs half shoving me aside, screaming and thundering over the wood like a herd of elephants.

I squinted at the group, trying to make out faces in the dark. No one looked hurt. No one was bleeding that I could tell. Nicole and Julie, Chad and MaryAnn, huddled in a group a few feet from the back stairs, but I saw no sign of Melissa or Byrony. I frowned at them, brain struggling to keep up with the things they said as for some reason sleep had turned the 'English is not my first language' button to full distortion.

"Oh my God," someone said.

"What was that?" I think Chad replied.

Jonah came up behind us, wrapped in a robe, and from the path leading to the cabin on the opposite end of ours.

"Is someone hurt?" he asked. "Someone better be hurt, or else I'm going to show someone a little pain for waking a man from his beauty sleep."

"It's not even midnight yet," Julie said.

"We were sleeping too," I said, taking Alex's hand and trying to make out enough of his face in the dark to tell if he was in the here and now or some nightmare battlefield of his past. "Alex?"

He blinked at me. I could see the flutter of his lashes in the pale moonlight. "Hurt? I have first aid training." He did? It made sense since he'd been a Ranger. Technically so did I, but no one looked injured.

"I don't think anyone is hurt." I looked at the group. "Where are Melissa and Byrony? What about Freya? Who was screaming?"

Julie raised her hand. "I screamed. Something touched me." She shuddered. "Nicole and I were doing an EVP session in the upstairs sitting room. Our room is right next to it. Something touched me. I screamed. Nicole screamed." She looked at MaryAnn and Chad.

"Don't look at us," Chad said. "I didn't scream."

"No you just hauled ass out the door when they came zipping down the stairs," MaryAnn remarked.

"You followed!" Chad defended himself.

"Focus please," I said. "Melissa and Byrony? Freya? Where are they?"

"Melissa, Byrony and her boyfriend Joe, were in the dining room messing with a Ouija board," MaryAnn said. "None of us wanted part of that shit. Freya went to bed, I think."

I tugged Alex passed them, my feet and legs freezing as we hadn't taken time to grab shoes, and made our way into the house through the back door. There was a bit of a sunporch off the back, enclosed, long and narrow, a space filled with storage boxes of crafting supplies, well organized towers of completed projects, and shadows. I paused when something seemed to move out of the corner of my eye, only when I turned my head, everything looked fine. Probably a trick of the light. Probably.

Inside the backdoor of the house, was the kitchen and the small sitting area attached to Freya's space. Her area was empty, dark, and quiet. I frowned at the made bed and silence of her space. There was giggling and noise coming from the dining room area, too loud to be anything other than human, so I followed the sound, through the kitchen and to the hall.

Melissa, Byrony, and a man I assumed was Joe, all sat at the table, surrounded by candles, and hunched over a Ouija board. Alex clung to my hand as I entered the space, a little angry as they hadn't bothered with anything more than paper plates to catch the candle wax and keep it from burning Freya's expensive table.

"Maybe it's time everyone went to bed? Since you can't see fit to check on people screaming five feet from you," I ground out, gripping Alex's hand like it was the only thing keeping me from strangling them.

"We can't help it if the rest are a bunch of babies," Melissa said.

"They are screaming at nothing. That's not our fault," Byrony added.

Joe laughed. "Kind of funny though."

"Not for the rest of us who are here to sleep and craft," Jonah pointed out.

"That's why you're in the cabin, isn't it?" Byrony threw Jonah's attitude back at him.

"If bitches weren't screaming for no reason, I'd still be asleep," Jonah said.

"We weren't the bitches screaming," Melissa replied.

"Something touched me," Julie whispered.

"Maybe it's time everyone goes to bed," I said.

"You're not the boss of us," Joe said.

Alex squeezed my hand, his eyes focused on the doorway behind us instead of the throw down at the table. I glanced back, not seeing anything. Not really. Just maybe... a shadow? The edge of movement? Was that a trick of light? Low to the floor like that? I frowned, studying the shadows now.

Freya appeared in the opposite doorway after a moment, also wrapped up in a robe like Jonah was. "Ladies and gentlemen," she said, flipping the switch and filling the room with light. I blinked away spots and tears from too much light too quickly. Checking the other doorway again, I found the shadow gone. I let out a breath I hadn't realized I'd been holding, but Alex's focus remained on the door.

"For those who wish to sleep, please head to bed, anyone who wants to do otherwise, please take your noise to the craft room, which is insulated to minimize sound." She waited a moment as if waiting for everyone to move, but no one did. "Anyone hurt?"

"No. Just afraid to sleep in our room," Julie said.

"Chad has the other king. He'd probably be willing to switch with you," Freya put Chad on the spot.

"Oh sure, yeah, no problem," Chad said, instantly making himself the hero. "Let me move my stuff." He headed toward the stairs. Julie and Nicole following at a slower pace.

When Byrony, Melissa, and Joe didn't move, Freya put her hands on her hips. "Guest rules state courtesy in not disturbing other guests."

"We didn't scream," Byrony said.

"Last request, move your game to the craft area, or call it a night."

"And if we don't?" Melissa challenged.

"Then you'll be finding yourself a new place to sleep for the next week," Freya said, unmoved.

Byrony rose, gathering up the board as she went. "We'll go out and play in the woods for a bit. I assume we are allowed to come back when we are finished?"

"As long as you're quiet enough to respect the rest of the guests, yes," Freya allowed. "Just because you don't plan on going on the retreat into the city tomorrow, doesn't mean everyone else has the same plan."

"I'm going tomorrow," Jonah said.

"So am I," MaryAnn stated. "I think Chad and the girls are too. We don't quilt, but I use a lot of that fabric for handbags that I sell."

I was too tired for this mess. Hadn't realized how tired until the adrenaline began to fade. And frustrated. Alex needed rest. Maybe I should have insisted he stay home. Now we would both be jumping at shadows.

I tugged Alex toward the back entry where Freya stood, and thankfully he followed at a subdued pace. It actually worried me a little, how silent he'd become. Was he seeing something scary? I hadn't felt anything. Not skin prickles or even an unease; well nothing more than being woken up to screaming could be attributed to. Had the shadow I caught a glimpse of been the cat? Perhaps even what had touched Julie and scared her?

Then there was Alex, silent and as pliable as a puppet in my hands. Was he experiencing an episode? Perhaps not even awake at all, but dreaming all this and moving where I led him? I gripped his hand, hating the idea of any of that, and not sure how to fix it.

Freya touched my arm as we passed. I noticed then that the back-door was still open, as was the middle cabin door, which was lit up like Christmas, glowing with inner light. Freya was also not dressed for bed, instead hair styled and makeup on. Was she doing a middle of the night photo shoot?

"You two okay?" She asked softly.

"I think so?" I replied, not really certain of anything at that moment.

Byrony's boyfriend was grumbling something behind us about them paying for the space too, so they could do what they wanted. I would have commented, but it just wasn't worth it.

"Head back to bed. I'll try to make sure the noise stays on par of those of you sleeping," Freya assured us. Jonah passed, patting me on the back as he made his way back to his cabin. I tugged Alex to follow me. He clung to the back of my shirt, breath warm on the back of my neck as he tilted his head to rest it against mine. He was focused on me. That was okay.

Alex trailed behind me, slow as molasses. I paused to turn and examine his face in the light of the kitchen and now illuminated back porch. His pupils were huge. Dilated like he'd taken something, though I knew he hadn't. Alex got horribly sick from most any medication.

"You okay?" I asked him, rubbing his cheeks with my fingers. He almost seemed to melt into my touch and sucked in a deep breath.

"Was dreaming of something…"

"Yeah? Do you remember what?"

"A light? A trail? Something in the forest."

Usually that was my dream. "How about we go back to bed?" I prodded him toward the door and down the stairs. He felt a bit like a ragdoll in my arms, easily steered, but sticking close to me.

"Don't go into the woods," he told me.

"I won't," I promised, reminded of our conversation before bed. "Not without you."

"They watch us."

That brought a chill to my bones as I led him to our door and into the house. This time I left the light on downstairs in the kitchen, enough to give a nightlight sort of feel to the small space instead of the relative darkness afforded by the drapes.

"Who watches us?" I asked Alex while he struggled to keep his eyes open. After guiding him back up to the bed, I found a washcloth and wiped down our feet, dirtied by the walk through the night, and pulled the comforter over us. Ice was shivering through my veins now, more than the chill in the air, instead worry over something Alex might have seen.

"Alex?" I whispered, thinking he'd already fallen back asleep while an edge of nervous anxiety began to trickle down my spine.

"Them," was all he offered, not opening his eyes.

I thought briefly about the shadow I'd glimpsed in the house. Admittedly I saw shadows a lot. Usually explained them away without thought. A trick of light. Something in my eye. Someone moving nearby. The cat even, when I was home alone. Only now did I think hard about that.

"Alex," I whispered, expecting him to be asleep.

"Hmm?" He replied, humming into my shoulder where he had buried his face.

"Did you see the cat again when we were in the dining room?"

He didn't answer for a while. Asleep? No, contemplating because he finally said. "Yes and no."

"What does that mean?"

"It had changed." Alex turned his face and opened his eyes to meet mine. "It didn't look like the same cat anymore. It was distorted. Almost angry looking. I think because of what they were doing in the dining room. It was getting bigger, angrier until the light went on. Not the cat anymore. Something else..."

"Was the Ouija board agitating it?" It was something I'd never been a fan of. But in general, I didn't mess with occult things. No opening portals or calling spirits. Even on the ghost hunts my shop hosted a few times a year, we searched for already active spirits. We did not demand their presence or call them into existence.

I watched other ghost hunters, or paranormal enthusiasts as they called themselves, do something called 'provoking the spirits.' This often entailed a Ouija board or some sort of angry verbal attack. I thought of it mainly as an American thing. Though I'd seen a few European ghost groups do the same.

The idea that attacking the dead, if that was what they were, was a good idea, stunned me. In my culture, the dead were respected, and only called upon to offer protection. They were ancestors, those who had come before, and treated with respect, not terror or even loathing.

There were legends of the dead coming back more as demons than ghosts. Pulled from their graves to right a wrong, but transformed into something greater than simply the departed spirit of a loved one. In fact, a lot of Japanese and Chinese legends feature spirits transformed into something else by ill intent. We didn't call those or demand their presence. We didn't agitate those.

There was a difference between the yurei, the departed, and the yokai, demons or higher beings. I'd always thought of the yurei as memories more than physical things. In America they were thought of as repeaters, little more than a cluster of energy going about the same actions over and over. It was a bit like a stain on the fabric of reality rather than a person. No conscious thought, only a simple repetition of emotion or activity. That's why people smelled perfume of their grandmother, or the pipe smoke of their grandfather. The yokai were more like what had taken Alex. Tricksters. Monsters. Demons. Things that manipulated the living to gain power, energy, or control.

I had thought the cat might have been a yurei, energy of a cat once loved and worshipped, imprinting itself in the bones of Freya's home. But the change, that wasn't the act of a yurei. Had it been the Ouija

63

board that had manipulated the spirit of the yurei? I hoped it hadn't been changed into a yokai by the group's interference. It would be sad to learn that Freya's beloved cat, who had engraved her delicate and loving memory into the house, had suddenly been shifted into something dark and dangerous.

Funny how it didn't occur to me to question Alex on the validity of what he saw. He could have still been dreaming, hallucinating, or a thousand other things. All I had seen was a shadow. It meant little in scientific terms. But I didn't doubt Alex's word. He hated admitting he saw things the rest of us didn't. Being with me, he didn't hide it as much. He trusted me not to judge him. And I didn't.

I bit my lip, staring up at the ceiling as a thousand scenarios rolled through my brain. Every option from full on exorcist horror stories to every ghost hunter in the world descending on Freya's B&B to catch a glimpse of the terrifying ghost cat turned monster.

"Hey," Alex said, which made me jump a little as I'd been so lost in thought. "You okay?"

No. I needed to work on something. Clear my mind, or even interrupt the thought process. But I hadn't brought any major uncompleted projects with, only small things to keep my hands busy.

Alex reached up to turn my face toward his, his eyes dark and half lidded. "Micah?"

"I..." didn't know how to articulate what I needed. There was panic, deep within my soul. The idea that we'd gone on holiday and come face-to-face with a nightmare kept rolling to the front of my brain. "I need a distraction," I whispered.

Alex shifted around in the blanket, pulling me from being the big spoon in our snuggle to him being wrapped around me, blocking everything but him from my vision. I let out a long sigh as his weight on me began to ease the panic and slow my thoughts a little. He stroked my face and hair, let me feel his heat and strength around me. It was grounding being in his arms. Alex wasn't some sort of over-muscled hero, but he was solid, and for that I was grateful.

"Tell me what you're most excited to see at the convention later this week," Alex said.

I blinked, trying to process his request through the tide of busy thoughts. They slowed like a production line caught with a broken cog, stuttered and jerking. "The convention?"

"Yeah, this textile thing? Reason we're here? We're moving forward right? Tell me what you're most excited to see. I've been looking at the class schedule and hope to catch a few myself."

"There are a few lines of fabric," I began having to reroute my thoughts. Some of the lines I thought he might like, with dragons and mythical creatures.

"Tell me about them. What sorts of patterns do you like best?"

And that was a loaded question. Because I liked so much, and yet had strong opinions about certain prints. I sucked in a deep breath and began to walk through my thoughts on some of the most popular lines. It didn't matter that Alex fell asleep in the middle of my explanation because I did too, somewhere in defining the political intensity of Alexander Henry prints to the wildly overhyped Kaffe Fassett florals. We both needed sleep, and who knew categorizing fabrics could be better than counting sheep.

CHAPTER 7

When we arrived at the breakfast table the next morning, both a little bleary-eyed and in desperate need of coffee, I was surprised to find only Freya and Grace wandering back and forth from the kitchen to the dining area. I didn't do mornings well, but Alex had woken me with sweet kisses and a mutual hand job, before dragging me to the shower and then demanding coffee. Which was why we were in the house right at eight and marching to the coffee pot.

"Hope it's like your coffee," Alex grumbled as he reached for the pot. "I'll still drink it if it's some Folgers crap, but yours is what I crave." It was, as Freya had been the one to introduce it to me. She had regular big brand boring coffee too, but the good stuff was there and ready to go. I waited for Alex to fill his cup, then took the pot to do the same. A bit of doctoring with almond milk and stevia, and I took a sip, enjoying the familiar taste and warmth running through my bones.

Alex took a drink, sighed almost pornographically, then downed half the cup before refilling it. "Heaven."

"I have those waffles you like," Grace told me. "Dairy free, and the chicken sausages. Always real maple syrup of course."

"Hmm," I said into my cup, not awake enough to form real words, but let her direct me toward the hotplate put aside for my special diet.

"Thank you, ma'am," Alex said to her. He followed me, and we loaded up our plates full of almond flour, dairy free waffles, and chicken apple sausages, all covered in syrup. I didn't normally eat this much in the morning, but we'd be out running around, with only a short lunch break in the middle of the day, and I wanted Alex to eat.

We sat down at the table, opposite the doorway where the ghost cat had been last night. I watched Alex's expression, but if there was something here, he gave no acknowledgment to it. None of the shadows looked out of place, even as I studied the spot for a minute or so.

We ate in our comfortable morning silence for a few minutes as the rest of the group began to trickle in. Chad first, with a plate loaded full of pancakes and bacon. Then Julie and Nicole, MaryAnn, and finally Jonah. No sign of Byrony and Melissa. But since they weren't going on the trip into the city, I assumed they were sleeping in.

Freya joined us, sitting beside me with her own stack of waffles and sausages. Since I'd had almost an entire cup of coffee, my brain was starting to come back online so I looked at her and asked, "Were you filming in the middle cabin last night?"

She took a sip of what looked like very milky coffee and nodded. "Tutorial. It's easier to film at night when everyone is in bed, and I have full control over the lighting."

"Sounds like a good way to lose out on sleep," Alex said.

"I plan to nap this afternoon while you're all in town. I release three videos a week, but the other two will be from the convention. The one last night was a basic tips video. Editing takes more time than filming, and I have to do that later too."

"You're not coming on the tour with us?" It shouldn't have surprised me. She lived close enough to Houston to visit any of the shops whenever she wanted.

"I've done videos from them all already. Plus I have a few projects to work on, so it's easier if I leave you guys to explore," Freya replied. "I'll be with you all at the convention later this week, but thought I'd give you guys some space to explore town."

I didn't really need to explore town and would miss her presence as I debated projects and fabric with myself. While Alex had enthusiasm toward my projects, he didn't understand a lot of what I said. Freya had years of crafting experience and I valued all of it immensely. Though I was likely to find much more at the convention, with all the new fabric lines, than I would at any of the in town quilt shops.

"Did Melissa and Byrony come back? I didn't hear them come in," Nicole asked.

"Sorry about the scream thing," Julie said, her face pink with embarrassment. "I think it was mood more than anything. Us jumping at shadows and suggestions."

"That's normally how ghost hunting works," I said. "People put things in your head, then you forget what is normal and begin to question everything. Sounds, the trick of light in your eyes, and then you start playing with your own emotions. Fear grows and you get chills, or an *off* feeling. All psychological." Having experienced the real thing, I now knew the difference. I spent a lot of time since my return analyzing everything I saw, heard, and felt. Sometimes to my detriment. Being rational was hard when you were afraid, and I hadn't quite mastered it yet.

"You don't believe in ghosts?" Chad wanted to know. "But it's your job."

It wasn't. Not really. And I didn't want to have this conversation over breakfast. It was far too early to discuss philosophy, but it was Alex who responded. "It's not really a matter of belief or not. Are there otherworldly and unexplained things out there? Yes. But do most people find that on a ghost hunt? No. It's suggestion and the human brain playing tricks on you. I think that's why we catch stuff in pictures and in audio we can't hear rather than in real life situations. It's so far removed from us, these echoes of the past, or whatever, that we need the devices to pull it out of the silence. Micah's shop is a craft shop, based in art rather than the supernatural. And we do tours, but it's a lot of history. That history includes some ghost stories, which often leads to suggestions that then make people claim they see ghosts."

"You've caught pictures. I saw them in your group," MaryAnn said.

"A lot of people have pictures outside the norm. Does that mean they are ghosts?" Alex shrugged, though I knew he was more convinced of it than I was. "But that's not why we are here, is it?"

"No," Jonah said. "I don't need to know if some spook is getting kicks by staring at me in the shower. But I do need some costume ideas for the upcoming year. Did you all see those sneak peeks of Yaya Han's new line?"

"I did," I said. "The mermaid scales she had last year shifting to dragon scales with an almost alligator look. I can't wait to see it in person. She also has some faux leather designs that look easy to work with."

"Boy," Jonah said, "you know the way to a cosplayer's heart. Did you see the shimmering latex? Made a bodysuit out of that last year and the boys couldn't keep their hands off my unmentionables. If any more people examined my package, I'd have to call myself UPS."

Alex snorted into his coffee cup. "I like him."

Jonah reached across the table, though it was too far to touch and patted the wood top in Alex's direction. "Same, Sugar, same."

"No bodysuits for me," Chad said. "But you should see the new mockup of the Infinity Glove that Freya's helped me with. It's amazing."

"Freya is amazing," I said pointing out my friend's strengths. She gave me a sweet smile.

"She is," Jonah affirmed.

Everyone else agreed and the group broke off into chatter about their projects. It became a round robin of excitement with everyone talking about their latest creation, fueled by Freya's support and helpful comments. By the time they got to me, we were cleaning up.

The sound of the bus arriving saved me from having to admit that I didn't have a specific project in mind, but dozens. The actual number of my UFOs, unfinished objects, I had no idea. Things were sorted and categorized by Skylar's super compartmentalization, however, my brain did not work that way. Out of sight, out of mind for me, at least when it came to crafts. Which meant I had a lot of started things or probably nearly finished things that I'd completely forgotten about in favor of a new idea because Skylar had put it away.

Alex refilled our water bottles and stuffed them in his bag. He was still using the faux leather tote I'd thrown together for him. I offered to make him something more elaborate, but he'd refused, saying he liked what he had. I returned to his side and he immediately reached for my hand, drawing me up into a little hug.

"What's this for?" I asked, returning the squeeze and then letting go as we made our way out to the waiting bus.

"Happy you're here," Alex offered.

"Where else would I be?"

He shrugged. I wondered if he'd had another dream. His brother warned me that sometimes when he woke up in a new place it could set off a PTSD episode, but Alex had been up and coherent before me this morning. He usually was. Not necessarily a morning person with a cheery attitude and zipping around the house, but awake and mobile, ready to move. Like a soldier, I realized. Which of course made sense as he had years of training under his belt.

"You okay?" I asked him.

"Yes."

The bus was one of those high-end things, with padded seats and TVs popping out of the ceiling. Only half the size of a normal bus, I estimated we had only twenty or so people on the tour. We got a listing of the shops from the guide on the way onto the bus, a stack of coupons, which I handed off to Alex, and instructions for getting back on the bus at each location.

Alex and I took up a pair of seats, him on the aisle, and me by the window. He bumped me with his shoulder, which made me look at his face again. He rewarded me with a goofy grin.

"You're a nerd," I teased him as he slid his fingers through mine and rested our hands in his lap. Surrounded by a group of old ladies and a few of their husbands, I worried we'd get some flak for touching in public. We were in Texas after all. But if anyone noticed, they said nothing.

"Guilty," Alex agreed. "Do you think we'll find some new fabric to replace the curtain into the sin cave?" The bus began to move once everyone was on board. The small group from the B&B sitting around us.

I blinked. "Sin cave? Oh, the back of the shop. Why does it need a new curtain?" Right now it had something that blended in and was boring. Since sex toys was a small part of my business I'd never put a lot of effort into the space.

"Everything else in the shop is custom and handmade inspiration, right?"

"Yes. But I don't make the toys." Since adding the one-off costumes I made to the shop, I'd had to move things around to create an area where people could try them on. They weren't exactly one size fits all. I'd found a market with capes, which took almost no time to put together, but a lot of fabric. In truth, I was running out of space. "I thought about adding a small area, taking part from the breakroom, and moving the adult section to a more enclosed space."

Alex seemed to consider that for a few minutes. "That would give us more room for costumes and quilts. But what about Narwal Dick-master's fans? Relegated to a closet. No one likes being in a closet."

"Narwal what?" Jonah asked catching only part of the comment.

I smiled and shook my head at Alex. "I could put some of Narwal's most popular design in the register case." In the main part of the store, beneath where we processed payments with an iPad, was a locked glass case of custom jewelry.

Alex's eyes went wide. "Like have dicks... big alien ones, right there for everyone to see?" His face went red when he realized he was

71

sitting on a bus filled with old people. The quilting hobby really did seem to be dominated by old white women, but we were in the South. "Fuck." He slapped his hand over his mouth.

"Alien dicks?" Now our whole group was interested. "I could use a big alien dick," Jonah said. "How did I not know your shop carries alien dicks, Micah?"

"It's a small part of the business. I have a couple artists who provide specialty pieces, and the rest is part of a company agreement I have."

"Specialty pieces?" MaryAnn wanted to know. "How special can a dildo be?"

Chad's eyes were huge, absorbing the conversation. Julie and Nicole laughed. Jonah fished out his phone. "Girl, let me show you pictures."

"Have you tried the alien impregnator?" Alex asked Jonah. "It seems to be a thing."

"I've seen videos," Jonah stated. "It looks capital H.O.T., *hot*." He showed a few pictures on his phone, which I couldn't see, to MaryAnn and Chad, both whose eyes grew wide and a bit shocked. "I have a bit of a collection. But what can I say? I like dick."

"Narwal Dickmaster strikes again," Alex said. "Converting another sweet angel to the darkside with his demand for obedience and subjugation. It's a growing religion."

"I must meet this Dickmaster of yours," Jonah said. He turned so we could see the pictures on his phone. There was some sort of bluish green phallic shape with segments and beads at the top. It looked sort of bug-like. "This is my favorite. It tingles in all the right places." There were a couple more angles of the dildo in pictures, and even a picture of it next to a book. The thing was huge.

"Wow," Alex said, suddenly at a loss for words. "I didn't know using a thing like that was humanly possible."

"Sugar," Jonah said, "This baby is magic. I'll send Micah the link so he can order one for the two of you to play with. If this Narwal religion has got a hold on you, wait until you meet the Scorpion King's cock. It is up there with the giant Spaghetti Monster, but instead of wearing a strainer on your head, you got a thick cock in your dock, nudging all those delicious things inside."

"Cock in your dock?" Alex tried to translate. "Wait, Spaghetti Monster? Strainer on your head? What?" He narrowed his eyes and looked at me. "Monster spaghetti? Does spaghetti come alive like some old blob movie and eat us now? Just how much did I miss while in the military?"

And for the rest of the bus ride to the first shop, I spent explaining what a Spaghetti Monster was, and how it had become a thing of pop culture. Alex looked several times back at Jonah's picture of the Scorpion King's cock. I ordered one to be delivered to the shop in a handful of clicks, wondering what Alex would do if I brought it home with us. Either way, as the tension left his shoulders, and he chatted with the group, even after they teased him, I was happy he'd come along. If anything, his ease with the others made my own anxiety fade.

CHAPTER 8

The first shop was large and filled with a lot of traditional prints and walls of Batiks. "Batiks are hand dyed," I explained to Alex as he marveled at the rainbow wall of color they were arranged in, like some horizontal cascade of fabric. "The quilt I made you had green Batiks in it. That leaf design, which looks sort of like it's dyed in the fabric rather than printed on top of it."

Alex stood out of the way of the people entering the shop, not really moving, but sucking in air for a minute. Was it too crowded for him? There were a couple dozen people in the shop, but there was plenty of space between us and everyone else.

I squeezed his hand. "You okay?"

"Taking it all in."

I couldn't help but laugh at the awe in his words. "The convention makes this," I waved at the walls of color, "look like nothing."

Alex turned his gaze my way and blinked several times, the words processing slow enough with him that I could almost see the wheels turning. "For real? There's more?"

"The convention fills a giant convention hall. Hundreds of booths, dozens of designers, classes, and even machines. It will be packed with people." Mostly Alex seemed okay in crowds, but I planned to keep a close eye on him. "I have a vendor pass, which means we actually get in for a sneak peek on Wednesday. It will be less crowded, but not all the booths will be ready, and there won't be other events like classes or those live tutorials." Ideally, I would find a few lines to carry in my shop and begin discussions with the line owners. It was much easier in person than trying to work through the bazillion walls of marketing directors for some of the larger lines. My goal was to aim for newer designers, establish a relationship, and help them build their brand.

"Your eyes got all glowy," Alex said to me.

I tilted my head and looked up at him. "Glowy? Is that a word?"

"Maybe? I might have just made it up. Um, excited?"

"I do find fabric exciting," I agreed.

"And calming."

"Yes." Because was that true or what? I petted the bolts in my hands, finding the texture soothing as well as thought provoking.

"Hoarder," Alex teased.

"That is the quilter's way," the lady at the cutting counter informed him as she took the bolts of fabric and the measurements I wanted. "We call it a 'stash' though, not a hoard."

"Like a pirate stash? I do like the dragon hoard thing better," Alex told her. He put his hands on his hips and struck a swashbuckling pose with a wide stance. "Arrr, do I make a better pirate than a dragon?"

The lady laughed at him. I smiled and put an arm around his waist. "You can be whatever you want, whenever you want," I assured him. He let out a deep breath and relaxed into my touch. "Pirate, dragon, merman, whatever."

"Oh, merman. That would be cool. Didn't Jonah say something about mermaid scale fabric?" His gaze scanned the shelves again, not finding scales I was sure, because this shop had none.

"There's a new trend this year in scales," the lady informed him. "Our shop doesn't have it, but a few others do. Some with metallics in them. Beautiful stuff."

"I'm sure one of the shops on the tour will have them," I said. I thanked the lady and we made our way back out to the bus. Julie and Nicole had a bag of Batiks. No one else seemed to have purchased anything. "None of the shops today will have apparel fabric," I told Alex.

"You made boxers for me out of cotton," he reminded me. "I thought a lot of clothes are made out of cotton?"

We found our seats and sat down to wait for the last of the group to return. "True. Cotton is useful. However, it's also stiff and limiting in regard to costume design and wearable fabrics. The quilt shops feature very specific cottons with tighter weaves."

"Apparel is a lot of synthetics," Jonah said. "Makes it softer in some instances, more malleable in others. Like latex—"

"The stuff gloves are made of," Alex said.

"Yes. Gloves are super thin latex." Jonah smiled. "Like condoms."

"We use a non-latex version of those," Alex said without thinking. "Fuck," he muttered. "Stupid broken filter."

I patted his knee. "It's okay. Latex, whether condoms, gloves, or even fabric, isn't porous. Which is why the gloves always feel powdery inside, to dry the sweat. What Jonah is saying is that latex is now mixed with spandex or a few other fabrics to make it more breathable, and softer against the skin. Most apparel fabrics are the same way. Jeans are no longer made with denim, it's cotton and spandex. Even true cotton is mostly used for quilting, as the rest is mixed with polyester. Everything is made to stretch and breathe."

"Which means you can make a bodysuit out of latex and not feel like you're wearing a full-body condom," Jonah said.

"You guys have such weird conversations," Chad said as he sat down behind us this time. MaryAnn slid in next to him.

"I point this out often!" Alex agreed. "It's how we find ourselves in conversations about the Scorpion King's penis and body condoms, and yet sounds completely natural."

"Sex is natural," I pointed out. Alex's cheeks turned pink again. I smiled and leaned over to kiss him. "You're adorable when you blush."

"I'm too old to blush."

I patted his knee again. He could think what he wanted. The bus started up, and we were soon on our way to the next shop.

"So do you hobby, Alex?" MaryAnn asked.

"Micah taught me to crochet, but I'm a newbie. Haven't done cosplay since before I enlisted. I do find all this stuff fascinating. Not really time for hobbies when you're serving."

"Have you been out long?" MaryAnn asked. "Or are you only on leave?"

"Out. Medical discharge," Alex said, not willing to go into it further. Technically his physical issue wasn't substantial enough to discharge him. Despite the fact that it made him nearly immobile some days as his hip joint locked up. His mental health problems had gotten him an official, while quiet, release. They didn't want what Alex had to say to be taken seriously. His recall of monsters in the desert didn't seem to scare them as much as I thought it should. Not disbelief, Lukas had said to me while Alex was missing. He'd met with Alex's superiors a few times. They had offered Lukas condolences, assuming Alex was dead, likely by his own hand.

Lukas had asked about Alex's memories, the death of the soldiers in his group, and that dark day in the desert. The military had brushed him off. But Lukas had discovered that, indeed, most of Alex's group had died that day. Two others' survived. One losing an arm, the other seeming to have gone mad as he, like Alex had been for a time, was now in a mental institution. Lukas implied that the military knew more than they let on, and it wasn't the training exercise gone wrong that they led everyone to believe.

It was something both Lukas and I agreed not to bring up with Alex. He didn't need the rehashing of the past year. He'd been scape-goated in a lot of ways; made to believe he was crazy. Which frustrated me. He had a good therapist now. Someone who let him talk and didn't tell him he was nuts. But I knew it was a daily struggle. He rolled between depression, anxiety, and being overwhelmed on a regular basis. Rarely showed it outwardly, but I did try to help him clear his head and focus when possible.

Skylar indicating that Alex would find a hobby on this trip, that was well worth the overpriced ticket I had paid to get him in. Having him along was a bonus of course. He was pleasant company, easy to joke and make light of himself first. And his childlike awe over new things was adorable. Though it made me a little sad to realize he'd enlisted so young, and spent a sizable part of his life in the military rather than experiencing the normal sorts of things most people did. He had never been on some stateside base working a desk job. He'd been overseas and in training almost non-stop. Which was why he sometimes had a hard time processing normal events.

"Alex is an amazing cook," I said. "He makes these peanut butter cookies that are super rich and tasty."

"I do like to cook, but I'm no chef," Alex agreed. "I'd like to learn how to quilt like Micah does. Or something with fabric. He takes scraps and poof it's suddenly a blanket, or a bag, or a pillow case. Magic."

"Once you get started it's hard to stop," Julie said.

Nicole nodded. "Even when you mess up those first few times. As long as you keep going, the magic happens."

"I want to learn magic," Alex said with a childlike wonder.

"Tomorrow is supposed to be a craft day," I told him. "We can find some things you like and I'll show you a few simple designs."

"I don't even know how to use a sewing machine."

"That's okay. If you can take apart guns and put them back together, I think you can figure out a sewing machine." I thought of something that Lukas had told me. "Didn't you fix a coffee pot with spare gun parts?"

"It's not like I put bullets in it or something. Just some screws and a few barrel fittings. The water was so hard it kept clogging. At least with the barrel fittings I could take them out and scrub them clean. The cheap plastic ones that come in most coffee pots don't ever come clean."

Everyone looked at Alex.

"What?" he asked.

"You used gun parts to fix a coffee maker?" Chad confirmed.

"Hardcore coffee drinker, right there," Jonah said.

"Guilty," Alex admitted. "I don't function without coffee in the morning."

"Oh, I'm sure you *function* just fine," Jonah teased him, flirting a little.

Heat turned Alex's cheeks pink again. "I don't actually. But that's okay. Micah doesn't mind." He was referring to the fact that he didn't wake up with wood like a lot of guys did. I think he worried that I thought he didn't find me attractive enough. But I knew that wasn't the case. It took very little effort on my part to ever 'turn him on.'

"Fuck," he cursed. "I keep saying stuff I shouldn't."

I squeezed his thigh. "You're fine." It didn't matter that the folks not in our group had moved to the other side of the bus and a few were giving us disapproving eyes. Everyone in the cosplay group knew I had worked in adult videos, and my cosplay had never been PG rated.

"He *is* fine," Jonah agreed. "You going to cosplay with him?" He asked me. "I could see him in some tight leather Witcher pants, or even the Assassin Creed outfit."

"Fake leather maybe," I allowed. Leather, and actual animal products in general were difficult to work with, breaking needles, and needing special treatment. "I think we will... cross that bridge when we come to it," I said, recalling the common saying.

I had some new ideas for costumes for Alex. Since he loved dressing up so much, my plan was to make him some things he could wear doing our tours, or even in the shop, and for fun, but had yet to run any of it by him. I needed to ask Freya for some help drafting the ideas first. From my head to paper didn't always translate the same. Freya, however, could take my verbal description, and sketch it, with notes, to something I could then turn into the guide for a pattern. I had yet to achieve her brilliance. So far the things I'd made weren't suitable for everyday wear, and I couldn't see us traveling around to cosplay conventions all the time.

We arrived at the next shop and listened to the instructions.

"Everyone will have an hour for the shop and an hour for lunch," the guide sitting up front beside the bus driver stated. "This area of town is filled with restaurants. You can either eat first and then shop, or shop and then eat. The store does ask that you not bring food inside."

Everyone murmured in agreement and we made our way off the bus. This shop was a bit more artsy. Some big name lines, of course, lots of modern colors, including the section of scales mentioned before, some handmade prints, and a lot of precuts. In fact, the stacks of precuts of all shapes, sizes, and colors instantly set my wallet on fire.

"Wow, you're super glowy," Alex remarked.

"Precuts are a quilters paradise," I told him.

"Was that English?"

I waved away his silliness. "Go find stuff. Ignore me while I spend all my money."

He dug in his pocket for a minute, then pulled out the stack of coupons, flipping through them and then handing one to me. I'd forgotten I'd passed him the mess. The coupon he gave me was for twenty-five percent off any order over one hundred dollars. I gaped at him.

"What?" He asked. "Go delight in your square things. I'm going to check on the machines." He wandered away to the far right side of the store which was set up with a dozen machines, including a few long arms.

I actually did get lost in the fabric for a while. When I checked out, I realized I'd been shopping almost an hour and a half and we needed lunch. Where was Alex? I didn't see any of our group in the store anymore. A few from the bus, yes, but not from the cosplay group. I thanked the woman at the counter, accepted the two giant bags and headed toward the machine area. Would Alex still be there?

He was.

Alex sat at a mid-arm machine. A large square in front of him at the machine, a quilt sandwich, we in the trade called it, fabric layered on batting layered on fabric. The free-motion sewing foot was on the machine, a round sort of hole of metal that made up the 'foot' pressing against the fabric. And Alex moved the square around, the machine buzzing as his foot rode the pedal.

At first I thought he was simply playing with it. Since there were two employees nearby, I wasn't worried. But as I got closer, I realized he wasn't playing at all. He used the machine at regular speed, instead of slowing the pace or even hesitantly pressing the foot pedal. His hands moved in a gentle direction, turning and shifting the fabric with little effort. Echoing... and restarting a new line of perfect quilting.

The two employees looked on in what seemed to be shock. Not that he was breaking anything, but that he had no hesitation in using a machine I knew he had never touched before.

"Alex?" I asked.

For a moment he continued, like he hadn't heard me. Perhaps he was in the zone, as they called it, super focused. I got that way often enough.

"Alex?" I called again.

This time he paused, foot easing off the pedal and his hands stilling the guide of the fabric through machine. He looked back at me, blinking, almost like he was waking from a dream. I switched the bags to one hand, hefting their weight aside, to touch his face.

"You okay?" I prodded when he didn't speak.

"Yeah, I think so," he replied. We both looked down at his little quilt square, probably a little over a half meter square, and found elaborate designs swirled over the space. From a section of detailed paisley feathers, rolling spades, and *fleur-de-lis* type symbols to elaborate pebble-like circles of varied size and shape, stacked upon themselves. His square was almost full. Maybe one of the other quilters had left it behind?

Alex pulled his hands away from the square, staring at it for a minute, then glanced around the room, before pushing away from the table to stand beside me.

"Thank you, ladies," he told the employees. "That was fun."

"I've never seen someone free motion that quickly and without rulers. I mean the long arm does it when programmed in, but your stitches are perfect," the older woman said.

"Like Judy's," the younger of the two confirmed. She put her hand over her heart. "I miss that sweet lady. She could feed a quilt through like that, transitioning from one stitch to the next seamlessly. Read the fabric and craft a stitch perfect for each section without hesitation. Real artistry. Won dozens of Guild prizes over the years for her work. Never seen anyone else do it in person. You must have years of practice."

"Thank you for letting me play with the machine," Alex said, tension tightening his shoulders. He reached for my bags. "We should get back to the bus, right?"

"We need food first," I told him, letting him take them as he rushed us toward the door of the shop.

"Don't forget your sample," the younger woman said. She took the square off the machine. "You did all the work. You should keep it. It's beautiful." She tried to give Alex the square, but when he wouldn't take it. I accepted it instead.

"Thank you," I told the women as we left. Once out on the sidewalk I grabbed Alex's arm and pulled him to a stop. "Alex?"

He was breathing hard, an edge of panic in his eyes. He gnawed on his lip, and I worried it would bleed soon. I took a step forward and kissed him gently, sucking his battered lip into my mouth and massaging it with my tongue before letting him go.

"Talk to me?" I asked. "I thought you've never touched a sewing machine before?" Certainly not a mid-arm. I didn't own one, though I had thought about getting one. Most people didn't know what they were. And to free motion quilt like that? Flawless, almost effortless.

Like someone who had never painted before, picking up a brush and in a few minutes producing a Michelangelo.

I had a thousand questions, but didn't know if Alex actually had any answers. No one magically began that skilled. It wasn't possible. Even an artist would have to learn the machine, practice how it moved, and get familiar with the motion of the needle.

"Alex?"

He set the bags at my feet, stalked a few feet away, running his hands through his hair, and pacing. I watched him, waiting for him to clarify his thoughts enough to share them. After several treks back and forth, I thought maybe he wouldn't say anything.

"I knew she was a ghost this time," he said suddenly. He waved his hand. "Or whatever. A spirit, or something. Not a living person."

"Okay," I agreed. "There was a lady with the two other ladies I saw?"

"No. Not exactly." He crouched down, closing in on himself for a minute, head over his knees, hands in his hair, which was a total mess now. He stared at the sidewalk for a moment, arms wrapped around his knees. "I let her use me."

"What?"

He stood up again and resumed his pacing. "She said it was sudden. She hadn't gotten to share her skill. Hadn't found anyone who could handle it, not even her kids. Said she would show me. Could tell that I was the right one."

"Wait... so the ghost lady was sewing through you?" I tested my understanding. I held up the square. "She helped you create this?"

"Yes and no. It was, I don't know how to describe it. I started very slowly. Those ladies showing me how to lower the foot thing and move the fabric. The other lady, she wasn't as solid. Not like that store clerk in the thrift shop was. She whispered that they have never mastered her skill. There was no one to teach her classes anymore. She offered to show me how to do a little. I said okay." Alex paused. "She touched me. It was cold. Not like the fire of the... well anyway, it was cold. She put her hands over mine and we started. I could feel a sort of memory. Not mine exactly, but enough of it that I could use it for myself. A muscle memory. The rest was easy. One design to the next. Like I'd been doing it forever." He stalked back to stand in front of me, his expression seeking. "I could probably do it again. Remember how, craft the lines of a thousand images." He waved his hands around. "I can tell you a dozen different patterns I would probably have never known before today."

Alex had a remarkable memory for things on most days. From languages to crafts, so the idea that some memory had settled on him, given him a glimpse at something he would never have experienced before, and burned it into his memory? That did not surprise me.

"Okay," I said, waiting for him to go on. Had this hurt him somehow? Or simply made him afraid that more memories would settle on him? It didn't seem like a bad thing, but I wasn't the one who'd been suddenly gifted with someone else's lifetime of experience. "How can I help? Did it hurt you?"

He let out a long breath. "I'm crazy."

"Weird. Not crazy." I bent to pick up the bags.

"You're not ready to dump my ass? Run screaming into the city begging someone to keep me away from you? I just told you a ghost lady taught me to ... sew? I don't even know what it's called."

"Free motion quilting," I offered. "I might run from the hair, but not your weird." I headed toward the nearest fast food place. "You need food. I'll fix your hair when we get back on the bus."

For a minute he didn't follow, instead standing on the sidewalk waiting, staring at me like he didn't understand how I wasn't rejecting him. I paused and looked back, before pointing to my chest. "Stolen by aliens or an interdimensional portal or Sasquatch or something for a couple of months, remember? Your weird is barely a blip."

His jaw dropped. But I turned around and resumed my course, hoping to find something halfway healthy for the both of us and make it back to the bus in time. Alex caught up a few seconds later, taking the bags from me, switching them to his opposite hand and taking mine in his. He squeezed my fingers, then rested the strength of his grip in mine, his heart pounding strong enough I could feel it through his palm. But he didn't run away. I hoped the message I sent him was clear enough. It was okay. Whatever it was. We would work it out. Weird came and went. I think we were both getting better at dealing with it.

CHAPTER 9

The rest of the tour went by smoothly. Alex remained close by my side. He was promising me sexual favors as we got back on the bus to head back to the hotel.

"I expect to be rimmed regularly," I told him as we sat down. "For at least a week."

Alex's face was so bright red, and he wouldn't look at anyone around us. "Stop," he whispered. "But yes."

"Boy, what did you do to get that fine man to promise to eat your ass regularly?" Jonah demanded.

"Bought him the dragon panel." They had all noticed it. It was that sort of thing which made people stop and breathe for a moment, taking in the details. A good painting could do that. I'd seen my fair share of 'fan' art at anime conventions over the years, so breathtaking that it could give any artist imposter syndrome. The dragon panel was in that line of workmanship. The beast almost seemed to pop off the wall in 3D splendor when we walked into the shop. A mix of positive and negative space, colors jewel bright enough to nearly glow at a distance, the dragon was anything but a mass-market print. The original had a gem-like luster to the colors that fabric dyes and paints could replicate only so much. I'd suspected when we viewed the digital panel, that the colors would be duller, more generic, but they weren't. Which was why the panel had cost so much.

"It was over a hundred dollars. For less than a yard of fabric."

"It's actually a little over a meter, which is slightly bigger than a yard," I said. "America's measurement system." I waved my hand.

"It's amazing. Looks like it's flying off the fabric," Alex said in awe. "Now if only we could have found some mermen."

"Never seen sexy mermen on fabric," Jonah said. "I've been a sexy merman a few times."

"Alexander Henry had a fabric with mermen on it, but they were skeletons," I said, recalling the print which was somewhere in my stash back home.

"Alexander Henry is weird shit," Jonah said.

"It can be," I agreed. Everything from day of the dead skulls and painted girls, to giant killer bunnies. I wasn't sure how the fabric line had become quite so wild.

Alex curled up beside me, nestling into my space. I could tell he was tired. I needed to get more protein in him. Maybe we'd have an early night after dinner, curl up and watch a movie on my laptop or something equally as easy. I suspected the anxiety of the day contributed to his exhaustion. The group broke into chatter, which I tuned out to focus on Alex. He had pulled a crochet hook and some yarn out of his tote and began working on another rose. I couldn't help but smile.

I wrapped my elbow around his and leaned into his shoulder and watched him work. I think it calmed us both. Him to have the repetitious movement, and me to watch him. He didn't have the same liquidity I did from years of experience, and his stitches weren't uniform in tension, but he was confident enough in each stitch that he flowed through a rose in minutes. Then he passed it to me to hand sew the few stitches that would pull the string into an array of petals. We worked that way the entire ride to the hotel.

Once we arrived back at the B&B, we took our stuff to the cabin, leaving everything inside and taking a moment to curl up on the tiny couch and hold each other. Dinner would be soon. If it weren't for the rumbling of Alex's stomach, we might have stayed there. I even thought of putting together sandwiches for us instead of going to the house for food, but finally sighed and got up, dragging Alex with me.

"Come on," I told him. "We can't be anti-social unicorns here."

"If I didn't smell fried chicken, I would disagree with you. You think it's the real thing?" He winced then. "Mom made it with butter-milk. That means you can't eat it, right? Fuck."

I tugged him out of the cabin and down the path to the house. "They will have something for me. Don't worry. Eat whatever you'd like."

Alex moaned when we entered the house to find a mound of real crispy fried chicken, mashed potatoes, homestyle gravy, and a dozen veggie sides. "I've died and gone to heaven," he muttered.

"Sweetheart, with the way you moan, a boy would think so," Jonah said as he made his way to the buffet area.

Grace pointed me to an area of grilled chicken and baked potato, for which I was grateful. I watched Alex fill his plate first, stacking it so high I thought he might explode if he ate all that. His grin was huge, like he couldn't believe his fortune. I patted his arm and pointed him to the table, then made up my own plate.

Freya came in with Melissa. They were arguing about something. It was rare to see irritation on Freya's face, but I could tell she was.

"Everything okay?" I asked.

"Byrony never came back last night," Melissa said.

"She's probably out with Joe," Freya said. "We are not babysitters. She's a grown woman in control of her own choices."

While I agreed with Freya, I could see how worried Melissa was. "Have you tried calling her?" I asked, certain she wouldn't be upset if she had and gotten through.

"No answer," Melissa replied.

"I thought you were going with them last night?" I asked.

"I did. We went into the forest. There's a part where the trail breaks off, and there are stories, scary urban legend stuff, so we went that way for a while, trying to find the spot." She flushed. "I got nervous. It was dark. Everything seemed so loud. Joe walked me back to the trailhead. I came back alone." She let out a long breath. "Scariest walk I've ever done in my life. Through the woods at night, alone."

"Maybe they decided to find another hotel for more games," MaryAnn pointed out as she put grilled chicken and a baked potato on her own plate, matching mine.

I glanced into the dining area to find Alex sitting at the table and eating. At least I'd get some food in him.

"We all rode together. The car is still parked out front," Melissa said. "Did they just walk to another hotel? Without me?"

"Maybe they wanted some alone time," Julie pointed out. "She and Joe have been together only a few months."

"In the woods? We have separate rooms. Why wouldn't they call? Or at least have their phones on? Reception in the woods is bad, but not impossible."

"Even if they got lost," Freya said, "there are plenty of places not far from here. They could find themselves at the gas station, or another house. I'm sure they are fine."

"But not here and not answering their phones," Melissa repeated.

A sick feeling of anxiety curled in my gut. The familiar weight of that dark monster sank down on my shoulders as my mind began to churn. What if? What if they were hurt? What if something had taken them? What if someone had taken them? Could someone have taken them? Why else would they be unreachable?

I made my way to the table, everyone else finding their own places, though Melissa didn't get any food. Alex was staring at the far doorway again in between eating. Was the cat back? I sat beside him, reaching for his hand, not sure if I could eat as my head filled with anxiety over a girl I barely knew and her missing boyfriend.

"What's wrong?" Alex asked me.

"Is the cat there?" I whispered, trying to focus on whatever it was he saw in the opposite doorway.

"Not exactly. What's wrong?"

"Byrony and Joe are missing," MaryAnn announced to the group. "Melissa says they didn't come back last night."

"From out in the woods?" Nicole asked.

"There are a couple houses nearby," Chad pointed out. "Maybe they got lost on their way back and stopped at one?"

"And didn't call?" Melissa asked. She held up her phone. "I've called them both dozens of times. Even walked out to the path, where it stops and breaks off, called and gotten nothing. Not even the sound of their phones ringing somewhere in the distance."

"What would you like for us to do?" Freya asked her. "We could call the police, try to report them missing. If the police don't think they are in immediate danger they won't start looking for a few days. There is nothing in these woods. Nothing bigger than a racoon or some deer. We haven't had wolves or bears for years."

"What if they fell and got hurt?" Julie said.

"Both of them?" Jonah asked. "Like at the same time?"

"Someone could have taken them," Melissa said. "Hurt them."

"Unlikely," Jonah said. "Byrony's attitude would have made a kidnapper return her by now. Or kill her."

"Not funny," Melissa snapped.

"They could be taken like Micah was taken," Nicole said in a quiet voice, her gaze falling on me.

An edge of tension and silence fell over the table. I could almost hear Alex's heartbeat in my ears, his anxiety rising like a cloud of emotion to cover us both. They all knew of my incident, having met them all long before it happened, but I didn't think any of them had actually been involved. None had helped in the search, not even Freya who lived the closest. I didn't blame any of them for that. Though the dynamics of our group had changed a little since then. Their hesitation to reconnect with me afterward had been clear, taking each of them several days and sometimes weeks to respond when I reached out. It was a normal response. Human even. The fear of loss and pain keeping them from compassion. I didn't blame them. Or at least I tried not to.

"This land isn't part of the state park," I reminded them all. There were a handful of similarities of those who went missing like I had. And a few that even I hadn't fit, since I'd survived, and some still questioned if I should have been grouped with the rest at all. "They are probably lost. It's a big forest area, and the cell reception out here is questionable. Technically if they walk in a particular direction long enough, they will end up in the state park." Though that was a couple miles of a zigzag type trek.

I pushed my plate aside, not hungry anyway as fear gnawed at my gut. The sun had already mostly set, leaving that final edge of purple-blue sky with a tiny hint of starlight until the moon completely rose. When I got up out of the chair Alex grabbed my arm.

"No," he said.

"I have flashlights in the car. Flares. Walkie talkies. Even a survival pack with first aid gear and thermal blankets." I felt heat flush over my face in embarrassment. "Your brother insisted I take them."

Alex did not look happy, but began to get up from his chair.

"No. You stay and eat. I'll go with Melissa to look."

"Not a chance in hell," Alex said. He pushed his plate aside. "I'll go help look. You stay here."

I narrowed my eyes at him. His protective side, while cute for stories, annoyed the fuck out of me. The idea of going into the woods at night scared the crap out of me, but I would not be left behind like some damsel in distress while Alex put himself in danger. "If you go, I go," I told him.

"We all go," Chad said, getting up from his chair too.

"Girl, I know you didn't volunteer us all to tromp around the woods in the dark," Jonah said.

"I'll help!" Nicole said.

"Me too," Added Julie.

"If we all look, we can cover more ground. Find them faster," Chad said rationally.

Jonah sighed. "Fuck. Not a single one of us is the outdoorsy type." He pointed to himself. "Nerd." He fluttered his hands around the room. "We are in a group of nerds. It's required for cosplay."

"I'm a nerd," Alex agreed. "But also, an ex-Army Ranger. Which is why I should go. Everyone else can stay here. I just need Melissa to tell me where she last saw them."

How many times had he told me in the past few days not to go into the woods without him? And he thought I'd let him go racing into the woods alone? I crossed my arms across my chest and met Alex's eyes with mine.

"Fuck," he sighed.

And that was how we found ourselves in the woods after dark.

CHAPTER 10

T he trail itself was a wide swath of path that curved and swung around in a broad arch. Even with only the handful of flash-lights illuminating the woods I could tell it was something people in the area used regularly for hikes, perhaps runs, or even peaceful walks.

All in all, the woods felt like normal woods. The trees large, but not that epic stretch that could be found in some of the national forests. Distantly the sound of cars echoed, mostly blocked by the trees, but occasionally finding its way through the darkness. The path from the house extended a couple dozen meters before turning into something that might originally have been a game trail reclaimed and widened by humans.

I had expected the area Melissa talked about leaving the path to be a sort of dead end. We walked over a kilometer from the house, fifteen or twenty minutes thereabouts, before finding the sharp turn that cut off the trail. It wasn't a dead end, so much as a tiny dirt line snaking off the path and into heavy brush. Alex gripped my hand hard enough to hurt, but I didn't pull away. We both had lights. Everyone had a torch or flashlight of some kind. The group was broken into pairs, a walkie talkie for each, plus our cell phones. Alex was not taking any chances.

"I don't feel anything," I whispered to Alex. No bugs or fire on my skin, only a slight chill from the evening breeze. "Do you see anything?"

He shook his head. "Stay close to me."

"Byrony?" Chad shouted. We'd been taking turns calling for them every few feet. "Joe?" We would stop and listen. It became a sort of stuttering dance of movement and stillness. Nothing but birds and bugs responded. I heard a squirrel a few times, watched them scamper away in a dark race of fluffy tails. Normal forest noise. The kind of silence that was easy to tune out.

"Is there another house nearby?" Alex asked Freya. "A neighbor you can call to see if they might have heard someone out here?"

Freya nodded. "Sure, let me call the Juarez family and see if anyone's seen or heard anything. They have a barn on their property that isn't used much. I don't know why Byrony and Joe would go there, but it doesn't hurt to check." She lifted her phone, but frowned. "I'll have to go back to the trail and see if I can catch a signal." She had no problem finding her way back that I could tell.

"Maybe they scared themselves and got lost," MaryAnn suggested. "They did seem to really like paranormal stuff. She and Joe have been talking about creating a YouTube channel for ghost hunting."

"It's a lot of work and equipment for little to no payoff," I said.

"Unless they are faking stuff," Chad added. "Then they get big TV deals."

We made our way a little deeper into the woods, this end of it a bit thicker with brush and the trail we'd followed off the path completely vanished beneath debris and overgrowth. Everything was dry and more brown than green, and it didn't look like anyone had been through here in a while. Alex was examining the area too, maybe seeing more than I was since he had military training.

"It doesn't look like anyone's been through here," I said softly.

"No," agreed Alex. "But the ground is pretty hard. Unless they stumbled through some leaves it would be hard to tell they came through at all. Dry places suck for tracking."

"Too bad it's not the rainy season," Freya said, finding her way back. "Nothing from the Juarez home, but I left a message for them to call and check their barn."

"Byrony? Joe?" Julie called.

"You bitches best stop playing!" Jonah shouted into the darkness. The group was getting a little more spread out than I would have liked, though Alex remained plastered to my side.

Melissa tried to call their phones. I don't know if she even had a signal but it was clear she didn't get through. Though everyone paused to listen for the ring of phones anywhere in the distance.

"Maybe their batteries are dead?" Nicole said.

"Or they turned them off for their goofy witchcraft stuff," Julie agreed. Which brought back the question, where were they? Gone almost twenty-four hours with no word?

"Let's create a line. Search for things on the ground, cloth, strands of fabric, marks in the dirt, leaves that look disturbed, anything that points us in a direction," Alex gave everyone clear instructions. "No more than five feet apart. Make sure the rest of the group stays in sight. If you have trouble or spot anything, call out. We'll cover more ground, faster this way." He didn't want to let me go. That was clear in his eyes as I tugged my grip free from his and took several steps away. The forest was dense enough that any more than the five feet or so, and you had to really look for someone's light. I couldn't help but be hyperaware of my light and my neighbors, including Alex, as a sort of safety net against anxiety.

We followed the regime for a little while. Slowly walking a few feet, examining everything around us carefully, and taking turns calling out then listening. I admit to falling into the rabbit hole of my thoughts after about twenty minutes into the search. When Alex had vanished, we had him on camera. There wasn't much area to search, even if the entire city had been put on watch for him. However, I wondered if this was how everyone had felt when I'd gone missing.

Had they set up grids and shone flashlights in the dark? Probably. I'd never asked as it had always been a touchy subject. Why the human brain latched onto guilt when there was nothing I could have changed about it, I would never understand. I hadn't asked to disappear, or for people to search for me. Would Byrony feel the same?

The change in my focus, the noise in my own head, once again distracted me from the things I should have noticed. The stilling of the wind. The absence of birds and crickets. But even my own overactive brain couldn't make me ignore the burning prickle trailing over my arms. It began slow. Almost a chill on my flesh rather than the usual ants. My skin tightened into goose bumps, the hair on my arms and the back of my neck rising. I stopped, blinking into the darkness as the feeling intensified.

There was movement ahead. Not an animal that I could tell. It was too big for that and moved... oddly. Like a person with an injured gait. Step, step, limp, step, step, limp. Large, lumbering, perhaps labored.

Fuck! Was one of them hurt?

I raced forward, darting around trees and brush expecting after a few meters to run into one of them, Byrony or Joe, and praying that Alex was following. I thought I could hear his footsteps behind me and didn't waste the few seconds to check. But as I rounded the last tree that I thought would reveal one of the missing, all I found was darkness. More trees like a wall of fortress defenses rather than a forest, and stillness. A complete absence of movement. No Byrony or Joe, no wind, no animals, simply darkness that comes from a lack of stars, moonlight, and all sources of artificial brightness. Even the light from my phone had vanished.

I stared, frozen for a moment, my brain racing through a thousand scenarios. But had only a half second to react when I realized the darkness in front of me wasn't normal, but more of a giant black mass of voided light, edged in a slate of devouring blackness.

For a few tense seconds I felt like I was staring face to face with something not human. Some undefined *other* perhaps. Then it moved, a sudden flight forward so fast I hadn't even enough time to draw a breath. It slammed into me with a ferocity that knocked me a meter or so backward, yet turned my skin to ice with its touch.

Panic came fast. I sucked in air, lungs screaming for breath. The sensation of cold terror rolling through me. Stars popped around my vision, not real ones, but flickers of warning signs from my mind, screaming that I wasn't getting enough air. It was a conscious effort to force myself to suck air in slowly, and let out long breaths, staving off passing out.

I immediately thought to run to Alex. Tried to get enough air to call for him. Only he wasn't there. No one was there. Not as far as I could see. My light was on, barely casting a glow in the thick darkness, but nothing else moved. And again, the silence encased me like a tomb of thick concrete walls muting life. I drew in a stuttering breath, forcing myself to calm, and focus. No bird this time, squawking or whatever it had been. No sign of a dimensional portal or whatever people claimed they thought I had seen that day. Simply me and the silence of absolute darkness. Which had touched me and left me cold.

I trembled. Couldn't stop shaking actually, partly the temperature of my skin having dropped and partly from fear. I swung around with the light, trying to find the dark mass that had touched me. Had that been some sort of portal? I couldn't find anything, just trees and more brush. Which direction had I come from? How did I get back? Had I stumbled through something? Was that possible? Was that where Byrony and Joe had gone? I knew in my gut that Alex would not have let me wander away from him. Even when I'd run, thinking I'd seen them, he would have followed. So where was he? Where was everyone?

I wrapped my arms around myself, heart pounding, body shuddering with the frozen tremble that wouldn't let up. I shined the light around, trying to find a sign of anything unusual. Shadows were everywhere, stretching from every tree and bush, moving with the light like some ancient dance of evil. Too much in my head reminding me of old stories, legends of tales told by people who claimed to have been touched by the darkness. Most driven mad by what they'd seen and experienced. Some possessed.

My stomach ached and cramped with intense anxiety. I had to fight the urge to throw up. The light caused the shadows, I told myself rationally. A play of trees and flashlights over bushes and branches. Nothing really moved. It couldn't move that way. The gloom I'd encountered hadn't been anything. Perhaps a pocket of cold air. Darkness wasn't a living thing; it was an absence of light. It didn't move on its own and manipulate the landscape.

Only something did. To my right a shadow took steps between the trees and for a moment I hoped that it was Alex. It was fully defined with the shape of a human, arms, legs, a head above shoulders I could make out, and a perfect silhouette. Or at least that's how it began. When I swung my light that way the beam died, leaving me staring at something dark again. Large like the first shadow I had encountered, but farther away, and the edges slightly more defined. More than a simple echo of the enclosed forest beneath towering trees, the shadow extended like a physical giant, arching across the distance, expanding, reaching for me with elongated arms and spindle-like fingers.

I opened my mouth to scream, frozen in fear, and yet angry with myself for standing there. "No," I said. "Not again."

I threw myself backward, a self-defense sort of roll, down and over until I was back on my feet and pointed in the opposite direction. I ran. I could sense it reaching for me in the darkness like giant hands carved from the trees themselves to drag me back to some other world. I didn't see the tree branch that wacked me in the face, making me fall backward and clutch my cheek and eye.

I expected blood, while my heart pounded in my ears and my breathing labored, but the only wetness I felt on my face was more liquid than the thick ooze of blood. It was the salty assault of tears I hadn't realized I was crying. My mind swirled and stuttered, unable to think of a solution to so many questions. The cold arch of something icy seeped into my flesh where I touched the ground. Fingers first, where I'd caught my fall, then my ass and legs, causing them to turn to jelly.

The ants beneath my skin, fire, intensified until every nerve in my body seemed to throb, the pain excruciating. I had to bow forward over my knees, gasping for breath, explosions of light in my head telling me I wasn't getting enough air. For a few seconds I wasn't sure how I survived, the agony making me wish for an immediate end. Folding in on myself did little to ease the hurt, but chased away some of the chill. I squeezed my eyes shut and tried to focus on something else, some thread of hope or anything.

Above the sound of my own blood pounding in my ears, I could hear something moving in the trees, stalking closer, and a looming presence of doom. Having experienced it several times over the years, I knew exactly what that feeling was. Had a vague sense of it before I'd first met Alex, and in those days before my disappearance. It was the weight of anxiety times a thousand, all pressing down on my soul, squeezing out any sense of logic or calm. Did it mean bad things for Byrony and Joe? Or just a warning for me?

I refused to look up, instead burying my face in my lap, curled around myself as though it would somehow put a stop to the terror. It didn't matter that it was cowardly, irrational, and part of a broken response to past trauma. Survival had narrowed to the noise in my head, and the feel of my limbs turning to ice while terror raced through my veins.

Sound came back in a whoosh of noise, almost too loud to bear. Shouting, cracking of wood, wind, voices, and a quiet mewling that I didn't realize was me until something touched my back and I screamed, full on murder scream over and over until I was gasping for air.

Strong arms wrapped around me, adding to the panic for a few seconds until the chill began to ease, warmth seeping into my body from the embrace. And the soft brush of textured hair on my neck and cheek helped me catch a breath. Alex.

"Breathe, baby, breathe," he whispered over and over while he rocked me, holding me in his arms, curled around me like a shield. "Breathe. That's it. Deep. In. Long out." He mimicked how I should be breathing, and I tried to follow. Sparkles decorated my vision, so even through the mild light of a nearby flashlight I couldn't see his face. "That's it, keep breathing. I've got you."

What if it was a trick? What if it wasn't really Alex but some monster? When had I started to believe in monsters? Dumb question. Two years ago on the hiking trail as I faced something I couldn't recall to this day. Was this the same? How long would I be lost this time?

"Breathe," Alex whispered. I felt his lips on my face. Light kisses that chased away the ice. If I could have crawled further into his embrace in that moment, I would have. And I couldn't stop trembling if I tried. Again my brain struggled to decipher the voices around me. Odd as it had never been a problem before this week in my entire life.

"You're freezing." He rubbed my arms, and wrapped himself tight around me. "Breathe, baby, keep breathing."

I let him hold me as the world began to refocus. The voices of the others took shape, but Alex showed no sign of letting go. He was still talking, though not to me. At some point my screaming had stopped, though I felt like a gaping fish, gasping for air, clinging to Alex with every fiber of my spirit.

"Call the police," he instructed someone.

"Because we found their board?" Someone... wait I think it was Jonah said.

"And a broken phone," Julie said.

"It's Byrony's," Melissa said her voice sounding strained, like she was crying.

"The police will have more people and dogs who specialize in this sort of thing," Alex pointed out.

"I don't understand where they would have gone," Melissa said.

"Maybe Joe did something," Chad said quietly. There was a pause and then he defended his statement, "it happens all the time. True crime stuff is littered with lovers hurting lovers. Always stupid reasons, but it happens."

"It's always someone you know," MaryAnn added.

"Joe would never hurt her," Melissa said.

"I'll go back to the trail and call the police," Freya said, heading away from the group.

Alex continued to rock me, and I swallowed great gulps of air, feeling it cool, and deep within my lungs. The group was scattered around us, close but not standing over us. I admit to feeling a bit embarrassed by my breakdown, though the terror had been legitimate enough to still have my heart racing. Alex peppered my face with small kisses and ran his hands over my back and arms.

"Keep breathing," he whispered. "You're okay. We're okay. I'm here."

"What happened?" I asked, not sure he would know.

He rested his forehead against mine, his face and eyes barely visible in the pale lights of the flashlights. "Later. Just sit with me. Breathe. Focus on me."

"Reverse of what I did for you," I pointed out, reminding him of the cemetery in which he'd had a PTSD attack over finding a body. Fuck… "Is there a body?"

"No," Alex said so softly I was sure only I could hear him.

I struggled to get up, pulling away from him now, anxious and scared but needing answers. He let me up, helped steady me as I got to my feet. When I looked around all I found were the obvious remnants of where Byrony and Joe had stopped. There was a backpack, a couple flashlights, a Ouija board, although the planchet seemed to be missing, and a handful of half-melted candles.

There were no signs of blood or even a struggle as the leaves and area surrounding their little camp seemed untouched. Alex reached for my hand, and I let him take it and pull me into a hug. His warmth began to seep through the cold still making me tremble, so I clung to him, breathing in his scent and basking in his heat.

"I don't know why I'm shaking," I told him. I was the rational one.

Always had been. Anxiety happened, and I'd had a couple panic attacks in my life. Emotionally overwhelmed was how I liked to think of it. Too much to process at once. This was that, and more, like a loss of physical control. Physically overwhelmed perhaps? Too much sensation? I realized then that the bugs were gone. That familiar crawling ooze across my skin had vanished, leaving behind the cold and Alex's body against mine.

"I felt something," I whispered to Alex, gripping him in a brutal hug as the realization sank in. Whatever I'd encountered out here hadn't been a simple shadow cast by light. "I think I saw something?"

"Hmm," Alex hummed against my face, where he pressed his beard to help ground me. "We'll talk about it later."

I *had* seen something. That was what Alex was saying without saying it. His sight, vision, ability, whatever it was, was so much more in tune than mine. If I only saw a shadow what had he seen?

"Alex?" I had to know. Even standing there in the forest, heart pounding, ears filled with the sound of my own terror, I had to know. "What did you see?"

"Byrony's ghost," he told me quietly, whispering the words into my ear so no one else would hear. "She went right through you."

I sucked in a breath so fast and hard that I choked. Alex continued to rock me, rub my back, and hold me tight. How could he be so calm? Byrony was dead? Was her body nearby? I had a million questions but couldn't clarify a single one.

"Her body?" I asked after a few minutes of contemplating.

"No idea," he answered. "I don't smell blood. I don't see anything nearby. But I'm keeping the group together. No one needs to find that."

"What about Joe?" I wondered.

This time Alex paused. I could tell he was thinking, debating on something, but he didn't answer.

"Alex?"

"I don't know," he admitted. "There was another... shadow? I don't know. Not as defined. Maybe Joe? Maybe something else."

"Did it feel like your demons?" Like the djinn or whatever it had been who had already claimed Alex and seemed to stalk us wherever we went.

"No."

I leaned into his embrace, resting my face in the groove of his neck. "This was supposed to be a holiday."

"Still can be," Alex acknowledged. "As soon as the police arrive, we're handing it over to them."

"What will you tell them?"

He shrugged and I understood. There wasn't much he could tell them. They wouldn't believe him if he said he saw a ghost. And if he did, they might even point fingers at him for doing something, though he'd been with the rest of the group the whole time. In fact, the entire group had been together all day. Perhaps Joe had done something and then killed himself? Of course my brain suddenly reminded me of dozens of news stories over the years of exactly that.

Alex kissed me on the cheek, and I turned my face to look up at him. "Stop thinking so hard," he told me.

"Can't help it. And you can't say you aren't doing the same."

He nodded, lips pulled tight into a mild grimace. "True. But this is not our doing, okay?"

"If we had stayed home?"

"This probably would have happened anyway. Blaming yourself only brings you unnecessary pain."

"Fucking truth bomb," I grumbled at him.

"There's a reason they say the truth hurts," Alex agreed.

CHAPTER 11

By the time the police finally arrived we were all sitting on the trail, exhausted, adrenaline gone, and I really wished we could go home, like back to New Orleans home. At least the dead there I knew of only in historical references. Byrony and I may not have been friends exactly, but I'd known her for years. Had my misfortune cast trouble on her? If so, what about the rest of the group?

Alex released me long enough to show them where they had found the stuff. The police questioned everyone. Sad how I predicted what they would ask. Too many times having experienced the whole missing person thing. They didn't recognize my name, for which I was grateful. I instantly blamed myself, as though somehow my disappearance made it easier for those around me to vanish.

"So you haven't known them long?" The detective asked me.

"I've known Byrony for a few years, but never all that well. More online friends than real life friends," I said. We hadn't really been friends at all. Byrony had a way of pushing people's buttons, and she had always disliked me. "I never met Joe until late last night. Saw him for only a few minutes before heading back to bed."

"They didn't indicate they were going anywhere?"

"Just out here to the woods to play their ghost games and not disturb the rest of us who were trying to sleep."

"Did anyone seem really upset with them? Like your host perhaps?"

"Freya?" I shook my head. "Annoyed mostly. I think we all were. It would have been different if we were at an actual hotel with very separated spaces. Though the group screaming might have woke people anyway."

"And they screamed because they thought there was a ghost?" The detective confirmed.

"That's what they said. I guess Byrony and the rest were doing scary stories or something. Alex and I went to bed. I think Jonah did too. And Freya came from the middle cabin where we do photo-shoots for our craft stuff." I tried to recall where everyone had been before they left. And couldn't recall anyone being unaccounted for. "Melissa went with them. She probably knows more."

"Did anything seem off about their relationship? Byrony and Joe?"

"Off how?" I wondered. "I saw them for two minutes."

"Did she defer to him, or was there a lot of tension between them?"

"I don't think so." I hadn't really been awake enough to notice. "Joe said something about they had rights at the B&B too. Like it was okay to keep everyone awake because they were, but that's all I remember about him." I glanced around trying to find Alex. He was a few feet away speaking to another officer.

"What about the rest of the group? Did you notice any tension between them and your friend or her boyfriend?"

"Everyone was sort of upset that they were playing. I think it was more that they'd been woken up. Sorry. I got woken up by screams and came running. My brain was a little slow to follow, so I probably didn't notice as much as I would have if I'd been more awake." I wasn't sure I was catching all this either. The panic mode had faded a little, but sat just below the surface waiting to pounce again. Too much adrenaline still coursing through me, and my gut churned like a cement mixer with the memories of whatever it had been that I'd seen.

"A lot of people run away when someone screams," the officer pointed out.

"Well my boyfriend reacted, and so did I. Maybe because he's ex-Army? If it had been me by myself, I probably wouldn't have gone running." Admitting to being a coward wasn't as difficult as it used to be. Years of living with the late night noises and people looking at me like I was broken while leading ghost tours around the city had taught me there were a lot of levels of brave, many synonymous with stupid. I considered myself a cautious sort of brave. Alex sometimes bordered on the other type. A mix of military training and white knight syndrome perhaps. Either way I wished he did less running headfirst into danger and spent more time thinking out other options. It just wasn't in his nature.

"If you think of anything else, call, alright?" The officer said.

I nodded, and waited until Alex was free from his questions, standing a few feet away, rolling from foot to foot with impatience and exhaustion. The trickle of conversations only half made sense around me. Freya talking about the plans for the group for the week. Julie and Nicole about their scare the night before. Chad about his short encounter with Joe, which led to nothing more than a back-handed insult about Chad's size. MaryAnn suggested that she'd heard the pair talking about meeting up with friends outside the group.

"Will you need a search party?" Alex asked the detective he was talking to.

"We'd rather everyone stay out of the woods until we've had a thorough search ourselves," the detective replied. "While there is some concern, we don't know there is actually anything wrong yet."

Only we did. Alex saw her ghost. I felt something...

I sucked in air, recalling the cemetery a month earlier and the mess of blood and bone. Lukas had questioned me at length about that night, thinking that somewhere in that mess lay answers to where Alex had gone. I remembered things a lot more vividly than I thought they'd actually been. A muddied mess of blood and a mangled corpse. Not the sort of thing people saw ever, even in the semi-realistic dark horror of movies. I'd had trouble shaking that memory. Not the first body I'd ever seen. But the only unnatural death I'd ever witnessed.

If I had to acknowledge the facts of what I'd seen, it had looked like one of those glass dolls, arms and legs normally made breakable, but wrapped around a fabric core. Only the limbs broken, smashed and mangled, center mass mostly intact, though twisted. A few seconds glance had been all it had taken to burn it into my memory for life. Like when people posted animal torture pictures as memes to 'warn' people that some asshole was doing something awful. Two seconds and the brain committed that horror to memory. I so didn't want that again. I was a simple tour guide and craft shop owner, not a medical professional or even a military member, former or otherwise. Death and destruction was not in my skillset.

"We will let everyone know if we need help with a search or have more questions," the detective told Alex. "You'll all be at the hotel for a few more days, correct?"

"Yes. A week or so. The convention we came for starts in a few days," Alex said. His focus fell on me. "Is it okay if we head back to our cabin?"

The officer nodded. I reached for Alex's hand and let him pull me into a sideways hug as we walked back to the B&B together.

"You okay?" Alex asked as we emerged into the backyard of the B&B.

"No," I told him honestly. I had a million questions while being so tired I could barely stand. Did I really want to know the answers? Find out that Byrony was dead somehow? Where her body might be? If some sort of ghost had touched me? The last question brought a million more, some based in legend, others in philosophy, a rolling tide of thought, emotion, and internal noise.

No. I was far from okay. The trembling hadn't stopped, not even when the adrenaline finally crashed leaving me exhausted and shaken. It had been years since I felt this... broken. Not since after my return from wherever and moving into a new place to hear whatever it was that continued to torment me. Those first few months I'd hid, burying myself beneath covers, and barely sleeping. Mind adding to the tricks the world around me played. The unease soaked into my skin in the same way it was right now. Leaving me constantly on edge. I had thought I'd finally gotten past it. Another lie my brain conjured to lull me into complacency.

Alex paused, pulling me into his arms and holding me. I didn't realize I was crying into his shoulder until he steered us away from the group. I heard the others protest behind us, but didn't care. No one needed to see my tears. I hated being vulnerable in front of anyone. Except Alex. He never seemed to judge me. I had no desire to join the group in the main house where I was sure they'd be debating Byrony's disappearance all night.

"Shh," Alex whispered. "You're safe. I'm here."

Was I ever safe? What *was* safe? Anything? Nothing? Alex's warm embrace made me feel safe mostly because I wasn't alone. He would face whatever I did, head on, if given the chance. That didn't mean he wasn't afraid. I'd seen fear in his eyes on more than one occasion. Though what terrified him was more my loss than things that went bump in the night. Was that the difference between us? He ran into danger to keep from losing those he cared about, and I hid from danger for fear of losing myself. Though if I were being honest with myself, the idea of losing Alex again, that would break me.

I'd unraveled too while he was gone. Lukas had come apart at the seams leaving me thinking more than once that he wouldn't survive the death of his twin. Many days I'd spent comforting Sky, assuring her she wouldn't lose Lukas over Alex's disappearance. Everyone spoke like Alex was dead, I suspected they'd done the same thing when I was missing, and it was brutal to hear. But I had been so focused on Sky and Lukas, that when I had time to myself, to think about how he'd been dropped into my life, a storm of humor, apprehension, and adoration, only to be ripped out just as suddenly, my world spiraled into chaos. Free time had not been my friend. The fine balance I'd walked since my own disappearance became an impossible dance while I teetered on the edge of a full breakdown. How often had I contemplated that I was the curse? That he'd been taken because of me? It was a heavy burden to bear.

Now I clung to Alex, like he was the last thing that could keep me from shattering completely. He held me, rocked me, kissed my face and hair, not caring at all what anyone else thought. It was one of the things I liked best about him.

"The middle cabin is open for you two," Freya said from somewhere to my left. "I finished the piece I was working on. And the cabin is all set up. Keys are on the table inside. Just lock up when you're done."

I heard her walk away and felt a thousand things all cluttered in my head. Cosplay was the last thing on the list. Even the elation of having Freya make me something was absent in the wake of all the internal noise.

"Well that's exciting," Alex said. "What does a cosplay cabin look like?" Alex pulled me toward the middle cabin instead of ours. I should have resisted, insisted we curl up together for the evening, hide from everything, but that wouldn't end the noise. And I knew that despite being exhausted, I'd be unable to sleep. Too much noise in the middle of all the silence.

Alex opened the door to the middle cabin and pulled me inside, locking the door behind us. The lights were on, illuminating the space. I took deep gulping breaths of Alex's scent and tried to focus on my senses.

"Down another rabbit hole," Alex said.

The space did sort of look like entering another world. While the photo cabin was the same size as the one we were renting, it was an open space filled with specific lights, screens, props, and racks full of cosplay designs made real. The space had no kitchen, though I knew there was a large bathroom in the back, instead it was broken up into a table area made for laying out and filming tutorials, and a big loft area with a bed made for photoshoots rather than sleeping. Expensive cameras were mounted in places designed to easily swivel or be set on timers to create pictures beyond what our phones could do even in the digital age.

A box sat on the table with a card next to it, which had my name written in Freya's delicate script. I took a deep breath, unwilling to let go of Alex to open the box. The trembling began to ease. Having walls around us helped, and watching Alex's awed expression did too.

"Wonder what she made you," Alex said guiding us to the table.

"It will be something sexy. It's what she does best."

"You don't need help being sexy," Alex said completely without thought. He wasn't trying to stroke my ego, that much I knew. He just found me sexy, and I liked that.

Alex reached out to open the box. Inside was an elegant, semi-sheer, baby doll dress in Gothic Lolita style. I'd never done Lolita as it meant a lot of lace and trim ribbons that didn't seem to fit me. And since leaving the sex trade I hadn't modeled anything other than sexy superhero wear for the most part. School outfits and bright colored wigs had been left in the past. The hiding of who I was became unnecessary. I'd become infamous rather than famous, and so the costumes had followed suit.

Standing there, staring at the dress, which would barely reach mid-thigh on me, I wondered if it had been anger or bitterness that kept me from the more feminine look I'd mastered prior to meeting Tim. Hot pants and skintight leggings could be sexy, in a different way. They were all I'd worn in years. Wigs and even the heavy eye makeup had gone the wayside. I'd let my hair grow out despite hating the color and the gentle wave that made it hard to work with. Another attempt to hide who I was, or become something I wasn't? I didn't know.

"This is gorgeous," Alex said. "And so soft. Material like this is usually scratchy, right?" He rubbed the edges of the skirt between his fingers. "Is this more polyester magic?"

I examined the edges. The entire design, which appeared made more out of the sort of fabric used for wedding dresses than normal cosplay. I'd have to chat with Freya about the cost. Would hate to have her spending a fortune on one little outfit for me. "Yes, mostly," I agreed. "Synthetics at least."

Alex held it up. "Do you want to try it on?"

No.

Something inside me screamed no like an echo of the broken past I'd been drowning in finally reaching the surface. I didn't want to be on that stage anymore, used like a doll for the pleasure of others. Was that what Alex wanted too? I knew I turned him on. The wigs, the eyeliner, the skirts, Alex admitted he'd enjoyed them. He had gotten off on the videos, been a fan, he told me more than once. But that life was in the past for both of us. Or at least that was what I thought.

In the end Tim only really got off when we were recording. He'd grown bored with me. No matter what dress, flirty makeup, or new toy I tried. It didn't excite him as much as camera angles and lighting. The production of voyeurism rather than the act of sex.

I could have left a hundred times. Had dozens of opportunities. Never said no because it was easier to stay. Until something ripped me out of his life and changed the world around me. Hardcore wakeup call, vanishing for a few months and then thrown back into a world that lost value with you so quickly. Tim tried to get back together, only I had felt like a broken doll, no longer pretty and able to hold my arms up in a way to make him happy.

Was that what Alex wanted too? A doll? A toy?

I reached for the dress, expecting to play my part, be the pretty femboy I had once been, all while feeling like a puppet, but Alex folded the dress back up into the box.

"Another time, maybe?" he said, smile warm rather than annoyed. Sometimes he was so confusing. I understood men in general. They were simple creatures. Me included. Easy to read, manipulate, please. Only, not Alex. He was easy in a lot of ways. His personality laid back. But to read, not so much. Just when I thought I understood him, he flipped the tables on me.

"You don't want to see me in the dress?" I asked, my throat feeling tight.

"Sure. But doesn't have to be now. It's pretty. Nice of Freya to make it. Didn't you bring stuff? I know you had a garment bag. What's in that?"

"Disney designs," I answered absently, thinking hard about what his motives might be. Did he have them? Or was that simply my brain in overdrive again?

"Like Sky's ice queen dress?" Alex stepped away to throw out his arms wide. "Let it go!" He sang, flinging his hands like he was casting spells of ice and building a palace. "Let it snow!" He didn't seem to know more than a few words of the song. "Finally watched the movie. The night you texted me but wouldn't let me come over. I watched it on Lukas's Apple TV. Talk about a gay anthem, right?"

My racing heart began to ease as he pranced around the room, singing horribly, the same words over and over since he obviously didn't know the song. He pretended to throw magic around like he was coating the walls in ice.

"Sky's dress didn't have the long cape thing. That was the best part. An ice cape. You have capes in the shop now, but no ice capes. I could totally be an ice king."

In truth I had been working on something very similar for him. A gender bender sort of thing. Since he'd loved Sky's outfit. I'd actually made him a few sets of things. None of which I thought would fit at all, as I had very little of his measurements before he'd been taken.

And didn't that put the skid on my racing thoughts. A reminder that Alex had been taken too. Perhaps not in the same way or even to the same place. Had he changed from the experience? I wasn't sure yet. Hadn't known him long enough before or after. But we had a lot of small things in common, and one really big one. We were both more than a little crazy.

"So, the garment bag? What's in it?" Alex asked. "It's like a pirate chest of unknown booty I desire to unlock."

"It's only a handful of things I've been working on. Wanted Freya's opinion on a few. Sizing, embellishment, etc. Nothing sexy, only fun stuff."

"For you?" Alex wanted to know.

"For you," I amended. "Mostly." After seeing some fan art of gender bending of many of the Disney characters, I decided to try my hand in designing a few. Everything I tried came back to Alex. How I could see him in leggings that looked like a mermaid tail, or a fitted uniform to echo Mulan's masculine side. The *Frozen* bend was easy and one of the first I'd completed, having enough fan art online to draw inspiration from.

The idea of making some of Disney's main characters, sexy, modern, and sort of male appealed in an odd way. Something I had never done before. I had started on sets of characters, though not all turned out usable. Which was why I'd planned to continue this trip even after Alex's disappearance. I needed the feedback. Something to occupy my mind other than anxious overthinking.

Maybe every cosplayer didn't start by growing up wanting to be a Disney Princess, but I had. However, envisioning myself in costume was still a struggle. Though for Alex? I had endless ideas.

"Have you ever wanted to be a Disney Princess?" I asked him.

"I loved *Mulan*. Best part was when the guys all dress up like geishas or whatever and climb the poles to storm the bad guy. I think I'm into the newer movies. *Brave, Moana, Frozen, Shrek*…"

"*Shrek* is not a princess movie."

"He rescues Fiona from a dragon. A kiss saves them. How is it not a princess movie?"

I blinked at him, trying to sort my thoughts, though thankfully they'd stopped running away in a million directions. "Because there is farting and bad jokes?" I offered.

"Bah," Alex waved his hand. "Technicalities. I think the fact that her parents are still alive, is the most unDisney-like part of it. What is with Disney and dead parents anyway?" He did have a point. Though there were a handful of Disney movies with living parents like *Mulan, Brave*, and *Moana*, they were more modern movies.

"What if I run and get the bag?" Alex surveyed the room. "I sort of feel like I'm on a set for a movie. It's kind of exciting. Can I dress up?" He put his hands on his hips and stood in a wide stance like warriors of old. "Feel like I could be on the cover of a romance novel."

I squinted at him. After tromping around in the woods and seeing Byrony's ghost along with whatever else had happened, and there he was shrugging it off like it didn't bother him. Only that wasn't true either. The tension in his shoulders made his back straighter, and he had to work to unclench his fists. He needed to unwind too. If he thought a little cosplay could help, I'd find a way to dress him up.

"Okay," I agreed. "None of it is finished, but okay."

Alex darted for the door.

"Wait," I called to him not wanting him to go running into the darkness alone. He paused. I walked him to the door and stood in the doorway. "Let me watch you get there and back. Bring your hair stuff too, so I can fix it."

"You're obsessed with my hair," he accused.

"I am," I agreed. "Touching it, smelling it, tugging on it when we have sex. Totally obsessed."

His grin was huge. "Hair stuff too." He leaned forward, kissed the tip of my nose, then darted across the lawn. Some inner terror in my gut clenched, almost expecting the darkness to open up and swallow him whole right there in front of me. But nothing happened. He let himself into our cabin, rummaging around for a few minutes before reappearing and making his way back across the lawn with the garment bag draped in his arms. He grinned like a little boy with a secret.

"What did you do?" I asked as we both headed inside.

He ignored my question and hung the bag up on a rack near the door. "I can't wait to see what you made."

Heat rushed up to fill my face. "None of it's finished," I reminded him.

"Finished in what sense?" He asked. "As in completed or as in

114

perfected? You have a way of hating on projects you don't feel turned out perfectly and calling them unfinished."

I sighed. He knew me too well already. "There are some things that didn't work out the way I wanted. I had hoped Freya would have some ideas for fixes. Other things are mostly done, they just need a bit of sizing."

"Mhmm." Alex unzipped the bag and began pulling out hangers, placing them on the empty rack to spread them out. "Micah?"

"Yeah?" I asked, absently cataloging the pieces I'd brought.

"Why is this all in my size?"

"Because I was using you as inspiration."

"While I was away?"

Away. Such an innocuous word. "Yes."

Alex stepped into my space and kissed me, full lips and mouth this time, devouring. I leaned into him, let him take the lead on whatever he wanted. I wanted to be putty for a while. To turn off my brain and not think. If only I had that ability.

"You're amazing, you know that, right?" Alex whispered against my lips. He kissed my cheeks again, stealing tears I hadn't realized were falling still. "Where to start? I think there's an icy cape in here?"

There was. The ice queen outfit I'd made for him I'd pulled from the fan art. Tight white leather-like pants, and an open shirt with blue shimmering threads. The cape attached to buttons at the shoulders, an iridescent blue train of icy snowflakes. I'd hand sewn the designs, tracing back to my youth and my grandmother's many lessons in embroidery. I'd never be the delicate artist she had been, but I could make a snowflake look real enough.

Alex looked around the cabin. "No open windows? Can I try this on? Fuck, I should have worn different underwear. Will purple show through these pants?"

"No one to see but us," I promised him though he was already stripping out of his clothes in a bit of a frenzy. He had to wiggle into the pants a little. Wear would loosen them. The fabric might have looked like leather, but it was part Spandex, so it would form to his body. Alex buttoned and zipped them, swinging his hips carefully to test movement.

"How do they feel?" I asked.

"Lighter than I thought. Tight, but not in a bad way. They aren't creeping up my crack, at least not that I can feel. Do they look like they are giving me a wedgie?" He turned his back to me, showing me his ass, which outlined in the pants, was firm enough to bounce a quarter off of.

"Looks good from here," I assured him.

He tugged on the shirt, again a little snug through the shoulders. I under-estimated how broad he was. But that was an easy enough fix. It was a bit of an old European style button up, with chunky caps on the sleeves, and a high collar. He let me adjust the collar and left the top few buttons open. I helped him tuck the shirt in the pants, smoothly, then attached the cape.

"I feel like I'm in a movie," Alex said. His eyes sparkled, all tension having left him. "My hair's not right though. The girl in the movie has a braid. Is mine long enough to braid?"

"No braid needed." I led him toward the bathroom and sat him down in the makeup chair.

"Wow, giant bathroom for a little house."

"Yes, but the ceilings are pretty low." There was a standing shower big enough fit several people, two sinks, and a long wall of counter space with a matching mirror for prep work. The room was made for costume changes, cleanup, and necessity.

Alex sat patiently as I worked on his hair, thoughts pulling together from the costume and his overall appearance. I smoothed his hair back into a ponytail to lie at the base of his neck, adding a bit of body to the top front, and even trimming down the edges of his beard until it curved in a perfect hug along his jawline. After a few minutes I stepped away to examine my work. The result wasn't something I had expected, but wow.

He sat sort of draped in the chair, cape carefully over the back, one leg up over the arm for comfort. Alex had a habit of draping himself over furniture. I didn't think he noticed it, though sometimes it looked posed. Or perhaps that was my brain thinking sexy thoughts about the way his ass looked when he laid on his stomach on my futon, or how inviting his chest was when he slouched in a chair, legs spread like a beacon of sexiness.

With his hair styled and trimmed, that odd sort of blond tipping of color he had, made him seem more like he was going gray, than blond. He had a mix of dark roots in spots, not from dyeing, his hair simply had that many highlights and lowlights. I wondered if he would actually go gray and thought the idea of seeing Alex peppered with white hair and even little crows' feet around his eyes suddenly really turned me on.

"Never knew I had a daddy kink before," I told him honestly.

He blinked at me, then pointed at himself. "Me? A daddy?"

"You are almost ten years older than me."

"I think I need at least another twenty years before I'm a daddy."

Looking him over, pants so tight they left little to the imagination, shirt open at the collar to reveal tan skin and a fuzz of soft chest hair, and that delightful beard... wow. My brain completely stopped, finding nothing else important at that moment but him.

"Okay, with the way you're looking at me right now I'm okay with being a daddy," Alex said, his expression serious.

"How am I looking at you?" I asked, knowing really, because I wanted to lick him, follow that line from his throat down his half-bared chest, perhaps even find a nipple under the edge of that sparkling shirt. All while I sat on the growing bulge stretching the crotch of the white pants, which had been made to look like newly fallen snow.

Alex squirmed under my gaze. "Like you want to eat me?"

"That a bad thing?" I asked, setting aside the grooming supplies and climbing onto his lap. His arms wrapped around me, pulling me close, settling my ass over his groin, where I rubbed myself against him to prove he wasn't the only one turned on.

"Not bad at all," Alex whispered breathily. "Just don't ruin the cape, okay? I really like it."

I unbuttoned the cape and let it fall over the back of the chair, free from any sort of damage, then devoured Alex's lips. He returned my passion, feeding at my mouth until we were both gasping for breath. I sighed, licking the edges of his mouth, but traced down his neck, over his collarbones and to his chest. Revealing one of his nipples by simply brushing back the fabric on one side, I nipped the little bud, watching it harden beneath my assault.

Alex sucked in a breath, giving me a sweet little moan.

"You know what's one of the best things about cosplay specific material?" I asked him in-between sucking on one nipple, and pinching the other with my fingers. His hips arched against me, pressing his cock to rub against mine. I gasped and took a deep breath to keep from coming from the friction alone.

"It makes you want to jump my bones?" Alex asked as he leaned into my touch. His fingers wound up in my hair, not pushing or pulling, just resting there.

"That too," I assured him. "However, it's made pretty stain resistant." I reached down to unbutton his pants and carefully slid the zipper down. The vibrant purple of his fitted boxer briefs peeking through the fabric made me smile. A wet spot began to grow and I pushed the fabric back to find his weeping cock hard and ready. Taking the weight of it in my hand I continued the teasing of his nipples, delicacies beneath the edges of that shimmering fabric, while I stroked him.

"Hey, you too," Alex protested. He always tried to focus on my pleasure.

"Oh, I plan on enjoying myself. Promise." I worked him with my hand, rubbing him, root to tip, taunting the sensitive head of his cock with my thumb.

He cupped the back of my head, forcing me upward to meet his lips again and devouring my mouth as though he were trying to force the heightened level of his passion into my mouth. But I didn't need it.

"Fuck," Alex groaned into my lips. "You too, please. Not just me. It's so much better when it's both of us." I could edge him for hours, and he wouldn't come unless I did. Other times I begged to watch him come apart. Those he had to work harder for. Alex was not a man who did voyeurism for sex. Not when he was the subject being watched. He didn't even watch well, often having to put his hands on me within only a few minutes after I began a sexy dance, or a teasing progression of touching myself.

"Yes," I agreed and shifted in my seat a little so I could unzip my own pants, and free my cock. I reached across the counter to squirt some of the hand lotion into my palm, and stroked myself firmly, twice. The sound of wet, slick flesh, filled the room. I squeezed Alex gently with my other hand. "This what you want?"

"Yes!" Alex cried. "Please, fucking please. Touch us." I slid our cocks together, taking both of us in hand, smearing the lotion and our precome between us, helping to slick the glide. It always took a few minutes of adjustment to get my hand right, comfortable, my ass resting firmly on his thighs. He gripped my waist, fingers caressing but not delicate. His lips returned to mine, arms around me, pulling me closer, begging for more.

I breathed out a deep breath, resting my forehead on his to stare into the intensity of his gaze as I worked us together. His hands dug into my ass, a firm grip to go with his adoring eyes. We danced together for a few minutes. A waltz of sweet kisses, moving hips, and gasping breaths.

I loved tasting his lips. He might not have the experience of other men, but he made it up with curiosity and passion. Alex got really good at mimicking what I did, nipping, sucking, a tiny bit of his lower lip sucked beneath my teeth. Eventually he'd get lost in the passion and his kiss would turn a little wild. More devouring than exploring. That was always how I knew he was close, which was good since I was too.

The tingle in my balls, rising fast, warned me the release was coming. I cupped my hand over the tip to catch most of the mess, and spurted into my palm.

"Fuck," Alex said long and slow, his cock twitching a little as his release followed mine. I caught most of this release on my shirt rather than his outfit, and kissed him on the lips for a few seconds before reaching over to the counter for a tissue.

Alex relaxed in the chair, like he'd gone boneless. His softening cock still peeking from between white pants and vibrant purple underwear. His shirt pushed open to reveal nipples still hard pink nubs begging to be touched. He looked like a debauched angel right then. A prince of some foreign kingdom who'd been led down the path of sexual awakening. I sighed as I looked him over, feeling my body respond again. I could have taken pictures and made a fortune by posting them up on porn sites.

"You are so hot," I told him.

He blinked at me, like his brain was still in orgasm mode, synapses misfiring. "*I'm* hot?" he muttered, like I was just too much to believe sometimes. "Come stick your cock in my mouth and I'll show you hot," he promised.

Of course that was all it took to wake me up again. Alex smirked. "Perk of having a hot younger boyfriend. Can I eat your ass too? You bought me a superhot dragon thing and I promised to dine on you extensively. I brought lube and condoms when I grabbed your stuff."

I gaped at him. "Were you planning to sex me up, sir?"

"Yes. Though I guess me being a hot daddy, helps, yeah?"

I sighed and crawled back into his lap to kiss him again. "Yes, yes, it does."

CHAPTER 12

To say we went to bed late was an understatement. After a bit more play in the cosplay cabin, I had insisted on taking a few pictures of him looking sexy, almost too sexy. One set I'd taken had been with one nipple showing, and his pants unbuttoned, underwear shoved down, leaving his delightful treasure trail and delicious skin on view. Not enough to make anything X-rated, that edge of naughty but still covered, that left enough to the imagination to keep people coming back. I had a few on my phone of more revealing pictures which Alex made me promise not to show anyone.

Sharing the pictures was not on my agenda. In fact, I planned to guard them a bit jealously. But I did get his full measurements and a few pictures of him looking very pristine, as much as an evening of sex would allow. His lips looked a little swollen from all the kissing, and I'd left a few little marks on his chest, but those were easy enough to cover with fabric. My clothes had taken more damage than his as I'd used my shirt to wipe up several ribbons of come.

By the time we'd gotten back to our cabin and collapsed into bed it was after two in the morning. So when Alex roused me to remind me we needed to go get breakfast, I grumbled at him the entire way until he shoved a cup of coffee into my hands and sat me at the table in the main house.

"You promised you weren't a morning person," I accused him.

He kissed my cheek. "Drink your coffee. You always feel better after the caffeine starts to kick in."

"Rather kick your ass," I mumbled into my cup.

"Kiss my ass?" Alex inquired, purposely misquoting me, I was sure. "What if I promise to lick yours later?"

Fuck, I was not ready for the lift that brought to my cock. It was too early. Not enough coffee and too much stress running through my veins. I glared at him. He stared back with a slightly lifted brow and a boyish grin. How could he be so adorable this early in the morning? His hair was a bit wild again, pulled back in a loose sort of top of the head ponytail. Not a manbun as he couldn't really get it to stay in that shape, but not quite a raging puffball. He must have put product in it already since the curls were large and ringed.

Alex leaned forward and kissed the tip of my nose. "The way you look at me."

"Coffee," was all I said, bringing the cup back to my lips and savoring the sweet butterscotch edge of flavor beneath vanilla creamer and stevia. I stared blearily into my cup trying to remember what the plan was for today.

"Yes," Alex agreed. "Coffee. Next we'll work on your food association skills with this new invention called breakfast."

I squinted at him, promising retribution for his teasing with a single look, but he smiled wider, obviously not deterred by my morning grumpiness.

"You guys are staying in for crafts?" Freya asked, obviously not able to read the not awake expression on my face.

"If you don't mind," Alex replied. "I think a day of crafting and maybe an afternoon nap is called for. Yesterday was a lot of travel, and then with the evening events..." Alex paused as if he were thinking of how to continue that line of thought, but changed course instead. "Do you think the police will want our help in the search?"

"They've been in and out all morning. Are still in the woods as far as I know. I think if they are in need of volunteers, they will let us know," Freya said. "I'd prefer everyone stay out of their way and let them do their job, so they can find Byrony faster."

Alex nodded. "That makes sense. We mostly plan to stay in anyway. And not that we dislike the food here or anything, but would you be willing to recommend some local places for dinner? I'd love to take Micah out for the evening, just the two of us. I think we could both use the distraction."

"Oh, I know some of Micah's favorite places." Freya proceeded to list off a handful of restaurants. Alex took notes on his phone. He was far too awake and organized this early in the morning. If I could drown in my coffee cup, I would.

Alex took my cup away for a moment, stilling my protest with a small kiss. When he returned it was with my refilled cup, and he set a plate down in front of me. Eggs, some fruit, and a thick slice of bacon sat on the plate. His own breakfast was a heaping mess of eggs and meat. I blinked at him.

"You need food too," he told me, then turned back to Freya. The rest of the group was beginning to appear for the morning with full plates, but a somewhat somber mood. I tried not to think too hard about that. Alex had worked hard to remind me that I wasn't the center of the universe for anyone other than him, so Byrony's death, if that's what it was, wasn't my fault. Did anyone else even know she was dead yet? I was so lost for what to do or say. How did mediums do this? Tell people they knew someone was gone? Watch lives shatter with careless words?

Maybe it was all a mistake. People had tried to tell me Alex was gone. None of them mediums, of course, because I'd always avoided the few true gifted I knew of in the Quarter like the plague. They looked at me in an odd way, like I wasn't right. It was one of the few reasons I loved being with Alex. Despite all he could see, either what he saw in me wasn't all that unusual, or it simply didn't scare him.

Hmm. Love.

I stared at him while we ate, studying the small things, and how we related. We both sat turned a tiny bit toward each other. He reached out often to touch my back, shoulder, or arm, affirming, but also comforting. I had tuned out almost everyone but him.

I didn't think we were one of those nauseating couples, all goo-goo eyes, but the trust was strong enough that I'd have him at my back any day. He finished most everything on his plate. I offered him the bacon from mine and he accepted. Maybe I could talk him into a nap sooner rather than later.

"Micah has some cosplay things he wants to consult with you on," Alex continued. "And I'm hoping we can do a little quilting today. We bought a bunch of fabric for that yesterday. I want to see the magic of how he turns squares into other shapes."

I tuned back into the conversation trying to catch up. Quilting yes, I could get Alex started on a simple project. Maybe even sketch out some new ideas with Freya, but I had a few of his pieces I wanted to tailor a bit as well, correcting the fit now that I had his measurements. It wasn't until that moment that I realized he was wearing the kilt I made him and a Simply Crafty T-shirt which read, "Crafting is my super power." The shirt had a bit of a Superman theme, reds and blues, faded in style. It was an older design I hadn't carried in years, and was worn soft enough to feel like velvet.

"That Lukas's?" I asked, suddenly distracted by Alex. The shirt fit him well, unlike most of Lukas's apparel, which was a size or so too big.

"Yeah, an old one. He said it didn't fit him anymore, but it's insanely comfortable." And it hugged Alex's arms and shoulders, outlining the lean muscle of his torso and the broad width of his shoulders.

Freya gave a light little laugh. "You two are adorable."

"Sugar just drips off them," Jonah complained. "Not fair to wave your 'got some' in our faces this morning," he gripped.

"Sorry," I whispered, feeling heat rise to my cheeks. Did something show on our faces that we'd used a little foreplay as life affirmation last night? I didn't think so, but I was also not fully awake. "I would love your help," I told Freya. "I have a few things I need to fix, and some ideas I've been trying to plan out but pencil to paper is not working for me." I tried to change the subject, hoping they would all let me steer it away from more sex teasing. Normally it didn't make me uncomfortable. Only now, with the subject also being Alex, did it bother me. Not really the thought of Alex and I together, but that other people thought of him in that way.

Jealousy.

Well, that was unexpected.

"I'm happy to help," Freya said. "I actually have been experimenting with a new design software. It was originally created for anime artists to help with 3D renders, but it's great for costume design. You can set the body shape and size, and then begin dressing them, even down to color and texture. It's a big help in visualizing ideas."

"Sounds amazing," Alex said. "Does it need a special computer to make it work? I think Micah brought his Mac." I had. It was in the cabin. Alex took my plate and empty coffee cup, delivering them to the kitchen before taking a seat back beside me. At least the coffee was beginning to kick in. "What is everyone else's plan for the day?" Alex asked. "Anyone else staying in?"

Perhaps it was the mood, or maybe they had all originally planned to stay in, but the entire group had projects to work on.

"I have a few designs I'm working on," Jonah acknowledged. "Might be for an unconfirmed TV show."

"Do they let you do that stuff ahead of time?" Julie asked. "I thought it was all time constraints and last minute hacks with limited materials?"

"Most of that is staged."

"Wow, talk about bursting our bubbles," Chad added. "I love that show."

Alex gave a raised brow in question since he obviously had no idea what they were talking about. I'd fill him in later.

"What about the rest of you? Are you working on costume stuff? Micah's stuff is pretty cool. Freya made him a gorgeous outfit too." Alex said. Which reminded me I had yet to thank Freya for her work.

"Did it fit okay?" She asked me.

"I didn't have a chance to try it on yet," I told her feeling bad about that since she'd gone through so much work. Would she be upset to know I wasn't sure I could wear it after all this time? I hated the idea of losing her friendship over my hang-up.

"We were focused on finding an outfit for me last night," Alex said. "Micah was pretty excited to show me a few things."

"In more than one way, I bet," Jonah teased. Everyone laughed. Alex squeezed my hand and a touch of pink dotted his cheeks. Yeah, totally jealous that anyone else could make him blush like that.

"Let me know before you leave for the week," Freya said, not seeming bothered I hadn't tried on her creation yet.

"It's beautiful," I said. "The craftmanship is divine."

Freya beamed. "I'm glad you like it, but again let me know if the fit is off anywhere so I can fix it. And be sure to send me your promo photos in it. I will start passing them around Instagram and my site. Build a little hype for you."

"Sure," Alex said, not really promising anything, I realized as he stood. "Let me run back to our cabin and grab stuff. I can't wait to see all of you work magic." He patted me on the shoulder, and I watched him walk toward the back of the house with a bit of a spring in his step. He seemed really excited to stay inside with a bunch of nerds working on cosplay costumes.

"That boy is fine," Jonah said. "Do you all see how that shirt fits? The muscles on that boy…"

"And he's super into you, Micah," MaryAnn added.

"More than Tim ever was," Nicole agreed.

"And really into your crafting," Julie said.

"Sounds like a good match to me," Freya smiled.

"We haven't been together long," I said. "But we seem to fit."

"Bet he more than *fits* you," Jonah said.

Chad threw a napkin at him. "Not everyone wants dick. Stop being one."

"Sugar, I'd even take yours right now," Jonah offered. "Haven't had one in a while."

"I can't believe you're all messing around when Byrony and Joe are still out there," Melissa said. She sat at the opposite end of the table, no food or anything in front of her, with her hands clutching the table. "We should all be out there looking."

"You heard Freya," MaryAnn said. "It's better to let the police do their job. What do we know about finding missing people in the woods?"

Melissa's gaze settled on me. "A lot."

Only none of them had ever searched for me. They hadn't left the comfort of their homes to traipse through the woods or grieve for a guy they made costumes with. And I understood, as I probably would have done the same for all but Freya. But it was far too early in the morning for me to be nice. There were parts of this group that had always carried a grudge against me. Whether it was my success, my youth, or something else, I didn't know. Only that sometimes I really grew tired of defending myself. My disappearance had made me realize that maybe they weren't my friends. And that was okay, they didn't need to be. Spending time crafting with like-minded people brought enough joy that we didn't need to be best buds. It did remind me of why I'd been so thrilled Alex had returned so I could drag him along. He might not have the same craft intensity of the rest of the group, but I liked his company enough for it to not matter.

"None of this is my fault. I didn't send them out to play in the dark. I didn't even invite them on this trip," I reminded them.

"Right, you hate Byrony," Melissa accused.

"I don't hate her. I barely know her."

"Barely know her but got into an online war with her over a couple pictures."

"That was a long time ago."

Byrony had copied a couple outfits I'd done. Not even some

general character cosplay, but original designs. She'd never owned up to it, though my followers had been the first to alert me to the photo evidence and point fingers at her. She saw my switch to sex on film as defeat, and flaunted another half dozen designs she'd stolen. Then I'd vanished, only to return and find her slandering me wherever she could. She even told her followers that I'd made the entire disappearance up to get attention. I left most of the internet crowds, changed my business, and spent very little time with any of the original cosplay group. Only the once a year trip, and last year Byrony had not even shown.

Was I still bitter about her theft and slander? Yes. But it simply meant we were no longer friends, and I made a point not to share ideas in any space she was also in, but it didn't mean I hated her enough to hurt her.

"I have no interest in anything she might say or do. We don't run in the same circles these days."

"And you're so benevolent."

"I'm more of the 'I don't give a fuck' mindset," I snapped back at her.

"Enough," Freya said. "I understand you're upset, Melissa. But whatever mess Byrony is in was of her own making. Take your blame elsewhere. Everyone is here to craft and relax."

"While she's still missing?"

"What do you expect us to do? Start racing through the woods and get lost ourselves? Get in the police's way? Trample any evidence they may have used to find her?" Freya asked.

"You always take his side. Micah has always been your favorite. You mentored him when he was barely old enough to be anything, and the rest of us fight for crumbs."

I gaped at her. Were we fighting over Freya? I glanced around the group trying to determine if I was the only one confused, but couldn't tell if anyone was agreeing with her or just as lost as I was. Was that why they all never seemed to like me much? Tim told me I'd been reading too much into ulterior motives, and that only got worse after my return. Maybe it wasn't all in my head.

"I give my time to as many as possible. And Micah showed a lot of potential at a very young age with no other support from friends or family. I'm sorry if that offends you, but I have thousands of followers, many of whom cosplay. All of you here are closer than any of them, and still you're ungrateful?" Freya shook her head. "I spend a lot of time looking over work for all of you. Time I could be crafting more videos and pieces of my own."

"Except interest in you has been waning for years," Melissa snarled at her. "It's why Byrony has been asking for you to give her acknowledgment among your followers, that her skill is at your level, that she's worth the fame. Instead you focus on a little boy with a broken past who doesn't even cosplay anymore. I didn't even want to come. Byrony said she wanted to try one last time to gain your support, instead you cast her aside again. This is all your fault."

"If anyone is to blame, Melissa," Freya said looking more angry than I could ever recall her being, "it's you for leaving them alone in the dark because you were too afraid of some woods. Byrony knew I would never promote her brand. Not after she spent the last five years cannibalizing everyone else's ideas. She wants fame without the work. I couldn't give that to her even if I wanted to."

"She copied us a few times," Nicole said softly with Julie nodding beside her.

"She copied me more than a dozen times," MaryAnn added.

"She copied everyone," Jonah said.

"It's part of what it means to be in the group," Melissa defended. "Collaborating…"

"Collaborating means actually sitting down and working out ideas with other people and everyone working on something together. She blatantly stole designs, from the colors to the trim and buttons without a single word of requested consent or acknowledgment," I brought up. "In fact, she told me more than once, that because she was a girl, she could make enough changes to an outfit I created to make it legally hers. Then threatened to sue me if I claimed otherwise."

But this was not why I'd come here. Time away from the long days of my small business had sounded like a good idea at the time. Company while I worked through ideas since Alex had been gone, and even feedback was supposed to be fun, a distraction at least. Being dropped into accusations wasn't my idea of fun.

I got up from the chair. "I'm sorry, Freya. Maybe I shouldn't have come. I'll take my stuff to the cabin and work out there while I call around to find a new place to stay for the week. I really don't want to be in the middle of all of this."

Freya put her hand on my arm. "Stay. You are in the middle of nothing. We are here to cosplay and craft. Let's focus on that."

Melissa screamed and slammed her hands on the table. "You're all so worthless." She got up and stomped up the stairs leaving everyone gaping behind her. Alex came in just as she left.

"Everything okay?" He asked, his gaze focused more on me than anyone else in the room. His arms were full of the garment bag and the shopping things from yesterday. If they hadn't been, I might have gone to him and buried my face in his shoulder. Instead I made my way to the craft room, needing to get out what was in my head because suddenly the internal noise had become deafening.

CHAPTER 13

F reya sat me down at the computer first. "Let me show you that software," she said, opening the giant Mac screen she had set up in the craft area. She logged in and opened a program. "It's not cheap in terms of software, but saves a lot of time."

She showed me how to input the size of the person, regular measurements, which I already had, and then from there I could choose from some basic designs and build on top of them. I played with it for a few minutes, creating a silhouette of Alex in his Frozen gear, but making the shirt a little more translucent and adding flakes to the side of the legs. I could probably play for hours with the software, and made a note to look it up later to buy for myself as it would be a huge time saver, but I needed something to clear my head. Something else to focus on, while still leaving me with enough capacity to think.

"Thanks, Freya," I said. "I'll play with this later. I think I'm going to show Alex how to do some quilting."

Alex spread out the haul of fabric we'd purchased yesterday, laying everything in a rainbow colorway. I made my way over to him and rested my forehead on his shoulder.

"Hey," he said, putting his arms around me. His warm breath

caressed my hair and I wished for a moment to go back to bed in his arms. Only my head was too busy to let me rest. "What do you need? Total distraction or thinking mode?"

A little of both really. "How about you pick something, and I show you some basic design? We can work on that for a while." I glanced at the set of mid-arm machines Freya had. "Then maybe you can try quilting again."

"Okay," Alex allowed, his tension rising with the mention of using his ghost-learned ability. We both had hang-ups. Maybe it was why we worked so well together. "Show me how you turn squares into something."

"Pick a set of squares," I instructed.

"Any of them? Doesn't matter the size?"

"Sugar, size always matters," Jonah piped up.

"Nope," I corrected. "I bought everything with ideas in mind. So whatever size squares you want. We can even mix and match."

"How about these? They make me think of strawberry lemonade or something." Alex chose a set of 5" squares, the colors a mix of of stripes, swirls and florals in coral, green, orange, white, pink, and black. I'd picked up the set because it reminded me of spring gardens, fresh berries, and bright colors. Alex seemed drawn to bright colors, though he rarely wore them. But I'd picked a few packs with him in mind.

"Sure," I agreed. "Let's do a disappearing nine patch."

"A disappearing what?"

I took the squares from him, stitched a set of nine together, three rows of three and then ironed it. When I laid them out on the cutting board he got really worried.

"What? All that work and now you cut it?" Alex gave me a squinty side eye.

"Do you trust me?" I asked.

"I guess." He sounded less than certain at that moment.

"You wanted magic, right?"

"Yes." This time more confident.

I picked up the large ruler, centered it vertically, and used the rotary blade to cut the block in half. Then, since I was using a rotating cutting mat, turned the entire thing with a little twist of the mat, to cut down the horizontal side as well, creating four blocks.

"Here is where your magic really happens," I told Alex as I separated out the blocks. "Turn this top right one, and the bottom left one." I turned the two, putting the larger uncut blocks pointing toward the middle, and suddenly it looked like a whole new pattern. "Now we sew them back together. It looks like we took a mad amount of time to make small pieces and sew them into these designs, when all we did is cut a block and turn it."

Alex gaped at the design. "Wait, do that again."

I flipped the blocks back to the way they had been, aligning the edges so it still looked like the nine squares. Then I flipped the top right one, which made the large print square point toward the middle, and a small square appear in the corner beside a couple of lines of green. The whole process made the piece *look* like you'd worked forever on it by sewing small pieces together. Except it was a simple block, sew, then cut, process.

Alex flipped the bottom left. Examining it.

"You can flip the other two as well," I turned them so the larger uncut blocks all faced the center, leaving small squares at each corner and the entire thing appearing as though it were bordered in green. "This is a cornerstone," I said pointing to the small square in the corners. "You can create a half dozen designs by simply changing how you lay out these squares after you cut them. That's where the magic is."

Alex studied the pieces, flipped them around a few more times before landing back on the first one I'd shown him. "Now I sew them together?"

"Yes, like we did the first squares, right sides together." I took them and sewed the new set of four squares together, then pressed it again.

"We made that."

"Yes."

"But it's tiny."

"That's why we make more and then put them all together. Quilts are made from many smaller blocks like this one."

His lips curved into a big oh.

"Do you want to try?" I asked him.

Alex shook his head. "I'm so worried I'll break something, or mess something up."

"I can fix pretty much anything you might do," I promised him.

"Except my anxiety about it," Alex admitted, indicating he knew it was an unreasonable fear.

"You would feel better if I sew and you watch?"

"I love watching you sew. It's relaxing."

"Okay," I agreed. Alex made his way back to our little area and began laying out the blocks.

"What if I change the order of the blocks?" He wanted to know as he laid out a bunch of squares on the large workspace.

"Keep the green in the same spots, since it creates a cohesive sashing, but change up the rest any way you want." He could actually change it all and make it 'scrappy,' though I had a feeling he was getting to the edge of his capacity of new learning for the day.

"More lingo," he grumbled. Alex went to work, laying out the squares, then bringing them to me to sew together. "You're like a super speed sewer."

"I also have years of practice," I reminded him. I cut and sewed, he ironed, and we rolled through four packs of squares like a well-oiled machine. Twice something bumped my leg and thought Alex was crouching in close, only when I looked up, he was perched on a chair about three feet away. I frowned and looked down. Maybe I'd dropped something. Nothing looked out of place in the dark underside of the sewing table. I probably needed more sleep.

The third time it happened I could have sworn it felt like what Jet often did when I was at home. In fact, I was so focused and chain piecing the blocks as Alex handed them to me, I almost thought that it *was* Jet, and that we were home. Only the sound of chatter from across the room made me look up and realize we were at the B&B. Jet wasn't there, but Alex had told me he'd seen a ghost cat.

I turned my gaze to him.

"What?" he asked, holding out squares, which I took, but didn't put on the machine.

"Is the cat near me?" I whispered to him. "The ghost cat?"

He looked at my feet, then back up to my face. Expression confirming a drop of a rock into my gut. "Yes. But she's normal right now. Just a cat. Do you feel the skin tingles?"

"No. I thought it was Jet for a minute..." And that made me catch my breath. No ants on my skin feeling, but I had felt something bump my leg. Had it happened before and I'd never caught it, or was this new from my encounter with whatever things had been out in the forest last night? I gripped the edge of the table, forcing myself to suck in air as I counted deep even breaths.

Alex rubbed my back in slow circles. "It's just the cat. I promise. She's acting like a normal cat right now. Mostly sitting at your feet."

"A ghost cat," I muttered.

"Yes. Would you rather it be a person?"

No. Absolutely not.

"Will we have time to finish this today?" Alex asked, holding out more squares. He was completely unbothered by the fact that a ghost sat at my feet. If he wasn't freaked out, I could calm down too, right? Focus on what we had at hand. We had already completed a half dozen blocks. "I've seen you finish putting together quilt tops in a day."

I had. Simple designs. Which is what we'd chosen. I took the blocks and continued to sew, working hard not to move my feet more than necessary to actually push the pedal down. Alex took to cutting the blocks, then handing them back. He did the ironing. I focused on sewing, racing through the blocks as fast as I could, and breathing deep while I chanted, "It's just a cat," quietly to myself.

We laid out the completed squares, Alex shifting one here or there every once in a while, until the batch was done. A good size blanket formed from the rows. The layout created a secondary design of diagonal lines from the turned center blocks. Alex played with it until he was happy the diagonals did what he wanted. Smiling in triumph as he placed the last square he'd been moving around for several minutes. He handed me the first two squares, adding one as I got through each one. I paused when the first row was finished to hand it to him.

"Iron that. Then give me the second row. We do each row, then sew the rows together."

He thought about that for a minute, but handed me the squares from the next row, then took the first to the iron. I glanced at the clock. Two and a half hours since we'd begun. It was a record even for me. Maybe ghosts motivated me too? The final row of sewing took almost no time. A quick nesting of seams, pinning, which Alex did with the two rows while I stitched the previous two. Finally it was finished, one big unit, which Alex ironed again.

He held it up. "We made this. And it didn't take that long."

"The magic of precut squares. The cutting takes up most of the time while quilting. There are machines that some of the bigger quilt shops have to cut squares or strips on demand, but not all of them have it."

"I'm sold. Squares or whatever, are the bomb." Alex grinned dancing around with our new creation. "What's next."

"You should eat lunch," I told him.

He waved a hand at me. "Are you hungry? I ate like four eggs and half a pound of bacon for breakfast. And did you see the strawberries? I must have had a pint of those."

I wasn't hungry, but I carefully got up and stepped away from the machine, worried about wherever the ghost cat might be.

I waved at Freya to get her attention. She was engaged in a conversation with Chad about the Cricut cutting machine, and crafting EVA foam for an Infinity Glove. She looked up. "Do you have any spare 108?" I asked her.

"Yes. Far left cabinet, left side. It's sorted by color," she said pointing to the distant wall of cabinets.

I headed in that direction, found the cabinet and opened it to find almost a full section, floor to top of the cubby, labeled 108. They weren't hanks of fabric like I had, but a section of full bolts, many solid colors, and a handful of prints. Alex appeared beside me with the quilt top, staring into the depths of Freya's organization.

"She's a hoarder too," Alex said with a bit of awe.

"Better organized though," I said. "We need to find a good back for our quilt. These fabrics are 108 inches wide, meaning they fit most quilt tops without having to piece together smaller bolts of fabric."

"Oh." Alex held up the top beside the wall of colors. "More quilting magic. How about this green with leaves?" He pulled out one in pale green, with metallic gold leaves.

"Sure. But we should stop for lunch."

"Or we could keep going and have an early dinner. How much is left?" He eyed the backing and the top. Did he remember the quilt sandwich part?

"All that's left is sandwiching the quilt, then the actual quilting. Are you ready to try free motion quilting again?"

"What if I can't do it?" he whispered. "The machine didn't feel as familiar when I was sewing the seams."

I set the fabric down and pulled him into my arms, tilting my head up to meet his lips. "Whatever happens is fine." There was fear in his eyes, but I knew he wouldn't let it hold him back. "If you can't do it, then we just put it on the long arm and set a design. No pressure."

"I want to be useful to you."

I stepped into his space and put my hands on his face so he could see only me. "You are. Just having you hang out while I sew is one of the few things that quiets my brain. Your presence, even if you were only napping while I worked, helps me out. Whether you craft or sew or not doesn't matter. I like having you close."

"I like crafting with you."

"And I love crafting with you too. Showing you stuff. Even with a ghost cat at my feet, I knew you were close and it was okay. I know this freaks you out a bit, but I think it will be alright. I would love for a ghost to stop in and give me some skill I could use," I told him.

"Careful what you wish for, eh?" Alex muttered. "The cat is still here. Sitting in the chair you were using."

I glanced at the chair as though I'd see something there. Nothing. Not even a divot where the cat might sit. I guess I wouldn't be sitting back down.

"You missed my point. Having you here has been great. I'm so happy you came along."

His cheeks pinked again. I worked to get us focused back on the project and soothe his internal panic about being gifted.

"Try to think of the finished quilt," I told him. "What color do you want the thread?" Freya, like me, had a wall of colored threads meant for top quilting. Some were variegated, some even metallic. I preferred heavier cotton thread for quilting, and found a pale peach I thought would work well, blending in most spots, visible in others. "How about this one?"

Alex took it and sat down at the mid-arm machine, threading it as though he'd done it a thousand times. The contrast between machines stark, as the mid-arm he sat at had an elongated neck, and was built into a flat surface with the table to allow more movement space. The free motion foot was already on the machine, feed dogs lowered. Alex wound a bobbin of thread, then set the machine to ready, a familiarity with the machine he hadn't had with the standard one.

"That's not normal?" He asked quietly.

"Normal for who? Why does normal matter?" I held out the quilt for him. "We talk about normal way too much for men who are not average in any way."

Alex grinned. "Your ass is beyond average."

"Perv," I teased him.

"But it's your eyes I love best. And those little freckles across the bridge of your nose."

Now it was my turn to blush. "Distractions aside, do you want to do this?"

He let out a long breath, adjusted the quilt into the machine, setting the foot on the edge, and stared at it. He ran through a fast outer basting stitch before re-centering the piece in the middle to work on one square at a time. After a minute he began to move, hands guiding the fabric with that same magic he'd displayed at the quilt shop.

"You okay?" I asked perching in a chair beside him, my back to the rest of the room, still keeping one eye on the chair with the cat, and one on Alex.

"Feels like I've been doing this forever," Alex said. I barely heard him over the whir of the machine, his voice small and uncertain. "Natural. But it's not really mine, yeah?" Alex said. "It's cheating."

"She gave you the skill because she knew you had the vision."

"You don't know that." He paused, having finished one of the squares in a mix of textured lines, curves, and designs that made the space unique and intricate.

"She said the others in the shop, and her own kids, didn't have the skill for it? A bit like art overall, I think. Someone can admire art, even love looking at it, but that doesn't mean they can create it. You can create it; she simply gave you the muscle memory in which to create the vision in your head."

He stared down at the piece. "I can sort of see what some of the different patterns would look like before I sew them. Even feel the direction I need to move my hands to get there."

"Okay. How do you feel about that?"

He frowned at me. "You sound like my therapist."

I laughed and leaned forward to kiss him on the cheek. "Does your therapist do that?"

"No, thank God. She's in her sixties."

"Does she promise to finger press you later?" I whispered into his ear.

He gasped, and I knew that tiny suggestion would make him hard. "Stop, your friends are here."

"Do you want to keep working on that, or take a break?" I prompted him, like I was offering more private things than getting him food.

He eyed me, then the quilt. "I think I can finish it pretty fast. I see it all in my head. Then we can head out for an early dinner?"

"Sure. I'll work on the binding while you do the quilting."

"Binding?" Again, he had no idea. It was interesting how specific the knowledge given to him by the ghost was.

I waved my hand at him and the machine. "Get to work with you."

"Wow, slave driver much?" Alex said, going back to his stitching. He kept most of the sashing to simple edge to edge swirls, made little flowers in the cornerstones, and full feathers in the larger squares. His seamless transitions made me stare in awe for another few minutes.

I had to shake my head to snap out of it. "You denied me sex. Therefore, I will make you work."

"Boy..." Jonah teased from somewhere behind me.

Alex's cheeks began to pink. "Didn't deny. Just want to finish... I can feel it. See it." He continued his stitching, flying through squares while I cut the binding.

CHAPTER 14

Melissa reappeared a handful of times and I worked hard to ignore her small interactions. Mostly she approached Freya. Very little ruffled Freya, but I could tell she was getting annoyed.

"They won't tell me anything," Melissa complained.

"Maybe they don't know anything," Julie replied.

"Let them work," Jonah said. "It's their job."

"Shouldn't they have a ton of people searching? Call for volunteers? Have hundreds of people combing the woods?"

"Real life is not like TV," Chad pointed out. "I watch a lot of true crime stuff, and rarely do they spend a lot of man hours and people searching for an adult. Kids, yes. Because kids get lost. Adults go missing and it's usually them escaping something, or them murdered and hidden somewhere."

"Micah vanished but wasn't murdered. People looked for him."

I sucked in air and sat down on my knees beside Alex. He was completely lost in the art now. Halfway through the piece, flowing over stitches flawlessly, a bit like the magic he claimed I had. I glanced around, wondering if the cat was still there.

"His was sort of a special circumstance. Vanished in a state park while surrounded by the people he came with. Even then I think it was Tim who began the search, and called for backup. The park rangers are used to people going missing, so they began to search too. That's normal for state parks, I think." Chad seemed a fountain of knowledge.

"We should push for them to search then," Melissa said.

"Those woods are less than ten acres. It is not a state park," Freya pointed out. "If anyone goes missing there, the police will find them if they are still there."

"But they haven't come back yet," Melissa said. "How do we even know they are searching?"

"Because we expect the police to do their job?" MaryAnn asked.

"None of you care!" Melissa shouted at them. "She could be dead and none of you care!"

I scooted closer to Alex, careful not to touch the leg he was using to press the pedal, but leaning against his hip. He paused and glanced at me, looking at the group for a moment before his gaze fell behind me. He frowned. Was the cat still there?

"Alex?" I whispered.

"Sit on my other side," he instructed.

I blinked at him, but crawled around to the opposite side of his chair and wrapped myself around his other leg. He returned to his sewing, occasionally looking up, and toward the machine we had been using. I wondered what he saw. The cat? Perhaps even Byrony's ghost? He didn't tell me, and I was okay with that. Instead I focused on watching him stitch and tuning out the others. Even as the argument escalated.

"We do care. That's why we are trying not to get in their way," Nicole defended.

"None of us are from here," Julie pointed. "Except Freya. I wouldn't know what to look for even if we were out there."

"How hard is it to look for *people*?" Melissa demanded.

"If you're so worried then why aren't you out there?" Jonah asked. "We all stood on the back porch watching the police for a while. They are in the woods. Not just one or two of them, but many. You saw them same as we did. They asked us all questions. Talked to everyone. If someone hurt Byrony and Joe, they are the ones equipped to help them. And as a black man, I can assure you, there are only a handful of things I trust the police with. Finding a famous white girl and her boyfriend, is one of them."

Melissa paced. And I could almost feel the anger and tension rolling off of her. Her hands were clenched at her sides and she vibrated with an energy that indicated she wanted to hurt someone.

I suspected it was more self-loathing than anything else. A frustration of being unable to really do anything perhaps. And I tried to understand, if it was Alex missing, I'd be freaking out too. But not on the only people I had for support right now. Alone in another state without Alex? I'd have turned to Freya and Chad and MaryAnn for comfort. Maybe Melissa didn't feel close enough to any of them to find something other than rage.

"The detectives on site said they would let us know if they needed anything," Alex said, glancing up a time or two. His gaze fell back to the other machine often enough that I worried at my lip over what he was seeing. "It's my understanding, that this early in the process, they are ruling out all possibilities."

"What other possibility could there be?" Melissa demanded.

"Dozens," Chad chimed in. "They got lost. They caught a ride with a friend. They wandered onto someone else's property. That one of them was hurt and the other took them to the hospital. There are dozens of possibilities. Not all of them mean they are missing or hurt. We see stupid drunk kids back home do really dumb things all the time. They get reported missing and someone finds them at a friend of a friend's house 'cause they were too drunk to remember how to get home."

"They weren't drinking," Melissa defended.

"Do you know that? You left them. They could have done anything after you left," MaryAnn pointed out. "Look. I'm worried too. But getting mad at us is not going to bring them back."

And wasn't that the truth? How many times after Alex had gone missing, did Lukas scream at me or Sky, or even his fellow cops? He lashed out until they forced him onto paid leave, requiring him to see a therapist before he had any chance of returning to work. He hadn't gone. Not until Alex came home. Sky said Lukas was going to therapy now, twice a week. It was that or give up his job. He hadn't really had enough time to experience change from his sessions, but I hoped it helped them both.

Finally, Alex stopped the machine, finished with the stitching. Edge to edge filled with design. He freed the piece from the machine and took it back to the cutting table, taking a wide berth around the machine we had used to sew it together. I frowned at the empty space.

"What's next?" Alex asked.

"We trim the extra off and bind it." I looked at the regular machine.

"Maybe we can use a different machine?"

"My regular machine is in our cabin." I glanced at the clock. It was almost three in the afternoon. "Why don't we trim it and then take it back to the cabin." I'd be thrilled to escape the group right now. The anger, frustration, and irritation was growing among them like a tangible thing. They still bantered back and forth, arguing about things they could do, should do, and whether or not the police would let them. Tuning them out was the only way I could breathe through all that aggression and the lingering sense of unease that filled my gut.

"Sure. Then we can head out to dinner." Alex laid out the quilt, holding up the ruler and rotary blade for me. Getting away from the house sounded like a good idea too. He kept glancing at the unused machine, gaze flicking to meet mine several times as he seemed to be telling me to stay away from it too.

I trimmed the piece with practiced efficiency, threw the waste away, and folded up the quilt, gathering the binding I'd created so I could finish it later. "I'll see you guys tomorrow morning for the first day of the convention," I told the group as I followed Alex to the door.

"You won't be back later?" Julie asked.

Not if I could help it. I needed to be away from them if I was going to last the rest of the trip without screaming at someone.

"Nah," Alex said. "We're going to eat out and then have a quiet evening in. I think we could both use the rest."

Everyone wished us well, except Melissa, who seemed to glare at us on our way out. I admit I didn't understand her. When Alex vanished, I'd spent a lot of time badgering the police and Lukas for any news. I'd also wasted a ridiculous number of hours watching the camera feeds from my garden, like it had some sort of portal he would magically reappear from. If Alex had gone missing from the woods, I'd be out there, either bothering the cops, or searching myself. Maybe they'd told her they didn't want her around? If she had bothered them as much as she was bugging us, then perhaps that was the case.

I sighed as we made our way across the lawn. There were police in the woods. I could see them, a handful of who seemed to be moving methodically through the area. So they were searching. Had they found anything yet? Perhaps were looking for evidence?

"The aggression did something to the cat," Alex said as we reached the cabin door and I unlocked it.

"What?"

"It was changing again. Like morphing into something big, dark, not defined. I think the negative energy did that." Alex stepped inside and set the folded blanket down on the small table beside my machine. "Let's not work on this right now. Let's go out."

I stared at him, trying to read his expression. It was worried, but not panicked. "You okay?"

"Mostly," he said. "I guess I sort of get what it feels like to be around someone missing now. I mean, I know she's dead. I saw her ghost. But I wonder if we should be doing something?"

"Have you seen her ghost again since last night?"

"No. Just the cat." He shivered. "Whatever it was changing into, it was something I hope to never see again."

145

"I wonder if that happens to all ghosts." Maybe that's what really transformed those lingering memories into something that terrified people.

"Perhaps those that linger," Alex said without really committing. Neither of us knew. I wasn't sure I wanted to. "You don't believe in ghosts," he reminded me.

"But I felt something, saw something. If not a ghost, then what? Ghosts are associated with bad and scary here in America. That's not how I was raised."

"Does that mean the ghosts are different here? Or the perception of them is different here?" Alex asked.

I stared at him as I stepped inside and closed the door, reaching out to wrap my arms around him. "Why are you so smart?"

"Not sure most people would agree with you."

"Most people are stupid."

"And you accept right away that what I saw was her ghost."

"I already told you, I believe you. You are not crazy. Or at least not any crazier than I am."

He sighed. "Rousing endorsement."

"Good thing we have each other. Do you want to go home?" I wondered.

"No. Your convention thing starts tomorrow. It's why we came."

"True. But weird seems to happen around us."

He laughed, more self-deprecating than humor. "Weird happens. We need a T-shirt that says that. Or magnets for weird. Or something." He stepped away from me for a moment to hold out his arms. "Is this appropriate enough dress for BBQ?"

"I love BBQ," I told him. "Probably my favorite thing about this country is BBQ."

He nodded. "Who knew? Well Freya knew, but I figured that's where we would go for dinner. But I have a stop I want us to make first."

"Okay?" I asked. "And yes, what you're wearing is fine. If Texans can wear assault rifles anywhere, you can wear a kilt and a Simply Crafty T-shirt to BBQ."

"Trust me? I have the address, you just need to get us there."

"All right," I said after a moment, watching Alex find his wallet and phone. "Hopefully less adventure and more BBQ?"

Alex's boyish grin eased some of the anxiety I hadn't realized I'd been soaked in most of the day. "Oh, yes."

CHAPTER 15

Before we could leave, we ran into one of the police detectives. He saw us headed to the car as he was coming out of the front of the house and made a beeline for us. My stomach flipped over. He was the sort of man you expected to be a detective, an older white male, with graying hair and a stern expression on his face. His hair was cut only a shade longer than a military buzz cut, so maybe it was growing out and was former Army like Alex? He also had a bump on his nose that meant it had been broken and not set right at some point in his life, though the imperfection fit his face well.

I couldn't recall if I'd seen him before. Though in the light of the afternoon he looked familiar. Had he been the detective who questioned me?

Alex held out his hand, the detective took it and shook it. "Detective Manning. Did you have more questions for us?" Apparently Alex's memory was working better than mine.

"I did, if you could spare a few minutes. A few things popped up when I pulled up your names."

Fuck. I sucked in air. Alex wrapped his arm around my waist, but nodded to the detective. "I've had an interesting few months."

"Interesting for sure. Called the NOPD, and there are a still a lot of questions about your disappearance and return," Detective Manning said.

"For me as well," Alex agreed. "But I've answered everything to the best of my ability."

"And Mr. Richards," Detective Manning said, "A bit of history with you as well."

"Years ago," I muttered.

"You both mentioned neither of you knew Miss Byrony Cartwright well." He said.

Alex shook his head. "Never even officially met her. One group meal and then an evening of noise which woke us up. That's all I know of her or her boyfriend. The evening meal, I admit I was pretty tired from the day's drive over, so I didn't pay much attention to her. And all I know of her trek out into the woods is that they were playing with a Ouija board and Freya asked them to take the game to the craft room instead of the dining room. My impression was that she'd encouraged the rest of the group to do a ghost hunt. But you'd have to ask them. Micah and I went to bed."

"It looks like you've had some trouble with her in the past?" The detective looked at me. "We have a social media expert who can give us a lot more information nowadays than a simple background check. There was some bad blood between you two?"

"Years ago. She stole some costume designs from me. It's a bit like stealing a painting and putting your own name on it. Bad form," I said. "I don't do design like that anymore. Got tired of people stealing from me and copying my ideas."

"Her friend Melissa seemed to think you were pretty angry about it."

"Melissa wasn't even around when it happened. As I said, it was years ago," I said. "I haven't spoken to Byrony in over two years." I shook my head. "I didn't even know she was going to be here. If I had, I might have found somewhere else to stay."

"Because you were so upset with her?"

"Because," I corrected, "she has a way of stirring up trouble and making things all about her. Did it at every retreat we had prior, and at least a dozen conventions that I know of. It's a part of her brand, I believe. Last I heard," actually MaryAnn had been talking about it while we sewed, "she had a way of starting fights with other vloggers to get more attention. I don't vlog. I barely cosplay anymore. My focus is my shop and my tours."

"But you came for this retreat. The others made it sound like you were getting back into the trade? That would put you at odds again."

"I came for a break from work and to go to the textile convention with a few people I know," I said.

"You're not getting back into the trade? Your host indicated she was helping you with some designs," the detective pushed back.

"Freya *is* helping with some designs, but not for cosplay purpose. The stuff I make is to sell in the shop I run. Though we do costumed tours sometimes as well. I currently have no plans to vlog or even blog my current designs." It was the first time I'd said it out loud. I hadn't told anyone yet. Not Alex or Lukas or Sky or even Freya that I had no desire to return to the influencer glory days I'd once had. Simply Crafty was my life now. And I really loved that silly little shop. Investing time and emotion into being an online doll for people to mock and shame? That was not anything I wanted to return to.

"Is this something you've discussed with the group? The others seemed to view your return as competition."

I waved my hand at the idea of it. "It's not happening. I don't want that spotlight anymore. Some of them want it too much. Being in that battle of who's better because they had more fans was never something I enjoyed. Byrony never understood that. It's why she kept attacking me. Even joined my Facebook group once, the one I use for my ghost tours. Started crap there. I had to block her and ban her."

"Wow, I didn't know that," Alex said.

"It was over a year ago. I tried to ignore her at first. You know I don't monitor that group a lot. But she had the admins up in arms."

"For someone who says he doesn't know her well, you seem to have a lot of information on her," the detective pointed out.

"Superficially. I've heard a lot of stories. Not sure they are all true, but plenty I've experienced firsthand to know some of them are. Do I know her? No. I didn't even know her last name was Cartwright. She went by Hayes online. I think she's from Oklahoma somewhere, but I'm not sure. Didn't know she was dating anyone. And really never even got introduced to Joe. She wasn't someone I thought about outside of this group. You know how you cut people out sometimes to focus on other things. That's what she was to me. Unimportant. Not a part of my life. Like someone you once worked with who always took credit for your work. Once you leave the job it doesn't matter anymore. She was never close enough to me for me to really put an effort into how we knew each other." I shook my head. "We had arrived not long before they went out to play games in the woods."

"And Melissa Umbridge? How well do you know her?"

"She's new to the group. Only been part of the cosplay thing a year or so?" I thought about it. "I honestly couldn't tell you what she cosplays as I've never seen her do it, only seen her name pop up in our online chats sometimes. I met her at a convention or two in the past year. Usually we'd have a group dinner or something as I don't cosplay much anymore. But other than that, I don't know much about her."

"Have you found them?" Alex asked. "Freya made it sound like the area is pretty small. I know where we were searching, we could still hear the road. So the woods can't be that big."

"They aren't. A couple acres in each direction before it hits someone's land or house. They could meander a couple miles by sticking to the woods and zigzagging a bit, but that's not what people normally do when they are lost. We aren't positive this is even a missing person's case yet. We are checking hotels and hospitals," Detective Manning admitted. "Joseph Dante was from here. So while Ms. Umbridge says Miss Cartwright's car is here, we have not yet located Mr. Dante's vehicle. He's not at home and had the week off."

"So they could be anywhere," Alex said. "Perhaps ditching a friend who wouldn't give them alone time?"

"Perhaps," the detective said, not looking happy about that idea.

"Ms. Umbridge is very worried," Alex said.

"And vocal," the detective agreed.

"If something happened to her friends I can understand," Alex said.

"True," Manning said. "The two of you are staying the week?"

"Yes," I said. "We are here for the textile convention, which starts tomorrow and runs through the weekend. I'm hoping to secure a few fabric lines for my craft shop."

He nodded, seeming to think for a few minutes. He pulled out a card and handed it to Alex. "If you think of anything, see anything unusual, give me a call."

"We will," Alex agreed taking the card and putting it in his pocket. "We're headed out to get food, but will be back later. Will your people need any help with the search?"

"We've already scoured the woods. They aren't large enough to miss a lot. So at this time no. Not unless we get another lead to the state park or something. We are checking lots for the missing vehicle."

"Let us know if you need help," Alex said. "We are willing to search if necessary, even though we didn't know her well. Her friend is very worried. I hope they just did something stupid and didn't tell anyone where they were going."

"You and me both, Mr. Caine," the detective agreed and let us go.

I breathed a sigh of relief as we finally got into the car. My heart was pounding. "They think I did something to her?"

"They are just covering their bases. It makes sense. Talk to anyone who has a history with them. If you've had words with her before that would bring up red flags. Our own disappearances probably make us look suspicious too," Alex said pulling on his seat belt. "Like we have a secret cult we are recruiting for. People who magically disappear and return without explanation."

"I'd like out of that cult," I muttered as I put the key in the ignition but didn't turn the car on. "You know she's dead."

"Sort of," Alex said.

"You saw her ghost. Do people who aren't dead have ghosts?"

"Maybe? I mean, yes it looked like her. But maybe it was a trick? Like the thing that took me playing tricks?" He let out a long breath and pulled out his phone. "When I was in the hospital there were a couple people like that. Empty? Soul gone from their body. All that was left was a shell."

Hospital. When Alex talked about the hospital it wasn't his recent short stay after he'd been found. It was his time in the mental ward. "Like their soul had left and all that remained was their body?"

"Mostly," Alex shrugged. "I once saw something in the hospital, next to one of those shells, a mass of sort of wriggling images. It was like it was trying to form a person, but couldn't? Like the person was so broken even the soul couldn't find its way back together. I don't know how else to explain it." He was quiet for another minute. "I never told anyone that before."

And it made sense. Alex's time in the hospital made him think he was crazy. Well, it began with that night in the desert, but expanded as he saw doctors and therapists who all assured him his mind was gone. Except it wasn't. Alex, for the most part, was solid-footed and common sensed. It was the whole 'seeing things others couldn't' that made people label him crazy. I wondered if that's how all the prophets got started.

"You were afraid that would happen to you?" I asked. "Your soul would abandon your body and not be able to form anything solid?"

"We don't know it didn't happen," Alex said quietly. "Maybe that's why I was missing."

Was that any less frightening an option than having him used as a puppet by some sort of unknown? Not really. "But you're here now."

"Yeah," he agreed quietly. "But in the woods, after I saw what I think was Byrony, I saw something like that. One of those rippling masses of images. Like a puzzle with multiple faces and body parts all strewn together." He shivered. "It was sort of monstrous."

"More sad," I pointed out, "especially if it's someone who was mentally ill, or broken. Perhaps that's what really defines the mentally ill. Sometimes their soul is scattered."

"Scattered. That's a kind word for it. I just don't ever want to be that way."

"Okay," I said.

"It helps to share, I think. I don't feel quite so crazy."

"I don't think you're crazy at all. At least not about the ghost thing." I wasn't sure what he saw, but knew he saw something. Like when my skin began to burn with that eerie sensation of spider webs or ants. Instinct on high gear? Something paranormal? I wasn't sure there was a difference.

"Thanks for that, at least. I don't think you're crazy either."

I laughed. "We'll be crazy together. Ghost cats and whatever."

Alex shook his head. "That was for real so weird. I've seen some odd stuff, but the way it changed from the cat to something… I'm not sure how to describe it. A mass of pain and anger?" He stared out the window, then sighed as his phone jingled. "Lukas has been blowing up my phone all afternoon. Now I know why."

"You think Detective Manning called him?"

"Oh yeah." He unlocked his phone and opened his texts. After a moment he snorted out a laugh, then turned the phone my way. There was a picture of Lukas with a "What the Fuck?" expression on his face. Above the picture, the text read: *My expression when the police call asking about my little brother. Call me, asshole.*

"Hey it's better than him screaming and raging, demanding you come home," I said. "Sky seems to have a calming influence on him."

"Maybe," Alex agreed. He hit dial on the phone and turned it to speaker. Lukas answered after the first ring.

"Why does it take you all day to call me you piece of shit," Lukas growled as he picked up the phone.

"Hey, asshole," Alex said with humor.

"Really? Really? Gone like two days and already in trouble with the police?" Lukas snarled through the phone.

"Love you too, big brother. And no, not in trouble. Don't know much about the girl or her boyfriend. Only met her once."

"Right, because you two aren't trouble magnets."

Alex sighed. "I'm going to hang up on you if you don't stop being a jerk. We have nothing to do with this."

"So you're going to stay out of the way and let the police do their job?" Lukas demanded.

"We have been," Alex agreed. "Shopping and crafting mostly. I can send you a picture of the quilt we've been working on all day when we get back from dinner. It's why I didn't call. We were bonding through sewing."

Lukas groaned. "Can't you just come home?"

"Convention starts tomorrow. We get a sneak peek at cool fabrics and stuff. I'm excited. And Micah is all starry-eyed." Alex looked at me. "I'm not a fan of the tiny house we are staying in. It's smaller than Micah's. Sort of feels like if I turn around I'll bump into a wall and break something. But the rest has been good so far."

"Tiny house? I thought you guys were at a B&B."

"The B&B has a couple of tiny houses in the backyard for extra private spaces," I added. "I thought it would be quieter for Alex and me."

"Yeah? How's that quiet working out for you?"

I heard Sky's voice in the background but couldn't make out her words.

"Fine," Lukas growled, more away from the phone than at us. "If anything else weird happens, I want you to come home."

"Define weird," I said.

"We are not in control of weird," Alex argued. "And weird is a very broad description of lots of things. Weird could be seeing a clown on a street corner or having the BBQ place we're going to run out of napkins. Doesn't mean we are leaving."

"Why can't you be the kid brother you used to be?" Lukas demanded.

"Not sure what you mean," Alex replied. "I never really did let you boss me around."

"You followed me a lot."

Until Alex had enlisted and gone off to make his own way. That was when the differences had really arisen. "I don't need to live in your shadow," Alex said. "I make my own now."

"Fuck," Lukas cursed.

"Hey," Alex interrupted his brother's cursing, "Micah and I are having fun. That's important, right?"

"Are you?"

"Yes. I discovered the magic of precut fabric squares today. And I am sort of good at this thing called free motion quilting," Alex said.

"Was that English?" Lukas asked, sounding a lot like Alex in that moment. "What is that?"

"It's the final top stitching to a quilt," I said. "The part that makes the swirls or lines on the fabric. Ask Sky and she'll explain it better with one of the ones I've made you."

"There is this machine in the craft room that is perfect for it," Alex continued. "It moves like a dream."

"It's a mid-arm machine," I said. "And Alex is pretty good. Amazing, really. He has a genuine talent for it."

Alex looked at me sideways. I knew he still thought the talent wasn't his. I wasn't sure that was the truth. Perhaps the skill, with the added years of muscle memory wasn't his, but the vision, that was. I didn't think you could gift someone with creativity. Memories perhaps, but not vision.

"What the fuck is a mid-arm?" Lukas grumbled. I heard Sky again. "A fancy sewing machine, fine. Whatever." He let out a long breath, a sort of frustrated sigh. "Just be safe, okay?"

"That's the plan," Alex said. "We are in the car right now, but Micah hasn't even started it. We are going to head out for food, but I wanted to call you first. Everything is okay there? Jet is okay?"

"The cat is fine. Grumpy as ever."

Jet was never grumpy with Lukas. He loved Lukas. "Is he not cuddling with you?" I asked. Was something wrong with my cat?

"He won't stop. He's on my lap or my chest all the time. And the second I come in, he's crying for my attention. He's a big attention whore. He has food and water. I don't know why he's so clingy."

He wasn't an attention whore, or normally clingy. Not really. Not unless Lukas was there. My cat *really* liked Lukas. "My cat is crazy about you," I told him.

"Your cat is crazy."

"Aw," Alex said, "Jet *wuves* you."

"Asshole," Lukas said, though he sounded much calmer now than when we had first started the call. "Both of you are assholes. I hate you both."

"You don't," Alex said.

"I don't, but I wish I could sometimes."

"Sounds like something you need to talk to your therapist about."

"Fuck you."

"Exactly my point," Alex grinned into the phone.

"Stop sounding so damn happy," Lukas complained. "This was supposed to be a boring trip for you."

"Boring how?" Alex wanted to know. "You told me to find a hobby."

"Sewing?"

"Lots of guys sew. Micah sews amazing stuff. A lot of which you own and use."

"Micah's crafty that way."

"And I'm not? Didn't you tell me I was the craftier of the two of us?"

"Asshole," Lukas grumbled again.

"Stop being so pissy. Go kiss Sky and leave Micah and I to our fun."

"You're really enjoying this?"

"Fabric shopping is great. Just wait until you see the dragon panel we found."

"I don't even know what that means," Lukas said. "Dragon what?"

"I'll show you when we get home. Just know I miss you. Take care of Sky, and we will call tomorrow. I promise to ramble on about what I see at the convention. It's the first day which is exclusive?" Alex looked at me.

"It's a vendor only day. Not open to the public yet. So the crowds should be smaller," I said.

"Sounds great to me," Alex agreed. "I'm sort of becoming a fabric whore," he told his brother. "And Micah won't save me from myself. I'm going to be working for free until the end of the year at least to pay for all the fabric I want."

Lukas laughed. "Micah's been adrift on that boat for years. But I gave you a card. It's your money. What you get from the Army. Use it. Buy what you want. You could probably buy yourself a fancy machine if you really wanted. If you're really into this hobby."

"I think they are expensive," Alex said.

"A couple grand," I added.

"Yeah, you have more than enough for that and a bunch of fabric," Lukas said. "Fine," he grumbled. "Go. Have fun. Keep me updated. And I better not hear from the police again."

"No promises," Alex said. "But we're off to get BBQ. Night, big brother!" He hung up before Lukas could reply.

I stared at him.

"What?"

"You're worried about him."

"Lukas? Nah. He has Sky. He's fine."

"Mhmm." I started the car.

"I want him to be happy. And not need me so much," Alex admitted. "So, like if something happens to me. If the shadow takes me back... he'll be okay."

"Yeah? If the shadow takes you back, what about me?" I asked him, pulling the car out of the lot.

"I try not to think about that," Alex said in a small voice. "I hope it doesn't happen, and cling to you in hope of a future. Meanwhile I worry something will happen to me and break your heart. Or even worse, something will take you and leave me alone and crazy."

I thought about that for a few minutes. "Would you be any less invested in what we have right now if you knew I was going to vanish tomorrow?"

"No. But fuck would that hurt. I'm kind of fond of your face, among other things."

"Same," I told him. "Now, where are we going first? You said something about a stop before dinner."

"Freya said there is a shop that sort of inspired Simply Crafty."

"Mae's Craft Emporium. I haven't been there in years. They are pretty old school. Don't have all the online options we do. But it's not normal inventory. It's handmade items and donated supplies. People give up their stash to them. So the fabrics are all out of print. Sometimes you can find a gem in all the florals."

"Sounds awesome to me. Do you remember how to get there?"

"Vaguely. Did Freya give you the address?"

Alex scrolled to something on his phone. "Yep."

"Let's go check out Mae's then."

"Is Mae an actual person?" Alex wanted to know.

"She was. Passed over a decade ago. Never met her myself."

"So this shop might be haunted?"

I gave him the side eye. "Stop looking for ghosts everywhere."

"Can't help it. They sort of just appear at random. You knew this from the get-go," Alex pointed out. "No backing out of my weird now."

CHAPTER 16

T he craft shop yielded a few gems, including a few old pattern books for quilting that I picked for Alex to browse through. They were hand stitching designs, some very intricate, but Alex was fascinated and wondered if he could do them with a machine. If Mae's ghost was in the shop, he did not point her out to me. We shopped, then ate enough BBQ that I felt like I could crawl into the backseat and sleep for a week.

"I don't think I've ever seen anyone eat that much," Alex teased me for the hundredth time.

"It was so good," I groaned, suddenly sad that Alex couldn't drive because I could really have used a nap instead of the forty-minute drive.

"It was good." Alex patted his stomach. "I have a food baby. That's what they call it right? Or does that only go with alien impregnators."

"I think it's a whole separate kink. Pretty sure one I'd fit right now too."

"I can drive," Alex volunteered.

"You don't have a valid driver's license," I reminded him.

He let out a long sigh. "I haven't had an episode in a while."

"I think you have to be a year from your last one before they let you test. But we can look into it when we get home." I got into the driver's seat, put on the belt and waited for Alex to get settled before starting the car. I was not a fan of SUVs normally since it seemed like it was more car than most people needed. However, for this trip, it was proving to be roomy and useful, as we had the back filled with stuff we'd collected at Mae's.

Once I pointed the vehicle in the direction toward the B&B I was kind of happy to be headed back early. The sky was growing dark already, as it normally did in the winter. Hopefully we'd be back before eight and have an early evening of watching something stupid on my laptop. I planned to finish the binding on the quilt we'd done today, since that would take an hour at most. Alex was usually happy to sit and watch me sew, or read. And now he had a half dozen books on quilting design to look through. Maybe it was the hope of an easy night that cursed us.

"What time does the convention start tomorrow? Are we going early?" Alex asked.

"It opens at nine, and I'd like to be there around that time. I have a few booths in particular in mind, that I want to visit first. But it's open until five tomorrow for the early crowd."

"Is the rest of the group going?" Alex wanted to know. I suspected he was worried that Melissa would tag along.

"I don't think so. None of them are vendors. I had to show some special paperwork to get in," I told him. "And since you're technically my employee, that's how you're getting in."

"Ah, I see. Another benefit of sleeping with the boss."

"I'm not your boss. Lukas is."

"I call that splitting hairs. Since you do my schedule and complete the accounting software to approve paychecks."

"But Lukas technically pays you."

"If that makes you feel better about bossing me around," Alex teased. "And finger pressing me."

I laughed. "You're a perv deep down inside, aren't you?"

"I think I am," he admitted. "But only with you. I have to work to not think of doing things with you to keep from getting hard. It's like you're my on-switch."

I got what he was saying, and couldn't keep the smile off my face. Alex didn't hold back, and that was okay. He told me things straight up and it helped to keep my anxiety in check. Often I had to remind myself that we were still in the teaching phase. Learning about each other, finding how we fit and where we bumped heads. I loved that I could turn him on without trying. But I admitted I wanted a bit more from our relationship than lust. We were getting there, I think. I hoped.

"So because you're a vendor and I'm an employee, is that why my ticket cost so much?" Alex changed the subject as he often did when the teasing danced on the edge of foreplay.

"Partially. More because I had to add you right before it started instead of having grabbed an earlier rate. Conventions do that a lot. You buy a year before the event and get admission for a quarter of the door price. But as a vendor my pricing was a bit different than the rest of the group anyway even though I don't have a table. It's all about tax IDs and paperwork."

"Do you have to show stuff at the door then?"

"Our IDs. Everything else is done. We'll get a special badge for the weekend that proves we are vendors. Gets us into vendor exclusive events and better seats at some of the other stuff. Some of the booths will offer special discounted pricing for us, mostly for networking purposes. And a lot of the young new designers here will be looking to make connections." I suspected a textile convention was a lot like most other types of product conventions. Big dogs trying to pump up their products, and the little guys trying to get noticed.

"That's what you're looking for, right?"

"Yes. Some new fabric lines would be great. But I also am hoping for a few pattern designers too. A lot of the bigger brands demand exclusivity, and I'm not a fan of locking out the market for those starting fresh."

"So we'll see fabric and sewing machines, what else?"

"Pattern designers, perhaps even Yaya Han, whom I know the group loves. I think she's been there before. A lot of products like scissors and cutting machines, maybe even some 3D printing stuff as that's moving to fabric now. Some of the larger quilt shops across the country will be there. Some YouTube personalities. Freya sometimes sets up a booth. This year I think she's doing a few classes instead of a full booth. The class and schedule list is saved to my phone." I pointed out my phone which was plugged into the charger. "A lot of the influencers will skip tomorrow. They are really only here to see fans and gain freebies from the companies trying to find people to push their products. We are not fans, we are industry. Even the hardcore cosplayers in the group, they are more industry than fans, though they might recognize some of the more famous ones."

Alex seemed to absorb that knowledge. "I'm not sure I understand what an influencer is?"

"An online personality. A character. People create them through social media to represent products or lifestyles through video and pictures. Their only talent is collecting followers. Think Kim Kardashian," I said.

I directed us to a quieter road, lined with trees per the GPS instructions on my phone. Had we taken this way down? I wasn't sure I liked driving it the way back. The street lights were few and far between, leaving long stretches of darkness on the two-lane road sandwiched in the middle of heavy woods.

"Who?" Alex asked.

"Big lips and butt. Pictures of her everywhere. How can you miss that?"

"Oh, I think I know who you're talking about. Girl with dark hair? Keeps popping out babies for some rapper?"

I laughed. "I guess. Sort of? Oversimplified, but yes, that sounds like her. Her family is pretty big too. They have a clothing line, but were rich before the whole reality TV thing made them infamous."

"I remember seeing something on TV when I was at Lukas's. Did you know he has like a bazillion channels? Never seen him sit down and watch TV though. He comes home and falls into bed, then is up at the crack of dawn and out the door. Maybe that was because of me? Invading his space?"

"I think it was the job. Plus, your brother is super serious."

"Didn't used to be," Alex protested. I knew he blamed himself for that. Worried that he'd messed Lukas up somehow and if he'd been able to stay in the Army, Lukas would be fine. I didn't think that was the case. Alex leaving for the Army and the constant worry, I think that made Lukas who he was. He buried himself in work trying to help others because he worried he'd missed saving his twin. Sky and I had talked about it, but neither of us brought it up to either brother. Some things couldn't be changed by simple words.

"Life transforms us all," I reminded Alex. "You're not the same guy you were before the Army, right?"

He sighed. "I think I still sometimes am. Like I look at him and think, 'Wow, he's put together' and want to be like him."

"Lukas is not as put together as he likes people to think."

"No," Alex agreed. "And I wonder if that's my fault."

"As you once told me: *You are not the sun, moon, and stars, yeah? You're not the sole center of the universe.* Not even for your brother." The GPS directed me to turn onto another side road. I really hoped it wasn't leading us to Timbuktu.

"Wow. That stuck with you."

I laughed. "Um yeah. You crushed my dreams. Telling me I'm a worthless toad like everyone else."

"I did *not* say that."

"Mhmm," I teased back. "Sure. Claim the fifth now that you've had me in bed. I see how you are."

Alex huffed. "You found me out. I want you for your body," he threw back, playing my game. "Oh baby, what you do to me."

"You're so bad at this."

"I'm a bit out of practice at sarcasm. Plus, I *do* like your body. But I'm kind of into a lot of other stuff about you too."

"Like?" I prompted.

"Are you fishing?"

"Yes. Needy tonight, I think. Since the police think I murdered some girl I barely know and all that." I silently wished that the police would find them.

"They don't," Alex said. "Well, maybe. Who knows how they think anyway? Shh, let me think."

"Don't hurt yourself."

"Har har. Well, I love how crafty you are. I feel like if we got stuck somewhere you could MacGyver a way out."

"I don't know if I'm that crafty. I think you're the more practical of the two of us."

"Fine, you'd have ideas that I could MacGyver. At least you didn't ask who that was and make me feel old," Alex said.

"My mom was madly in love with him. My dad thought he was stupid, but let her watch the reruns for years, even bought her the boxset of all the seasons a couple years back. But making duct tape lockpicks? Yeah, not my level of craft. What else?"

Alex grinned. "I love your freckles. I know you hate them, but I love them. And your eyes." He sighed. "Those are physical things so let me think more... I love the way you engage on the kid's tour. The voices, the animation, the life you give to the stories you tell. I can tell you care, not just about the history of the city, but about those kids."

"I want them to like history. History is important."

"Especially with how bad the American education system is with history, but that's not what I mean. You create a sense of magic around a lot of the things you do. The stories, the art, the creativity, and the passion for the shop. Even those goofy shirts you think up sayings for and design. That's all part of the magic."

"I'm not really magic," I whispered. What would happen when that magic bubble burst and he saw me for who I really was?

"Oh, I know. You're not magic. And I never said you were. See, people aren't magic. But only people can create it. Magic is an emotion. A stilling of your breath as you stare at a painting or hear a song that gives you goose bumps. The way you tell stories, the way you craft, those things make people stop and breathe. Sometimes think. The ones who can at least. There will always be those who are brain dead." Alex smiled and patted my knee. "Don't discount your magic. Not everyone finds theirs."

"Yours might be the quilting," I pointed out, feeling a little teary-eyed suddenly.

"Maybe," Alex said. "Just know that when I look at you, I see Micah. Who teases me, and makes me smile, who dances with me, and is patient when I ask stupid questions about a world I wasn't part of for a long time. And who creates magical things to cast away the fear and anxiety and build a new future. I'm thrilled that you let me be a part of it. Whatever this future is you're building."

I felt something inside shift, like some wall cracking, or ice chipping away from a part of me I hadn't realized had been broken. Sometimes Alex really said stuff that blew me away. His magic, I realized in that moment. Not the sewing, or at least not only his new quilting skills, but his ability to see past the façade. Alex wasn't fooled by masks or pretty words; he saw down to the soul.

"Are you crying? Did I do bad? I'm sorry," Alex said.

"No," I sniffled and wiped my eyes with the shoulders of my shirt. "Something in my eye." Like having a boyfriend who got me.

"Right. Super dusty in this brand-new rental car with the windows shut and air on."

"Jerk," I grumbled at him.

"Do you need more praise?"

"Your brother is right, you are an asshole."

"But your asshole," Alex agreed. "You can play with it later. Or I can play with yours. Or we can cuddle. I'm good with it all. It's weird that it's dark so early."

"It's barely after seven," I pointed out, "not that early. This is normal back home too. It is November." It wasn't completely dark yet. An orange glow met the horizon in a narrow band leaving a tiny glimpse of the disappearing daylight.

"Are we taking the scenic route back to the B&B?" Alex asked, staring out at a few passing fields and a lot of trees. The area surrounding the road was heavily wooded. "This isn't one of those haunted roads is it?"

"Um, I think all roads in Texas are haunted. But no, not scenic route. Just not the highways. I didn't want to take the long way around. Are you seeing anything weird?" I glanced at him, trying to keep my eyes on the road as this was also deer country. I didn't need to hit a deer because I wasn't paying attention.

"A feeling," Alex said. "Not seeing anything but dark and trees. But anxiety…"

"I don't feel anything." Nothing other than normal apprehension for driving on country roads with the oncoming dark. "Keep an eye out for deer or other animals. Cows maybe." I said as we passed a small field that looked like it could have been a pasture of some kind, then we were back in the trees.

"Cows are not small animals."

"But common here in Texas."

"Didn't know Texas had so many trees," Alex muttered, his gaze locked on the road and the surrounding area.

"Parts of it," I said. "The west side of the state is pretty gross. If you drive across to say get to New Mexico or something. Lot of cattle farms. You can smell them for miles. Makes me question eating beef every time I pass."

"Gross," Alex said. "Well, not beef. I love beef, but the stink. I can imagine."

"No. Most people can't really get the true ick of it until they get close. Imagine regular cow farm times ten thousand and there you go." I'd driven that way twice, both for conventions, and would never do it again. Next time if I had to go that far west, I'd fly.

"Totally gross," Alex said.

Suddenly he gasped, and I reacted by slamming my foot on the brake as a shadow streaked into the road.

The car screeched and lurched to a stop, but didn't completely stop the collision. A shadow hit the car, not the other way around.

Like it had been hurdled from the darkness and into my path, it slammed into the front of the vehicle, making a loud bang from the hood, then fell backward.

I sat gasping for breath, staring into the headlights. Horrified. Had I just hit something?

Alex put the car into park and jumped out while I struggled to process the last thirty seconds of my life. Light illuminated the road and the tip of something laying on the ground which didn't look like an animal. My stomach flipped over as I realized I could see a head of hair.

I climbed out of the car slowly, filled with terror, and wanting to throw up everything I ate. Fuck, fuck, fuck. What the fuck? We were in the middle of nowhere! Not a streetlight as far as I could see, only the headlights illuminating a still form. Alex leaned over it, the body, whatever it was, so I could only partially see. I expected the front of the car or even the road to be covered in blood and gore, only there was nothing. Not even a dent in the hood.

"Call 911," Alex told me. I didn't move, still stuck there gaping like a fish out of water. "Micah! He's alive. Call 911."

Alex's command broke through the terror for a moment. I raced back to the car and fumbled for my phone, ripping it out of the charger and carrying it back to Alex even as I dialed. I couldn't speak anyway. Couldn't breathe. Stupid panic attack.

Alex took the phone from me as the operator answered, and said a bunch of stuff I couldn't make out. Something about finding someone in the road. I stared down at the crumpled form. He didn't look like he'd been hit by a car. Instead he sort of lay there curled up in the fetal position, shivering, breathing roughly, and muttering things that didn't make any sense. The pale light on his face outlined enough of his features for me to recognize.

Joe.

Somehow we'd found Joe. Lying in a road in the middle of nowhere. I looked around, trying to determine anything that would serve as a location marker, but didn't know enough of the outskirts of Houston to recognize more than trees and road.

Sound vanished with a whooshing pop. Not the usual subtle shift to silence, but a full blanket of it. I stared at Alex who was still talking to the operator, but couldn't hear any of what he said, and the man on ground. His lips moved, but was he actually speaking? Was it him or me?

Only the pounding of my own blood in my ears surrounded me, an echoing rush of my racing heartbeat. It blocked out everything else.

I raised my eyes to the woods in sudden terror as my skin began to burn. Something was there. Shadows lined the trees in the darkness. Hundreds of them, like some sort of Halloween horror movie come to life. They writhed and danced undefined, at least to my eyes, but my skin prickled with a thousand needles. I could have ripped my skin off in that second and felt less pain. Nothing could be as horrific as the feeling of being covered in fire ants, except maybe the wall of moving shadows around us.

Did Alex see them? Would they look like people to him, or light swallowing shadows, like they did to me?

Somehow I'd taken a few steps past Alex and Joe. When had that happened? I didn't remember moving, but could feel my blood pounding. A throbbing in my chest that made my ribs hurt. Was it just me? I turned back toward Alex, hoping to reach him, touch him and chase away the terror. Only I came face to face with something...

Monstrous.

More than a shadow it towered in front of me like a wall of shifting—people? Emotions? Faces? I wasn't sure how to describe it. Only that it looked like the monstrosity of multiple people mashed together in a soup of shadows. Dozens of eyes and mouths gaping, screaming, reaching for me.

Hadn't Alex said he'd seen something like that? A scattering of faces and perhaps the manifestation of a shattered soul? This was far beyond anything I could have imagined from his description. More like

Frankenstein's monster, with parts cut out and sewn together haphazardly, all still moving, dozens of soundless mouths shrieking of horrors. I screamed, noiseless to my ears, but could feel the strain in my lungs. Couldn't help it. Instinct and instant reaction as I fell backward, stumbling far enough to tumble off the side of the road and into the shallow ditch. It moved toward me, floating, running without legs?

Whatever it was came at me, a nightmare like I'd never dreamt, twitching and following me. I scrambled backward out of the ditch, rolling to my feet and running in the opposite direction from the road.

The darkness seemed to swallow up everything around me as I fumbled my way around trees and tripped over unseen rocks or roots. I couldn't breathe. Couldn't pull in enough air, partly because of the running, and partly absolute terror. It wasn't fair. I didn't see stuff. That wasn't my curse. Feeling things and occasionally hearing things was bad enough. Seeing things like Alex did? I didn't think my sanity would survive.

I realized in that moment, that while I said I believed him, and tried to assure him he was normal, at least for us, I'd been paying lip service. My own fear kept me from thinking too hard about what he saw, and what would happen if he wasn't the only one who had a curse of that intensity. But it was a cop out. Alex was a much stronger man than I. He'd have turned around and faced it already, instead of becoming the rabbit like me.

I ran on, not really seeing anything, only darkness and occasionally the sturdy width of a tree smashing into my shoulder to redirect me. I didn't see the car until I slammed into the side with a thud, bouncing backward with the force and landing painfully on my back, head cracking on the hard ground.

Stars circled my vision. I blinked upward, into a canopy of trees, a car smashed into the woods at my feet. Sound came back with the small plink of liquid falling, a drip like a broken faucet, as the pounding in my ears faded, my ragged breath reaching my ears, and then footsteps, a crunch of leaves and gravel.

I tensed, head still reeling, but instinct screaming at me to get up. I would have if my body cooperated. Instead all I could do was lie there, gasping for air, waiting for the horror to reappear and do whatever to me. Perhaps add me to the mass of terrifying faces gaping and screaming.

"Micah?" Alex appeared above me, his face a welcome sight. "Fuck, you're bleeding." He touched my head. There were other footsteps in the dark. Did he hear them? I tensed. "Breathe, baby. I've got you. Breathe."

I struggled for air, chest aching from the effort. Heat trickled down the side of my face and lights began to appear in the dark. Alex didn't seem alarmed, but maybe he didn't see them? I gripped his arm, trying to form words when I still couldn't breathe.

"I think he's in shock," Alex said. "His head is bleeding. Is there a medic?" He was looking up toward the lights and not talking to me. "Micah, can you hear me?"

Someone knelt beside me, light illuminating a uniform. "Might have a concussion," someone said. Fingers touched my head. I knew they weren't Alex's because he was holding my chin between both hands.

I must have whimpered or something because Alex whispered comforting things. "Shh. It's okay. You're okay. You're safe."

Was I? Where was that thing?

The area brightened with dozens of lights and voices now. Cops. I could see the mass of uniforms moving around us, and the EMT crouched beside me.

"Micah?" The EMT said. "I need you to respond. Can you hear me?"

"Yes," I whispered. The word came out more like a wheeze. I had thought sound returned before that moment, but it all slammed down on me like a bomb of noise. A dozen voices, the crunching of rocks and leaves, Alex's soft words, the EMT's questions. And the police examining the vehicle I'd magically found during my escape.

"Is it the missing vehicle?" One cop asked.

"Plate matches," someone replied.

"Anyone find the girl yet?" Someone else asked.

And that's where I lost consciousness.

CHAPTER 17

I wasn't out long. There was a ride to a hospital, and a trip to the ER, in which they insisted on doing x-rays to check for a concussion. I threw up a couple times, which had them giving me nausea meds. But I sat in a small room in the ER waiting for the nurse or one of the doctors to return. They had already stitched up my forehead. Two whole stitches. At least it stopped bleeding. Maybe Alex and I would have matching scars.

Alex stayed with me most of the time. Though the police arrived and asked him to step out to answer some questions for a while. I wondered when they would ask me. And wasn't surprised when it was Detective Manning who came into my room, with a nurse behind him, and took the chair Alex had been sitting in.

"Mr. Richards. I'd like to ask you some questions," Detective Manning said. "Your friend insisted your nurse stay here for the questioning, to ensure it doesn't stress you too much."

"He has a concussion," the nurse said, tight-lipped.

"Mild, from what the doctor said," Manning pointed out.

"Still a concussion," the nurse said. "If he starts randomly chatting or spouting confessions, I'm shutting this down in favor of his sanity and freedom."

Confessions? To what? I blinked at them both. "Okay." My heart still raced, even though it felt like hours had passed since seeing that monster. I was exhausted and would have preferred Alex to be at my side while I was questioned about something I had no real way to explain. We hadn't talked about it yet, what I had seen. Hadn't talked much at all other than to the constant roll of nurses in and out of my room. My head hurt, but it was a dull throb. In fact, my whole face ached. I vaguely recalled smashing into the car at a full run, a bit like a bug hitting a windshield. Only the curve of the car had kept me from major damage, or so the doctor had mentioned earlier. I'd have liked to curl up in bed, wrap myself in Alex's arms and sleep for a week until the pain finally faded. Would have been nice to have Jet on my pillow too, protecting me from scary mutated people monsters.

"You saw Mr. Thomas in the road?" Manning began.

Huh? "Mr. Thomas?"

"Joe? Byrony's boyfriend?"

"Oh. I didn't see him. Not really. I saw a shadow. Alex must have too because he gasped. Did that press of imaginary brakes thing. I slammed on the brake. Didn't mean to hit anything."

"Do you remember hitting him?"

Had I? No. The shadow had run into the stopped car. "No. I stopped before that. Wasn't going that fast. Was worried about deer."

"Not a lot of deer in that area," Manning said.

I shrugged. "Lots of trees, makes me think deer."

"Do you remember your panic attack?" Manning asked. "Mr. Caine was on the phone with a 911 operator when he said you had an attack and ran."

I had seen something. My stomach churned again. The nurse gave me one of those blue plastic-rimmed barf bags. I gagged but nothing came up. "Sorry," I muttered after a moment. "Yes, I remember the panic attack."

"Most people shut down for a panic attack."

"And some people run," I said. "That's why it's called fight or flight or freeze. I have training in handling other people's attacks." Mostly

PTSD, but Sky had them sometimes too, ever since she'd been attacked last year.

"Except your own?"

"Haven't had one like that in years. Not since…" those first few weeks after I'd returned.

"Since?"

"You know about my disappearance," I snapped at him. "After I returned I had them for a few weeks, but they faded. Sometimes I still get anxiety attacks, but not full panic attacks like this. People don't normally find people in the middle of the road on a dark stretch of woods. That freaked me out. Wouldn't that freak you out? I remember my heart racing, blood pounding in my ears." Something came at me and I'd run. Would he think I was crazy? Probably. I had no desire to be dragged to whatever nearby psych ward they had for evaluation.

"Mr. Richards, your heart rate is up now. Take a few deep breaths please." The nurse interrupted. She was a kind African-American woman who gave Manning a hard face, but focused her attention on me after a few seconds. She patted my arm. "No need to send you into another panic attack. Breathe. Another attack will just make your head hurt more."

"It's mild?" I asked, vaguely remembering a doctor having stopped in briefly to tell me about my scan. I wasn't sure the nausea was related to the minor headache, or the memory of whatever that shadow had been.

"Yes. You hit your head pretty hard, but it's nothing terrible," the nurse assured me. "Nothing some rest won't cure. Doctor thinks your nausea is from the panic attack rather than the concussion."

It struck me then how quickly the police had arrived. We'd been in the middle of nowhere, or so I'd thought. The GPS had us a good twenty or so minutes from the B&B. How had the police arrived so fast? "I ran into a car. Were we by another road?" I couldn't recall seeing one.

"Nothing but service roads other than the one you were on,"

Manning said. "Funny that you found that car in the middle of a panic attack."

"Is Joe okay?" I asked. "I think it was Joe in the road. I vaguely remember seeing his face."

"Do you have a reason you drove that way tonight, Mr. Richards?" Manning pressed.

"I was following the GPS on my phone. Avoiding going around on the big highways and coming back inward. The GPS said it was a fifteen-minute time savings." I said, recalling how my phone had been plugged into the navigation system of the SUV. "I think you can pull up records like that, right? Tell where my phone has been. We did a bit of shopping, then dinner, then the route back. All mapped through my phone since I don't know the area all that well. Only been here two or three times before."

"We are pulling your records. And Mr. Caine's."

Did that mean he was keeping our phones? I hoped not. It would really suck to have to navigate the city without a phone. I knew people used to do it with printed maps, but didn't think picking up a paper map while driving was the best of options. "Are you taking our phones?"

"We've already pulled the data from them. One of my guys will drop them off with you before you leave the hospital," Manning said.

"That's fast."

"We have a great tech unit and your boyfriend has been very cooperative." The way he said it made it sound like I wasn't being cooperative.

"I've told you everything I know."

Manning seemed to think about that for a minute. Finally he asked, "How many people are in your cosplay group?"

That was an odd question. "The one here? I don't understand. The online group has a couple hundred thousand."

"I mean the exclusive group. Those of you who do the meetups like this."

Oh. "The number changes a little. People come and go. Those who came were the main group. Chad, MaryAnn, Julie, Nicole, Jonah, Byrony, Freya, and myself. Melissa, as I said is new to the group. There have been some others in the past. A few I've met, but none that I was ever close to. I've only been to five or so cosplay group specific meetups myself. Though if they are in a city nearby, I try to meet them for a meal. Sometimes we'd catch up at conventions, but we all used to travel a lot so it wouldn't often be more than two or three of us at a time." I tried to recall some names. Most of the group members were women. That was sort of the norm with cosplay. Not because men didn't cosplay, but because they didn't really ask for help and network to improve their skills. "There was a girl named Sarah for a while. She was Californian, I think."

"When was the last time you saw her?"

"I met her like three years ago, but haven't seen her in probably two years. She was into the sexy cosplay thing too." I shrugged. "I had a bit of trouble happen in that time, so maybe I missed when she left."

"Do you remember any of the others who have left the group?"

My head hurt. "Maybe? There was an Amanda, but she wasn't in the group long. I recall a handful of names, but no one I really had time to talk to."

"Do you remember why Amanda left?" Manning asked.

"No. I wasn't close to her at all, and make it a point not to get into other people's business."

"Are you close to anyone in the group?"

"Freya," I said. "She's probably the only one I talk to outside group events."

"How close are you to Miss Pedjic?"

"She helped me get my start as a professional cosplayer. I've known her for years."

"But do you visit her outside of group events?" Manning prodded. "Or she visits you? Since you live in different states."

"No. We talk sometimes through Facetime."

"About events not related to the cosplay group?"

"Sometimes." Though mostly it was related to crafting. Occasionally something came up about our personal lives. I realized in that moment that I wasn't as close to Freya as I thought I'd been. She, much like most of the other people I called 'friends', had been put in a box set aside for one purpose, crafting comradery. "I guess I never really thought about it before. At least not really in those terms," I admitted. "I keep them at a distance." I did that with everyone. Or tried to. Some had gotten through my barriers, like Sky and Lukas, and now Alex.

"Why do you think that is?"

"I don't know. Guess it's something I'll have to bring up with my therapist," I snapped back, irritated that he was pointing out my flaws. "I'll call you when she has an answer for me."

"Your boyfriend seems to know you well, if that's any consolation," Manning stated. "He pointed out that you keep parts of your life compartmentalized, including acquaintances."

"Good to know my boyfriend sees my flaws."

"He said you didn't seem as close to the group as you were to him, his brother, and your friend," he checked his notes, "Skylar. I asked him why that was. He seems to believe it's part of your healing from past events. Do you agree or think there is something else that separates the groups?"

"Again, I'll check with my therapist and get back to you."

Manning sighed and got up. "I may have more questions later."

I blinked at him. "You know where to find us."

"You don't plan on going home?" he asked.

"We are here for an event. You might think we are cold and unfeeling to stay, but I really didn't know Byrony," I said. Would Alex want to go home? This trip kept getting weirder and weirder. I had so many questions of my own. "Would you stay if you'd arrived for an event and someone who just happened to be at the same hotel went missing? At a bigger hotel we probably wouldn't have even known she was gone."

"I might not stay if I knew someone staying at that hotel had done something to her," Manning said, offering up the most I'd gotten from him the entire conversation.

I frowned. "Did you find Byrony? Do you think one of the group hurt her?" Alex said he thought he'd seen her ghost, but worried something was tricking him. I'd come to think of the supernatural as bad, though Alex didn't seem to think so, and thought maybe something otherworldly had gotten Byrony. Hadn't even thought that anyone in the group could possibly hurt her. "I can't see anyone in the group doing something like that."

"But you said you don't know any of them all that well," Manning pointed out.

"Well no. I don't. But I guess I don't look at everyone I know as though they are a potential danger?"

Manning looked me over. "You're very lucky then, Mr. Richards. Or naïve." He shrugged. "We'll be in touch," Manning said and left the room. The nurse glanced at me and followed him out. A minute later Alex reappeared. He came around the side of the bed and took my hand before leaning close to kiss my cheek.

"I threw up," I told him. "Don't kiss me. I need a toothbrush. BBQ doesn't taste so good the second time around."

"That's why I kissed your cheek," Alex said. "The nurse will be back in a little bit with release instructions."

"What about the car? And you can't drive," I said. I closed my eyes a moment and startled awake when the nurse came back in, not realizing I'd fallen asleep that fast. The adrenaline was finally wearing off.

"I should be mad at you," I told Alex.

"Yeah?" He asked.

The nurse removed the IV and blood pressure cuff. I had to work to focus on her. I would not be driving. Alex helped me out of the bed, steadying me with his arm around my waist. He had a handful of papers in his grasp, and led me to an offered wheelchair. I didn't think I needed it, but the nurse insisted and wheeled us out to the curb where our SUV idled. Was Alex going to drive? He wasn't supposed to. I frowned as I got out of the seat, but Freya appeared, opened the side passenger door for me, and Alex helped me in. I had a thousand questions, but waited until we were all strapped in and on the road.

"The detective said you told him stuff." What was it Alex had told him? Oh right, my issues with letting anyone close to me. Was that really a secret? "Never mind. It's stupid."

Alex tugged on my seatbelt to make sure it was buckled, then reached for my hand. "It's not stupid if you want to talk about it. It's not stupid if it upsets you."

I didn't. At least not right now. I had questions. "I'm lost," I told Alex who was sitting beside me in the seat behind Freya, who was driving. "Catch me up? What happened? Everything is sort of a blur."

"You have a concussion," Alex said. "The whole left side of your face is a big bruise. You must have turned your head at the last second else you'd have a busted nose. The concussion is a mild one, and you cut your forehead on the side of the car you found. They updated your tetanus shot, since they couldn't find one on record for you. If your arm hurts the next few days, it's because of the shot. Chad dropped Freya off at the hospital. The police drove the SUV to the hospital, and gave me the keys. I gave Freya the keys so she could drive us."

"Oh," I said, finally dropping pieces into place. "What time is it?" Only now did I recall dozing a few times in and out while being moved around the hospital, to the room, and to be scanned and back.

"After midnight," Alex said.

I groaned. "Sorry, Freya."

"It's fine. I'm glad you're okay. It sounds like you had a rough night." She said. She took the highway, instead of the back roads I'd followed. "How are you feeling?"

"Tired," I said.

"We'll be back soon," Freya told us. "So you can rest."

"Did they find Byrony?" I asked. "Is Joe okay?"

Freya seemed to tense at the question, but Alex patted my hand. "We'll talk about it tomorrow, after you've gotten some rest. The police didn't give me much information, and I was more worried about you than anything they found," Alex said. "You hit that car pretty hard. I was right behind you, but my fucking hip locked up, slowing me down, else I'd have caught you before you ran into it."

I let out a sigh and locked my fingers into Alex's, squeezing for a moment. I needed to talk to him anyway. Just him. Tell him what I saw. Had he seen it too? The last thing I wanted was to spill all of it in front of Freya and have her think I was as crazy as I felt.

Crazy. Fuck. That was what Alex was afraid of. Had been for a while. And now I was teetering on the edge of the same thing. Did I want to see things? No. I, too, wanted to be normal. Was there a choice? Alex indicated he couldn't turn it off. Had never really determined until recently that the things he saw weren't what everyone else saw. Perhaps he didn't witness the horror like I had. Maybe he only saw them as people. Had it been Byrony in the road? A collage of all her emotions and lifetime of memories squashed into one form? It hadn't looked like Byrony, but it wasn't like I stood there and examined it either.

I let out a long breath of air and clung to Alex's hand, eyes closed, trying not to see the world around us. More memories I didn't need. Almost like a nightmare. Was that why Alex didn't want me to go into the woods? Had he seen this thing before the night he'd seen Byrony? Perhaps he'd known somehow that I would find the car. I didn't realize I dozed until Alex roused me again, and I found us stopped in the little lot outside the B&B.

"I can clean up the room Byrony was staying in if you two want to stay in the main house," Freya offered.

"Thank you, but we are fine in the cabin," Alex answered for us. He helped me out of the car, and held his hand out for the keys. Freya got out and handed them to him.

"Let me know if you need anything," she said.

"Thanks again. Sorry for the late night," Alex said. He hit the button on the fob to lock the car. "See you in the morning." He directed me around the house and toward the cabin.

"I'm okay," I promised him. "Just tired." Though I admit to clinging to him as we walked the lighted stone walkway to the cabin. Every sound, every shadow, every dark corner made my heart pound, and by the time we got to the door of the cabin, I was trembling.

Alex opened the door, reached inside to turn on the light and tugged me in behind him. He locked the door then wrapped me up in his arms. I couldn't stop trembling. Was that still the shock? Maybe the concussion. I'd never had one before. Alex was breathing hard, not crying, but focusing on deep inhales and exhales, like I often did when I needed a minute.

"Alex?" I whispered. What had he seen? His sight was always so much more intense than mine. If I'd seen some hideous monster in the dark, what must it have looked like to him?

"Better to talk about it in the morning, I think," Alex said after a minute. "Things are less scary in the daytime."

I opened my mouth to protest, but he pulled back enough so I could see his face and how tired he looked. He shook his head. "Not tonight. For my sanity, too. Let's get you cleaned up and in bed."

"I feel gross," I said. Hospitals always did that to me. The scents of disinfectants, and other people, drugs, and latex, among other things, always seemed to cling to my clothes. Plus I'd thrown up, and felt like I could still smell that too, though I didn't think I'd gotten any on myself.

Alex led me toward the tiny shower area. There wouldn't be enough room for the both of us. Rubbing off together required no space between us, actual washing did. And I was too tired and strung out for the rubbing off.

"What's that look for?" Alex asked as he turned on the water and began to tug off my clothes.

"Wishing I wasn't too… everything to sex you up."

He grinned. "Tomorrow."

"I hope my head doesn't hurt still." I let him strip away my clothes and watched him gather it up into a pile, then I stepped into the small shower. The water was hot and I let it cascade over my back, avoiding my stitches and my aching face.

"Be right back," Alex said. He vanished from the bathroom, leaving me in the small glass enclosed shower area for only a minute or two before returning with a fresh pile of clothes. Undies for both of us, and a T-shirt for him. Alex did not like sleeping naked. Part of his time serving, he said. Always be prepared in case they had to jump up in the middle of the night and fight or something. I only slept in undies because it made him less embarrassed by the way his body responded to me. Another reminder that we were new together, adjusting and learning. Was I worth the effort, I wondered again?

He opened the little toiletries bag I'd brought with and pulled out a bandage. "I knew I'd thrown some waterproof ones in here. Let me put this over your stitches so I can I wash your hair."

I stepped closer to him, away from the spray and let him brush my hair back to apply the bandage. "Is there blood in my hair?" I asked.

Alex nodded. "And leaves and dirt."

"Gross." I turned back toward the water, avoiding putting the injured side of my face near the downpour. Alex stripped out of his clothes and squeezed in behind me, bringing in my shampoo and a small washcloth. I leaned against the wall, resting my chin on my elbows as Alex washed my hair, then carefully used the washcloth to rinse away the rest of the dirt all over my body. I was half asleep when the water was turned off, but mind still racing, not quite letting me succumb again.

"Were the police already there?" I wondered out loud. They had been there too soon to have responded to the 911 call.

"They were following Joe's phone. Got a hit off a cell tower nearby. Sounds like they were searching the area."

"So they knew he was close…" I sighed, relaxing into Alex's touch even though I felt sort of numb. Had they given me something at the hospital? I thought I vaguely recalled some sort of painkiller. "Was he alive? Is he alive?"

Alex sort of hesitated, but finally said, "Physically, yes."

That was an odd answer. Alex reached for the towel, and carefully dried me off.

"What about you?" I asked waving at his body, though he looked clean.

"I showered while you were dozing. Want to brush your teeth?"

"Yes, please."

"Will you fall asleep over the sink if I don't hold you up?"

"Maybe. No promises."

He helped me into my undies, then I leaned against the sink and watched him dress. Boxer briefs for him, and a T-shirt. Then we both brushed our teeth. The minty freshness helped ease some of my anxiety as the last of that acid was washed away. The stairs up to the loft felt like climbing Mount Everest. Alex helped me into bed, then vanished back downstairs, where the lights went out. He left the one near the door on, for which I was grateful, and returned to curl up next to me.

"Alex?" I had so much emotion floating in my gut, it began to well up, like a rising tide of anxiety. I was about to jump out of bed and start pacing when he rolled over, trapping me beneath his weight, and weaving his hand through my hair. It was a sudden stop to the anxiety, like he hit pressure points or something to turn me to jelly.

"In the morning," he said. I reached up and wove my hand through his hair, delighting in his curls and the weight of it on my palm. Having him close helped. I closed my eyes and tried to focus on having him in my arms instead of the craziness of the past few hours.

CHAPTER 18

The morning arrived far too quickly. Alex rousing me with a huge cup of coffee and a handful of aspirin helped. I thought for a minute I'd have preferred a blow job to wake up, until my first sip of coffee, and realized Alex knew me better than I knew myself.

"How are you feeling?" He asked quietly. "Dizziness? Pain? Light-headed? Nausea?"

"Tired," I grumbled at him, sipping my coffee and relaxing.

I watched him move around the cabin, taking out clothes for us, putting away the things we had gotten from the store yesterday, cleaning and packing, keeping us organized. Alex did organized well when he focused. Him in skinny jeans and a Simply Crafty T-shirt hugging his shoulders did not help me focus. Had his ass always been so cute or was it the jeans accentuating the curves that helped?

"I feel like one of those anime characters drooling over a lover," I muttered into my coffee.

Alex looked up and rewarded me with a sexy smile. He stalked the few feet to where I sat in a chair beside the door and leaned over to kiss me. Since I was already dressed and cleaned up for the morning, leaving coffee as my only flavoring, he lingered over my lips. I sighed into his mouth, wishing I could take him back to bed.

"You still want to go to the convention right away this morning?" Alex asked.

"Yes." I was actually tempted to go today and then say screw it to the rest of the week and head home. If I could talk to a few people today, get contact information, and make a few connections, we wouldn't need to attend with the bigger crowds and could leave behind the madness of the last few days. I was tired of being a suspect. Tired of having people stare at me like I knew stuff or was hiding things. Just tired of having to be the put together guy people remembered from a time long past.

"Drugs must be helping," he said after a minute. "You're not flinching when I kiss you."

Had I reacted before? I could recall something prior to the coffee, but figured it wasn't important enough to matter. "Does it look awful?"

"I hope people won't think I'm beating you when we're out and about," Alex said. "You're pretty colorful on that side." He waved a hand to change the topic. "I have an Uber coming for us."

"Huh?"

"Taking you to breakfast first, then the convention. Not a good idea for you to drive. So rideshare it is. What do we need with us?"

"We're not going to the main house for breakfast?"

"No," Alex said firmly. "I already sent a message to Freya. We'll eat, then spend some time wandering around fabric. We could both use the distraction."

"Okay," I agreed, wondering what he had seen last night. "Are we going to talk about last night?" We actually had a lot to talk about. I had an endless cycle of questions on my mind.

He threw himself into the seat next to me, a frown defining the lines on his face. It was rare for him to look as old as he did in that moment. More the age of his soul seeping through than the physical age. The strain of life on his skin had always appealed to me about him. Small imperfections that drew my attention. Maybe I did have a daddy kink.

"You're so hot right now," I told him.

He gave me a self-deprecating smile. "Don't distract me with sex if you want to talk about spooky stuff."

I sighed. "I hate spooky stuff, but can't bury it under the rug forever. Might as well get it out already."

He reached out to grasp my hand. "Tell me what you saw? You don't normally see stuff, but I know you did."

I sucked in air and closed my eyes as though that could somehow stop the memory. "Something," I admitted. "A mash of people maybe? Like a wall of writhing flesh with faces melted into it? A nightmare? Hell, I've never had nightmares like that, not in all the years of being tormented by the noises at night." And that had been after I'd seen shadows in the woods. I could recall them for the few seconds before I'd come face to face with that monster. Had those been real too? "Shadows in the woods too, before."

"And when you stopped the car? Did you see Joe in the road?"

"Not at first. I saw the shadow at first. Rushing across the road. Then I saw Joe. But I had already stopped. You reacted before I did. You saw him first?"

"Coming up off the side of the road, yes, not lying in it."

"So you saw movement too."

Alex nodded and seemed to think about that for a minute. He got up and refilled my coffee cup, turning off the pot before he made his way back. His silence was unnerving. Silence was one of those things I'd learned to spend a lot of time analyzing. Ours wasn't normally a tense silence, more one filled with thought. This one was a gauge of what he wanted to say versus what he thought.

"Don't temper yourself on my account," I told him. "I know I sound crazy too. But I lost sound," I finally said, adding to the stretch of thoughts I knew were running around his head. "It happened the first time when I was on that trail two years ago. Everything vanishes. I can feel my heart pounding, but can't hear anything. Just the pounding in my ears. That happened this time too. Didn't come back until I was on the ground."

Alex looked at me now. "So you didn't hear me calling you?"

"No. Didn't know you were behind me at all."

He gripped my hand, squeezing it hard.

"Alex talk to me. What did you see? Was it like what you saw when you were in the hospital?"

"Yes and no? In the hospital, those things were smaller, less defined, and limited to one person. This other thing… Honestly, it's hard to explain. In the road, that thing that was a mash? What did I see? Death. No other way to describe it. Saw it once before, overseas. Large, solid, defined, yet not. Thought I was seeing things. Too much heat and sand. Saw it wandering an open-air market. There were so many dead that day, on the other side, but I guess it's all the same. Dead is dead. And the death I've seen didn't wander around in a black cloak with a sickle in his grasp. More liked a bloated monstrosity devouring souls…"

I gasped at him because that was exactly what I'd seen and it still made me sick to think of it. I had to work to breathe, counting careful numbers and staring at my sewing machine because every time I closed my eyes, I saw it again.

"Lots of mythology around Death, with a capital D," I said after a few minutes of getting control of myself. What did that mean for the afterlife if there was one?

"Omens and stuff, yeah," Alex agreed. "My brother has a lot of random occult books at his place. Plus you have a ton in the shop. I've been reading as much as I can. Trying to find answers to things no one really knows for sure, I guess?"

"What about Joe?" I asked. "That shadow? He's not dead. You said he was breathing."

"Physically not dead," Alex clarified. "I think that thing, Death, or whatever it was, was chasing Joe's soul. Or spirit. Whatever." He waved his hand. "I guess the terms don't matter much. It formed out of the darkness, coming up off the side of the road and lunging toward Joe's spirit. But yes, Joe is alive. Breathing." He sat in silence for another minute, then added, "Empty. In the psych ward, I met a couple guys like that. Empty. Like they were just shells of people instead of actual people. I didn't understand why. Thought maybe it was the meds that made them so lifeless. I know they were guys who attempted suicide and were considered to have failed. But maybe that's not right? Maybe they didn't fail, but killed what was inside instead of the physical part?" He shivered.

"Wow," I whispered. "That's heavy." And terrifying.

Alex let out a long breath. "Yeah. A lot in my head today."

I guess that made two of us. "If that thing was Death..."

"It's not always like that," Alex said quietly. "I've seen people just vanish after they die. The spirit or whatever. Fuck. It's crazy to think back at all the things I've seen and realize it was not as simple as I first thought. Then there's the ghosts that linger. Why didn't Death, if that was what it was, come for them? Why do they stay?"

"Unresolved things, maybe? Why did it come for Joe if he's still alive? Why did it look so monstrous? Is Death really so awful?"

"Some death," Alex said. "As I said, I've only seen it once before. The people who died were from a suicide bomber. A couple dozen, I think. They triggered it in an outdoor shopping plaza. Lots of innocents. Women and children, and a handful of soldiers they thought weren't on their side. Senseless death, a lot of it. Maybe that's the key?"

"That would mean there would be more than Byrony out there in those woods," I said, thinking about the mash of faces. "Or does it travel long distances to gather random people? We don't know why she died. Are we sure she's dead? Or maybe she's like Joe." Stripped of her soul or something. And wasn't that an awful thought. "Maybe it was a murder suicide, like Joe killed her and tried to kill himself but only separated his soul from his body?" Crap that was too heavy for me this early in the morning. I took a long drag of the coffee, a thousand things in my head. "Did the police say anything?"

"Not really."

"Did they confirm she's dead?"

"No," Alex said. "What did Manning ask you?"

"About the group mostly. Who's in it, who has left, etc."

Alex seemed to think about that for a minute. "Have a lot of people left?"

"You do realize the actual cosplay Facebook group has a couple hundred thousand people in it, right?"

"Not that," he said. "I mean your inner circle. Freya, Byrony, Chad, Bobbsey twins, pretty black boy, sorry, I've forgotten their names."

"Nicole and Julie and Jonah. You think Jonah is pretty?"

"Never met a prettier boy than that who still wanted to be a boy," Alex said. He glanced at me. "Oops. Was I supposed to say you're prettier? Does it help that I like your pretty better than his?"

"Why am I dating you again?"

"My witty sense of humor and my hot bod," Alex teased doing a little shake of his hips.

"You do have a fine ass," I admitted.

"Still not answering my question. Who has left your group?"

"A handful of people. I'd have to look up some old chats and make notes."

"Can you do that?" Alex wanted to know.

"You think this is happening because of the group?"

"Not a big believer in coincidence."

"Wouldn't that mean that I've attracted something to them? Since the weird and paranormal seems to follow me?" Wasn't that an awful thought. Would I have to distance myself from everyone just to keep them safe now?

"What did we say about centers of the universe?"

"It's a valid question," I said. "Weird follows us."

"Yes, but we don't know this is actual paranormal weird and not people weird."

"There's a difference?"

"Sure. People don't need help doing fucked up things all the time. Don't even need to be overseas to know that. Watch the news. Stupid is fatal and highly contagious."

"But we saw Death, or whatever, and that would mean paranormal weird," I pointed out.

"Except that paranormal weird can show up whenever it wants. Maybe it's drawn to people weird."

"This is a very dizzying conversation. I think I need more coffee. Fuck. And all I wanted was a little holiday from weird random ghost shit," I grumbled into my coffee cup, which was sadly empty again. Alex got up and refilled it from the last in the pot, not even bothering with creamer and sweetener. I didn't really need them anyway.

"Distraction will be good. Fabric is fun," Alex said.

"It can be."

"Do you want to discuss what made you mad last night? Something that I told the police?" Alex prodded.

"It's stupid."

"Not if your instincts made you mad about it. Obviously, it bothered you."

"It is stupid. I know I compartmentalize. I didn't think of it in such simple terms until last night, but it's not a surprise that you would see it. You see everything about me. That's unnerving. Makes me wonder when the other shoe will drop."

Alex blinked at me, processing my words. "Okay. I don't think I see everything about you, but I'm not going anywhere."

"Mhmm," I said, uncomfortable with the direction of the conversation. I'd have rather talked about death in that moment, than my own past and shortcomings.

"I'm not."

"You don't know everything about me," I said.

"No," he agreed. "But that's why we are still in the teaching phase, right? Learning about each other, seeing where we fit? Because we're more than just a spark." Our eyes met and held for a minute, and I could almost feel the way he saw me. It wasn't a look of adoration and sublime devotion, but it was filled with kindness and hope. He wasn't throwing me on some pedestal for worship, or even down on a bed to ravish. Alex was looking for a partner, good or bad. I knew that before we'd ever gotten involved. He needed someone to focus on. I thought I'd be okay with me being that focus, except he saw so much. Would he hate what he learned? Would I annoy him with my overthinking like I did everyone else?

I sighed. "You should know some stuff about me."

"Like?" Alex asked.

"I have a lot of self-esteem issues."

"Funny, for a guy who used to have sex on camera, but okay, and that's not really news."

I threw him a glare. He just smiled back that silly boyish upturn of his lips that made me want to kiss him. "Stop being so cute."

"Can't help it, I am what I am!"

"Jerk."

"A cute jerk and your jerk."

"Asshole," I added, without any heat.

Alex nodded. "Okay. I can be. My brother calls me an asshole often. And since we're twins, I think that means he's one too. What else?"

"I don't do relationships well."

"I think we're doing okay."

"We haven't been together that long."

"No, but that's okay too. Again, not going anywhere. I'm into you. Do I need to spell that out in a different way?" Alex stared at me. What did he know that he was trying to make me say? I had been at the hospital. They'd had access to some of my records, that was obvious since they'd looked for a tetanus shot, though my last one had been overseas. Maybe it hadn't been my medical records at all, since Freya knew my dirty little secret. I didn't think anyone else in the group did.

"I've struggled with an eating disorder in the past," I said, coming out with the one thing I really never talked about. Tim hadn't known. I'd lived with him during the worst of it and he hadn't had a clue.

Alex did not seem surprised. "In the past?"

I sighed. "I have not relapsed." I was not purposefully throwing up or avoiding meals. It wasn't as much of a struggle to actually sit down and eat as it once was. I didn't calculate calories in my head as I used to. "I've just been distracted."

"You get distracted at home a lot," Alex pointed out. I did have the bad habit of forgetting to eat while I worked on projects. Having him around made me more aware of time and when I needed to feed him, which meant I was eating more regularly.

"I'm okay," I promise. "I'll even bring it up with my therapist again. It's part of our routine anyway."

Alex sighed and leaned forward to kiss me on the lips. He took the coffee cup out of my hands, setting it aside and carefully climbing onto my lap. The small seat didn't make it all that comfortable for either of us, but I liked having him in my space. The intensity of his focus was the hard part.

"I like you the way you are. Don't change anything about yourself just because you think it will make me like you more. Okay? Losing weight, cutting your hair, wearing a certain style of clothes, I don't *need* any of that. You, as you, turn me on. You know that." He held my face in his hands. "And I'm crazy about your brain. The insane mess of thoughts racing around your head, and the deep focus in your eyes. So if you're going to change anything, do it for you, okay? Because it's something you want, not because you think it will make me stay."

"Okay," I agreed. "I can promise to try. Can't promise I won't think about stuff. My brain wanders a lot." Negative thinking, my therapist pointed out, was all pathways we created for ourselves. Recreating more positive routes was work most people weren't willing to do, but I'd been trying. "This seeing things mess has got me in a spin," I admitted. Thinking scary things that Alex had probably experienced himself over the years.

"We aren't crazy," Alex said. "Isn't that what you tell me?"

Did I still believe that? We'd seen Death. How many people would it take to lock us up if we spoke those words to anyone other than one another? I had a lot of unvoiced thoughts about this whole thing.

Would saying them ease the burden or make me feel crazier? "Do you think there are more bodies out there? By the car I mean."

Alex pressed his forehead to mine and closed his eyes, breathing in deeply. "Yeah."

"We stumbled on something."

"We did," he agreed.

"What do we do about it?" What could we do? Would the police find anything? If we pointed them in that direction wouldn't they just suspect us?

"Trust the police for now." He laughed, but it wasn't a funny laugh, it was a pained one. "Never been a fan of the police, you know."

"Your brother is one."

"Right? That's been a mess. I see him. Know how he thinks. Know he's not a bad guy. He takes care of people, but he sees a lot of the world as bad. Assumes guilty first. They have to sometimes to stay safe." He let out a long breath and sat back, perching in my lap, still half on his knees to remain balanced. "First year out of the academy he got shot by a ten-year-old boy. Was a gut shot. Should have killed him. I was overseas so didn't hear until like a month later. Was so mad. Told him he needed to find a new job. He said he would if I would."

"But neither of you did. It's not your fault he's in a dangerous job any more than it's his fault you were."

"Yeah," he said, but didn't sound convinced. "I'm home now. Was thinking maybe he could work the shop instead."

"And drive us both nuts by being there all the time? He *loves* solving stuff. Have you seen him during some of his cases? Yes, he's stressed, but man, when Lukas is on the hunt, he's like a fucking bloodhound. Don't ever sit down and watch True Crime with him. He'll bitch the whole time about the incompetence of the people involved in the case and how obvious the killer was. It's how his mind works." Having known Lukas for a while, there were a few similarities I could see between the brothers. Lukas's tenacity wasn't all that unlike Alex's focus. They simply had different directions that drew them.

"I want him to be safe," Alex said.

"He wants the same for you. Even when he's an asshole. And honestly, he hasn't been injured on the job in like a year or so."

Alex frowned at me. "A year? What happened a year ago? I never heard about any injury."

Uh oh. That was right, we hadn't talked about the Sky thing yet. It was probably better to hear it from his brother than from me. "Maybe ask Lukas when we get home? But he's fine."

Alex narrowed his eyes at me. "Not fair."

"Not true," I told him. "You weren't here when it happened. No reason you should be stressed about it now. Everyone is fine."

"Is this the Sky thing you guys won't tell me?"

"Eventually you'll have the details. I think Lukas and Sky should fill you in. I was only a concerned third party at that time."

Alex growled and got off my lap.

"Don't be mad at me," I said, not wanting a rift between us in all this mess.

"I'm not. Or at least trying not to be. It's really not your place to tell me what happened to my brother and his girlfriend. Fuck. Siblings suck."

"I wouldn't know."

"Why didn't your parents have more kids?"

"They wanted to travel the world." At least that was what they told me.

"You're lucky."

"Sometimes. Mostly it was just lonely."

He frowned and paced for a minute. "Let's get food. I could use a heap of eggs and bacon right now." He glanced at the coffee cup in my hand. "And you need more coffee." Since I agreed, I followed him out to the lot where we waited for our Uber.

CHAPTER 19

We got to the convention shortly after ten, which wasn't bad. I texted Freya while we were waiting in line to get inside. She did not like the idea of me leaving after today. Even when I promised not to ask for a refund on the hotel costs. I didn't want to short change her when I was the one itching to get home to the safety of my little house and the elaborate garden wards. That did not seem to be the concern on her mind.

Freya: *We came to hang out as a group.*

I came for the convention and to work on some stuff with you.

Freya: *We haven't really taken the time for that. Let's get together this afternoon.*

I wasn't sure I would have the energy this afternoon. Not after the convention and whatever drugs keeping me moving right now had worn off.

Freya: *We have a bunch of group activities planned for the week.*

I knew that, though I wasn't really looking forward to it. Spending hours brainstorming over costumes used to be fun. Now I wondered if I'd be looking at everyone as suspects. Which of them were dangerous? Was it all in my head? We really hadn't had confirmation that they had done anything yet. Seeing ghosts wasn't an exact science, so how could we be sure we weren't misled.

Alex gripped my hand; his brow rose in question. Obviously my mood was on my face.

"Just arguing with Freya about group time," I told him.

"Tell her you'll get back to her after we are done wandering the convention today. You need to focus on your plans for the store. That's why you paid extra, right?"

And leave it to Alex to be very clear. I nodded, and told Freya exactly that. She shot back something about me returning to design and modeling, but I shoved my phone in my pocket to ignore her. One problem at a time. Apparently, I would have to sit down with the group and explain that while I may do some costumes and even an occasional photoshoot, I would not be returning as an influencer of any kind.

Surprisingly, just before we got inside, we ran into MaryAnn. She waved a hello. It was odd to see her alone, though I didn't think she and Chad were a thing, only good friends who happened to live close to each other. They were together a lot of the time.

"Hey," I greeted her.

"Morning, wow your face looks bad. Are you okay?"

I flinched. Alex squeezed my hand. "He's a little bruised but fine. I didn't know any of you guys were coming to this early open thing."

"Oh, yeah. I've been working with a company on some fabric design. Apparel really. Been doing testing for them." MaryAnn held up a garment bag. "Have a few finished pieces with their new line to display. Plan to talk to a few of the techs and designers to give feedback. I'll be spending a lot of time in their booth over the week talking about the designs I did. Even have a couple patterns up for sale."

"Wow, I didn't know you had branched out," I told her.

"I think I'm getting tired of the scene," MaryAnn admitted. "Still get a lot of likes and follows when I do one of my morphing videos and go through a half dozen costumes. But it's a lot of work for little payoff. I've had a few designers over the years approach me with ideas. This was the first fabric one that I really liked."

"Sponsorship is good," I said, remembering my influencer days. Ad clicks and sponsors were how we made money and expanded our user groups.

"I've been a purist too long. Since I have a regular job, it was fine. But I really love the transition of characters. Been teaching classes back home to kids just learning how to cosplay. And doing one of those work design programs that help low income people get jobs."

"Sounds more satisfying than being some online caricature," Alex said.

We got to the door and showed our IDs, getting our specialty lanyards, indicating we were industry rather than public. MaryAnn's was the same. Hers sponsored by a company I'd been seeing pop-up more and more lately in apparel fabric.

"I hope so," MaryAnn said. She turned toward us and gave a little wave. "I've got to head to the booth and get set up. See you guys later, okay?"

"Sure," I agreed.

"Definitely," Alex said. We watched her walk away. Alex looked around the giant convention center, his eyes wide. "Holy fuck this is huge."

"A lot of ground to cover," I said.

"Okay, do we start walking or do you have a plan?"

"Start walking *is* my plan," I told him.

His gaze was locked on a center area which arched the length of the convention center with an open space of machines. Hundreds of them. "I didn't know there was even that many sewing machines in the world."

"Do you want to hang out with the machines while I search fabric?"

"No. I want to look at fabric with you."

His answer made me do an internal sigh of relief since I hadn't really wanted to wander alone. There was something about exploring a convention with someone who mattered to you. An edge of joy experiencing something with someone else. I reached for his hand and he took mine, and we picked a direction. "But we can look at the machines before we leave, right?" Alex asked.

"Of course." I had thought of trying to find a quality mid-arm for sewing, especially since Alex seemed to be really good at it. We went right first, heading down the first row in a slow stroll of appraisal, happy to be together, and a keen eye for anything good.

B y lunchtime I was starving, which was odd for me, and Alex was playing on a mid-arm machine that I'd already indicated we would be buying. It was a non-digital machine, without one of those touchscreens and all the bells and whistles of most of the mid-arm machines that did embroidery as well. He sat down with the sample and began to flow through a dozen stitches, some of them from the books I'd found him at Mae's. The sales people had tried to get him into one of the machines with lots of extras, but he waved them off.

The one he'd chosen was more of an industrial type, high speed, a lot of programmable stitches, and a metal frame. It would need a special table, something to inset the machine and give Alex more space, but that was something we could solve when we got home.

Home. I couldn't wait to get home with Alex. Why had I come again? Oh yeah, fabric. In my pocket I had a handful of cards, contact information, and sample swatches. We'd bought our fair share. Even finding a treasure trove of gnome fabrics that Alex pulled out his credit card for. He'd purchased a kit for a large quilt, which was part paper pieced.

"I have no idea what that means," Alex admitted as he handed over his card. "But we need to make this for Lukas."

"I'll make you do the cutting and the quilting," I agreed.

He'd also fallen in love with a handful of small designer pieces that he thought would make good gifts for his parents. And one giant unicorn set for Sky.

"Not sure Sky is into unicorns," I told him.

"Everyone is into unicorns," Alex said, buying the piece while I wondered if there was a way I could tone down the glitter vibe a bit.

"Okay," I agreed. Finally he'd caved to the need to play with the machines. And that had been fine because I needed a break from all the color and bluster of the overstuffed fabric booths and chatty merchants.

Alex looked at me wide-eyed when he heard the price. He stopped the machine and got up, as though he was afraid he'd break something so expensive when he'd just been using it like a master. In fact, his skill had a group of folks gathered around, watching as though he had put on a show instead of simply been playing with the machine.

He'd sat at almost two dozen machines, even playing with a few long arms before settling on this one. The nearly 3k sticker price didn't surprise me at all. It was a quality machine. Simpler than I would have chosen, but I could see why he liked it. And since it was a brand I trusted and had used before, the price tag didn't really bother me.

"I didn't realize it was so expensive. It looks so basic," Alex whispered to me as I waved one of the sales people over. "What are you doing?" He asked in alarm.

"Do you have that machine here? Can we get one?" I asked the woman who responded to my call.

"We do. We also have a twenty percent industry discount," she said pointing to our badges. "Let me have one grabbed off the truck for you."

Alex gaped at me. "Micah…"

"What?" I asked.

"It's three grand. For a sewing machine."

"Closer to twenty-four hundred before tax."

"Don't just buy that for me," he protested and dug in his pocket for the card Lukas had given him. "Is there enough on my card for it?" And that was how bad he wanted it. I would have bought it for him, but was pretty sure he needed to know it was his too.

"How about we split it?" I said. "You'll obviously use it, and I will too since it's industrial enough to work for costumes as well as quilting. We'll need to find a good place for it in the flat. And an expandable desk with an inset."

"Split it?" Alex asked like that was a foreign concept. We had been splitting the cost of food all week at his instance to pay for stuff.

"Would you rather buy it yourself and stick it at your brother's place?"

"I'm not likely to use it unless you're around."

"Okay then," I said. We headed over to a desk area to fill out the paperwork and pay. "We'll have to take it back to the hotel. Can't exactly tote it around with us all day."

"Do you want to leave already? Or see if they can hold it so we can pick it up later?"

"I'm starving," I admitted. "Would like to get real food instead of the greasy stuff outside. And my head hurts." It was a mild headache, more from noise and too many people than from the concussion. "So a nap would be nice."

"We only got halfway around," Alex said. We had found Mary-Ann's booth and spent a while talking to her about the designs she'd done and the fabrics in the new line she had used. "You haven't gotten to see everything yet." He frowned at the giant section of machines. "I got distracted."

"We have the rest of the week," I reminded him. Having already found a few fabric lines I liked, and talked to people to get their contact info, I had made a good dent in my plan for the week. I might want to go home and hide in the sanctuary of my place with Alex, but I couldn't justify the expense of the trip at all if I did that now.

MaryAnn crossed the field of machines just as they were delivering our machine to us. "Wow! Look at you guys!"

"We didn't exactly think this through," Alex said, bags heaped at his feet of fabric, patterns, rulers, and samples. I had two entire bags of samples. Perks of being part of the industry crowd. The sewing machine… we'd need a large Uber to get that back to the hotel. I was pretty sure it would fit in the SUV I'd rented, but we'd have to wiggle stuff around when we were on our way home.

"I wanted to find you guys and see if you want to have lunch with me and Chad. He's picking me up, will drop me back off. Can probably take you guys back to the B&B as well," MaryAnn said.

"Wow, that'd be great, but I'm not sure all this will fit."

"He's got a Highlander. Plenty of room. We were thinking some place quiet, maybe that Asian place you showed us the last time, Micah."

"Hmm, Takamatsu. Japanese, Chinese, and Korean, with a sushi bar for those who like it. Good variety." My stomach grumbled at the thought of katsu don and miso soup.

"I guess that's a yes?" Alex said. "If it's okay with Chad. We don't want to interrupt you. Not sure if it's a date or something."

"Oh no. I mean no, not really. Chad and I are..." She paused long enough for me to wonder if I'd read their relationship wrong. "Something. Though not the typical couple. But more than friends."

"I had no idea," I said. I mean I guess might have, but since I'd known Chad was asexual, I hadn't thought he'd find himself in a relationship. Though I could see how that was flawed thinking. Something else I'd have to work through with my therapist, since that wasn't a judgment my mind should have leapt to.

"We've kept it pretty quiet, so no big deal. I don't want you guys to feel weird about hanging with us. The group has been off enough about this Byrony thing," MaryAnn said.

"Yeah, her disappearance has certainly caused a bit of stress," Alex said.

"Oh, I don't mean that. Byrony does this sort of thing all the time, to cause a stir or get attention. I mean her attempt to take over the group and force Freya into retirement." MaryAnn waved her hand. "But that started before you guys got here, so maybe Freya didn't tell you?"

I had no idea. "Was Freya thinking about leaving the market?" I couldn't imagine her doing anything else. She'd been an influencer before there had been enough of an online presence to influence, beginning with traveling to conventions and posing for thousands of pictures. "I never thought she'd leave the business. She loves designing and photography so much."

"She does. But she's been doing it so long and she misses traveling more. I know Grace was talking about taking over the hotel for her, and Nicole and Julie have been working on plans to help manage her vlog as she travels. She was going to do a study in costuming in different cultures. I think she was even working on a book," MaryAnn said. "Freya would need a really good reason to stay."

Wow, was I out of the loop, or what? "I feel bad. I had no idea."

MaryAnn shrugged. "You've been doing your own thing. You love the shop and it shows. We were actually all a little surprised when you came this time. I think it's the reason Byrony came at all, she didn't think you'd show."

"I don't understand that, she and I were nothing to each other. We didn't talk. We weren't friends. I barely knew her," I said, feeling like the blame for her disappearance would fall back on me again. Originally, I'd really debated on coming at all. Had purchased the ticket and reserved my space, but thought I might cancel. Then Alex had dropped into my life full of inspiration and entertainment, quashing my loneliness. My desire to brainstorm with the group had shifted to focus on him, rather than rebuilding anything I might have had previously.

"She didn't feel that way. Always saw you as a rival. And when Freya mentioned you'd asked for her help with some designs, she flipped out. Like you returning to the group would keep Freya here, and oust her from taking over the vacuum Freya's departure would create in the cosplay influence world." MaryAnn's phone beeped.

Only I had no plans to ever return to cosplay influencing. "I don't think I have that kind of power over Freya," I said.

"She adores you," MaryAnn said. "Would do anything for you. I think that bothered Byrony so much too."

"Yeah, Melissa made that clear," Alex said, not looking happy. "We can't control how other people feel."

"Of course not. But everyone is excited to have you back. New, old blood in the group. New inspiration," MaryAnn said. "Especially with Alex's influence. We all think you'll bring great things to the group."

"Everyone except Byrony," Alex said. I felt a little sick. I needed to get the group together and explain I would *not* be returning the way they thought I was. And I really was beginning to think coming at all had been a mistake.

"Right," MaryAnn agreed. "Anyway, Chad's outside. Let me help you guys get stuff loaded." She grabbed a few bags. Alex had the rep from the booth wheel the machine on a dolly to the door where we found the SUV idling. Thankfully everything fit with very little jostling.

"Thanks for the ride," Alex told Chad as he took his place behind the driver's side, and I sat beside him. MaryAnn took the passenger seat.

"Apparently you guys planned to do some shopping while you're here." Chad said.

"I don't think most of this was planned," Alex remarked, glancing back at the heap of bags.

"A lot of it is samples for my shop," I said. Some of the apparel fabrics wouldn't really fit into the mix of craft supplies I had in my shop, but I'd play with the samples anyway. Perhaps create a new line of easy to wear cosplay items to sell. "The machine is Alex's new baby."

Alex flushed. "Micah will use it too, but well, I mean…"

"Watched you quilt yesterday and was shocked. Where did you learn that?" Chad asked. "My grandma used to hand quilt stuff. I remember watching her as a kid. Never got into it myself, but still have a half dozen of those quilts she made for me. Takes skill to do it by hand and to move the machine like you did? That was amazing."

"It's more like moving the paper around the pencil," Alex said absently.

"Right, which is a different skill set," MaryAnn said. "I've done some decorative stitches on fabric. Takes a lot of focus and time. You did it like you'd been doing it forever."

"It's just sort of natural for me," Alex said without elaborating.

We parked at the restaurant, which didn't look like much from the outside, but had a nicely spread out layout inside. There was a sushi bar, and actual bar section and then a large dining area. We got a table in the middle of the dining area. I didn't even need to look at the menu as my heart was already set on the chicken and rice bowl with egg sauce. Alex browsed the menu, while MaryAnn marked the sushi request card.

"This will probably be the group's last big get together anyway," Chad remarked folding up his menu.

"Why's that?" Alex asked. "I thought you guys did this a couple times a year at different events?"

"We did. But we've reached the end of an era, really," Chad said.

"It's really sad, but everyone is older now," MaryAnn added. "Moving on to other careers and interests. Me to professional costume design, Jonah to modeling and TV, the girls are opening up a shop, and even Chad is starting a non-profit. You were sort of the pioneer in that, Micah," she said. "Not the videos as much as the shop. Chad and I watch snippets of your tours all the time."

I looked at Chad. "You're starting a non-profit?"

"Teaching sewing to kids," he nodded. "I follow the Instagram pictures of costume stuff you do," Chad said. "I love those gloves you do for the kids. Can you show me how to make them before you leave? We've been doing some classes in low income areas teaching some basics. That would be a fun project for them."

"Wow, sure. I can donate some supplies too," I said, more than a little shocked that they seemed to follow my career. "I don't do a lot of big costumes anymore. More everyday small things, capes, gloves, hats, headbands with ears, or clip-on tails. Never thought of offering classes."

"Not sure we have the space or the time between the shop and the tours," Alex pointed out. "Maybe a once a month thing if we can find a place to rent space? Something people could schedule ahead like the children's tours."

"Teaching kids is amazing," Chad said. "I love the time cosplaying when everyone wants a picture with me and I get a couple thousand likes, but nothing compares to when you show a kid something new. Their eyes light up and the world opens for them. I mean, I'm from Michigan. We've had some ultimate crap dumped on us, communities abandoned. A lot of people left or gave up hope. But kids are still growing up there. If I can inspire one or five or fifty kids that they can be more? Then I've done my part."

"Wow," I said, stunned. Chad, the burly ex-football player, who had always taken on the role of dumb-jock, seemed to really have it together. "That sounds amazing."

"It's not full-time yet," Chad added. "But we have the non-profit registered, all the paperwork filed. We've got a few partners in the community. Freya's donating a few machines. MaryAnn's new vendor is sending some fabric. Lots of small area donors of supplies and talent. We've had basic mending classes, how to read patterns classes, crochet and knit classes, and even upcycling classes."

"There will be a lot of expansion to the non-profit in the new year," MaryAnn said. "Part of why we are here, to make connections at the convention with suppliers."

"If there is anything we can do, please ask," Alex said.

"Agreed," I said. "And I can teach you a couple basics while we're here. The gloves are easy, so are the capes. The ear headbands don't even take any sewing."

"We'll probably take you up on that," Chad said as the waiter appeared to take our orders. "Most of the group is contributing something, whether it's skill, or even a promise to visit and host a class. Every little bit helps."

"We hope the group continues," MaryAnn said. "Maybe expands in a different way. Like meetups to teach classes or at major shows. I don't think anyone is giving up cosplay, just changing our focuses a little."

We ordered, and I couldn't help but be dropped into a food for thought mode. How out of touch had I been? And hadn't I blamed them for not reaching out? Only they were all busy creating amazing things too. Yes, I'd been floundering for a while, but I'd found a paddle and was working my way through the edge of troubled waters into a new career. Had the others been doing the same?

Alex squeezed my hand under the table and I turned to look at him. He made a silly face, tongue sticking out, eyes crossed. "You're so weird," I told him.

"You love my weird," he said, tapping the chopsticks like they were drumsticks instead.

"I do," I admitted.

His cheeks turned pink.

MaryAnn cooed at us. "You're adorable."

"You love my weird?" Alex asked again, looking me straight in the eye.

"Yes." Then I realized what he was really asking. We hadn't said it, had we? It was always something I hesitated with, again compartmentalizing. Yes, it was soon, but the time he'd been gone was brutal, lonely, and uninspiring. If he were ripped out of my life again, I wasn't sure I'd hold it together. "Yes, I love you, and your weird."

His face turned pinker. "Really?"

"Do I need to have it skywritten? Translated into Farsi? Paper piece it into a quilt?"

"No," he said and leaned over to kiss me lightly on the lips. "I thought maybe because we were still learning...teaching...whatever, that it was too soon."

"It's okay if you don't feel the same yet," I told him. "Emotions are complicated things. And we have plenty of time to learn about each other."

"I do though," Alex said, almost stumbling over his thoughts as much as his words. "Love you, I mean. Am crazy about you. Your brain, the endless swirls of how your mind works, always creating, the well of knowledge, and well... I'm pretty fond of your face too. But I love you for being you."

I smiled at him and accepted another light kiss. "Then I think we're on the right path, yeah?"

"Yes," he breathed.

"I'd do anything for you," I admitted. "So don't be stupid. Stay close to me."

"Plan on it," Alex said. And since the food arrived, it saved us from having to hear too much of MaryAnn and Chad gushing over how adorable we were.

CHAPTER 20

There was something different about having uttered the words. Not a bad something. More a solidifying of the bond between us. An agreement that we were on the same page. I worried that I'd become comfortable with Alex too fast, needing his calm assurance in my space to function, but he seemed as focused on me as I was on him. We still had a lot to learn about each other, but we had time for that. So long as the paranormal kept out of our business.

After our meal and returning MaryAnn to the convention, Chad took us back to the B&B and even helped us load everything into our cabin, though the new machine had to go in the SUV. Alex insisted on covering it with fabric so no one would try to steal it. I didn't point out that if someone wanted something to steal, a giant box covered in fabric wasn't going to deter them.

But getting to curl up with him for an afternoon nap? That was priceless. I slept hard wrapped in Alex's arm and one of our quilts from home. He roused me slowly with kisses, though mostly to my face.

"Lower," I grumbled. "Don't you owe me an ass kissing? Or licking?"

"Yes, but we've been invited to a special event and there's not enough time. So maybe later?" Alex sounded hopeful. "I was trying to let you sleep but it's almost five thirty. We'll have dinner soon."

"I'm not hungry and dinner isn't until seven."

"Dinner is early tonight. And we both need to eat. I need more protein and some bananas. Man, I've never wanted bananas so much in my life as I have in the past two weeks."

I opened an eye to stare up at him. "Do we have any left in the kitchen?" I'd gotten him a sizable supply from the grocery store we'd stopped at before arriving.

He flushed. "I ate them all. Dunno why I'm still craving them so bad."

"Potassium," I said absently. "I think I packed some electrolyte water packets somewhere. Your brother gave them to me before we left." My brain rolled slowly through all the events of the last few days and the morning. I sat up and stared at him, able to see most of the tiny house space from my position in the loft. The industrial machine I'd brought sat on the small table, a scrap of quilt sandwich in it, filled with designs. "Did you nap?"

"A little," Alex said. "About forty minutes or so. I didn't want to wake you. Was hoping you'd wake up on your own since you didn't sleep well last night."

"I've heard a concussion will do that to you," I remarked without feeling. In reality, Alex had to wake me every two hours last night to check on my head. Each time I'd fallen back to sleep quickly, but it still made for a rough night. My sleep schedule was going to be really off by the time we got home. "Wait, invited to what?"

He held up an envelope, scrawled with our names in fancy text. "Iron Cosplay?" He asked, like saying the words would bring clarity. It did for me.

"Wow. It's been years. Three maybe four since we did one as a group?" I took the envelope from him and opened it to read Freya's delicate writing scrawled as a fierce challenge. "I wonder if everyone is going?"

"Is it anything like the Iron Chef?" Alex wanted to know. He was practically thrumming with excitement.

"You're a super nerd, you know that, right?" I asked him. "Yes, it's a race to create a costume with limited and shared supplies in a certain time frame. The invite says there will be prizes awarded."

"You love me anyway, you already said, nerd or otherwise," Alex said.

"I do." I stared at him. "Odd, right?"

"'Cause you're not a big old nerd in disguise yourself?" He flopped over on the mattress next to me. "Are we going? Please? Can we be super nerdy and Iron Cosplay or whatever it is?"

"Yes, we can go. There will be a handful of these type of events at the convention too," I pointed out. We'd already browsed the brochure of event scheduling and Alex had highlighted things he thought sounded cool. I was less interested in the process of craft and more attuned to the supply. Alex, new to the entire thing, wanted it all. So we planned to make as much time for what we could.

"But those are all with strangers. At least we sort of know these people."

"Small groups are less intimidating. It's how I got my start in the group at all. Was part of the online group, networking with people while doing the photography. Before I met Tim. Went to a cosplay convention in L.A. The group invited a handful of us to meet up. We ate dinner, hung out, and did an Iron Cosplay the night before the con started so we all had something new for each day. It was a mess, and everything fell apart as we wore it, but it was a thing. It's how I met Freya, and Chad and MaryAnn. I think the girls and Jonah showed up at the next event a few months later. We did the Iron Cosplay thing each time."

"Didn't sound like it was on the agenda here. Did they stop doing it?" Alex asked.

"Yes. I'm not sure why. I wasn't able to make it to every event. At that point I was traveling across the world. So sometimes it didn't happen. When I moved to the States and in with Tim, I had less time and money to do the conventions, though would go to one or two a year. I think the last one I remember having an Iron Cosplay at was right before I went missing."

Alex ran his fingers along my bare arm, which I hadn't thought was soothing until that moment when the hard truth about the past crashed down on me. "Do you think they stopped because of me?"

"No," Alex said instantly. "You said you already hadn't been going as much. So maybe enough of you being in one place to actually do it became an issue? Then there was that mess with Byrony. Sounds like she was never well liked in the group but often a part of it? When did she join up?"

I shrugged, trying to think back to all the events. "Not long before I vanished, we all did a New York thing. She was there. We did an Iron Cosplay at that one, but she didn't participate. Melissa did. I don't think Jonah was there either though." I frowned trying to sort through memories. "It's hard to pull out pieces when so many events are similar and held in the same place year after year."

"I hear you there. Lots of military memories that all jam together. So how does this Iron Cosplay thing work?"

"Usually we are in groups and have a set goal for a costume. There's a pile of fabric and other craft supplies and then the sewing machines. It's limiting because you can only use what's in the pile. Other than thread that is. And you have to share the machines. I did a lot of hand sewing because too many of us needed machines," I explained.

"Well at least we're in groups. I'd be completely useless on my own," Alex said. "Dinner is a little early tonight, at six and the cosplay thing starts at seven. It does have a little notation at the bottom that asks no one be consuming alcohol before attending the event."

"Oh yeah, that happened once." It had been the one time I'd had Tim with and sort of my fault. Tim had gotten quite drunk because he was bored by the whole cosplay thing. I'd tried to leave him in the hotel room, but he'd insisted on coming along. He'd sat in the corner muttering comments to everyone as they worked. "Yeah…"

"Do I want to know?" Alex asked. "Drinking, much like medication, and me don't mix. So I don't do it."

"Lukas doesn't either," I said absently. "Maybe something in your genes?"

Alex reached up and pulled me into his arms, rolling me over on the mattress. "Serious face," he grumbled at me.

"Sorry. Lots in my head, memories and stuff. Not all good." In fact, few of the memories I had, ever popped up as positive at first. It took effort to remember the good stuff over the bad.

"How's your face feel? Your head? Tummy okay?"

"Mostly fine. The nap really helped." I analyzed how I felt. My face ached with the dull echo of the bruise, but it was bearable. My head didn't hurt at all, and my stomach was… empty. "Hmm, maybe I am hungry."

"Good. Sounds like it's a make your own pizza night, but we can do pizza without cheese," Alex didn't sound bothered by it, as it was something we did a couple times back home, even ordering from big chains a handful of times. "Would bananas be weird on a pizza?"

I laughed and tugged out of his embrace. "Let me find those water things. It's supposed to restore electrolytes."

"I hope they taste better than Gatorade. I hate that stuff." Alex followed me downstairs and to the kitchen area in which I'd tried to organize stuff. The packets were in the small cupboard beside the stairs in which I'd stored the coffee supplies. He took one of the packets and turned it over to read the label. "Doesn't look scary."

"Not sure your brother would give us anything that looked scary. He's more obsessed with your health than you are," I pointed out and dug through the fridge for a fresh bottle of water.

"He's always been that way. But he does it to Sky too. Saw him do it." Alex opened the packet and added it to the water, then recapped the bottle and shook it.

"Does it to me too," I admitted.

"Does Lukas know about your eating thing?"

"Yes. So does Sky. I was in rehab after I left Tim. Lukas did a lot of driving me back and forth."

Alex tried the water, taking a sip and then a long drag of half the bottle at once. "Okay, that's not bad. Lemonade flavor is okay, weird aftertaste, but not bad."

"There are more flavors in the box. Nothing banana flavored, sorry."

Alex set the water down and wrapped me in a hug, breathing deeply.

"You okay?"

He let out sigh. "Yeah. I think. Anxiety up, not sure why. Happy you're here with me though. Excited for Iron Cosplay and more of the convention tomorrow. Can't believe we bought such an expensive machine."

"It's actually a fairly simple one on the low end of the price range for mid-arms. They can run up to twelve grand."

Alex's mouth fell open. "Holy fuck!"

"That's back at the shop," I reminded him.

He laughed.

"Let's go get food," I said and tugged him toward the door.

"And Iron Cosplay. Dun dun da-duhn...."

"I think that noise is more indicative of a crime tv show."

"Okay well I've never actually watched Iron Chef. Is there a secret to winning Iron Cosplay? Wonder what the prizes are."

"Freya usually has good stuff. I won a computer one year. In fact, my MacBook," I pointed to the computer sitting on the table, which I still had and used to this day. "Four years ago or so, I won it in an Iron Cosplay."

"Okay now I'm superhyped. I won't be much of an asset though, since I don't know a lot about sewing costumes. Maybe I'll just watch," Alex said suddenly looking very worried.

"We are usually in teams. However, it's often not teams of our choice."

He stared at me. "Fuck. Means I probably won't get to team with you."

"Probably not. But you can sew straight lines just fine. And you have ideas. That helps. The key is to think simple. Don't pick some crazy hard costume idea like Cloud from Final Fantasy. The simpler the outfit, the more time you can spend getting it to look legit." I lead him out of the house and across the path to the back of the main house. Everyone was already gathering.

"Legit. Man, I wish I were more up on what's popular right now in anime."

"Doesn't have to just be anime. Think games, cartoons, even movies. One-year Chad was a Minion. It was a hoot. He looked more like a giant Twinkie, but the effect was there." I stepped into the kitchen where there was a bustle of activity. Grace was handing out trays of dough. A long line of toppings were set out on a table, then each one going into the oven. "Do you know what a Minion is?"

"We watched that in the psych ward," Alex said. "Goofy things with like one eye, working for the weird bald guy who turns out to be a big softy for kids."

"Yep, that's it."

"I could probably be a Twinkie. Saw banana Twinkies at the grocery store recently. Wonder if those are any good."

"I'll buy you a box and more bananas after we leave the convention tomorrow. We'll stop on the way back to restock our kitchen," I promised.

"Hmm, banana," Alex moaned almost sounding sexual.

"What were you up to out there, sleepyheads?" Chad said from his spot in line. "You feel better?" He asked me.

"Yes. Much. Don't mind the weirdness of my boyfriend. He's low on potassium so he dreams of bananas." I accepted a plate of ready to top dough from Grace and found a place in line, Alex following behind me.

"I dream of your banana too," Alex said with a straight face, his gaze focused on the table full of toppings. They had a great variety, tons of meat, a half dozen types of sauce, ones with dairy clearly labeled, and a long row of veggies. No bananas.

"You can have my banana later," I said.

He blinked at me like it took a minute to process, but grinned. "And your donut hole."

"I don't want to know, do I?" Chad said.

"You really don't," I agreed.

"Ever read a gay romance?" Alex asked him. "It's eye opening to say the least. I think I'm supposed to be sexing him up more often, but he hasn't protested yet. Some of the novels I read have sex every twenty pages."

"Sounds exhausting," Chad remarked.

"Right? I'm not as young as I used to be. But even then, not sure I had the energy for that." Alex said as he began to build his pizza. "Craft," he waved at me with a spoon. "Fill your pizza with worldly delights."

"He's funny when he's had sleep," Chad said.

"He's funny all right." I made a face at Alex, not something I normally did, but crossed my eyes and stuck out my tongue. Alex copied me, making an even funnier face with his eyebrows askew. "Stop, you brat," I laughed.

"Yeah, yeah. Food then craziness."

"Oh my God," Chad said. "You're going to be one of those cosplay partners aren't you?"

"One of those?" Alex asked. I didn't think he could put more meat on his pizza and still call it a pizza.

"Big ideas, insane ideas that somehow you make happen against all logic."

"That's him," I agreed, choosing an olive oil and garlic-based sauce. "You can have cheese," I told Alex. "You don't have to skip on the cheese because I do."

"Hmm," he said. "Maybe. Do we get more than one of these?" He held up his eight-inch round plate.

"We can," Chad said. "Just have to ask. I usually eat three." He patted his belly. "The crust is so thin and crunchy, they are divine."

I loaded mine up with chicken, basil, and a half dozen veggies before making my way to pop it in the oven. Freya was on oven duty, adding pies, and taking out completed ones to pass them off.

She patted me on the arm. "You're staying for cosplay?"

"Yep. We're both pretty excited. It's been a long time."

"Years since we had this much of the group together," Freya agreed taking my pie from me to add to the oven.

"And the last one?" I asked. "MaryAnn said you're planning on traveling a bit."

"Expanding the vlog. Starting a cosplay around the world book," she agreed. "Everyone seems to be heading in different directions."

"Girl, you went out of your way in prizes this year!" Jonah said as he entered the kitchen to retrieve his finished pizza. "A Tula Pink machine bundle? That machine is worth eight grand!"

"That was MaryAnn's doing," Freya said.

"The clothing line I'm working with offered it. They are giving away two more at the event, but since we're all for the most part, influencers, they gave one to us. Only caveat is that they ask we use some of their products and display some at their booth," MaryAnn said. She got her pizza and headed to the dining room.

Alex and I grabbed bottles of water and followed them to the table to wait for our food. Along the front wall of the dining room a table had been set up covered with prizes. The Tula Pink sewing machine was there, along with a couple iPads, a MacBook Pro, some cosplay design books bundled with patterns, and a stack of fabric bolts. Freya really had gone out of her way this year.

"Wow!"

"What's a Tula Pink?" Alex whispered to me.

"She's a fabric designer, quilting mostly, but the machine is an embroidery machine." I couldn't recall him playing with one at the convention, but he'd been more focused on the space of the mid-arm, and Tula's machine was nice, but had only a thirteen-inch neck rather than the eighteen-inch neck the machine we'd bought had. "Her machine has some really cute custom stitches, like rabbits and cats and even cat food bowls."

"What? No way," Alex leaned in to look at the side of the box and the example of the stitch. "Oh those are cute. And a year worth of fabric supply. How much is that? Like a year's worth for me is probably less than it would be for you the fabric hoarder," Alex said.

"I think there's a certain amount of yardage, overall it's not a bad machine. And I like a lot of Tula's prints. I'll point out her stuff to you tomorrow when we go back to the convention."

"I think I like the one we got better, but I can fight hard to win if you want. Well, all this stuff is pretty amazing. A MacBook, I could use that. And those design books look interesting." Alex examined everything. "Even a few gift cards for some places that sound like fabric shops?"

"Right?" Jonah said. "I don't need any of that, but that doesn't mean I'm not going to work my ass off to win it." He sat down with his pizza.

"Oh crap," Alex said doing a little hop and racing back to the kitchen where Freya was waiting with our pizza. "Sorry," he said. "Just wowed by everything so far."

She smiled at him and patted his hand, then handed him his pizza. "I think you're going to love Iron Cosplay. It's all about thinking on your feet."

"Well, ma'am," Alex said, his southern drawl sounding really heavy in that moment, "As an ex-military man, one of the things I do best is think fast on my feet."

I got my pizza and headed back to the table, Alex in tow, the group chatter rising up around us. Everyone was starting to sit and eat, and talk about the upcoming cosplay. Everyone except Melissa.

"Anyone seen Melissa?" I asked. "She okay?"

"Haven't seen her all afternoon," Nicole said.

"Police came by earlier," Julie added. "She went with them."

"Did they find Byrony?" Alex asked.

"I've not heard any updates," Freya said.

"The police didn't say anything when they were here," Julie added. "They just took Melissa with them. I wonder if they think she did something."

"Melissa would never hurt Byrony. Didn't they find Joe already?" Nicole asked.

"Let's not dissolve into that mess again," Freya interrupted. "We'll find out more when we find out more. For now, let's focus on food and the evening cosplay."

There was a grumble of agreement.

"Let me run over the rules for all of you while you eat," Freya said taking her place at the head of the table. Alex nudged me and pointed in the direction of the doorway to the craft room, was the cat back? I couldn't see anything out of the ordinary. Maybe last night had been a fluke.

"Is the cat there?" I whispered.

"Yes, but she's a normal looking cat right now."

I sucked in a relieved breath and focused on Freya and the rules for the upcoming event.

CHAPTER 21

"Everyone will be broken up into pairs," Freya began. "To create an even number, I'll be joining in."

"I apologize ahead of time to whomever I'm paired with," Alex said. "My sewing skills are minimal so far."

"But his imagination and enthusiasm is unlimited," I added, patting his hand.

"The objective is to create not one, but two identifiable costumes," Freya continued. "Fully wearable. Judgement will be made on a list of criteria, including workmanship, design, innovation, originality, accuracy, and overall balance." She passed out copies of a piece of paper which had a list and boxes to check with a one through ten option. "We are peer judged as always. Meaning once the time is up, everyone gets a little runway show and gives score. Ten points to the best in each category. Then we'll add everything up to designate prizes."

"Are we winning as a group then?" Jonah wanted to know. "How does that go for prizes?"

"Yes, wins are considered group wins. First place gets first choice from the table, and down the list. Hopefully no one will fight over anything in particular. There are a lot of great items on the table," Freya said.

There was a murmur of agreement.

"What's our timeline?" I asked.

"We begin at seven," Freya glanced up at the clock. It was twenty 'til. "Then we have until ten to complete our projects. I will allow for an extra ten minutes to put them on and ready for the presentation, that includes adding makeup or hairstyling."

"Not much time for hairstyling," Nicole said.

"Or makeup," Julie agreed.

Freya nodded, "All part of the planning. As always, think ahead, plan, converse, and prepare. We all know that final stop in time comes faster than any of us realize."

"No kidding," Chad agreed.

"Costumes should also be solid enough to wear tomorrow," MaryAnn added. "The company offering up the fabric and a lot of the prizes wants us to do a little walk through show tomorrow afternoon. It's nothing but a runway type thing in which they will briefly talk about the fabrics used, but keep in mind they do want to see them."

"So we'll be wearing these in public tomorrow?" Alex asked, his eyes going huge.

"Yes, but only for a few minutes. They have a changing area in the back of their booth so you won't have to spend the whole day in costume," MaryAnn answered.

"This is so cool," Nicole said.

"One of our best contests ever," Julie added.

"I have so many ideas," Jonah said.

Freya got up and went into the kitchen returning with an empty mug and a sheet of paper. "Let's draw our partners then. Alex, since you're the newest to the group, how about you go first?"

"Oh boy, talk about Johnny on the spot." He wiped his hands off on a napkin and waited for her to fill the cup with slips of paper and hold it out. He shuffled around for a bit before choosing, then opened it and read it, "Jonah."

"Damn!" Jonah said. "I get the hot boy. I can work with that."

Alex's cheeks turned pink.

Freya held out the cup for me. "Nicole," I said after pulling my paper.

She smiled at me. Julie got Chad. And MaryAnn got Freya. That pair would be hard to beat.

"Everyone finish eating. The fabric is stacked on the table in the craft room and we'll start exactly at seven, so no talking about costume ideas until then," Freya said returning to her chair with a huge smile on her face.

"Good, I need more pizza," Chad said getting up to rush back to the kitchen.

"Me too," Alex added. His plate and the heaping mess of meat he'd put on it was gone. I was still working on mine. "You need anything?" He asked.

"Another bottle of water please?" I pointed to the dredges left in the one I had.

"Sure thing." He vanished back into the kitchen and I went back to eating and staring at the opposite doorway looking for shadows. If the cat was there, I couldn't see it. Maybe the whole seeing thing had been because I'd been overstressed or special circumstances.

Alex returned a few minutes later with another pizza, this one covered in more plant things than meat, peppers, olives, mushrooms, pineapple, tomato chunks and even large fresh basil leaves. He handed me a bottle of water. "Okay?"

"Yeah," I said, finishing up my pizza.

"So simple is key you say?" Alex said. "I can't imagine winning against a group like you. Everyone has been doing this for years."

"I'm a bit out of practice."

"You still make costumes all the time," Alex said. "Just finished a few for me."

"It's a little different under pressure."

"No kidding!" Alex agreed. "Look at those prizes. I've never seen such great stuff for a small group like this."

"Sounds like a lot of it came from donations from the company MaryAnn is working with now. Maybe I need some sweet deals like that."

"If you can find some quilt companies to do the same. Unless you plan on branching out to apparel fabric in the shop. Not sure where you'd put it." Alex looked thoughtful. "Most of what you carry now are those folded bundles."

"Fat quarter or half-yard bundles," I said.

"Right, more terminology, anyway, can apparel fabric be done that way?"

"In a bundle? Maybe specific to a pattern. Give people the yardage and accessories to make something. I don't know if it's ever been done as most people order the knock-off stuff from China that falls apart after one use." Maybe something basic like the cape. Could that be cost effective if I got a deal on the fabric?

"You're thinking," Alex grinned.

"You inspire me," I admitted.

"Inspired enough to win?"

"Maybe."

"What would you pick if you won?" He asked.

"I'm hoping for the computer software bundle," I told him looking at the table. The design software Freya had showed me was added as a pair to the MacBook. I didn't need the MacBook and that would be one of the first things to be chosen, but I really wanted that software. Glancing at the specs of the software and I knew I'd need the computer to make it work as my machine was too old. Which was likely why it was set as a bundle.

"I thought you'd want the sewing machine," Alex said. "Since it's fancy and super expensive."

"It's great," I agreed. "And I've always wanted an embroidery machine for some of the projects I work on, but we just got the machine I'll probably use the most. The Tula machine is more a dream toy than a useful thing to me. In reality I don't need any of it. I do okay. I could buy any of that."

"But that's not the point of the contest, right? The cool stuff is to motivate us to do our best and win."

Maybe. "What would you pick if you won?"

"The books probably, or the fabric and patterns. Though having my own computer would be nice. I wonder if that machine is too fancy for Chad's non-profit to use? The kids he taught would get a kick out of that right? Even if it stitches cats or bunnies or something."

"Oh," I looked at him with wide eyes. "That would be way cool. Can you imagine those kids he's teaching? Have them make something and finish it off with a cool embroidered dragon or something?"

"Man that would have been sweet when I was a kid." Alex said. "Maybe make some gnomes for Lukas. Weird how he's into gnomes and I like dragons. Gnomes are so... weird."

"There's a story behind the gnomes," I said.

"Yeah?"

I glanced up at the clock. "No time for it right now. Less than two minutes before we start." I got up and cleaned up my plate and cup.

"Crap." Alex shoved the last of his pizza in his mouth and got up too, balling up his napkin. He chewed fast and swallowed as we took our stuff to the kitchen. "I need to wash my hands. Any last words of wisdom to share?"

"Look at the pile of fabric and the first thing that pops into your mind for characters discuss that with your partner. Might be a color or a specific pattern, whatever inspires you and jumps to your attention. The two of you may branch out with ideas but it's a fast place to start, and gut instinct usually helps. And remember: simple. If you pick a simple costume, putting it together goes fast and you can spend more time on embellishments, hair, makeup, and accessories," I offered. "It's the little details that often win this thing."

Alex nodded, his eyes scrunched in thought. We both took turns using the small downstairs half bath to wash our hands and then joined the group waiting outside the closed double doors of the craft room. I couldn't help but feel a bit of anxiety in my gut, so much like excitement that they echoed each other. So close it was almost impossible to tell them apart. I'd have preferred to work with Alex, but maybe it would have hindered me too as my plans for him were never simple.

Nicole would be easy to work with. She was smart and resourceful. The fact that she was a petite blonde helped keep our options open.

Freya stood next to the door. "I'm going to open the door, and everyone pick a corner for their group. You'll have ten minutes to discuss with your partner before the rush for fabric. Then it's off to the tables. Everyone ready?"

There was a murmur of agreement. I caught Nicole's eye and she nodded, moving closer. Jonah pulled Alex away. I had to fight down the urge to grab Alex back, more as my safety blanket than worry Jonah would seduce him. Alex was tuned into me, so he threw me a warm smile and mouthed, "Good luck!"

Then the doors opened.

It was a bit of shock of color and fabric. Instead of it being stacked on the cutting table it was on a cart, bright colors, some incredible designs of varied widths, and what I could tell even from a distance was textures. Knits to cottons to leather-looking polyester. It was the fire red that caught my eye first even as I moved around the room, meeting with Nicole and finding a spot. If Alex and I hadn't spent the trip to the convention the first day discussing anime he'd seen, I might not have been drawn to it. But the fire made me think of Inuyasha. Alex said it had been one of his favorites growing up, especially when Kagomi shouted "Sit, boy!" at him. Which I pointed out wasn't quite the same in the non-dubbed version, but he didn't care.

Nicole turned to me. "Ideas?"

"Inuyasha and Kagomi," I blurted, but tried to keep my voice down.

Nicole glanced back at the fabrics. "All the colors are there, but it's missing a bit of 'Wow' factor."

"I was thinking of the 'Sit, boy!' thing. So like dog ears and rolling circle over the head." A single pose could make an outfit. Have one pose mastered, the outfit detailed to fit that snapshot, and you were golden.

"Oh," Nicole's mouth echoed the big O as the idea came together in her head too. "Okay, so we'll need red, white, and green. I can whip out that school girl outfit in less than an hour. Do you want to be Inuyasha or Kagomi?"

"Inuyasha," I said, still not feeling any desire to do the dress thing. Especially not a school girl one. I really hoped Tim and the videos hadn't ruined that for me forever.

"Let me pull up some pictures," Nicole said.

"Okay, one representative from each group will race to the cart and get what they need in fabric. Thread, beads, buttons, zippers, and other basic supplies are on the box on the table and open to everyone at all times. But get the bolts you need. Once I say ready, set, go," Freya said.

"Can we trade fabrics if we need to?" Chad asked. "Since they are full bolts instead of pieces?"

"Yes. Anything you're done with put back in the cart and it's free game."

"Sweet," Jonah said. He looked at Alex. "You want to go or me?"

"You," Alex said. "You know more about the texture stuff than me."

Jonah nodded and took a stance like he was ready to run a marathon.

"You or me?" I asked Nicole.

"You can go. You know what we need."

And I did. Those of us from the group lined up near the table, ready to move. Focused on what we needed and waiting for that starting mark.

"Everyone on your mark. Get ready," said Freya, apparently MaryAnn was choosing for them. "Go."

Everything else faded in that moment other than the fabric and the plans I had. The red was perfect, a linen which would help with the drape, though a little thin, the white was thinner than I expected. I grabbed the green and some muslin to help with the weight of the white and rushed back to Nicole. I held out my finds. "The white is thin," I remarked.

"We can make it work."

Nicole and I worked side by side. Measuring, cutting, and ironing pieces to ready them for stitching. Thankfully Freya had brought in a few extra sewing machines, so there was one for each group. I had no idea what I would have done if I'd been forced to hand sew everything.

I glanced up once or twice to find Alex and Jonah huddled together in their area. Alex seemed to be working hard to do what Jonah directed him. The two of them had a heap of green, brown, and orange fabric. I wondered what they'd thought of, but had enough to do that I had to focus on.

Nicole wasn't kidding about putting together the school girl outfit. White skirt with green embellishment, white top with green sailor collar, and even the small red accents taken from leftovers of my fabric. Her ease at creating the pleats had me gaping at her for a minute. It was a bit like magic. No pins or struggling to hold the fabric for the skirt in place, she put it under the machine and folded in the pleats as she sewed.

"Wow," I told her as I fished the drawstring through the pants I'd finished.

"What's wow?" She asked.

"No pins," I waved at her.

"I've made thousands of school girl skirts," Nicole said. "I was worried you'd pick something we had to use lycra or spandex for. I hate both of those fabrics with a passion. Those need pins."

I laughed, understanding exactly where she was coming from. "They make great body suits and leggings."

"And wobble all over while you stitch," she grumbled turning out her corners and pressing her seams together. "Don't forget we'll need time for accessories."

"I'm on it." I pointed to a batch of wood beads I'd found. She grinned at me and we continued to work, a rush of mad costume-making science.

Nicole held up her finds from the wig trunk with a long black wig and a snow white one. "I need to do some styling," she said. "Do you have the ears ready for yours?"

I held them up, hoping the white with pink insides stood out enough against the fall of the snowy hair. I also had the headband which would give the little swirly thing often depicted as dizzy in anime.

"Need to finish stringing the necklace," I told her.

She held her hand out for it. "Go change. I'll need to fix your hair. Mine is easier." She glanced at the clock. How had it gotten so close to ten?

"Holy crap! I didn't realize we were that short on time."

"Go change," she waved at me. I grabbed up the heap of fabric that made up my costume and rushed off to the bathroom. Couldn't wear my normal clothes under this, even with the billow of the fabric. Too many lines would interrupt the drape. The red had enough stability to it, but the white underlaying was thin and showed too much.

It took me an extra minute or two to get the ties all in place and adjust it based on the mirror. But it was only one of those waist-high mirrors, so hard to see everything. I raced back to Nicole. She looked me over and nodded. "Shoes off, he's barefoot most of the time."

"Oh," I said. "Right." I kicked off my shoes and added them to the pile while she went to change. Nicole reappeared in the schoolgirl outfit and helped me adjust the wig until it stayed, then she clipped the dog ears on, and took a few minutes fiddling with the headband with the spinning thing. If I were more tech-savvy, I might have been able to make it actually spin, however, the best we could do was make it pop up when I pulled a little string. The entire contraption needed to be strung through my costume.

"Ten minutes until stopping point on the costumes," Freya called out. "We'll have an extra ten for hair and makeup, but sewing will have to stop. If you have anything that needs stitching, finish it now."

I heard a lot of frantic running of sewing machines and was glad we were done. Nicole was fussing with my hair. "Get your wig," I told her.

She scrambled for it, and seemed to find hers easier to handle than mine. But hers was also a lot shorter and finer. I handed her the other necklace I'd been working on; it was made to look like the broken jewel she and Inuyasha had been searching for, pieces chipped off. The jewel itself I'd crafted from melting a bit of soap in the microwave, cooling it in the freezer, and cutting it to form the gem-like edges.

This time she gaped at me. "This is amazing."

"Legit, right?" I asked. "Authentic. And useful when we're done since you can shower with it. I do soap making for the shop when I get tired of working with fabric."

She grinned. "We are going to rock this."

"We are," I agreed.

"Sewing machines off," Freya called. "Ten minutes for last prep." And that was okay, as Nicole and I fiddled to perfect our costumes. Maybe we wouldn't win first, and that was okay. I felt amazing. Creative juices flowing, happy instead of anxious, and excited to see what everyone else had created. It was almost like time had reversed and all the bad had vanished. And for those few hours it was an incredible feeling.

CHAPTER 22

Time was called and everyone stopped. I looked around into the sea of the room and saw characters, incredible, believable characters. Everyone was smiling and laughing. That was the magic of cosplay, becoming someone else for a little while and leaving all the troubles of life behind.

"Head to the main hall. We'll use the entry for pictures and judging," Freya announced. We filed our way out of the craft room to find Grace waiting for us with a camera.

"You all look amazing!" She said.

"We'll do one group at a time," Freya instructed. "Strike your pose in the taped box and we'll get pictures. The rest of us, there are clipboards with the criteria sheets. Put the name of the characters at the top and check the boxes to place your votes. MaryAnn and I will go first."

The two made their way to the box marked in tape on the floor at the end of the hall. There were lights set up with a plain background, making it look like a photobooth.

Freya and MaryAnn posed as Grace began snapping pictures.

"I hope we get copies," I heard Alex say. "Left my phone in my other pants."

There was a murmured laugh and consensus. Freya and MaryAnn had gone the sexy cosplay route which was often their trademark. Gender-bending Mario and Luigi from Mario Bros., their super short, cutoff shorts showed off a lot of skin, and their revealing tops with sort of push-up corset-type shirts, outlined boobs for miles. Their hair was pulled up and styled into sexy ringlets in ponytails and baseball caps, and they looked more like supermodels than game characters. However, this was the sort of cosplay they were both famous for. They rolled through a few poses, old pin-up style, none particularly specific to the game.

Nicole nudged me, holding out a clipboard.

"Sorry!" I said. Embarrassed to have been staring when I was supposed to be voting. I went through the sheet, giving high marks in some areas, and mid-range in others. I'd seen them both do this particular costume before, and much more accurately. A few hours didn't give time to craft the shirt and screen print it too. Some pieces looked more taped together than sewn, a little disappointing from two such skilled seamstresses.

Next up was Chad and Julie. And those two were... wow. Chad had to lumber to the spot and crouch a little to fit in the lighting area. Hagrid and Hermione from Harry Potter had been their choice. Julie's ratted out hair, a fluffy mess, resembling the movie character, and she'd done good work getting her Gryffindor robe accurate, right down to the patch. She held a handful of old books, and a golden-looking hourglass necklace which looked put together from EVA foam, and probably spray painted.

Chad's costume was a leather-like robe. The bulk beneath it meant he'd used pillows or something as it didn't lay quite smooth, but still gave breadth to his size. The mess of hair on his head and face had to have come from Freya's wig trunk and was close to the real thing. He had no other props, and the overcoat was pretty plain. In general, their costumes were good. And people would stop, ask for their photos and pose with them if they were at a convention. However, when it came to overall skill, detail, and accuracy, it was lacking a little. With more time they could have added some things to Hagrid's design to make it stand out. I wondered if the leather-like material had made them lose time, or just sheer size had caused them trouble.

In general, they had gone with simple, only two overcoat type items and some accessories, but other than a few bits of Julie's outfit, hadn't taken the time for small details. They also didn't have a good set pose and stood a little awkward together. I gave them high marks for inspiration and creativity, but mastery and accuracy were low.

Next up were Jonah and Alex. As they stepped into the square it was the first time I really looked at them. Couldn't miss the bright orange of Jonah's outfit, or the pea green of Alex's top.

Jonah had done a gender bender as well, taking on the role of Velma in her fitted orange sweater and short skirt with knee-high socks. He'd found Mary Janes somewhere and fake glasses. He didn't bother with a wig, instead using his shaved short hair as a sort of backdrop of what Velma's hair had been. He looked like a smart, sassy, and with some sort of bra underneath, sexy African-American Velma. Lots of hip and a good show of leg, an illusion of fabric creating that very feminine look. They'd constructed a magnifying glass thing out of EVA foam. It was huge, and sort of comical, but a fun detail.

Then there was Alex. I had to smile. If anyone made a better Shaggy than Alex, I had yet to meet them. His wild hair and full beard added to the full stoner effect. The pea green V-neck shirt, white undershirt with long sleeves, and brown pants fit well, hugging his lean frame and making him look like the tall and lanky detective from cartoons of old. He'd let his hair down and obviously run his fingers through it a little to make it look like the messy stoner, and at some point, he'd retrieved the one pair of dress shoes he'd brought with to add to the outfit.

He hugged a pillow, big and brown, and stitched in black thread to the outline of a very particular dog. It even had the words "Ru-Roh" stitched above the dog's head in a thought bubble. While his Scooby wasn't anywhere near as large as the real Scooby had been, since I was pretty sure the dog had been a Great Dane and the size of a horse, he was a good two feet tall. The pillow cut to look like a sitting Dane, with the stitching perfect enough I wondered if Alex had done it with his quilting skills. The two of them did a few sneaking poses hunched over the magnifying glass, looking shocked, or searching, and even a fake kiss as a Shaggy and Velma thing was a cannon side story.

"I really hope we get copies of the pictures," I said to no one in particular while scoring the list for them. They got high marks for originality, creativity and even execution as all of the pieces looked like real clothes with authenticity to the series. Even Alex using his own hair. They rolled through a few silly poses, like Velma slapping Shaggy's ass, and we all laughed. They were a pair that would have crowds lined up.

When they left the box, I grinned at him. "You're amazing!" I said to Alex.

His cheeks turned pink. "You guys are amazing. Go... do your thing." He waved at the box. Nicole and I headed over to get ready. Thankfully the box was large enough for the 'Sit, Boy!' pose. She held out the jewel necklace just inches from me and said, "Sit, boy!"

I did my whole fall to the ground and pull the dizzy string thing. An uproar of laughter echoed across the room and I worked to hold the silly pose while I heard the click of the camera and murmured voices. Nicole and I did two other poses, one of which showed off the clay fake 'nails' I'd created to make me look like the half-demon, lunging at her, and her looking serene. And the last one was a fake almost kiss, like we were reaching out for each other.

When we left the box, Alex greeted me with a kiss. "I love Inuyasha!" he said. "You make a great half-demon."

"I'm wicked that way," I promised him with a wink.

"Brat," he whispered fiercely to me. "These pants hide nothing, behave."

I glanced down to find him giving me a little half lift and smiled.

Freya collected all the sheets and Grace began helping her tally points.

"Did you stitch Scooby?" I asked Alex.

"Yeah. A fabric sandwich design and Jonah helped me turn it into the pillow. He said he could probably make a plush but there wasn't enough time."

"You guys did great," I said.

"It was all Jonah. Never seen anyone cut pieces so fast that fit perfectly once sewn together."

"And that man of yours," Jonah said, "damn he can sew. I was like sew this to this and he whipped right through it. Not even a problem with the knits once I changed the needle."

"Except the skirt. He had to do that. Pleats?" Alex looked down at the skirt Jonah was wearing. "Pleats are evil things."

"Right?" I agreed. "Nicole slammed through hers like it was nothing. I think I need more practice."

"Sewing clothes fast is part of fashion design," Jonah said. "Skirts are easy. Too bad Velma didn't rock an A-line. Would have finished it in half the time and better to show off this fine ass." He patted his own butt.

"Who created the magnifying glass?" It looked a bit like one of those giant foam cheese head things I'd seen on TV. Or even the big foam bat they had at some sports events.

"That was me," Alex said. "Foam is pretty easy to work with. Since we had sheets of it available and a couple of good craft blades, I did that while Jonah was finishing up the hems."

I grinned at Alex who was too creative for words sometimes. "You're amazing."

"And goofy," he said.

"You make a sexy Shaggy," I said touching his face. I really liked his face.

He leaned to kiss me, which was more complicated with all the hair I had, but he managed it.

234

"Aw," Jonah said. "A Shaggy and Inuyasha crossover love story. Not sure the cannon universes will ever be the same."

We laughed.

"Alright everyone. Numbers are tallied. Everyone ready?" Freya asked.

"Yes," came the unanimous shout from the group. We all huddled together, excited, still teeming with the adrenaline from the contest, and everyone grinning, feeling good.

"There are no losers here," Freya continued. "Everyone has done amazing work. And everyone gets a prize. We'll go in order, first to last, based on points. Everyone will get their scoresheets when we're done so you can see the feedback provided by your peers. Once each group is called, they can step up to the table and choose their prizes." She held up the paper like it was one of those Grammy envelopes. "First place wins for originality, authenticity, and use of physical form to fit the characters as well as execution. Amazing that this is our newbie with one of our old pros, Jonah and Alex as Velma and Shaggy. The Scooby pillow got lots of comments," Freya said as she announced.

Alex's mouth dropped open. "What? No way." He glanced at Jonah who was dancing and strutting about in his sexy Velma costume. "How? I mean…"

"Boy," Jonah said, "don't look a gift horse in the mouth. We worked our asses off and look fannn-TASTIC." He headed to the table. "Plus, you had my fine direction. There is a reason I'm a rising star."

Alex followed Jonah to the table his expression still reading as shocked. I wasn't surprised, more thrilled that he'd had such a positive time. He appeared to be glowing with happiness and excitement. The two of them looked over the table. I expected Jonah to take the sewing machine and Alex to take the books and pattern set he'd expressed interest in. Instead Jonah choose an iPad bundle, and Alex picked the computer and software set. I gaped at him as he returned to me.

He winked, holding the computer to his chest, his smile so large it brightened his face. "This is what winning feels like?" He said. "It's amazing. No wonder you guys do this sort of madness."

"Next set of winners," Freya began when both Jonah and Alex were back with the group. "Gets high marks for props, poses, and structure of their pieces, everyone loved the 'Sit, boy!' pose. Nicole and Micah."

"Oh, that's us!" I said jumping a little as I had been more focused on Alex instead of myself. Nicole tugged me to the table. I contemplated getting the pattern and book bundle Alex wanted, but felt bad, since I could buy any of that for him that he might want. In fact, there was nothing on the table I couldn't buy if I really wanted it. I was blessed that way, having a successful shop.

"What are you thinking of picking?" Nicole murmured to me.

"If I take something to donate do you think anyone would get mad?" I whispered back.

"Donate to who?" She asked.

"Chad's non-profit."

Her mouth formed an O and her eyes got big. "Good idea."

"That would give them still a choice for themselves," I whispered back. "What are you thinking?"

"I'm thinking I don't need any of this but like the idea of those kids he's helping. I honestly had more fun just doing this event than winning any of this stuff."

We were on the same page. "What if I pick the machine to donate?"

"Okay, then I'll do the pattern book set," Nicole said.

I was a little sad for a moment, not getting to give those things to Alex. But again, reminded myself I could give him whatever he wanted. Hell, he could probably pick stuff for himself and buy it if he wanted. He was not helpless even if his finances weren't as solid as mine. "Okay."

So I picked the sewing machine and she grabbed the bundle. Some of the items left were a couple convention ticket bundles, with fully funded tickets to several conventions across the USA, a Cricut cutting machine and a batch of supplies for it, and bulk fabric supplies from several apparel lines. They really had gone all out in their prizes for our little group. We returned to the others and I searched for any disappointment on Alex's face that I hadn't picked the book bundle, but there was none. He smiled at me and kissed the tip of my nose after I set the machine at our feet. We would do our giveaways after everyone picked prizes.

"Third place winners, goes to Chad and Julie for Hagrid and Hermoine," Freya announced. I found that a little odd since Freya and MaryAnn's outfits had a bit more polish than Chad and Julie, but maybe that had just been my opinion.

Chad and Julie made their way to the table. Chad picked one of the fabric supply sets, and Julie took the Cricut bundle. "I'm giving the fabrics to the non-profit," Chad announced without ceremony. "It will help keep the kids in projects for a while."

"That leaves Freya and I last," MaryAnn said. She made her way to the table, picking up one of the last apparel sets.

"Did you guys do that on purpose?" Julie asked suspiciously. "Make yourselves last?"

"Whatever do you mean?" Freya said serenely. "Why would we do that?"

"'Cause you were the ones to get all the prizes for us," Jonah said. "I wondered why your costumes were a bit less polished than usual."

"We worked hard on these," MaryAnn defended, putting her hands on her hips.

"The L on your hat is made from paper and colored with a crayon. Girl, that is not normal for you," Jonah remarked pointing to her green hat.

Freya waved her hand like it wasn't important. "What's important is that everyone had fun. It was great to see such imagination and determination from all of you. I can't wait to have you all on my channel for an interview."

"Wait, what?" I asked.

"I thought we were just doing the booth thing tomorrow," Julie said.

"And I'll be having a little show with everyone featured on my YouTube channel," Freya said.

"Can you use the pictures of us and not do an interview?" I asked. The last thing I wanted right now was to be back on the YouTube influencer stage.

"Don't you want to show off your costume? I thought it would be a great introduction to your new influencer page. And you can do a tutorial with the fancy new sewing machine you have." Freya said, seeming confused.

"Oh, about that." I picked up the sewing machine and offered it to Chad. "I picked this so I could donate it to your non-profit. I wanted to make sure you still had a choice too, or else I'd have left it for you."

Chad gaped at me, shock looking very real and funnily Hagrid on his face. "Are you sure?"

"Yes. I don't need any of this stuff. But your non-profit sounds amazing. I would have loved having something like that when I was a kid."

"And this stuff is for your non-profit too," Nicole added, handing over the bundle she'd picked. "Lots of patterns and books for them to try. I can buy any of this myself. Would rather give all this to you guys."

"Really, you guys?" Chad seemed lost for words and his eyes suddenly became glassy with tears. I grinned and threw myself in a hug at the giant man with a soft heart. I wasn't normally a touchy guy, but the night had filled me with emotion. He hugged me back and then accepted a hug from Nicole too. "You're all amazing, and jerks too, but amazing. You have no idea how much this will help."

"The clothing line I'm picking is going there too," MaryAnn said, "but Chad and I already discussed that."

"I look forward to talking with you all about the non-profit on my channel. We can even open up a fundraiser," Freya added.

"Do we have to go on YouTube?" I asked.

"I thought you were going to return to doing influencer stuff?" Freya asked.

"Yeah, about that," I said slowly. "I'm pretty happy with my shop, the tours, and the tiny bit of cosplay I do. Influencing is a lot of stress and judgment I don't really want or need. It also takes a lot of time video editing, photo editing, responding to comments, a lot of which are just rude. Those are things I don't want to spend time on." I looked at Alex wondering what he thought. We hadn't really discussed it either way. He supported whatever I did, no matter what I did, and I loved that about him. "I'm happy with what I have. I don't need to be in the spotlight for any of it. In fact, I prefer not to be."

The group stood in what seemed to be shocked silence for a minute or so. But Alex's smile was huge and he kissed me on the nose again.

"I will support you in whatever you choose," he promised.

"But I thought you were coming back," Freya said.

"We were all sort of looking forward to your return. Your designs have always been so good we were all motivated to work harder to catch up," Julie said.

"That's just it," I said. "I don't want you all to look at me and think you need to 'catch up' to anything. The passion and originality come from inside." I put my hand on Alex's Scooby pillow. "And this was amazing, inspired, and well executed. None of that needed me to be involved. You're all branching out into incredible things. My amazing thing is my shop, which I love. And I'm sort of into this hot stoner guy who inspires me."

Alex grinned at me. "Woot. The half-demon is in love with me." He did a little dance, looking silly and adorable all at once.

"Your shop would be busier if you had the influence to drive people to the website," Freya pointed out.

"It would probably build hype," Nicole added. "We still do pictures and stuff, and will do classes and online tutorials to drive business to our new shop."

"We do okay," I said. Maybe I'd expand into tutorials down the road, but for now I liked the simplicity of the shop. "I'm happy where I am. Really. You guys are all great. I'd forgotten how much fun this was, even while being stressful." I looked at the clock, and it was after eleven p.m. "How about we call it a night? Ride this high into a good night of sleep for the convention tomorrow? I'll do the booth thing, and Freya if you really want an interview, that's fine. I'll direct people to the shop website since I won't be reopening my old influencer one. Hopefully that's okay with everyone?"

"Works for me," Alex said. "I love Simply Crafty. If you guys haven't checked out the website yet, there's amazing stuff for sale. We should add links too," Alex said. "For the non-profit and everyone else's websites. Tutorials and all that. Redirect traffic that might be interested in that sort of fun quirky stuff, as that's what Simply Crafty specializes in."

"I'd love to link our Etsy shop to your page," Nicole added. "We do mostly accessories with a cosplay flair, but that sounds like it would fit."

"Sounds good to me," I said. I did most of the web work myself. Years of video editing and website building had taught me a lot. The only thing I hired out for was the actual sales platform programming. That part of the site worked like a well-oiled machine now. "If you need help building a sales platform independent of Etsy, let me know. I've got a friend who did mine for a really reasonable price. He also maintains that part of it for a small monthly fee. Mostly all I have to do is print off order sheets and pack stuff up. It runs like a dream. Cut out the middleman charging all those fees on every sale."

"That sounds great," Nicole said.

"Holy crap, I'm super tired all of a sudden," Alex said.

"The adrenaline fading," Chad agreed. "Maybe we should all call it a night. We gotta do the convention tomorrow."

I nodded and everyone else seemed to be in agreement.

"I'll talk about the details for the booth cosplay event tomorrow over breakfast," MaryAnn said. "See you all in the morning."

I grabbed Alex's hand and made my way back to the craft room to gather up our clothes. Alex gave the doorway opposite the dining room a wide berth again and I frowned as I studied the space, finding nothing out of the ordinary again. "Everything okay?" I asked him as he gathered up his stuff and we headed toward the back door.

"Nope, everything is good," he promised.

We stepped down the backstairs and followed the stone path across the dark yard lit only by the small path lights. "Are you mad at me for not getting the books?" I asked.

"What? No. Never." He held out the computer. "This is for you though. Maybe I should have given it to Chad's thing too?"

"The software is probably a little advanced for the kids in Chad's group."

"That was my thought too." We reached the door to the cabin and let ourselves in. It took a few minutes to get out of the costumes, putting them up so they wouldn't get messed up or dirty. The clay nails put on with double-sided sticky tape would have to have new tape added tomorrow, but I found a bag for them so they wouldn't get broken.

I didn't bother with anything else, leaving only my undies as I waited for Alex up in the loft. He apparently had the same idea, appearing in the loft in just a t-shirt and his undies. His wild hair making me reach for him. "That was amazing," he said, curling up with me on the bed.

"A lot of excitement in cosplay. A lot of frustration and hard work too."

"No kidding," he said. "I'm glad you wanted to go. It was fun."

"I'm glad you did it with me, even if we didn't get to work together."

"Well now you have fancy software to figure out designs we can do together."

"Yeah. I'll have to set it up. Do you want my old computer then? Still works great, even if it won't run the new software." My old computer was a MacBook Air rather than a Pro. So it was smaller and lighter. I would miss that about it.

"Sure. It will give me something to research paranormal cats on, other than my phone."

"Was the cat back?"

"Hung out in the craft room most of the night, perched on the top of one of the shelves. It wasn't until after everything was done that it got weird."

I thought about that for a few minutes. "Wonder why."

"That's why I need to research. But that's for another day. Right now, it's bedtime since we have a convention to attend tomorrow." Alex dragged himself up and turned off the light. I sighed and rolled over to center myself on the bed and in his arms, which is where I was happiest at that moment.

CHAPTER 23

Waking up to the tickle of Alex's beard on my face made me sigh.

"Is that a good sigh or a bad sigh?" Alex asked. "I brought you coffee."

"Remind me again that you're not a morning person?" I growled at him.

"I think everyone in the world is more of a morning person than you before coffee." The scent of coffee made me open my eyes and stare up at him. He had obviously been awake awhile since his hair was tamed and he was fully dressed.

"And here I thought you were offering me morning sex," I said.

"Before coffee? Do I look suicidal to you?"

I couldn't help but smile as he did know me well. The years of being rolled over for a good time had long passed, and oddly, I didn't miss them at all. I preferred a quiet morning of snuggles, coffee, and crafts to porn star style morning sex. Maybe I was getting prudish in my old age, twenty-three wasn't all that old, but I wanted to be awake enough to appreciate the man in my bed.

"See there's a crack in the grump. Drink your coffee. As much as I'd like to skip breakfast with the group and do our own thing today, we have that costume thing to get details on. Never realized how antisocial I can be until we got here," Alex held the cup out until I sat up and took it from him. The first sip was heaven as usual. The smooth, creamy vanilla flavor with a hint of butterscotch, rolling over my tongue and down my throat made me close my eyes and breathe. The scent helped too. Coffee and Alex.

"You smell good today," I said to him.

"I don't smell good other days?" He quipped.

"Not what I meant."

"Mhmm. I dug out the body wash stuff Lukas gave me instead of just using yours. Felt bad always using your stuff. Didn't want to use it up."

"You don't smell like Lukas. He uses cologne."

"But I mix well with your coffee is what you're telling me?"

"Yep," I said into the cup. "I'd totally be down for morning sex with you... after coffee."

Alex laughed. He leaned forward to kiss me, which I allowed despite the niggle in the back of my brain about my own morning breath. "Drink your coffee."

I settled into the cup of creamy butterscotch coffee, and after about ten minutes dragged my lazy ass downstairs to the bathroom to shower and clean up. Alex refilled my coffee cup as he danced around the house, organizing and cleaning as was becoming his habit. His tastes in music were a bit more eclectic than mine as I'd learned on the drive. He could appreciate pop music and had even added a few songs to his playlist that came from the Top 40 stations, but in general he preferred rock. As I combed my hair and washed my face, Bad Wolves' remake of the song "Zombie" by the Cranberries rolled on repeat between a handful of Adele R&B and Lewis Capaldi's heartbreak stuff. Alex only had a few dance songs in his mix, like Bruno Mars, Jason Derulo, and even the duet of Justin Bieber and Ed Sheeran, which I knew he'd got from listening to me play it, while the rest of his picks slid from the grunge of classic Nirvana to the nonstop angst of Three Days Grace.

Alex sang along unabashedly, his voice while good and pleasant, lacked training of any kind. I suspected if he had training, he might actually be the sort of phenomenal that made people superstars. He wasn't casually good like a lot of people were, but that firm and confident tenor strength of a lot of rock greats. It never ceased to stun me at how good he was at so many random things without really trying. A true jack-of-all-trades, I supposed.

His tone became a little breathy after a while, sounding a bit like he was running or something. Not really possible in the small space. I finished cleaning up and returned to the main area to find him following along with some sort of kickboxing exercise video on my computer. He had the sound off and was just following their moves to the beat of his own music. It all looked like he'd done it before, with no jerkiness of movement or hesitation. Punch, kick, squat.

"Hey," he said a little breathless. "I'm so out of shape."

"You look good to me," I said letting my gaze roll over him. Sure he was still thin and needed to put on more muscle, but I suspected it wouldn't be a challenge for him to get back to tip-top shape now that he had stable living conditions. I'd never been into gym bunnies or drawn to every man with a six pack of abs. I liked my men scruffy with something to hold on to. Feeding Alex back to a normal weight was on the top of my list for more than one reason.

He grinned, stopped, and ran his hand over his beard. "I'll have to find a gym or something back home. Used to run every day, or hike with a giant backpack. We had a couple routines too, random stuff we did to keep in shape while we were waiting on orders. Our troop was never one to sit around with our thumbs up our asses. I think the ghost tours helped. Running around NOLA chasing after ghosts and hauling boxes for you. What a way to keep in shape."

"We need to run away from ghosts, not toward them," I told him as I rinsed my cup in the sink.

"You might be in the wrong profession."

"Jerk. I'm a craft shop owner. You said so yourself."

"And a legendary tour guide of the most haunted city in the world," Alex said.

"I think that might actually be Paris, but you'd have to Google it."

He reached for me, pulling me into his arms and settling himself around me like there was no place he'd rather be. I really enjoyed his regard and hoped it stayed this way for a while. Before him, I had to admit I wasn't a very touchy-feely person. There was something different in the way he held me, hugged me, and swept me into the warmth of his personal glow that made it all okay.

"Breakfast with the group, then off to play with fabric," Alex reminded me, kissing my forehead and then my nose.

"I love fabric," I sighed.

"I know where I rate," he teased.

"Slightly above fabric," I said.

"Mhmm," he agreed lips meeting mine for a deeper kiss.

"This will not get us out the door," I said into the kiss, his body pressed to mine. "You, thrown on the bed so I can have my way with you, but not out the door."

He laughed and pulled away. "Okay, okay, let's get this over with." He reached for my hand and tugged us toward the door when someone knocked. We both stopped like deer in headlights. Was someone coming to get us? The crackle coating in the glass on the door made it impossible to make out whomever was standing outside. Alex opened the door.

Detective Manning stood there.

"Morning, Detective," Alex greeted him.

"Morning. Do the two of you have a minute? I have a few follow-up questions I'd like to ask." He waved at the house.

Alex and I stepped back in unison to let him in. The space suddenly felt very small. Three people was far too many for this tiny house. "We were just headed to breakfast before going to the convention," Alex said. "How can we help?"

Detective Manning pulled out his notes. "When the two of you stopped for Joe, did you see anyone else out there?"

"No," Alex said. I wasn't sure how to answer without sounding crazy. Yes? A shadow? A monster of many faces?

"How about you, Mr. Richards?" Manning pressed. "Something spooked you, made you run. What did you see?"

"Just shadows," I said, deciding to go with the basic truth. "Maybe reflections from the headlights. I don't know what it was. It was why I stopped in the first place. I saw a shadow."

"Joe in the road," he confirmed.

"I guess."

"You don't sound very certain."

I shrugged. "Shadows are shadows, right? Tricks of light and our vision? I'd think you'd get more answers from Joe at this point."

"Any idea why he was out there?" Alex asked. "It was a bit of a drive away from the B&B where their phones were."

"One phone. They had one on them. Notes from one of Miss Cartwright's discussions online indicated they were seeking out ghost stories. Hunting for something called the 'Rake,' have you heard of it?"

"In legend, yes," I said. "It's a very thin looking man-like creature with long limbs and claws that began in rumor on reddit a few years ago, I believe."

"Is that something you experience often in your ghost hunting tours?" Manning wondered.

"A Rake? Never. Not even the garden utensil type as we live in the Quarter of New Orleans," I said. "Our tours are specific to New Orleans history. And since the Rake is a new monster, I'm not sure I've ever heard of anything showing up in the Quarter. Never even done much research on it, though I think it pops up in the paranormal groups sometimes. Much like the Loch Ness monster does."

"You said they were talking to someone online about it. Like from our tour group page on Facebook? If that was the case than Byrony was on there as an alias since she was blocked from the group," Alex said.

"Why was she blocked?" Manning asked.

"Because she irritated the moderators. Why ask us? Doesn't Joe have better answers?"

"Mr. Thomas has been very incoherent. He's been remanded to medical custody for the time being."

"In a mental ward?" Alex asked, obviously recognizing the comment for what it was. "Is he a danger to himself?"

"He's had some self-harm attempts," Manning admitted.

"Could he have hurt Byrony then?" I asked.

"We're pretty sure he did, just not set on the motive yet."

"Motive," Alex said. "She's dead?"

"She is. I'm sorry. I know neither of you knew her well."

"Wow," I said, feeling a cold bit of numbness settle in my gut with the confirmation. "I guess I didn't know him at all, but wouldn't have thought he'd do something to her."

"There's still a lot to learn," Manning said. His stoic façade made me wonder how many bodies he saw in his lifetime to make him that cold. I barely knew her and suspected she was dead, but still found myself shocked by the announcement being official. "You don't seem all that surprised Mr. Caine."

I glanced up at Alex, his expression wasn't much different than Manning's.

"I'm an ex-military man," Alex said. "Seen my share of bad. And that girl has been gone a few days. I follow the news enough to know that's never a good sign. I probably would have been more surprised if you had found her alive and partying somewhere while her boyfriend had a breakdown. I guess I just don't have as much faith in humanity as Micah does. You wouldn't be here still asking questions if it were a simple partner abuse case."

"No," Manning agreed. "We do see those all too often." He stared at my face, and I knew he was seeing the bruises and the stitches but recalling other people. At least I hoped he was.

"You know how I got these," I said. "Car in the woods."

"Why was the car out so far? Was that even on the GPS?" Alex looked at me.

"I don't remember seeing anything."

"Service road to get to coordinates to see the 'Rake,'" Manning said. "Mr. Thomas's phone was plugged into the GPS much like yours was. They were a little off location, but not far. Must have stayed in the car longer, possibly looking to spot anything from the safety inside the vehicle."

"Do you think there's something out in those woods, Detective?" Alex asked. "A Rake?"

"Mythical monsters, no. A human one, sadly, yes."

What did that mean?

"Anyway," Manning pulled a wad of paper out of his back pocket and unfolded the mess, trying to straighten it out. "If I show you a conversation we pulled from social media, can you tell me if you recognize the names?" He was looking at me.

"Um, sure. I don't spend much time online, but I can look at it."

He held the stack out. They did appear to be stuff taken from both my group and the cosplay group. I glanced over the names first. One from my group was one of those random photos people took that could show something spooky or not, and this one did look like a section of woods. Nothing obvious about the photo screaming it was of some undiscovered cryptid, but when I read the comments I got clues where to look. In one of the distant corners there was something slightly paler than its surroundings. Humanoid with shoulders and a head, but lanky, proportions off. I frowned at it, trying to recall if I'd seen it before. Whatever was in the picture could be a Rake, or at least fit the description of one. The poster was one 'CosplayGambler' whose avatar picture seemed to be of Gambit from the old X-Men comics. Dozens of people responded. Neither Alex nor I had, as we both went by our normal names. And none of my admins had either, as the poster must have stayed with the rules to the group.

The stuff CosplayGambler shared to the cosplay group was pretty standard low-level cosplay stuff. Pictures of outfits he or she wanted to make, non-gender specific, questions about materials, comments on other people's posts. Nothing set off red flags. Other than the odd

Rake photo, which they claimed to have snapped themselves while out in the Texas woods.

The last few pages were messenger conversations. One a group chat with Byrony and Joe, both using their regular names. They were talking about the photo and what the location had been. It wasn't until then that I realized Joe had been in my group. He'd responded to the original photo. So while Byrony was blocked, her boyfriend had stayed, to what? Spy on me? Because the spooky content was so great?

"Well obviously Byrony and Joe. Though Byrony was not allowed in my group. Apparently Joe was in it though I don't know why. I don't recall having him in a tour previously, and most in the group have attended one of my tours at some point. I don't know who 'CosplayGambler' is either. I can send a message to my admins and see if they know," I said, handing back the papers. "You think this person might be involved?"

"Let's just say that they've been around a while. Had conversations with two other former members of your cosplay group that you've mentioned before, Sarah and Amanda," Manning said. "Did you know both girls were reported missing some time ago?"

I blinked at him while those registered. "Like how long ago?"

"Like since they left the cosplay group. At this point we're going over both of your groups with a fine-tooth comb."

"The cosplay group isn't mine. It's Freya's. She might know who that is."

"I plan to ask her. We will be talking to everyone in the group today."

"Did you find more than just Byrony out in those woods?" Alex asked. He must have picked up on something I hadn't. But his brain worked that way.

"Why would you ask that?" Manning asked, seeming surprised, but also not answering the question.

"You said it's not a case of Joe hurting his girlfriend. You're looking for this third person who seemed to be chatting with all the missing girls. Though Byrony isn't missing anymore. You said she's dead. Something tied you back to the groups," Alex glanced at the stack of papers, "and to narrow it to this one person, who happened to have trackable conversations with the other two missing girls. Did you find them as well?"

Manning said nothing and that was confirmation enough.

"Fuck," Alex cursed. "Next vacation we get beaches and private cabins instead of cosplay fanatics," Alex told me.

"There are fanatics everywhere," Manning said.

"Serial killer ones?" Alex asked. "Because let's be clear. What I'm getting from your questions and lack of specific answers is that multiple women from the cosplay group are confirmed dead by mysterious circumstances in some random Texas woods? That doesn't happen every day, right?" He held up his hand then. "Okay if the statistics point to yes, I don't need that in my head."

"You're far too observant," Manning remarked.

"My brother is a police detective. Comes with the territory. What do we need to do? Should we head home? Is it safe here?"

"I can't answer that for you. I don't know. This could be one of the members of the small group. Or someone who follows them around," Manning said. "Social media makes stalking people a lot easier these days. We have cops who specialize in the digital side trying to pull apart their profile, get a real name. Honestly, at first, I thought it was Richards," he looked at me.

"Me?" I was shocked.

"You and Cartwright had a history. I thought you might have played a prank that went wrong. That was before everything else. The rest doesn't fit. Sarah actually vanished while you were gone. Vanished yourself, or whatever," Manning said.

"What sort of prank?" Alex asked.

"Mr. Thomas had a gun. This is Texas after all. We think he was shooting at something and accidentally hit Miss Cartwright. The initial shot wasn't fatal, but the wound without care was."

Alex frowned. "There's only one member of the group who lives in Texas though."

"Freya wouldn't…" I said.

"We are certainly looking at her specifically. However, her alibi is pretty sound. Since she runs a hotel and does quite a few events each year, she's got a lot of records. And again, we can't find much for ties between her and the missing women. Has she said anything to either of you that might sound suspicious?" Manning wanted to know.

"No. She's been very polite and accommodating. Though she did seem a little annoyed with Byrony that first night we were here," Alex said.

"Because they spooked the group," I added. "Woke everyone up because they scared people silly. I was annoyed too." I looked at the detective, a thousand thoughts in my head. "Freya's always been very approachable, and helpful to everyone. I don't know why anyone would think she'd hurt anyone."

"One of the others in the group mentioned she might be eliminating competition," Manning said.

"That would sort of be all of us, wouldn't it? Since we're a cosplay group?" I thought about that. Not believing that Freya's fame was at all dependent on everyone else's failure.

"The same type of cosplay? Sounds like Miss Pejic is a big name."

"She is," I agreed. "One of the biggest in the world. But there are others. Some in the group, some not."

"You used to be a big name yourself?" Manning asked.

"I guess? Had a few years of being invited to special events and offered product deals of stuff. But that was a long time ago."

"Before you disappeared."

Everything came back to that, didn't it? "Technically, I was working in a different trade then as well." Had been doing the porn videos for almost a year prior to that.

"What made you change trades?" Manning wanted to know.

"My boyfriend at the time, mostly. It sounded interesting. And I was growing bored of always trying to think of new videos, costumes, and pictures to take to keep people interested. It's a never-ending need for content. Absolutely exhausting in my opinion. So I transitioned into something that was less work." Having sex on camera, posting a video once a week and getting a couple million views, that had been easy. Thinking of new dirty ways for people to see me on my knees dressed up as a fem boy and acting out scenes, that became work. In the end it hadn't been all that different from the influencer roll. New content brought added revenue, but people by nature were quickly bored and moved on.

"Some in the group were suggesting you would be returning to the influencer roll," Manning said.

"And that would make me want to kill Byrony and some other girls a few years ago, why? What would I gain?"

"Their followers, perhaps? Is that how it works?"

"Not at all," I said. "Influencing is a very visual persona created for a certain group. Everyone has different tastes. Even if someone follows sexy cosplay, which is what Freya and Byrony did, technically I did as well, though it's not likely their fans would go from them to me. Because I'm male. There might be some crossover, but my target was mostly gay men. Their targets are straight men and women who are into lifestyle stuff, hair, make-up, etcetera."

"Men don't follow other men for lifestyle stuff?"

I laughed. "Men follow sex. The only thing I offered, other than pretty pictures, was the occasional tutorial on costume creation. And that stuff never got interest like my sexy cosplay videos did." Or the porn. It was one of the reasons I didn't want back into that market. I wanted my existence to be about more than just sex.

"Do the women ever see themselves as competition?" Alex said. "Since they are sort of in the same market?"

I shrugged. "Maybe. I've never seen it within the group. Everyone's been pretty helpful to each other. I always thought we had the mindset that growing the community was better than narrowing it. Though I know Byrony butted heads with a lot of people for stealing

LISSA KASEY

ideas. I think if she'd asked and been more open about sharing, it probably wouldn't have been an issue."

"Did Sarah or Amanda take ideas?" Manning asked.

"Not that I know of, but again, I didn't know them well."

He sighed.

"I'm sorry. I wish I knew more. I've sort of been outside the group for a while."

"We will find something," Manning stated. "These people trip up eventually, miss a clue somewhere, a link they forget. Whether it's your friend or not, I advise you both to be careful. You might not be the normal target, as the victims so far seem to be women, but sometimes when these people are cornered, their regular rational flies out the window for self-preservation."

"We understand. We'll keep an eye out. Thank you, Detective," Alex said, offering the man his hand for a handshake. Manning took it and let Alex see him out.

I stood in the small living area of the cabin feeling a jumble of emotion and numb all at once. Alex wrapped his arms around me. "It's gonna be okay," he said.

"It's not Freya," I said.

"I know she's your friend..."

"But not really. I'm not any closer to her than I am to the rest of them." I stepped out of his embrace and threw my hands up in the air in frustration, even taking a moment to tug at my hair. "Because I'm broken and don't let anyone close to me."

"You're not any more broken than the rest of us," Alex said. "It's okay to be upset when something you thought was right is wrong."

"I'm not going to just accuse her. He said they didn't have any proof and she has an alibi." Why I needed Freya to be innocent, I didn't really understand. Maybe it was because once upon a time she'd been the first to see potential in me? She hadn't brushed me off as some annoying kid from a faraway land wanting to escape his strict parents. "I wouldn't be who I am now without her," I said finally.

254

"Maybe," Alex agreed. "But she was only a point on the path. You've had a lot of other points, people, friends, events, that got you here." He rubbed my back which helped me focus on my breathing. "You are who you are meant to be right now, and I think that's pretty great. Regardless of how you got here."

I turned to stare up into his face and had to sigh. He was that sort of male pretty I never knew I wanted until him, but those eyes were magnetic. Deep wells of emotion, drawing me in, *seeing* me, and still liking what he saw. I could list a hundred things about him that made me want him. Some stupid, small and silly, others intense and odd, like his ability to see things others didn't, even if that meant the paranormal. The more I learned about him, the more I liked.

"More than a spark," I said as I touched his cheek.

"Yes," Alex agreed. "So stay with me, yeah?"

"Planning on it."

"Good, let's go get breakfast and try to pretend things are normal."

"I'm not hungry," I said, feeling almost sick at the thought of eating.

"We'll just get some fruit or something."

"Might be eating with a serial killer," I grumbled.

"Maybe. Either way, stay close to me. If things get weird, we'll find another hotel."

"Weird how? We sort of thrive on weird." I let Alex tug me out the door and toward the main house, hoping for a chance to get our instructions for the later show, a banana, and get the hell out of there.

"Good question. Weirder than usual."

I sighed and clung to him. It was too early in the morning, and I hadn't had nearly enough coffee to deal with this sort of drama.

CHAPTER 24

Unfortunately, drama was what greeted us at the backdoor in the form of raised voices.

"You all are a bunch of fucking psychos," I heard Melissa shout. We entered the kitchen, finding the group scattered between the kitchen and the dining room filling plates of food and readying for the day. Melissa stood near the entryway, bags and things piled at her feet. "I hope you all know you're staying here with a murderer."

"The police said it was an accident," Julie said.

"Shot by Joe. Nicked a vein or something," Nicole added.

"Can we not talk about this during breakfast," MaryAnn asked.

"Fucking psychos, all of you!" Melissa screamed. "Byrony is dead, and you're all about fucking breakfast?" She pointed at Freya. "Don't you realize how insane she probably is?"

"I'd prefer if you wait for your taxi outside," Freya said.

"I'd prefer you go jump off a cliff," Melissa snarled at her.

"Woah," Alex said putting his hands up and crossing the room to Melissa. "Let me help you with your bags okay? Some air will be good for you. Breathe. I know you're upset and you have reason to be." And that easily he took over, leading Melissa outside to the front porch, carrying her things. He glanced back at me, but I nodded to him that I was fine.

Chad was the only one not in the kitchen. I realized a moment later it was because he'd been talking to the police because he appeared with Manning beside him while I was gathering up fruit for Alex. Manning headed toward MaryAnn next. She gave him a warm half-smile and nodded as he led her to the craft room.

Grace paced the kitchen. "You okay?" I asked her.

"It's not Freya," Grace said in a huff. "That man wants to pin this on her. But it's not Freya. This whole thing is a mess that started with that Byrony girl."

It sounded like this had begun a lot sooner since two other girls were found, but I didn't point that out. "I think the police are looking for whoever did this."

"The police are monsters," Grace said.

"Some of them I'm sure. But Alex's brother is a police detective. He's a good guy. It sounds like Detective Manning is looking for the right person, asking questions and trying to get the facts straight. If he wanted simple, he could have arrested Freya already because she's the only one of us that lives here in Texas. But he's asking questions, talking to everyone, and researching. I don't believe it's her either," I admitted. "But getting in the way will only make his job harder. Someone is out there hurting people. We can't let that go on, right?"

Grace let out a long breath. "You're right. You always were one of the smarter ones in the group." She patted my hand. "Let me get you a portable bowl for all that fruit. I'm assuming you boys want to get on your way." Since I had filled a small bowl with berries, topped it with a couple of bananas and was trying to figure out how to wrap it with paper napkins to keep everything in place while Alex calmed the masses, she must have read our intentions.

"Thank you," I said. "Alex loves bananas." Which actually sounded like more than affection for the food when I thought about it. Nicole, who stood nearby, snickered. "Nothing out of you," I teased her.

"Didn't say a word," she said with her hand on her heart. She handed me the banana she'd taken too. "Give him this one too. Poor boy needs to eat."

"I'm feeding him up," I protested, like his malnourished state was somehow my fault.

"Mhmm," Julie joined us. "Too busy feeding him your banana to give him real ones."

I gaped at her.

"Girl," Jonah said entering the kitchen to fill his plate with eggs. "Plenty of protein comes from that banana. Protein makes a fine strong man."

Both girls laughed.

I groaned at the bad joke. "We just stopped in for breakfast to get the details on when and where we need to be for the costumes later."

"The show is at two," Freya said from the doorway to the dining room. "At the Haut Apparel booth. There's a dressing room area behind it, but I'd say be there early enough to get changed. If you drop the costumes off here at the house before you go, I'll bring them to the convention for you, so you don't have to worry about going back out to your car to get them."

"That would be great," Julie said. "We always end up in the bus lot anyway and having to take the bus over. It would be such a hassle to get out to the car and back."

"I have a vendor parking badge," Freya said. "Since I'm doing classes all day. It's easier to leave a lot of the supplies in the car when it's parked right next to the building."

"Thanks," I said. "We'll drop them off. I didn't pay extra for the vendor parking." I'd thought about it, but the extra cost when I knew I wouldn't have to haul big boxes around hadn't seemed worth it at the time. The separate bus lot would be fine as it was only a ten-minute ride over to the convention center.

Alex reappeared in the kitchen. I held up my stack of accumulated bananas for him. Grace returned to give me a big take-out type salad bowl for the fruit.

"Fill it up. Plenty of room," Grace said.

"Thank you," Alex told her, taking the container and my little bowl to combine them. "We were going to head out right away. There's a class at nine I want to jump in."

I nodded, though only vaguely remembered the schedule Alex and I had discussed. Too much on my mind. My gaze met Freya's and she didn't seem upset or worried, just sad.

"You okay?" I asked her.

"I've had better mornings, but I'll be fine," she assured me. "Go. Have fun. I'll see you at the convention later. My first class isn't until eleven."

I ran back to the cabin to grab the costume bags, and dropped them off before making my way to the car. I was seated and nibbling on fruit before realizing that I was in the passenger seat and Alex was driving.

"Um, you don't have a valid license," I said.

"I don't plan on getting pulled over," he told me, eating a banana while he steered us out of the B&B lot. "You're a little out of it. That means I drive or we get another rideshare."

"We could carpool with one of the other."

"No," Alex said. "Someone in that group is shady."

"You don't know that for sure." But I didn't stop him to take over. Alex actually drove with exceptional care. Full stops, signals, brakes, yielding to others when I would have pushed through with impatience. He followed the GPS on his phone, using the longer highway route. His phone rang about halfway there. Alex used a button on the steering wheel to click answer. I hadn't even known that was an option.

"Brother mine, tell me what you know," Alex said into the sudden lack of the radio as the phone connected. The GPS still showed on the screen on the car, but the phone said 'Lukas'.

"You do know police information isn't public information, right?" Lukas asked drolly over the line.

"Hi, Lukas," I said.

"Hello, Micah. I thought you were supposed to be keeping this jerk in line? Not chasing monsters or anything?"

"We aren't chasing anything," Alex said. "I just want to make sure nothing is chasing us. I didn't get much from Manning this morning, but enough to make me worry."

"Manning has a good reputation. Smart, resourceful, good solve rate, and often ends up with bigger, more complicated cases. I know he called the department here to ask about both of you. And there are whispers about the FBI getting involved, which means a big body count. I can't pull case details without risking my job," Lukas said.

"I wouldn't ask you to."

"I can say what has been released to multiple media outlets is limited, but I know there are more than three bodies."

"More than three," Alex echoed.

The words sank in slowly. Byrony, Sarah, and Amanda. Who else? Why?

"Word is they were looking for some military type drones to scan wooded areas for the possibilities of others. I know there's a big request out for cadaver dogs. Some people are talking about a new serial killer. I think you guys should come home," Lukas said.

"We don't know if this is related to us or the group at all," I said.

"Three members of the group dead, that's what Alex confirmed for me already," Lukas said. "Sounds like more than a coincidence to me."

"In a group that has thousands," I protested.

"Yet these three were part of the small group that actually meets up for costume stuff, right?" Alex asked.

"Manning did not confirm that they found Sarah or Amanda," I said.

"Not in so many words," Alex agreed. I really hoped neither of us gave away that Alex was driving instead of me. Lukas would freak. "I plan to keep us separate from the group as much as possible. Claiming we are doing lots of classes, and if I see anything as a threat we'll leave."

"The whole running into a guy in the middle of the road wasn't bad enough?" Lukas said.

"At least we found him, got him help," Alex pointed out.

"And led the cops to the car and the missing girls by accident," I added.

"Right, and tell me exactly how that happened? You stop to help a guy and end up running into the woods, which leads to cops and a trip to the ER?" Lukas demanded. Alex and I exchanged a look and must have been silent for far too long because Lukas cursed. How much had Manning told him? "I know you're both fucking weird so just tell me."

I heard Sky in the background trying to soothe him, but it didn't seem to help. Telling Lukas we suspected we'd seen the incarnation of Death, or whatever, would hardly calm him down. "I saw a shadow," I said. "Not a person shadow. Something moving where there shouldn't have been. It's why I stopped. It's why I ran. I don't normally see stuff."

It was Lukas's turn to be silent. Finally, he said. "Ghosts?"

I sighed, readying myself for another debate on the American view of dead people. But Alex interrupted. "Not exactly. They were mostly shadows. I didn't see any people-like things either. They didn't look like ghosts to me." He paused and gulped. "That first night that Byrony went missing, I saw her ghost like she was standing right in front of me. She was that clear. Joe's too, but he's still alive."

"Physically," I whispered.

"Yeah," Alex agreed softly. "There were shadows in those woods too. The ones behind Freya's house. Undefined, mostly. I guess I'd begun to think of the shadows like that as the really old dead, or maybe just not human at all."

Lukas growled. "Come home. No messing with more supernatural shit. We just got you back."

"I don't think most of this is supernatural related," Alex said, surprising me. We'd seen a lot since arriving. The ghost cat that morphed into something dark, the mass of shadows, and the Death thing. "I'm not getting that vibe."

"You're not getting that vibe..." Lukas sounded like he wanted to reach through the phone and strangle his brother. But it was then that I realized I wasn't really either. I'd felt a bit of it in the woods that first night when something touched me, but it hadn't stayed. More passed through me. Then on the road, the silence, created by the panic attack which had me dashing into the woods, it hadn't been the same.

I remembered the feeling of wriggling flesh, like I'd been dropped into a pit of fire ants, totally unbearable, every single time I stood in front of the LaLaurie Mansion. The weird bird chitter that echoed into the darkness until all other noise was snuffed out hadn't happened either. More a tuning into my own heartbeat pounding and ears flooded with the sound of blood pumping. Not that vacuum of all sound. Did it mean all we had encountered was less terrifying? No. But perhaps not the demons we normally dealt with. Whatever these supernatural things were, they weren't directed at us.

"Maybe the killer is the target of the activity?" I asked Alex. "Instead of us. Which is why it's less intense."

"A sort of karma perhaps?" Alex said. "Maybe. Or a signal that whatever they are chasing is the true darkness in all this. But whoever is killing these people is human."

"That's usually how homicide works," Lukas said dryly.

"You guys have Marc's death as unknown," I pointed out. Marc had been another tour guide. He'd been murdered by some sort of ritual gone wrong. The darkness had killed him, I was pretty sure, though didn't know how exactly the police could ever pin that down.

"Can't put it on the dead woman. Have no proof, though everyone thinks it was her and her niece," Lukas said. "Coroner said his death couldn't be determined exactly, since he was cut into pieces. Internal explosion is not a thing."

"Gross," Alex said. "We're eating breakfast."

"In the car? You shouldn't eat and drive."

"I'm not eating," I said, my stomach still a little queasy from the news this morning. The few pieces of fruit I'd had weren't sitting all that peaceably. He didn't need to know I wasn't driving either.

"Whatever," Lukas griped. "Finish your convention thing and come home in one piece. I don't want to have to travel to fucking Texas to bring you both home in body bags."

"Will you continue to poke around?" Alex asked.

"As much as I can without getting into trouble. I'd rather you both come home now."

"All the victims have been women so far," Alex pointed out. "Not that it's a good thing, that they are women, just that we probably aren't the victim of choice."

"That we know of. As I said, there are more bodies and I don't have details. We have no idea if that is a common denominator or a coincidence. I'll see if I can find pictures of the missing girls. Maybe they looked alike," Lukas said.

"Byrony was a redhead," Alex offered.

"Amanda was African-American," I said. "I think Sarah was blonde."

"Not helping, Micah," Lukas said. "Common traits, not different."

"I barely knew any of them. Sorry." I said, again feeling a little broken for the constant need to push people away before they hurt me too.

Alex reached over and patted my leg. "We'll see if Micah can find anything from the group once we're back at the cabin for the day. We'll send you pictures and any info we find."

"You are not detectives."

"Nope," I agreed. "We are cosplayers shopping for fabric in T-minus ten." I pointed Alex toward the bus lot and he slowed to follow the orange vest people waving flags.

"Nerds."

"Happy nerds," Alex said. "Wait until I show you our new sewing machine when we get home. It was like super expensive. Later, brother." He clicked the dash button again and hung up the phone, steering us into the next available spot. He parked and turned off the car, then looked at me.

"What?"

He let out a sigh. "I have to fight the instinct too."

"What instinct?"

"To protect you. To be an asshole caveman and take us both home. It would be the smart thing to do."

"We don't know that anyone is out to hurt us. Or that it's related to the group at all. We tend to run into crazy things without trying."

"And we just randomly stumbled across Texas's latest serial killer? Who just so happened to have killed three girls related to an online cosplay group that all of you are in? Sounds like a lot of coincidences."

I sighed. He was right. He reached across the seat to touch my face. He was gentle, but it still hurt as he reminded me of my bruises. "You've already been hurt. Let's try to see as many of the booths as we can today and maybe head home early?"

"I thought you had a bunch of classes you want to go to?"

"None of that matters. Not to me. I can find tutorials on line. I can't replace you."

I let out a long breath because Alex had a way of saying things that hit hard, without trying. "Same," I said lamely. "Stay close to me, okay? Don't follow any black-eyed kids into the woods."

He frowned at me.

"What?"

"I don't remember ever telling you that. The night I disappeared, my demon showed up as a black-eyed kid. Offered me help in getting you back."

I blinked at him, thinking back to his description of his abduction by the djinn or whatever it had been. But it wasn't his description I was thinking of. It was the video of his disappearance. Something that niggled in the back of my brain the dozens of times I'd watched it. Like there was a face there in the brush.

A black-eyed child.

Pareidolia, I'd convinced myself, as much of what the paranormal Facebook group found could be attributed to the human brain latching onto the idea of a face or a shape. I'd read plenty of stories about black-eyed children. The rule was not to let them in. The always cried for help and if you followed them you vanished. If they knocked on your door and you let them in, you died. More myths, or at least I had thought so.

"Micah?" Alex prodded.

"I think I saw something in the video of your disappearance."

"A black-eyed child?"

"Yes. Maybe. I don't know." I bit my lip. "I don't normally see things."

"Or maybe you do and just brush it off like I did for so many years."

I sucked in a deep breath. Alex squeezed my hand, making me look at him again.

"I like your weird," he promised. "Even if it scares you, it's okay. Our weird fits together just fine."

I felt tears burn my eyes. No. I was not going to cry while sitting in a public parking lot. I'd always been a little weird, right? First dreaming of cosplay and crafts in a very scattered way which had bothered my father a lot. Then becoming a porn star fem boy, and finally as this lightning rod for the supernatural. "I don't want spooky to be drawn to us."

"I'm not sure it is. Seeing it doesn't mean it's drawn to us. Just means we are less likely to walk through the ghost of grandma Jane, right?" Alex gave me a stunning grin, kissed me on the lips and turned to get out of the car. "Now we have fabrics to browse. Think of all those smooth cottons beneath your hands."

"Lots of stiff metallics too," I added as I got out and followed him toward the bus. He let me take his hand and we swung them like we were little kids.

"Stiff..." Alex chuckled.

"Perv."

"Only for you, babe." Alex pulled me into a hug and kissed the side of my head before we got on the bus and found an empty seat away from all the grandmas.

CHAPTER 25

The day actually went pretty smoothly. We got through most of the rest of the booths, spending enough time browsing to buy another heap of fabric and even meet a few more budding designers. Alex hopped around a handful of classes, standing on the edges, listening to the overview of what they had to share.

He'd spent more time interested in fabric than the machines this time since he had chosen the one he wanted. As the time neared for us to do the costume thing, my anxiety grew. Normally I didn't mind dressing up. I liked being someone else. But the crowd in front of the booth began to extend out into the aisles, and there was a lot of murmur about seeing some cosplay stars. I was not a star by any means. Not anymore. Three years ago, maybe. A baby at twenty, I'd done my share of conventions, with people waiting to see me, snap my picture, and get a signature. A lot of the female cosplayers started as young as fourteen. I'd been sixteen when I made my debut, then spent almost four years in the spotlight, being small and cute, attracting a lot of unwanted attention as well as adoring fans. I didn't feel like that person anymore.

And I had a growing unease with my hardcore porn past. At the time, I'd thought it empowering. Only looking back now, realizing I'd let Tim treat me like a sex doll, did it feel demeaning. It was why I ultimately gave it up. Not my disappearance or even the end of my relationship with Tim. Other guys messaged me all the time, volunteering to be my 'daddy' or to 'use me' or a million other things. In general, I'd thought sex on screen wasn't a big deal. If I ever did it again, it would be much different, with me in control. I wasn't a kid desperate for affection anymore. Okay, so I was an adult desperate for affection, but I had boundaries too.

Would people recognize me? It was one of the reasons I had no desire to dress in any sort of girlish costume. No school girl. No dresses. I didn't want anyone to look at me and think of the little boy I'd been. It wasn't me anymore. I wasn't even physically the same guy. Not as thin or delicate, since time filled out my face and my body. Could I still pull off looking like a girl? Probably. With the right clothes, wig, and covering part of my face, but I didn't want to hide like that anymore.

Alex squeezed my hand. "What's up?"

"Regretting this cosplay thing," I said.

"You love dressing up."

"Not for crowds like this. Not anymore."

We headed toward the booth, trying to find someone in charge to lead us back to the changing area and where Freya had promised to have our costumes waiting.

"You made an amazing Inuyasha. Why don't you design more stuff like that for yourself?" Alex asked.

"Not much occasion to wear them."

"That's never stopped you from designing for Sky or me. No reason we can't have random costume nights at the shop. It's a craft shop. We specialize in random."

I paused to look at him. Again, he was right. I sighed. He smiled that boyish grin that made me want to curl into him forever. "Stop seeing me so clearly," I grumbled at him. "It's not fair."

He waved an employee of the booth over and got us led to the back where a bunch of hanging fabric had been created into dividers for makeshift dressing rooms. There were dressing bags hanging on a rack with names pinned to them. Alex grabbed ours.

"Did you give everything over to Freya this morning?" Alex asked with a frown. He lifted my bag a few times. "It feels really light. The red part of your costume was heavier, I thought."

I took it from him and it was extremely light. The bulk of the fabric from the red outer layer alone had weighed more than this. "I gave her the whole thing. Wig and all." I knelt at Alex's feet, hoping I was out of everyone's way and unzipped the bag. My heart flip-flopped. It wasn't my Inuyasha outfit. It was the baby doll dress Freya had made me. I zipped it back up, my heart pounding, emotions rolling through me in waves of anger, terror, and sorrow.

"Maybe they just made a mistake." Alex went to the rack and pushed through all the bags. "It should be here." He paused to unzip his own bag. It was his Shaggy costume, untouched. "Fuck."

I stood and put the bag back on the rack. Emotions slamming down on me. The wall I'd spent so much time erecting inside me to keep them back, shattered in an instant. Silence descended again. Not paranormal this time, but my own shutting out of all noise. Too much in my head. A thousand questions, thoughts, emotions all so jumbled I couldn't even pull out a single one in that moment to form a coherent thought. I could barely breathe. All I felt was Alex's arm around my waist. His breath tickled my ear but I couldn't hear him, not until he wrapped his arms around me in a fierce hug.

"Hey, breathe," he said. "It's okay. No one is going to make you put that on. I'm here."

Freya and MaryAnn appeared, both in costume, but neither wearing the ones they'd designed last night. No, these were fully polished feminized versions of their Mario and Luigi outfits with super short shorts and T-shirts that revealed more of their breasts than they hid. These were the type of costumes that made them famous, the crafting, the detail, and the sex. That too, made me even madder. We'd all busted our asses to make costumes in a few hours, that they insisted we wear in public and not have time to polish, while they came out looking like rock stars in stuff that had obviously taken weeks to complete. Were they trying to make us look like amateurs? It wasn't going to hurt my business since cosplay wasn't my venue anymore, but the rest of the group still had real attention focused on them for their design. Yet there was no warning? No note that they would be showing up in full gear and the rest of us would be Johnny-on-the-spot? Oh, except me. For some reason I'd be in a pro costume too, half naked, and relegated to the role of the fem boy again.

I don't think I'd ever really related to the comment 'I saw red' before. But I'd also never been so angry. Anger was easier than sobbing hysterically or running away. And I was fucking pissed.

"Where is my costume," I demanded of Freya.

Her smile faded and she frowned. "Right there on the rack with the rest of them."

"*My* costume. Not that doll clothes crap you made me. I didn't make that. What kind of insanity makes you think that I am going to wear that in public? This convention isn't even cosplay related. There are more old people here than those under forty and you think I'm going to dress like that? I thought this event was to display the fabric sold by these people, not put on a sex show."

"She made your costume from Haut Apparel fabric," MaryAnn defended.

"*She* made it. Not me. Where is the costume I made?"

"We thought you'd have a great rerelease debut with the outfit Freya made," MaryAnn said.

"I've already made it clear I have no intention of returning as an influencer. And the fact that you two show up wearing these super polished costumes while everyone else wears things they scraped together in a couple of hours, what the fuck are you trying to do? Damage everyone's reputation?"

"That's not the intent at all," Freya said. "The company just wanted to show some pictures of their stuff. We've been working with their line for a while. Having the variety will show people how versatile their fabric is, for pros and for those in a hurry."

"Except my costume. Mine wasn't good enough to be in public?" And that made me even angrier. I'd worked hard on that, finished seams with perfect top stitch and created a realistic costume that could have been judged top of the line. My only gripe had been some of the fabrics, which had been thinner than I'd have liked, and the drape hadn't lain right. Had I more time I would have chosen other fabrics, but that was part of the process. The idea that they decided my hard work wasn't good enough? I wanted to break something.

"Your costume was great," Freya said. "We just thought this would create more buzz. You'll look absolutely stunning in it. I'm sure Alex will agree." She looked at him for some sort of approval.

"I have no intention of ever wearing the costume you made me. I'm not that person anymore. And I'm really beginning to think my place isn't in this group now. I'm not a sex doll, and Alex doesn't want me to be either. I'm sorry if that's all you ever want to be, but you don't get to force me into that role."

Freya looked like I'd slapped her. She sucked in a deep breath, turned and stalked away.

"Freya worked really hard on that," MaryAnn said. "She wanted it to be perfect for you."

"Maybe she should have picked something that better fits my personality now instead of who I was five years ago? Proves how little any of you know me or obviously care to know me. I'm done with all of this." I was so mad I wanted to chase after her and demand my costume back. I had worked hard on that. But in reality, it didn't matter. It was just some fabric. I could make another if I wanted. Instead, I left the dressing area and went in search of the manager of the booth, planning to explain the mishap and offer repayment for the donated sewing machine if they were upset about me not appearing in their event today. And I would not be appearing. In fact, this whole convention was over for me.

I hadn't realized Alex had followed me until he touched my back lightly, as I was explaining to the guy in charge what had happened. "We can pay for the machine," I added at the end. "Since we donated it to the non-profit. It would be unfair to ask for it back."

It would hurt. I would never have spent eight grand on an embroidery machine. Neither Alex nor I would ever use it. I vaguely wondered what finances I could move around to free up enough cash for that. We'd both been spending a little recklessly.

"It's fine," the manager said. "We'll use the non-profit as promo. I would have liked to see the outfits you created. Do you have pictures you can send?"

I didn't. And that made me angrier. Something else Freya had taken.

"Not yet. But we can take a few over the next few days. Once we get Micah's costume back," Alex said. "Can we email them to you? We feel really bad. I know that machine was expensive. We have some other prizes too. Freya said you guys donated most of it. I can return the computer and software."

"We only donated the sewing machine and some fabric," the manager corrected him. "Anything else was donated by the group. And helping the non-profit will be good press. We've already talked to the co-founder quite a bit today and are donating more fabric and a few more simplistic machines."

"There's Chad," Alex said, waving to Chad as he was entering the booth area, obviously looking for the changing booths. He headed our way.

I didn't realize how upset I really was until Alex hugged me, and Chad was walking away toward the dressing area. I had completely missed their conversation, too tuned into all the noise in my head. The manager was back to chatting with customers and directing people. Alex steered me out of the booth and toward the exit.

"If we return our machine we could pay back half of the cost of that machine," I whispered. "I'm so sorry. I know how much you want that machine."

"A quarter of it, and no. We won't be returning our machine. Chad is trading the fancy one in for a few smaller ones. So the company will do another giveaway for it. Make a big to-do about the non-profit and get good press. We don't need to do anything," Alex said. He led me out of the convention to the area to wait for the bus and I realized his hands were full with our purchases and his garment bag.

"Sorry. Let me help with some of that."

"I'm fine. It's just stuff. All in bags."

"We'll have to give back the computer."

"How about you not worry about that right now?" Alex said. The bus arrived, and I picked up two bags despite his protests. We rode the entire way back to the car lot in silence. The noise in my head deafening. I stared out the window, working hard to count my breathing, and keep from dissolving. Wasn't I better than this? Wasn't two years long enough to heal? Perhaps it wasn't all related to my disappearance at all. It was me being broken again.

We made our way to the car and loaded up the back. I stared at the driver's seat, knowing I should take it, but not at all in a clear head space to do so. Dammit.

Alex hugged me hard, pressing my face into his shoulder and squeezing me until it was difficult to breathe. "We're fine. I promise. Fuck, I can almost see the noise in your head. I hate seeing your eyes so dark. Lost."

"I thought she was my friend," I whispered. And that was the bombshell. Despite keeping her at a distance, I had believed Freya was a friend. Even confided stuff to her I rarely shared with anyone. No, she wasn't as close as Alex or Sky, but I'd trusted her, looked up to her.

"Even friends make mistakes. Let's go get a late lunch. You think your favorite Asian place is open? That was pretty good."

"Not hungry," I muttered.

"You haven't eaten anything today."

"Fruit," I said.

"Two strawberries is not enough to sustain anyone." He led me to the passenger seat of the car.

"I should drive," I said.

"No," Alex said, getting in on the driver's side. "Not until you've eaten and had some rest." He steered us out of the lot, and commanded Siri to set a route for the Asian place. "At least have some miso soup. You love miso soup," he said as he drove.

"It's very stereotypical Japanese," I grumbled.

"And you're half Japanese, so why does it matter?"

"It was never enough you know, not in Japan or China. It's why I didn't stay. People saw my eyes, my light hair, they made judgments. It's not much different here really. Only here they judge the shape of my eyes and face. Gay men judge me for being too pretty. Everyone says I'm too young to be a business owner or to know so much history. It's a losing battle wherever I go."

"What are you battling for?" Alex asked.

"Acceptance." Someone to love me for being me. Whether it was my odd mixed heritage, my nerdy interest in crafts and sewing, or my endlessly noisy brain, I wanted to be loved. That was when the dam burst. Anger washing away with tears and the realization that the small world I'd built up around myself was so fragile and mostly an illusion.

Alex leaned over to pull me into a hug. I hadn't realized until then that we were stopped in the lot of the Asian place which had been much closer to the convention center than I had remembered. He held me while I sobbed, the weight of my past heavy on my shoulders. I was the odd guy out. Had been even before I'd been taken by who knew what. Now I could see creepy things and couldn't hold a relationship together.

"I love you," Alex said. "No matter how much you hate yourself right this minute. Know that I love you, accept you for who you are, adore all your quirks, and look forward to learning more about you every day."

"I thought I had it together," I said quietly into the wet shoulder of his shirt. "But it goes back further than my disappearance. There's a lot more than that."

"Yeah," Alex agreed, not sounding surprised.

I sighed. "You see me better than I see myself and I wonder how you don't hate me for that."

"You've been hiding from the world a long time. Existing without really living," Alex agreed. "But wasn't it you who told me you wanted to move forward? Learn to live again? That's the whole reason you still decided to come to this, even when I was gone, right?"

It had been. I'd thought getting back with the group would thaw that part of me I'd put on ice. The part that cared too much about everything. Only it wasn't the group that thawed me, it was Alex.

"You can't storm into my life, take over, and vanish again," I said, balling the front of his shirt up in my fists. "I won't survive. I barely survived..." when it took him.

"I'm not going anywhere," he promised. "I'm into you, remember?"

"But we didn't get to choose," I whispered. "It just took you." And once something had taken me too. That hadn't been a choice either.

"So we stick together as best we can. We can't see the future. There could be an atomic bomb dropped on us tomorrow. Best we live in each day, right?" Alex asked.

I let out a long sigh. "I really don't want food." Mostly I wanted to wrap myself in him and forget everything else in that moment.

"Is that your head or your stomach talking?"

"Both." My stomach churned with anxiety. Food wasn't going to sit well, and I'd rather not be tempted to throw it up and ease the pain. I also didn't want to go back to the B&B. Funny how memories could turn so quickly from good to bad.

Alex was looking at something on his phone. "I'm going to call around to find us a different hotel."

"We could just go home," I whispered, feeling about ten years old right then and needing my space, my cat, and my boyfriend.

"By the time we pack up and get back in the car it would be really late. I think we should stay somewhere else for the night and head home tomorrow. After the whole finding random people in the road thing..." *Death...* the word went unspoken. "I'd rather us not drive at night." He looked at the clock. It was almost four. Where had the time gone? By the time we made it back to the B&B it would be after five and then we'd have to pack up our stuff. Could I even hope to get my costume back?

Alex clicked call on his phone and spoke a moment later. "Yeah, I'm wondering if you have any rooms available for the night?" He paused to listen. "Two adults. One bed is fine." He listened for a moment. "No, that's great. We just have to grab our stuff. Can I make a reservation and be there in a couple of hours?" He dug out his credit card and gave them the information. "Thank you!"

When he hung up, he stared at me. "Place we're going is outside the city, but I didn't want to try anything close to the convention center. If they had anything open it would cost a fortune." He turned on the car. "Let's go get our stuff."

He started to back out, but glared at the back up cam, and the hanging garment bag. He reached back and took it off the hook, dropping it on the middle seat and giving him a full 360-degree view through all the windows. It was then that I realized maybe Alex had wanted to be seen in his costume. He'd worked hard on it. It was actually his first in over a decade at least. And I'd deprived him of that. I was such a selfish jerk.

"I'm sorry," I blurted.

"For what?" He asked as he steered us back out onto the road.

"Taking you away from the cosplay thing. Your costume was good. It should have been seen. People would have loved you."

"Micah, babe, I'm here for you. This costume thing, this fabric thing, it's only fun because you're here. Would I do any of this without you? Not a chance. I hate crowds on the best of days. Show off something I made? No. Too long out of the game of wanting to be the center of attention. If life as a soldier taught me anything, it was that standing out got you the wrong sorts of attention. Would I have done the show? Sure, but only because you wanted me to. Because your eyes lit up with the idea of making something and showing it off. So don't tell me you don't like cosplay anymore. You love dressing up, creating characters, and being seen."

"Not half naked," I grumbled. Even my newer stuff, which was sort of pin-up sexy, was more about the curve of a hip or butt than showing skin.

"No, and you don't need to be half naked to be sexy. Hell, I wore that ice king thing you did for me, more covered up than I could recall being outside of a uniform, and felt sexy as hell."

"You were sexy as hell," I said recalling him in that chair, half hard, and outlined in stretchy leather-like fabric. "Fuck, you're so hot."

He laughed, and it was a sexy sound. "So let's go get our stuff, settle into the hotel and have a night in, yeah? Away from the group? All to ourselves?"

And didn't that sound like the most incredible idea I'd ever heard?

CHAPTER 26

The trip back to the B&B was uneventful. No one was there. We loaded up the car in silence. Triple checking every nook and cranny for stuff. I didn't want to leave anything behind. Alex was texting someone off and on. I suspected he was letting Lukas know we would be on our way home tomorrow.

Fitting everything in the car was a bit of a jigsaw puzzle. We had gone a little nuts with the fabric. But we got everything squeezed in and still had enough room to see all the way through the car.

"We should drop the computer off at the main house," I said. Grace would probably be there working on dinner. There were lights on inside. I wondered about the ghost cat. Had it been a sign of bad things to come? Perhaps responding to Freya's moods? Maybe Freya was the killer. Though I couldn't imagine why. Her fame surpassed everyone in the group, and it sounded like she had plans to branch out into more than an influencer roll. Was she eliminating competition?

"Freya says to keep it. Says I won it fair and square. She said she used part of the group registration fees to pay the prizes so everything was covered," Alex told me. He held up his phone. "I wanted to make sure she knew we were leaving."

"I don't want to talk to her," I said, anger not really faded at all. "Can you ask her where my costume is? I'd really like it back."

He nodded, texted and waited a minute. "She says she doesn't know where it is, but will find out."

I let out a long sigh.

"Let me run in and check the craft room for it," Alex said.

"You don't have to."

He patted my knee and got out of the car. "I'll just be a minute."

I got into the passenger seat and put my seat belt on while I waited for him. He raced up to the front door and opened it. Instead of letting my mind stir up more rage with overthinking, I opened my phone and browsed Pinterest, saving costume and quilt ideas I liked. Alex returned a few minutes later empty handed.

"It wasn't there. Grace said she hasn't seen it," he said a bit breathlessly. "Sorry."

"It's fine. It's just a costume. I can make more."

"But you worked hard on it," Alex said. "Unfair of them to keep it."

"The least of our worries right now. I should probably drive," I said again, feeling bad for letting him drive without a license.

"Let's worry about that tomorrow, yeah?" He started the car and drove us toward the directions on his phone. The hotel was less than ten minutes from the B&B, a tiny thing in a short row of retail type places. There were only two floors, and Alex darted inside the main entry to grab our key while I waited.

He returned and handed me the little envelope. "Normally, I would have requested the second floor," he said. "But the guy told me which window we are on the first, and I can park right in front of it. That way if anyone messes with the car, I'll hear it."

"Had a lot of car break-ins in your life?"

"Yeah. Before I left for the Army it happened at least once a month when I was at my part-time job. Lukas got his broken into all the time while he was at school or college. Even when we never left anything in the car. I think it's why he still owns an older vehicle. No bells and whistles to tempt people. Especially since his car is parked most of the time."

"I've never owned a car," I confessed as Alex parked around the side and in the last spot right next to a window. "Most places I lived had good public transportation. And the rest were short-term, so I borrowed a car from a family member."

Alex shrugged. "Cars are stressful. You don't own a car. A car owns you. Repair costs, gas costs, insurance, it all adds up, even if you don't have a car payment. But I'd like to get my license back, so I can drive if I need to." He motioned to the car. "Legally. But I think Lukas will let me borrow his should we need to go anywhere we can't get to by trolley back home."

He got out of the car and dug through to find his duffle bag. "I stuffed clothes and bathroom stuff in here for tomorrow. Anything else you need for the night from the car?"

I blinked at him as I got out, pointing to the quilt we'd brought. He grabbed it, and my laptop bag, and handed them to me before locking the car. We made our way inside through the keycard access side door and down the hall to our room. It was basic enough, bathroom, queen-sized bed, TV on a big dresser, and a table shoved in the corner. I put my computer on the table. Alex opened the curtain for a second to confirm the car was parked right there, and it was. Then he stripped the bed of the blankets and laid out our quilt.

He kicked off his shoes and unzipped the duffle bag, taking out a bag I'd made that I knew was filled with toiletries for the both of us and setting it on the counter in the bathroom. I watched him move, focusing on him as I breathed, and let a moment of peace begin to roll through me. He latched the metal door lock and paused to look at me.

"You okay?" He asked.

"Sure," I said absently.

He frowned. "You gonna take your shoes off and stay awhile?" He glanced down at my feet.

I looked at them too, and absently toed my shoes off, leaving them near the table. "Are there any ghosts or anything in this room?" I asked him.

"No," Alex said.

And that was settling. No ghosts. No cosplay group. Just four walls, a locked door, and Alex.

"What do you need?" Alex said crossing the room to wrap his arms around me. He touched my face, gaze searching, concerned. "There's a couple fast food places across the parking lot. I can go grab us something to eat. You should eat."

"I don't want food."

"What do you want? You know I'll give you whatever you need."

I felt a smile tug at my lips, thinking a cascade of naughty thoughts since we were alone at last and in a place where I didn't feel vulnerable. "You don't know what you're promising."

"I do," he said, his body responding to something he saw in my face, because his breath hitched, and I felt him harden against my thigh. "Fuck, anything."

I shoved him back on top of the bed. He landed with a little bounce and waited, watching as I crawled on top of him, straddling his hips and reaching for his face. Our lips met with fury, a heat of need, my demand of possession. He was mine. He wanted me. Looked at me like I was his world. Saw me in ways no one else did. Sometimes that scared me, but right now it made my body sing. It was easy to turn the anger to lust. The emotions weren't far apart, and I could never be angry with Alex.

I devoured his mouth, tasting every crevasse, memorizing the flavor of his tongue, and sucking on his lower lip while grinding my hips into his. I could come this way, a mess of fast frottage, but wanted more. Needed to see his pupils blown wide from pleasure, body trembling, breath labored, sweat glistening on his skin.

There were a lot of parts of our lives where I felt older than him, more experienced. Often it made me sad, realizing so much of my youth had been strained, while somehow, he'd survived with some portions of his innocence intact. His years in the military had tainted him in other ways, colored his vision of politics, war, and power, but everyday life sometimes awed him. However, in this instance, his body beneath mine, I reveled in my knowledge. Fantasized about a thousand ways to make him come, and teach him the ins and outs of our bodies.

"Please tell me you at least packed lube in that bathroom bag," I begged.

"Course," he said between kisses, his hands cupping my ass to slow the drag of our erections together. "Condoms too. Wasn't sure what we'd need."

I thought about that for a moment. A thousand thoughts in my head. Doubts, questions, anxiety.

"Hey," he said. "Don't go all quiet, share the train of thought."

"Condoms?" I asked.

"I don't need them if you don't."

I let out a breath I hadn't realized I'd been holding, and bit his lip lightly. "Let me go grab the lube." He did one more small sway of his hips, a nearly painful glide of our dicks trapped by fabric, and it was so good. "Fuck." Now I was copying him. Swearing like an Army man. He was rubbing off on me. I gave a dirty little laugh as I pulled away and went to find the lube. "I'd like him to rub off on me," I told my own reflection, not caring how silly it sounded.

"You can rub off on me whenever you want," Alex promised from his spot on the bed as I returned.

I stripped off my shirt, unbuttoned my pants and shoved them down before getting back on the bed and dropping the lube beside us.

"No fair," Alex said. "I want to be mostly naked too."

"I want you completely naked," I said, tugging his shirt up and off, then pushing at his jeans. He didn't even try to keep his underwear on. He shoved them and the jeans off in one go, kicking off his socks. He tugged my underwear down until I had to crawl out of those and cast them aside. When our bodies met it was like a roaring fire of heat.

"Fuck," Alex groaned as I slid my body against his, sweat almost instant and mixing with the precome from both of us. His hands went back to my ass, cupping my cheeks and pressing our bodies together, increasing the slickness. He breathed out a long breath like he was trying to keep himself from coming. "What do you want? Need?"

"You," I answered immediately.

"Yeah?"

I realized then that he was really offering me anything. Willing to do whatever I wanted. I could have turned over and told him to eat my ass for the next few hours and he would have. And wasn't that insanely hot?

He smiled up at me. "Share what's on your mind."

"Ass eating," I said. I liked that he was beneath me, thought briefly of sliding into him. How long had it been since I'd been on the giving end? And then was suddenly struck with an image of him riding me. Well fuck wasn't that hot. "You riding me," I added without thought, and instantly regretted it. What if Alex never bottomed? Would he get mad?

Alex rolled us over, startling a gasp from me. "What do you want first?"

I couldn't breathe. Had my cock ever been so hard? I groaned as he gripped it and ran a slow squeeze over my length, adding lube, I realized. He fingered the head, teasing my foreskin and the sensitive underside. "I should stretch you," I whispered to him. "Don't want to hurt you…"

"You just want to play with my ass," he teased.

"Yes," I sighed. "Always."

He captured my lips with his, tasting me, teasing me with his tongue while his hand worked me to a fire. I could have come just from his lazy stroking, it was maddening, almost tight enough to hurt, drag slow enough to keep me on edge, but teetering so close. I wasn't sure I would last more than a second of him around me. Maybe I should have gone with the ass licking first.

He smiled, moving a little above me, breathing in my air and meeting my gaze. I felt him then, the tip of me at his entrance, both of us burning up. He pressed down, and I held my breath as he swallowed the tip of me, his body tight and clenching at the intrusion. I couldn't help but cry out as I slid in, a steady glide until I was fully encased. His body rippled and shifted around me, accommodating my size, which had never been small despite being the fem boy of all my former equations.

"Fuck, you're huge," he groaned.

"Am I hurting you?" I prayed not, he felt incredible, soft and tight, squeezing me and guiding me deeper.

"No," he said almost in a growl. "Good, so good." Alex closed his eyes, leaning back a little, shifting his hips a time or two as though trying to find the perfect seat. I felt a tiny bit more give, my balls resting against him, his pressed between us. He groaned, glanced down, and then reached between us, where he stood hard, and jutting against my stomach, adjusted his balls, the weight of them hot and sweaty. I slid in a little more, until he was fully seated. He let out a long breath. "Fuck, it's been so long. Never been this full. Feel it everywhere. The stretch is so good."

We both sat like that, breathing for a minute, me trembling with the need to move, his body still shifting and clenching around me, adjusting. He rocked his hips a little, his breath hitched and eyes fluttered.

"Fuck," he said drawing out the word.

"Like that?" I asked, mimicking his movement and adding a bit of a pressured shove up into him.

"Yes…" he sat back hard against my hips. "Yes, fuck me please. Do that again. Hard."

I reached for his hips, something to hold as he rode me, shoving my hips upward as he pressed down into me, friction gold. We rolled together, not a dance, but a wicked slam of circling hips. I could tell each time I grazed his prostate because he gasped and trembled, eyes deep, pupils wide, eyelids fluttering. It wasn't like videos, with the full pullout and shove back in, no, this was a balls deep glide of only a few inches, his heat like lava. And the way he looked at me wasn't that absent interest in only my body. He gazed at me, seeing me, focused on me in a way I realized I hadn't been comfortable with in the past. Not with anyone but him.

"I'm so crazy about you," I told him, tracing a hand up his chest, playing with his hair, and the sweat, pinched at a nipple, teasing it, drawing more decadent sounds from him. Alex might have been thin and needing to be fed up, but he was still beautiful, breathtakingly so, body moving above me. I traced his lips and face for a moment, marveling at the high cheekbones and soft beard that tickled my skin. Couldn't help the sweet sigh that left my lips as he caught my palm and kissed it. I was close, dancing on the edge of release, fighting that final explosion because I didn't want it to end. Not even for a second.

"Yeah?" He gave me that boyish grin I loved so much with a mix of added lust and desire. "Want me for more than my body, right?" He teased as he rode my cock like something out of a dream of an incubus.

"Fuck yes."

He guided my hand up to his hair, let me take a firm grip and tug his face back down to meet mine. The angle wasn't as good this way, not as tight or deep, but still enough to make me tremble as I tried to stave off my release. I would have reached for him, squeezed his fine cock and teased him to release before me, but it was trapped between us at that moment. His movements adding to the friction.

I sighed into his lips. "Don't want to come yet," I told him. "Want this to last forever."

He smiled against my mouth, the feeling a funny tickle of his beard and the soft flesh of his skin. "We have all night."

Alex reached back, and I wasn't sure what he was planning until I felt a finger where our bodies joined. A press of the digit against his hole and our bodies. I paused, but Alex didn't. The fingertip pressed in beside my cock and it triggered a thousand things at once. Dirty thoughts of Alex fingering himself, the stretch of his body around me and that digit, and lots of longing to put my own fingers inside him until his eyes fluttered back in his head.

Then there was his body's reaction, a clenching, almost bucking frenzy of movement, muscles gripping me in a vice but still sliding until I couldn't hold back the climax. It poured from me like his body was milking it from me. I spurted inside him as he continued to ride me, his finger pressing in a little further, causing another ripple effect.

I screamed into his lips, my entire body coming in a way I couldn't recall ever happening. A tightening of everything, an explosion of all senses, body, brain, and soul. I might have even lost consciousness for a few seconds because I gasped, and opened my eyes to Alex kissing my face. We were no longer moving, at least not intentionally. Our bodies were still locked together, sweat pooling between us. His come warmed my belly and dripped down my sides. We both spasmed a few times, bodies clenching and unclenching around each other, like an ongoing play of mini orgasms.

He danced small kisses around my face, palm on my chest over my heart. "I love you," he said softly.

I smiled, realizing my hand was still gripped in his tight curls, aching with the strain. I hope I hadn't hurt him, though he didn't look unhappy in any way. "Holy fuck," I grumbled into his kisses.

"That's back at the shop," Alex said. "And I don't think we need it. We do just fine on our own."

And wasn't that the truth. He slid off of me and I was instantly saddened by his absence. "You should be permanently attached to my cock," I told him.

He laughed. "What would people think?"

"Fuck people," I said.

"I'd rather it just be us fucking," Alex said.

"Oh, yes. Most definitely. Plus, you still owe me ass eating," I pointed out.

"Right!" Alex reached up to untangle my hand from his hair, then sat back and lifted me, flipping me over with such ease I was laughing until his face dug between my butt crack and found my hole. He delivered a few experimental licks, leaving a trail of saliva, then breathed his warm breath over it. "Careful what you wish for," he said.

"Even I can't get it up right away," I told him. Though I was half hard anyway, simply from the thought of his mouth on me.

"We have all night," Alex promised, using his hands to spread me open and began to dig his tongue into my hole. "I think I can make you come a half dozen times yet tonight." And he set about doing just that.

CHAPTER 27

I felt Alex's kisses on my face and my eyes fluttered open. "It is not morning yet," I grumbled at him. "And I don't smell coffee."

He laughed lightly. "Actually it's just after ten at night and I'm starving. There's a Subway across the parking lot. I'm going to run and get food for us."

"My legs are jelly," I told him. "Not going anywhere." I reached for him. "Stay with me."

He let me wrap him up in a hug and shared in a long kiss, but he was dressed so I couldn't grope him properly. "You need food too," he said. "Neither of us have had anything all day."

"Fasting is good for us. Reduces aging," I told him absently running my fingers through his hair. "I think there's science." Of course my stomach took that moment to let out a loud growl. "Traitor," I said.

"Mhmm," he said, kissing me again. "You nap. I'll be right back. We can talk science tomorrow."

"Take your phone," I said.

"Of course. What sort of sandwich do you want?"

"Meat," I said smiling, half teasing. "All the meat. Never enough meat."

Alex's laugh was wicked and delicious. "I'll give you all the meat you want." He delivered a long lick to my torso, making me remember the half dozen times he'd brought me earlier with his mouth. "Extra pickle too."

"You could stay and do more of that," I offered though wasn't sure I'd stay awake long enough to play.

He tugged the quilt up over me. "After food. Nap. I'll be right back."

I sighed and settled into the bed, closing my eyes and apparently falling asleep that quickly because when I opened them again, he was gone. I frowned at the dark silence of the room, wondering what had woken me. Alex couldn't have been gone long. I rolled over to look at the digital clock radio and was startled to find it after midnight.

Wait. Hadn't Alex said it was after ten when he'd gone to get food? I sat up, my entire body aching like it had had a good workout. Technically it had been a while since I'd been quite so vigorous with sex. I'd been careful with Alex previously, letting his shyness dictate what we did. Tonight, he'd given me reign, and I'd taken everything I wanted and begged for more. Just remembering made me half hard again. Why wasn't he back yet?

The room was dark and untouched. Alex's duffle sat in the chair. His shoes were gone. I climbed out of the bed to the window, pushing the curtains aside for a moment. The car was still there. Where the hell was Alex?

A lead ball began to form in my gut. Had the shadow thing taken him again? I reached for my phone, unlocking the screen, hoping for at least a text explanation from him. But there were only a few from an unknown number, which I didn't open, instead going for the list that popped up from Freya's number.

Had she done something to Alex? I hadn't thought her the killer, though plenty of signs pointed to her. Maybe I was just that bad a judge of character. What did that say for the rest of my life and the people I cared about then?

I'm sorry. Freya's first text read.

LISSA KASEY

I should have thought it through. I know you're happy where you are. And I'm glad you've found Alex. He seems good for you.

It was stupid. Keep the computer and software. Please don't stop designing. You've amazing talent even if you're not running around with media attention.

I'm sorry you're leaving early, but I understand.

Alex says you're very angry. And while I'm sad that it's at me, I'm happy because ever since your breakup with Tim you've been very reserved, almost cold. I've worried for a while that he really damaged you.

It wasn't Tim who hurt me. I wasn't sure it was related to our relationship at all. It had been my disappearance and how the world had treated me afterward. Like I'd been at fault, the victimizer instead of the victim. Always looked at with question, doubt, and accusations. How dare I make people worry? How dare I make people search for me? How dare I ask anyone to care about me?

But you've been so happy this trip. You look at Alex and your face lights up. You spend hours working on crafts and smile not realizing anyone is watching. You reach for him without worrying about anyone else. I think he's lightened your heart. That makes me happy. I can see he inspires you.

I just wish I didn't have to lose you as a friend...

There seemed to be a long pause after that one as the time change showed an hour or so mark.

I haven't been the best of friends to you, and I'm sorry. Was wrapped up too much in myself. That's my failing. Having a career and fame is great until you realize how much you have to give up for them. I'm glad you saw that so soon and didn't waste your life alone like I have.

Please call me when you get home, so I know you're safe. As soon as I find your costume, I'll mail it to you. I shouldn't have listened to MaryAnn's advice anyway and let her switch them out. I'm so sorry. Love, Freya.

I stared at the long trail of texts, read through them a half dozen times. Nothing about it screamed insane murderer to me. Nothing about what she said made me think she would have taken Alex.

I tried calling Alex. His phone just rang and rang, then clicked to voicemail. I didn't leave a message. My heart pounded with worry.

Maybe the shadow had taken him. Alex said he thought that the paranormal wasn't drawn to us, that this time wasn't really about the shadows that dogged our steps, but instead about the people around us. Maybe he'd been wrong.

What if it had been waiting for the right moment to grab him? A time when the rest of us weren't watching? But why give him back at all then? He wasn't healed from the last round.

I pulled on my clothes and shoes, trying to think through the panic. Did I have the detective's number? Maybe I should call him?

I dug through my wallet and realized Alex had that card, not me. Fuck.

I called Alex again. Nothing. Texted him, begging him to reply. Maybe he had gotten distracted at Subway. For two hours? My brain thought that was stupid even as I grabbed the spare room card, car keys, and darted out into the hallway and down the corridor to the main outer door. He hadn't been wrong about Subway being across the parking lot. It was in a small strip mall kitty-corner to the hotel, dark and closed. I raced to it anyway, the sign on the window saying they closed at eleven. Early for a Subway, but I saw no sign of employees or Alex.

Fuck.

My phone was clutched so hard in my hand I didn't realize I'd dialed until the faint buzzing ring echoed through the silence of the late evening. Standing in the parking lot there was nothing moving, no cars, no bugs, no birds, just the ringing of the phone. My heart raced, and I searched the surrounding darkness with my gaze, terrified of what I'd see, but hoping for a glimpse of Alex.

"Micah?" A voice came through the line, close enough to Alex that I felt a momentary leap of joy that it was Alex, only to realize it was Lukas instead. The subtle difference in their tone a mild Southern drawl for Alex, and a more polished city edge in Lukas's. I must have gone too long without answering, though I put the phone to my ear because Lukas said, "Micah? What's wrong?"

"He's gone," I whispered, feeling the words whoosh out of me like

I was a squeaky toy crushed underfoot. I dropped to my knees, suddenly unable to breathe. The weight of the idea of him being taken again enough to undo all my hard fought for calm.

Panic attack. Full loss of vision and air like a punch to my gut. Everything narrowed down to the frantic warning signal going off in my head.

I could barely make out Lukas's words. A string of curses and the slinging of accusations. Things already racing through my mind that didn't need help taking hold. I was really good at self-blame. Shouldn't have taken him from home. Maybe if he was home with Lukas, he'd have been safe. Maybe if he'd never met me, he would never have been taken.

Then Sky's soft voice filled the line.

"Micah, sweetie, breathe, okay? Count with me. Focus on my voice, breathe. One, two, three..."

I fought to suck in air and focused hard on her voice. It was the only thing grounding me in that moment, despite the fact that I was curled up in a ball on the warm pavement, in the middle of a parking lot, phone pressed to my ear. The wheezing draw of my lungs, eased a tiny bit, letting in cool trickles of air.

"That's it, breathe," Sky continued. I heard Lukas in the background somewhere still raging, though couldn't make out his words. "I had a feeling both of you would have PTSD about Alex's disappearance," Sky said. "Can you tell me what happened? Keep breathing."

"He's gone," I whispered, my heart feeling as though it had been ripped out and were laying in front of me, barely beating on the black pavement.

"Did he say where he was going? How long has he been gone?" Sky asked.

"Subway. But I'm there now. It's closed. It's been hours. I fell asleep." Just uttering those last three words broke me. I hunched down and sobbed into my knees. I'd failed him again. He'd given me so much in such a small amount of time, and I'd failed him, let that thing take him. I'd walked around the last two years thinking I was finally healed from it all, above the pain. Except I hadn't healed, had I? I'd just buried it all until Alex arrived and gave me a reason to plant seeds instead of bury memories. Fuck.

"Micah, sweetie, it's okay. I need you to focus for me. Do a few things so we can find him, okay?"

"He's gone," I said again. "It took him again."

Sky sucked in a breath hard enough I heard it over the phone. "Do you know that for sure? Did you see it?"

Like when he'd vanished on video? There one second, poof, gone the next. I remember those first few nights being home, sitting outside in the darkness, terrified, yet hopeful that he'd return. Only I'd been greeted with nothing but silence.

"No," I said. "I fell asleep. I failed him."

"You didn't. It's okay, we'll find him," Sky assured me, but she was hundreds of miles away. Lukas with her, one of the few people I would have trusted to take over the search. But he too had fallen apart the last time. "Lukas is going to try his phone. Do a trace. He set that up before you guys left. Has both of your phones set to trace."

"Already tried calling. He didn't answer," I said with my face in my knees. I trembled, the phone sweaty against my ear as the evening was warm and humid, unusual for so late in the year. My heart pounded in my chest and I traced the cracks in the ground with my gaze, trying to find anything other than the panic to guide me.

My phone buzzed, notice of a text. I pulled it from my ear to click over to the texts, maybe it was Alex. It wasn't. Instead the unknown number again. I flipped it open and frowned at a long slew of texts from a number and area code I didn't recognize.

You shouldn't have hurt her.

Your cruelty knows no bounds.

We were supposed to all be together again.

Why are your feelings more important than ours?

You don't get to make demands of us.

We didn't ask for much.

Why is he more important than us?

You swore we were friends.

Was this Freya? Maybe some hidden phone she had? A twisted personality or something? Us? We? Who was we?

You can't have it all.

We all give up things we love to succeed.

Sacrifices are necessary sometimes.

My heart skipped a beat. Had whoever this was, hurt Alex?

I texted back: *Did you take him?*

There was no immediate answer. I heard Sky calling for me and flipped the phone to speaker. "Micah?" She sounded panicked now.

"Someone texted me," I said. My mind raced with a million possibilities. Maybe it hadn't been the shadow that had taken him this time. Maybe, like he'd mentioned before, it was some sort of human monster. "Maybe someone took Alex? I don't know the number. They wrote 'Sacrifices are necessary sometimes.'" I trembled at the idea that this was all my fault. What if this killer took Alex and hurt him because I wasn't doing what they wanted? I'd dragged him here, into this mess with a group I didn't really know anymore. Had I ever? What kind of insanity was that?

Lukas was back on the line. "Read me the number so I can trace it," he demanded.

I did, feeling more like a robot than a person. A thick breeze began to chill my skin. I could almost feel something watching me. The heavy weight of doom lingering in the distance. Familiar and yet different. What was it Alex said to me before. Not my demon, his. Was this his demon? Out there watching me? Was that why it felt different and rewarded me with silence instead of terrifying noises?

Those nights when I sat outside my flat waiting for him, searching for him, sometimes I'd felt this way. Like an animal in a snare waiting for the predator to come and end it all. Except it never happened. I'd cried myself to sleep at night wondering how he'd survived a year on the streets and mental wards to be stolen from me in a short few days.

A text came back from the unknown number: *Yes.*

Fuck!

I texted back: *Take me instead. It's me you're angry with. Me who did you wrong. I will pay the price. Where are you?*

The eerie night silence lingered for far too long. No reply. I waited and waited, heart pounding. I needed him back.

"Micah?" Lukas called.

I watched for a text. "I'm here."

"I've got a trace going on all of you. I called the detective there, Manning. He didn't answer, but I left a message. I need you to stay somewhere he can find you."

The text bubble popped up on my phone. They were writing a reply. Instead of a text, a link appeared in the window indicating it was a map. I sucked in air as I clicked it and it pulled up my direction app. Too far to walk, I'd have to drive. I headed toward the car.

"Micah?" Lukas demanded.

"That number sent me a map," I said.

"Forward it to me so I can send it to the detective. Do *not* go there."

"They have Alex," I said as I got in the car and plugged the phone into the computerized console.

"And are dangerous. Micah! Be reasonable. What will you do to stop them? You're not a secret ninja or anything. Just because you dress up as one sometimes, does not mean you're a hero."

Ouch. That stung more than I thought it should. But that was part of it, wasn't it? Why I ran around New Orleans following ghost stories, and played with things most other people avoided. Not for a lack of fear, but because I felt like a coward. That was a virtual kick to the nuts of reality. I clung to Alex because he wasn't afraid of all the things that terrified me. And no matter how much I might pretend that it was all nothing, I still trembled in terror at night when the noises began.

Fucking noises. Nothing but sound. I'd wished to be deaf some-times, when the screaming started, or Jet walked agitated around my apartment while I tried to block out the terror with a craft. All leading back to one event.

Something had taken me, holding me for months and doing who knows what. Then I'd returned home to a life shattered and tormented by stupid night noises. I spent my evenings terrified, hiding, cowering in the corner of my home. How useless was I?

I backed the car out of the parking spot and headed toward the lot entrance to a flurry of chatter over the line. It was the least I could do, right? If someone was angry at Alex, wanted to hurt him because I'd left the group, that was on me. Cowering in the hotel room would not save him.

"I'm tracing your phone, Micah," Lukas warned. "If I have to send every cop in the state of Texas after you, I will."

"Good. Maybe they'll save Alex," I grumbled into the otherwise silence of the car. It was a short trip on the highway, then off a side road, toward the state park, which made my pulse race. That was the last thing I wanted. Wandering in some national park alone at night. Lukas and Sky chattered through the phone, though I turned them down until I couldn't hear more than the tone of their voices. Sky was trying to soothe, and Lukas was ranting. I didn't need either of their comments right at that moment. Terror rolled through my veins, even as my brain demanded courage. It was very contrary and frustrating. So many memories and thoughts at once, it was a wonder I could stay on the road. I glanced in the rearview mirror and almost ran off the road.

I slammed on the brakes and pulled over to suck in air and stare into the reflection. Slowly I turned my head, hoping it was just a trick of light, perhaps a play of the headlights over the highway. But no, it wasn't.

There was a fluffy white cat sitting on top of the covered sewing machine like it didn't have a care in the world. It didn't look like a ghost. Everything about it looked 100% legit, fur, blinking eyes, twitching ears, and all.

I gasped, trying to breathe for a minute. Then whispered, "Precious?"

The cat's head turned my way, glowing orange eyes meeting mine. Its tail flicked a few times before it turned away and stared at the backseat. Was something else in the car? My stomach heaved and I stared at the spot too, expecting something to appear. Only nothing did.

The GPS droned on about getting back on the road. I let out a long sigh of air and pulled back out onto the road.

"Micah?" I heard Lukas again, but was annoyed so I hung up on him. Alex was missing. There was a fucking ghost cat in the car. And a possible psycho killer was directing me to a state park. Did the presence of the cat mean it was Freya? Could the night get any worse?

CHAPTER 28

The lot the GPS directed me to wasn't the main entrance of Sam Houston State Park, it was one of those outlying road stops, with little more than a dirt parking spot. No other cars were in the lot and there were no streetlights nearby, just my headlights. I sat in the car staring out into the woods for a minute.

Was that a light in the distance? Was that Alex? I turned off the headlights and put the key in my pocket. Even taking a second to unplug my phone. Had to turn the sound off since Lukas kept calling, and texts began to roll in from Sky. Nothing from the person who sent me the map.

I got out of the car, slamming the door and locking it. For a second I glanced back inside to see if the cat was still there, and it was. Only it wasn't alone now. A child sat in the backseat, only half illuminated and semi-translucent, by the pale moonlight.

It stared forward into the trees, blank, lifeless looking, and absently stroking the back of the cat. Something out of a horror movie. Eyes nothing but black voids.

Fuck, fuck, fuck. I stumbled backwards, falling on my ass and breathing hard, expecting it to follow me, or suddenly appear beside me. Only it didn't, and when I got up and could see back into the car, both the child and the cat were gone.

I trembled and sucked in air, the smell of pine, dirt, and leaves eerily familiar. In the distance there was a faint light. It didn't move, change or shake. Perhaps it was another parking lot.

Or Alex.

Or the killer.

I balled my hands up into fists, gripping my phone in one and ready to turn the flashlight on at a second's notice, then made my way into the darkness.

There was something about the dark, stretching distance of woods at night that really messed with a person's senses. Shifts in noise, owls, rustling leaves, branches, all of it echoed into the darkness in a roll that didn't seem to really provide direction. I did my best to not trample through the brush like I was marching to my death. I also didn't text the unknown person back to let them know I had arrived. No need to give them a chance to randomly shoot me or something before I even got close. Was Alex here somewhere?

I tried his phone again, a text, and then calling, hoping I'd hear the ring. Only there was nothing. Just the wind and a vaguely increasing sense of doom. It took a few minutes and a half dozen meters of distance to realize it wasn't anxiety projecting that feeling in my gut, the heaviness was back. Warning bells inside my head screamed I wasn't alone, something was watching me.

Twice I glanced back and thought I'd seen the child again, only to freeze, double check, and find nothing there.

"I'm going insane," I whispered mostly to myself. "Going, ha, already there." Coming here, following the directions of some unknown who might be a murderer, that was insanity. I should have stayed at the hotel. Waited for Manning or some other cops to arrive. Lukas would have gotten them moving, even if they'd have brushed me off. I tried to convince myself that doing this meant I wasn't a coward. But that was a lie. I was really good at running away. It's why my relationships didn't last, and I never lived in one place for long, hard to run away with commitments.

A branch cracked somewhere nearby, making me pause and search the darkness. At least my eyes were mostly adjusted to the low light. However, it meant that wind moving brush made everything look like shadows. After a minute or so of nothing else, I began forward again. That distant light still not moving.

Several horrible thoughts flickered through my overactive brain. What if Alex was already dead? What if that light up ahead was just his body laid out for me to see? What if Freya had taken him, slaughtered him, and planned to do the same to me? Even if I escaped, I'd never trust again. It sounded like a long and lonely life to live. I had to pause, focus on my breathing for another minute or two, before pushing myself forward.

Not far from the light, perhaps a couple dozen meters, my skin began to prickle like ants crawled across it, fire trailing across my skin in a thousand needle pricks. Alex would have seen it, whatever it was. All I got were a million tiny cuts that made me feel like I should have been oozing blood. I stared out into the dark edges of the woods and the distant trees, almost demanding to see something, anything that would explain how I felt. Even face-to-face with that monstrous nightmare Alex had called Death would have been a more welcome sight than the vast stretch of nothing.

Not close enough to reveal the light, or anything ominous like wavering in the darkness. Too hard to see it anyway. There was no movement, no shadows, no people. I was alone. Always so fucking alone. I'd dared to hope that with Alex I wouldn't be. I glanced back and thought I caught a glimpse of the child again. Fuck. Was it playing with me? Leading me on this chase? Why?

If it had Alex, what did it need of me? Perhaps just to show me what it did with him? I didn't want to see him used as some sort of puppet. Could it control more than one person at a time?

I'd been a puppet before, led around by the strings of other people's expectations. First by my father, who still tried to pull strings to this day, and then by Tim, now by some unknown member of the group or even a paranormal monster. What the fuck did they all want from me and why couldn't they do it themselves?

In that moment the rage welled up again, so long had I shoved it down, that it seemed to bubble out of me like lava from a volcano explosion. I spun around, cursing the darkness and the anvil of shadows covering the long stretch of woods. The one light, a good twenty or thirty meters away, did nothing to illuminate all the spaces between the trees.

"What the fuck do you want from me?" I growled into the darkness. "You bring him back. He's mine. You already had him, used him up. I haven't even finished fixing that, you worthless monster! You want to control someone so bad, take me! Give him back and take me. I'm the useless one, buried in my fucking past full of mistakes and disgrace to my family. I'm the one walking around like I'm already dead and letting everyone pull my strings. Should be easy right? Just do it!"

Alex had been the hero. Fighting and surviving battles for a country that abandoned him when he'd survived. He took care of Lukas and me, and gave everyone an edge of humor and joy that seemed impossible to sustain these days, even when he struggled himself. I remembered him dancing around the cabin, or wrapping his arms around me to deliver kisses, or his tiny smiles during his focused concentration while he sewed. The world had so few left of the pure in heart like Alex was. This monster, cold, heartless demon, whatever the fuck it was, couldn't have him.

A whoosh of wind staggered me back a few feet and everything dropped into silence. No noise from the woods, the wind, or even my heartbeat, which had been slamming through my ears only moments before, but a vacuum of sound. I blinked and there it was, standing in front of me.

A black-eyed child.

Not the shadowed edges of something like I thought I'd seen in the video, or even a vague outline like that night we'd found Joe in the road. This was solid, almost glowing in the darkness, yet monochrome. I was sure if I reached out, I could have touched it and it would have felt solid. I couldn't tell if it was a boy or a girl, only that it was a mix of grays except for the eyes, which were pools of gaping darkness. If the form of a child was supposed to make it feel less threatening, it failed miserably.

It stood only a meter or so away, expression bland, while my skin burned, crawled with that nasty sensation of bugs, and dripped with sweat like I was bleeding. And maybe I was. Bleeding from all my pores sounded like a gruesome way to die, but maybe it would be fast. Faster than dying of loneliness.

I swayed before the child, barely able to hold my feet, body trembling, hand clutching my phone to my chest, though I couldn't feel it in my grip, just the pressure of my hand closing down hard, an ache of muscle. My lungs wouldn't move more than a tiny fraction, leaving my air supply low, and vision swirling.

The child stood in absolute stillness like a statue, not looking at me, but into the distance where the single light remained. The wind didn't rustle their hair and they took no breath that I could tell. All I could focus on was the dark pools of their eyes.

Alex wondered about these things, wanted to give them definition, as though putting them in a labeled box would help ease the terror of them. I had a box for them too, a large one that didn't erase the fear. Yokai. Demons. Not of this world, but wandering among us.

Every instinct I had told me to run, only I wouldn't, not this time. For Alex I would stay, let it do what it would, as long as it meant giving him back a normal life. Even if it wasn't with me.

I gasped at that thought. So far gone for him and not realizing it until that moment. I'd never believed in instant love. Attraction sure, and Alex hit all those buttons, but love? I was a cynical bastard on the best of days. Yet he still made me smile. Even before coffee and when the world kept throwing shit my way. He hugged me and made the world right. It would be okay to be gone if I couldn't have him. Better that way maybe.

I flashed back to that day on the mountain trail. The noise, the silence walloping me into stillness, the waver in the road, the pain on my skin, and the darkness. Almost like the child's eyes, so deep, endless, welcoming. That day hadn't been filled with thoughts of the man I loved. No. I'd been seething with irritation and anger. Planning to recreate my life, start over, reinvent myself because I hated everything I'd become.

For the first time I reflected back and could remember in detail how I felt that day, that deep well of black reflected something inside me like a mirror. Revealing the self-loathing. Anger at my own weaknesses. And an almost suicidal level of depression. All balled up into a glowing mass of throbbing pain inside me. Shoved down, pushed aside, while I tried to move on from all of it, without really acknowledging any of it. How much work had I done, pretending to heal my trauma, only burying it instead? Going through the motions of moving on, I was a fraud.

This was why my skin broiled whenever they were near. Not some sixth sense, but an arising of self-hatred putrefying my soul. They awakened the darkness inside me, things I couldn't ever run from because they were part of me. A lifetime of failures. Reflected them back at an intensity that made me want to run screaming from myself. Worthless, pointless, useless.

I squeezed my eyes shut like that could somehow block the pain.

Had Alex seen that too? Probably. Nothing about me seemed to surprise him. And maybe he had seen all the flaws, but what had he said? That he loved me anyway?

I recalled the night in the car when we'd found Joe. How his words had cracked something inside me. Opened up some sort of sense of peace. A dream that I wasn't really alone. He had said, *when I look at you, I see Micah. Who teases me, and makes me smile, who dances with me, and is patient when I ask stupid questions about a world I wasn't part of for a long time. And who creates magical things to cast away the fear and anxiety and build a new future. I'm thrilled that you let me be a part of it. Whatever this future is you're building.*

I was more to him than a sex toy. More than a pretty thing to look at or a way to make money. He didn't expect me to follow his rules or respect him just for being older. He watched me cry, held me while I bled, and gave me back all the passion I threw his way. He seemed to like that sometimes my brain was a storm of ideas, jumping from one to another, and my silence never bothered him.

Until I rid myself of all this self-loathing, how could I be worthy of him? Was that why it kept taking him?

When I opened my eyes the world around me sparkled with new illumination like I'd taken off sunglasses to reveal the truth, not only about myself but about the entire world. Shadows lessened, and structures and shapes outlined in colored lights. Even the child pulsed with a faint orange radiance. Fire. Hadn't Alex said it was fire? The djinn of legend were beings of fire.

Energy snapped and fizzed in my free hand. I looked down to find a ball, a glowing hunk of what appeared to be steaming shit. It weighed a ton, and was hard to hold up, yet looked like nothing at first, until the colors became shapes of memories, and swirling feelings, all those unwanted terrors, self-hatred, and loneliness. All gripped in my fist like I was unwilling to let it go. Why would I hold onto something so awful? What was it gaining me, other than weighing me down? I stared at it wondering why my instinct was to keep it. And that's what my gut said, keep it, we'd worked hard for it, and it was ours. But what was the point? Letting it weigh me down wasn't going to bring Alex back to me.

If I wanted to move forward, I'd have to either let it go or learn to work past the weight of it. If I let it go, would it release me? Could I finally move forward? Or would it always be an anchor keeping me in place?

Wasted energy, I thought, staring at that glowing pile of shit. All of it was a waste of energy, life, power, and love. This constant fear that had ensnared me for the last two years, only finally easing when Alex came into my life and brought his sunshine. What he'd broken in me was the cycle of self-loathing. Chiseled away pieces of a wall to keep out pain, and covered me in warmth.

I flipped my wrist and dumped the ball, letting go of all that hate, anger, and bitterness. It dropped away, like a lead weight shoved free from my shoulders.

The orb hit the ground and blasted outward in a booming circle of radiant color. When it touched the child, they shivered, colors flowing over them briefly as though it were absorbing the energy. Then it lifted its head to stare at me, expression changing to one of interest.

I stared back, unmoved by the dark eyes of swirling terror. Yokai. Demon. Black-eyed child. Djinn. Ghost. Normally I never called them, knew better than to make demands. Locked in my own sorrow they had ignored me, found me uninteresting, despite knowing I was sensitive to their presence.

Now they found me tasty. My emotion, power, life, whatever. That was what had drawn it to Alex, wasn't it? People gravitated to him because he was a source of light in the darkness. He was a beacon of warmth; I merely reflected his glow.

I sucked in air, willed my heart to stop racing, and swallowed back the fear, waiting for the child to respond, do something, other than stare at me with that unnerving gaze. This wasn't death. Not anything like that writhing mass of souls I'd seen on the road that day. Would they give me Alex back? Perhaps an exchange, my energy for his. Mine might not be as bright as his, but I was willing, so long as he could be free.

They seemed to look us over, but shook their head.

Marked. I heard the word, a breathy whisper echoing through the silence, but the child's lips didn't move. The only sound, like it was in my head instead of a real spoken word.

Who was marked? Alex? Me?

The child's hand breezed over my wrist, not touching, more a wave, and agony erupted from my skin. I screamed, couldn't help it, felt like it was burning me to the core. A pulsing energy scorched over my arm, an imprint of blues and greens, and seared flesh swirling like an elaborate tattoo on my wrist. The ball of self-loathing seemed to reappear in my grasp as though I'd never let it go, weight slamming back down on me.

I should have known it wouldn't be that easy to release the baggage of the past.

The etching curled up my arm, and I could feel it racing over my shoulder and across my chest, tracing line after line until every inch of me throbbed in agony like it was being cut into my skin. The pain insanely intense and brutal, yet not unfamiliar.

As the glow faded, leaving the mark slowly vanishing beneath my skin, I realized it couldn't be a new infliction. A tug on my memory echoed back to that walk in the park, the silence, the pain, and darkness. A buried memory of torment, and the first arrival of that horrific touch, a mark. Claiming me. For what?

Marked. They said again. *Not ours.*

What the fuck did that mean? Something else had marked me? So we couldn't do an exchange? My life for Alex's? I glared at the vanishing glow on my skin, lines going from thick nasty burns, to ink lines, to nothing. Felt the weight of it through my entire body. Instead of trying to release the ball of trauma that clung to me, I crushed it beneath my fist and let another emotion rise. A whipping fire of anger, burning away the sadness and loneliness, leaving only room for determination. Rage poured over me. Not buried or shoved aside this time, but the living fire-breathing dragon of a lifetime waiting to be set free.

Alex liked dragons. He'd like this fire too, right? He'd be okay if I wasn't meek and obedient? If I wasn't always the guy to diffuse the conflict and tell everyone it was okay? He'd still love me when the last of the ice melted from my soul, right?

The world flickered for a moment, starlight and moonlight flashing out for a few seconds around me. Darkness overtaking me. A heat settled in my gut, while pain throbbed over my skin, a reminder of the mark that might have faded but still bound my soul. It wanted control, I realized. The way the mark snaked through me, like the fire, fueling negative emotion, seemed self-sustaining, until it met with the cooling force of my affection for Alex. From that came a trickle of other emotions, love for Sky, dreams for Lukas, and even distantly the warmth of my parents, all bits of sand falling onto the fire, squelching the worst of the blaze.

Marked.

I thought about that for a moment while I stood in the war of emotions. Something had been feeding on me for the past two years. Slowly devouring my positive energy, keeping me stagnant in pain, afraid, and lost in the dark. That was why the child couldn't use me. There wasn't enough of me left to offer it anything.

Alex had been returned to us in shambles, unwell, and used up, on the verge of death. In some ways, their use of him had been kinder, faster. They could have killed him, left him in a ditch somewhere. Instead they had given him back to us to restore. My own demons, they were killing me slowly. Perhaps that was why others who had vanished like I had, had all been found dead. Why it decided to let me live only made sense when I realized how much it still had control. And that was terrifying.

Marked. The child agreed and nodded, seeming to agree with my thoughts. Did that mean Alex was marked too? He had a faint scarring on his palm that he hadn't had before all this madness had happened to us. Perhaps his mark was different than mine.

I thought about why they would have returned him, and it was really the same reason I'd survived. We would be useful. They could feed on us. Find us with ease, and take another joyride. Did that mean I'd been used like Alex had been? Was there a way to remove the marks? Or did it only end when we were dead?

The child provided no answer, merely took a step back.

Sound and definition returned all at once, my heart pulsing hard, the wind blowing, leaves shuffling. Even the sensation on my skin faded. They weren't taking me today, and I realized they didn't have Alex either. If they had, they wouldn't be here right now. Did that mean Alex was out in the woods somewhere? That didn't make sense either because the child would be there, right? Watching him? Hadn't he said they watched us?

I glanced up at the trees and wondered if it was more than just Alex's demon who watched us. Was mine out there too? Was it different? Like another type of creature, or simply another version of a black-eyed child?

I stared in the direction of the light again. These shadows didn't need artificial lights and text messages. They took me in broad daylight and Alex while he was on camera. A little forest gained them nothing.

I balled my hands into fists, angry again, irritated by the lack of answers and clarity. Alex had said he didn't think this mess was paranormal. He'd also begged me not to go into the woods alone. Had he seen all this coming? Who was messing with me? Not a what, but a who this time.

Odd how the fear faded that fast. Sure I'd shoved it down beneath my anger, but the weight of doom, that felt like something outside of me. An impression imposed by something else. More of an eerie 'I'm here,' presence to remind me I'd never truly be alone. The child stayed where it was, staring back into the distance again. Uninterested in me.

Watching. Only it wasn't looking toward the light anymore, but back toward the lot and my car. Was someone there? I could still sort of see the shape of the car, but no lights anywhere in that direction. Whatever was out here with me, dragging me into the night, wasn't the paranormal monsters that had marked Alex and me. Those monsters didn't need elaborate ploys and abandoned woods. They could find us anywhere. Which meant whatever was out here was human, and really pissing me off.

CHAPTER 29

I turned away from the child and stalked through the woods, anger raging, feeling the weight of it intensify with every step. Heart pounding even as the light began to illuminate a small area of woods. I don't know what I'd expected, other than maybe some horror of Alex's shattered body laid out with elaborate lighting. However, all that sat in a small clearing was a flashlight/lantern and a box.

Of course the box conjured up a million scenarios and nightmares, but I examined the surrounding area with my gaze, clinging to a tree, hoping that if someone wanted to gun me down, they'd have to work for it. There was no sign of anyone. Simply the light and the box.

I approached it slowly, waiting for something to jump out at me. Nothing moved. I stood a few feet away, waiting, and watching the trees.

"Alex," I called. My voice echoed a little, but no other sound filtered back to me. I picked up a stick, about two inches thick and a yard long, and nudged the box. For all I knew it could be a bomb or Alex's severed head. The box wasn't locked, and appeared to be a cheap sort of thing that could be bought at any craft store and then decorated. I'd done similar in my life for costume props. Nothing popped out of the box and it didn't explode.

When I opened the lid, a scream shattered the silence. Not mine, but human and horrific, like someone was dying. I dropped to my knees, searching the area for the sound, straining for the direction, though it felt all around me. It wasn't *my* scream, or anything like the sounds I normally heard at night. More like something out of a horror movie. It didn't sound like Alex either, not masculine enough to be his voice, even in pain.

Was someone else out there hurt? Had they taken another member of the group? Technically everyone had plans that would take them away from our get togethers. I might have been the first, creating the shop and a new life, but Jonah had the show, Nicole and Julie their own shop, Chad and MaryAnn, his non-profit, and Freya expansion into traveling. I wondered vaguely about Melissa. If she'd done all this to get rid of Byrony who always put her down, or maybe because she hadn't felt like she was part of the group. Or was it someone we didn't even know?

The scream echoed again, ahead and to the right, up higher than where I knelt. I closed my eyes and let my hearing trace the sound, the way it bounced and traveled. I'd spent a couple years studying sounds in the dark. There was someone out there. Messing with me? Trying to make me afraid with screams in the night? Hadn't Detective Manning said something about Joe shooting Byrony by accident because something scared him? Were they trying to scare me?

I thought back to who I might have told in the group that I heard things since my return. Had I confided that in anyone? Freya, maybe. But if I had, it had been years ago. If Alex hadn't heard the noise himself, I'd have never told him. He didn't need the torment any more than I did, and I really hated when people looked at me like I was crazy.

Another sound rose up from the darkness. Some sort of mess of birds or apes. If I hadn't been hearing something stalking me at night for the past two years, it might have frightened me. But this noise was too faded, and distant, almost like a recording. The breeze felt almost icy against my bare arms, a fast cooling of the sweat of fear. I'd survived staring into the face of more than one monster. This seemed more like a show, and not a good one.

Someone was fucking with me. And it wasn't cool.

I snarled at the darkness and got to my feet, kicking the box over. The lid popped off and out rolled a handgun. I didn't know anything about guns. Had never held one in my life. Never even cosplayed with one. This one looked small and relatively new. Alex probably would have known the make, model, and caliber of bullets.

I didn't even try to pick it up. A gun was of no use to me. Even if there was some sort of monster in the dark, I was not going to run after it, shooting. I was more likely to shoot myself by accident with a gun, than any attacker. Again I was reminded of Joe and Byrony, frightened by something. The 'Rake' even, if I went by what they'd been searching for. I was pretty sure whatever was out here wasn't a mythical creature created on reddit.

A note had been taped to the lid of the box. It read: *Save yourself.*

From what?

The scream echoed again, closer this time, followed by a replay of those odd recorded noises. Did that normally fool people? Maybe those who'd never heard what I had.

For a moment I wondered if Alex actually heard the same thing I did. It wasn't like I could record it and play it for him. Had tried that a dozen times or so to prove to the police I wasn't nuts. But whatever was making a fuss out in the woods right now was neither mythical beast, or my demon.

I glared into the darkness and hit the light on my phone, holding it up to illuminate as much as it could reach. New phones had flashlights with intense power. When we'd gone in before we left home to get Alex's new phone, I had upgraded mine as well. The one-click on the phone face blasted a flood stream of brightness into the woods. The glow stretched several meters.

It was then I saw a glimpse of movement. Something slim and

willowy creeping through the brush. For a few seconds it seemed to turn my way and reflect the light.

My brain processed what I was seeing with a quick warning of apprehension as it reminded me of something similar to the 'Rake' pictures posted online. Thin with long wispy arms and an almost alien-like head, and iridescent eyes. It had an odd half-hop of a gait, paused as though it were waiting for me, and then turned, scampering off into the brush. If I hadn't known what might be hiding out there, I might have actually been scared. It looked pretty legit.

Before the most recent events, even after I'd been taken and returned, I'd never been a big believer in random paranormal monsters. Knowing the little about the Rake's history, I had to say it was one of the least believable stories I'd ever heard. I'd probably get on board the Bigfoot train before the Rake. And there was no skunk smell, that thing had looked hairless, not like a giant man-ape. In fact, the reflective sheen of the creature's 'skin' almost appeared like some of the more luminescent fabrics I'd seen at the convention these past few days rather than anything possible in nature. Animals, in general, had evolved to hunt and hide. Reflective skin would make it really hard to hide, especially for something supposedly as elusive as the Rake.

I narrowed my eyes in the distance, listening for the sounds again. Someone in costume. Did they have Alex? They better hope he was okay because if they had hurt him, I'd teach them what the darkness was. They had no idea what followed me, that black-eyed child, and the monsters that tormented my home at night, maybe even that death collage of souls I'd run into on the road. Were they all tied to me? Maybe. I'd be happy to share it with whoever was playing games with me right now.

I gripped my stick and raced into the woods after it, phone held up more like a lightsaber, spearing the darkness with a brutal intensity. Lukas said I wasn't a hero, even if I cosplayed one sometimes. But I was done being the coward, the puppet, and the sidekick.

Someone was messing with me, possibly hurt Alex, and I was about to break someone's kneecaps.

The scream, half strangled, came from my left, and I shifted my run in that direction. Man, I needed more exercise than sewing, city tours, and vigorous sex with Alex. My legs felt like jelly, or maybe that was still because I'd had vigorous sex with Alex. I certainly wouldn't be putting the kibosh on that any time soon. As long as I got him back. My lungs worked harder than I could recall in a long time, but I kept up, the tip of my light still illuminating the creature's back.

My heart pounded hard. It was running now. All out. Twisting and turning like it had been in these woods a hundred times. And maybe it had. I wondered if this was another spot filled with the bodies of missing cosplayers. Was it some sort of game, scare them to death? Or into an accident that left them dying? Or did they straight up kill them when they ran out of energy or something? What was the point of giving me a gun? Were they suicidal? If I knew how to use it and had been willing, I'd have shot them by now. Though I suspected the stuff they showed on TV about people hitting what they aimed at while both parties were running, was probably a stretch of the truth.

The uneven terrain gave me nightmare ideas that I was half tripping over unmarked graves, even while I was gaining on it. It didn't run like an animal anymore. It ran like a person, arms and legs flailing, while I was catching up. I might have been short and on the small side for a guy, but I had speed.

Had to lower my phone to pump my arms a little harder. I stretched out, using the stick for added length to jab at the creature, hitting it once in the shoulder. It stumbled a little, but not enough to let me catch it, and then again in the lower back. This time I hit it hard enough to send it into a spin.

It clipped a tree and tumbled down a small hill with a very human "Oof!"

I should have thought a little more about racing after it, as I leapt down the small hill, expecting more ground, but encountering more of a narrow ravine, with a bigger drop than planned, and a thin strip of water. Only my trusty stick kept me from completely breaking an ankle or falling on my face into the stream. The creature rolled and landed half in the water, and I was on it, stick to its neck, realizing I'd dropped my phone when I hit it.

Fuck!

The small bits of moonlight filtering through the heavy foliage, revealed little. All I knew, from touching it, holding it down, even as it kicked and struggled with me, by the shape of their body, was that it was female. My heart flipped over. Freya?

My gut still wanted so badly for it not to be her.

I couldn't reach for the hood and partial mask, not while holding her down. Instead I shifted my weight, flipping her, sitting on top of her, and pressing her face into the water until she sputtered and shrieked at me, trying to buck me off. That voice I recognized, and it stunned me long enough that she succeeded in shoving me to the side and rolling away. Water dripping from her face, washing away some make-up, mask askew, but leaving the reflective contacts. Her body-suit cleverly made with dark edges to make her appear thinner, emaciated, and pale.

"Great costume, MaryAnn," I said. "But I'm kind of lost on the entire point of all this," I told her. "Is this some sort of game? I have to say I'm not amused."

"This isn't a game," she snarled.

"Does Freya know what you're doing?"

She shrieked. "You have no right to even say her name!" She lunged at me, not hitting me but grabbing the stick and shoving me backward hard. I landed half in the small stream with a splash, but managed to catch the stick. She dragged me back out without trying as she tried to take it back. "It was supposed to be that worthless boyfriend of yours! Not you."

I yanked at the stick, trying to wrestle it from her as she didn't appear to be otherwise armed, but she'd given me a gun. "Why Alex?" I demanded.

"He took you from the group. You hurt Freya because of him. She was so excited to be a part of your return." She pulled at the stick hard. I let it go at the last second and she fell backward from her own momentum. I leapt for the stick, sweeping it up and jumping away.

"What's the point of all this? Kill Alex and then what? I come back to the group? Didn't seem to work for any of the others you killed," I said, keeping a good distance and trying to find my phone. It must have landed face down since that stupid flashlight thing was hard to turn off. Or it had landed in the water.

"I haven't killed anyone," MaryAnn defended. "They all saved themselves from their worst fears."

"How's that?" I jabbed the stick at her when she started to get up. She crawled backward a little, struggling in the mud for traction.

"Freya told me all about your boyfriend's issues. How he was in a mental ward before. Would have been easy for him to just end it."

My gut turned cold. "You wanted him to kill himself?"

"It was the easiest way to get rid of him. You don't need him. You had us."

Wow, crazyville. "What about Chad? I thought you had a thing with him?"

She laughed and it sounded more than a little unhinged as she got to her feet. I held out the stick to keep her away. I wondered if my phone was up on the top of the ravine? It was probably only two meters or so of a steep incline. "Chad's sweet. Would do anything I asked him to. Except apparently bring Alex to me."

Was that where Alex was? Chad had him? "Everyone is leaving the group, why are you focused on me and Alex?"

"You hurt Freya. Byrony hurt Freya. Everyone treats her like crap when she does so much for us. Everyone needs to be punished."

"And the other missing cosplayers? Did they hurt Freya too?"

"Yes," MaryAnn hissed. "She gave you everything, made you a star, and you abandoned her. Now she's having a hard time keeping followers and product deals because of her age, and you could have helped!" She bent slowly, keeping back, but pulled a hunting knife from her boot. "She even made you that costume for your debut. And you rejected it."

"Does Freya know you're doing all this? That you punish people who hurt her?" I backed away. There was no way I was getting up that ravine without her stabbing me in the back, and the narrow bank of the stream didn't give me much space to move. I suspected we'd landed more in some sort of bog runoff to the nearby lake. It would be a good place to hide a body. The only way out was past her. And I wasn't exactly trained in combat.

"She doesn't need to know."

"But Freya's going off to travel too. Leaving you behind, what will you do?"

"I've got her tied up with contracts to the same fabric line I'm in. They wanted her anyway. We'll be together all the time."

So she'd been manipulating us all. "The gun was stupid," I told her. "I don't know how to use one." She came closer, and I jabbed the stick at her, making her step back. She limped a little, and I wondered if she'd hurt her leg in the fall. That could be to my advantage.

"Didn't seem to matter to anyone before."

"Americans are obsessed with guns. But I'm not American," I reminded her.

"You going to try some kung fu shit on me?" She taunted.

"That's a racist stereotype. I'm Japanese and Irish. And even if I were Chinese, not many of them know kung fu."

"Whatever." She stalked at me, grabbing for the stick, knife held up like one of those slasher movies. It wasn't really a good way to hold a knife in general, not enough force behind it. So when she grabbed the stick and tried to slash me, I shoved the stick hard, and kicked out toward that limping leg. Must have landed enough of a blow to hurt because she screamed and collapsed inward a little, as if to protect her core.

I used those few seconds to roll around her, drop the stick and run. The narrow stretch of ravine lasted a couple more meters before spitting me out on the side of the lake. I could see the swimming area in the distance, with the lifeguard tower and parking lot. Of course, the fact that they were empty and in the wrong direction didn't exactly help. Without my phone I would be forced to run forever, and my energy wouldn't hold out that long. The area surrounding Sam Houston National Park wasn't butted up against housing, or even small businesses like gas stations. In the middle of the night, there was no one. I thought hard about what options I might have.

If I followed the road out from the beach would it lead to a main road? Somewhere I could flag down help?

MaryAnn came after me, no longer as quiet as she'd been the first time. I'd obviously done some damage. The sound of her barreling through the trees let me know that she was moving slower and breathing hard. I actually curved around the edge of trees, racing for the beach as though it were humanity. Running on sand is not as glamorous as they make it look in movies. It was awkward, a stumbling gait as the sand gave beneath my feet. I had almost made it to the parking lot when something dark appeared, looming before me.

I slid to a stop, almost landing on my knees as my balance vanished. My gut felt like it had taken a sucker punch, and I gasped for air.

Death. It writhed before me. The same broken/mixed face monster I'd met on the road that day. Huge. Like it was more than three meters tall and two wide, the darkness of stitched together faces whipped around it like tentacles covered in screaming mouths. I fell backward, too close to really move around it and hearing MaryAnn still coming. I glanced back to see her only four or five meters away. Too close. Did she see it? She didn't stop.

She came at me with the knife again, face contorted in rage. I scrambled around, crab walking backward, away from the darkness, but not fast enough to really get away from her. She hit the black mass full force, smashing into it, and for a moment I thought it would actually slow her down. Instead it seemed to burst apart like smoke, covering her in darkness for a few seconds before she leapt free of it, flying at me with the knife.

"Freeze!" Someone shouted. Lights suddenly blazed, and I couldn't see anything. Not the darkness or MaryAnn.

MaryAnn screamed in rage. I blinked away tears at the brightness, barely able to see her standing illuminated with her back to the lake, the dark monster Alex thought was Death, dancing behind her like some mythical Cthulhu of nightmares.

The next few seconds transpired so fast it all happened in the time it took me to suck in a breath. She raised the knife to lunge at me, but someone smashed into her from the left, at the same time I heard the movement of cloth and click of weapons.

Alex was suddenly there, wrestling the knife out of her hand kicking it away. I worried for a moment about the police, as it had been their light that brightened the beach to near daytime levels. Would they shoot him? Except Manning was there, rolling MaryAnn over and handcuffing her. Reading her her rights. Another officer picked up the knife with gloved hands and put it in a bag.

I reached for Alex, wondered for a few seconds if he was a figment of my imagination. Maybe I had died. Fuck.

He rolled over, keeping his distance from the Death thing, which still stood there, and came to me. His hands were all over me. "Are you okay? Fuck. I thought we were going to be too late. Did she hurt you?"

That last bit of ice on my heart shattered and I grabbed him hard, wrapping my arms around him, like somehow I could meld with him and keep him there forever. "Where the fuck were you?" I demanded.

"Long story," Alex grumbled. "I'll explain in a bit." He eyed the Death thing warily. "Once we're off this beach."

MaryAnn fought the police, using her weight to try to throw them off balance, while they treated her with kid gloves. She got away for a second, and my breath caught, fearing she'd come at me even though she was unarmed, but she ran toward the water instead. She had reached the water and was wading in before the police dragged her back.

Alex wrapped his arms around me and breathed for a minute

while they dragged her toward the distant parking lot full of cars. One of the cops appeared near us and held out a phone. My phone.

"Thank you!" I told him, reaching for it. "I dropped it."

"We were tracking you," Alex said. "For once my brother's paranoia pays off." He helped me to my feet and guided me slowly away from the beach. The Death thing still waited there, though it was fading. And it was odd how the police who moved around seemed to naturally avoid it like they could see it, but I was pretty sure none of them could.

"You're freezing," Alex said, rubbing my arms.

"I'll have one of my guys give you both a ride back to your car," Manning said. "And if you're willing, Mr. Richards. I'd like a statement from you."

"Okay," I said. "As long as Alex can stay with me." I gripped Alex's shirt. He didn't look hurt at all. "I'm not letting you out of my sight again."

"Same," Alex said, putting a possessive arm around my waist. He looked at Manning. "A ride to the car would be great."

CHAPTER 30

I had to drive us to the police station because we were being followed by cops and Alex didn't have a license. The adrenaline began to fade as soon as I got in the rental car. We sat with silence between us for a while, radio on low, playing whatever Top 40 station had been programmed in. Alex kept a hand on my thigh while I gripped the steering wheel with both hands, a billion things in my head.

"I saw it," I said after we got on the highway, cops in front and behind us now. I knew MaryAnn was in one of those, but didn't care which as long as we were back among civilization. "The black-eyed child. The thing that took you."

Alex put his hand on my shoulder. "I'm sorry."

"They've marked us," I confessed. "The child said I was marked by something else, so it couldn't take me. I felt the mark. Remembered some things."

"Yeah?"

"Not like where I went or anything. Just feeling the mark." I blew out a long breath. "Not something either of us can see without some sort of help." Sometimes when I moved a certain way, I could still feel the lines, though looking at my body several times, pushing up sleeves or even my shirt, I saw nothing. It almost felt as though it had marked my soul rather than my body. Which of course led to a big internal debate about the existential presence of souls. "It's a way for them to find us, and use us again."

"We suspected that already," Alex said.

"It's been two years," I trailed off... since it had taken me. Why wait so long? Just to let me live and fuel itself off my negative emotions? "I need to learn to not focus on the negative. I think that gives it strength."

"Okay," Alex agreed. "How can I help?"

He always had such a simple viewpoint on things. There was a problem, let's fix it. "Stay with me? I know I sound like a little kid being all needy, but right now you're my sunshine."

Alex laughed. "You are my sunshine, my only sunshine." He began to sing. "But seriously though. We're in this together. You help me get through the day. Sometimes with distraction, sometimes with snuggles." He paused for a minute, apparently thinking back to our early evening because he added, "I really like our snuggles."

"Lots more where that came from," I promised.

"Sure. But everything else is okay too. And when I annoy you because you need alone time, just tell me."

I nodded.

"So tell me about MaryAnn? What happened?"

"Shouldn't I wait to tell the police?"

"I'm not sure it will matter. They have Chad's statement."

"Wow, right. Oh, and you went with Chad?" Chad was a big guy, but I didn't think he could have just overpowered Alex and taken him by force. Not with Alex being ex-Army and Chad nothing more than a desk jockey.

Alex sighed. "Yeah, stupid right? He said he could get your costume back, and I knew you worked hard on it. But then he was just driving around for a long time, seemed pretty upset. I started prodding him with questions."

"Has he been helping MaryAnn this whole time?"

"Doesn't sound like it. She's only taken to clinging to him for the past few months. He says they really don't have a relationship at all, other than friendship and the non-profit. Sounds like she convinced him that me and her were working on a surprise for you? Which is why he had to convince me to go with him, and drop me off in a secret place."

"That's really shady."

"Yeah," Alex agreed. "And stupid of me to go with him. He could have been armed."

"Was he?"

"No."

"MaryAnn left a gun for me."

"Have you ever used one?"

"No. It was stupid and useless. I thought, what the fuck am I going to do with a gun? So I picked up a stick instead. Swung my fair share of sticks in my life. Even cosplayed as a ton of samurai. Figured I could swing a stick like a bat better than fire a weapon I'm more likely to hurt myself with." I felt heat fill my face as I thought back with a bit of embarrassment to the rage that had fueled me for a while. "I got pretty mad. Sort of ran at her... didn't know at the time it was her, only that someone was messing with me... with the stick like it was a bat. Looking back now, it was a pretty crazy thing to do."

"She could have had a gun."

"Odd that she didn't, right?" I said, thinking back on it. "It sounded like she trusted her victims to 'save themselves.' Which meant suicide, I think." At least that is what she had planned for Alex. "I guess Chad made her mad by not bringing you. She had to change her plans last minute."

"He started off headed in that direction, but I got him talking."

"You were gone a long time. I sort of panicked."

"Sorry." Alex squeezed my forearm. "We were in his SUV a long time. He drove around forever, while I talked to him, worked out was happening, and finally convinced him to take me to the police station where I'd find Manning."

"Why didn't you answer your phone?"

"He asked to borrow it. Claimed his was dead and he needed the GPS. I could have tried to wrestle it back once I realized what was going on, but we were on the highway. I didn't think forcing us to crash was a good idea."

"No," I agreed, following one of the cars off the highway. "I called Lukas. He freaked out of course. I got the messages from MaryAnn. Or at least I guess they are from her. Followed them to the park."

"She must have decided since she couldn't have me, she'd try something on you."

"I think Freya told her about the night noises I hear. I know I didn't tell MaryAnn. But she attempted to scare me with screams and animal noises. None of it like what I normally hear. It's what made me so mad." I thought about that again for a while. Wondering what Alex heard. "Maybe we all hear it differently."

"Maybe," Alex said. "Doesn't matter when it does what it's supposed to, right? Scare us? Disrupt sleep which leads to more anxiety?"

"I guess?" I wasn't ready to tell him yet that I suspected the marks that linked us to whatever paranormal, was feeding on us, especially the negative emotion part of us. Fear, anger, sadness, all those things fueled them. Of that I was certain.

I turned into the lot of the police station and let them direct me to a spot. We waited in the car as they pulled MaryAnn from the back of the squad. Her face was bloody. She hadn't been that way when they put her in the car. Her expression was blank as they dragged her toward the door. She moved more like a rag doll than a person, the spirit seeming to have vanished from her. From being caught? Or something else.

She turned back our way for a brief second and I gasped. A dark shadow lingered over her shoulder, only a small hint of what we'd seen, but clear enough to know it was Death, that horrible monster, who stood beside her. Her eyes were blank, even with blood trailing down her face.

We got out of the car as Manning waved to us.

"Is she okay?" Alex asked him. "She didn't look hurt like that on the beach."

"She was banging her head against the window of the car. We've already called for an eval." Manning held the door for us and we followed him into the station.

"Eval?" I whispered to Alex as we were led back to a room.

"Psych," Alex said. I remembered she'd run through Death, the shadow version of it, and jumped into the water. Why?

"They could have shot her."

"She's a woman," Alex pointed out. "Her hood had come down showing her hair, and her clothes were wet. We knew because Chad had confirmed it was MaryAnn, but seeing makes a difference. If it had been you and you'd gone running, they would have shot you, despite them knowing you weren't the suspect. Bad training. Most cops just don't see women as the same threat." He was silent for a minute and I could tell he was working through something so I didn't push. Finally he added, "I think her going through that Death thing...I think it made her suicidal. Her trip into the water, and fighting police, those were attempts. Psych evaluations don't normally happen this fast. Not unless there's something else going on."

Now I had a lot to think about. Was that why Joe had been so broken? Had the Death thing killed or taken MaryAnn's soul when she ran through it? Or did it just make her want to end it so it could take her? What would have happened if I'd hit it? For the first time since this mess started, I was happy I had actually seen it, even if it left a terrifying memory. At least I hadn't touched it. Maybe I'd be lucky and never see it again.

Chad sat in a chair near a desk. He glanced up at us and flinched. His eyes were swollen from crying and he looked tired. "I'm so sorry," he said. I wasn't sure who he was talking to directly, but he looked at Alex and me. "I'm so sorry."

We passed him and took seats in a small office. It wasn't the sort of thing I'd expected from an interrogation room, since it had a real desk and pictures on the wall. Manning's office, I realized after a moment. Not an interrogation room.

"I'll be right back with you guys," he said as he waved us to the chairs.

I took a seat and set my head on Alex's shoulder beside me, breathing deep as exhaustion rolled over me. I really hoped this whole mess was done.

"You still want to go home after this?" Alex asked.

"Yes, please."

He kissed my forehead, and I was grateful to not be alone.

B y the time we got back to the hotel and into bed, it was after four in the morning, and I crashed like I couldn't recall ever having done before. Alex woke me some time later with kisses and coffee. "Sorry, it's just Starbucks," he said. "They don't have our normal stuff."

I blinked at him and sat up to take the coffee, noticing the clock said it was after noon. "Fuck," I said into the cup, which was hot, but not nearly as good as the coffee I made at home. Awake no more than five minutes, and my brain was already working at warp speed.

"You are beginning to sound like me. Cursing all the time. What would your mom say?"

I snorted. "My mom curses like a sailor, much to my father's dismay. Did I miss anything this morning?" How long had he been up?

"Talked to Freya for a bit."

"Oh." A thousand things rolled through my head, ever the flowing tide. I sighed. "Did Freya know?"

"Doesn't sound like it. Though I've only heard from her via text. She said she's at the police station answering questions. Said MaryAnn has been here a lot to visit her, working on costumes and planning events over the past few years. She is pulling up a lot of records from the B&B and the group." Alex crawled onto the bed beside me, and I scooted over until he could wrap his arms around me and we both could lean against the headboard while I nursed my coffee.

"Let me guess, those visits corresponded with missing group members?"

"Yeah," Alex agreed. "They still aren't sure how many. Freya mentioned she put a post-up in the group about missing members, but since it's so large, it will be hard to locate who's left and who vanished. Sounds like she'll be going through the last few years of events."

"That sucks. This is all insane. Was it some kind of obsession? I still don't get it." I sucked down half the cup of coffee despite the scalding heat of it. "I need more coffee."

"Sounds like it was something like that. I'm not sure we'll ever know all the psychology. People have odd triggers. I suspect Freya will need a good therapist. Can't imagine how hard it must be to have someone so focused on you, they murder people just to try to keep you happy." Alex ran his hands through my hair. "Car is packed. We can pick up more coffee on the way home. Unless you want to stay for the rest of the convention."

"Absolutely not."

"Good."

I sighed and relaxed into him, resting my head on his shoulder. "Move in with me," I said. It was fast. Everything about our relationship was a whirlwind of events, but I needed him close. He made me want to be a better person for him, not as afraid, and willing to stand up for myself.

"I'm half living with you already, you sure you want that?"

"Yes. You're mine." Until the yokai returned and called in their marks. I'd hold tight to him until then.

He kissed the top of my head. "Okay. Finish your first cup of coffee and if you're still saying the same stuff once the caffeine is flowing through your brain, we'll make it permanent."

I gripped the collar of his shirt, looked up at him, and kissed him.

"You are mine," I said. "I'm a possessive bastard. I'm crazy about you. Love you. Sorry I'm not more vocal about it."

Alex's smile was like sunshine. "I'm okay with that. You be you. You don't need to change anything for me. Ready to go home?"

"Fuck yes."

The drive home was filled with Alex singing to the radio and hand stitching the binding to the quilt we'd almost finished. I'd been a bit surprised, but apparently he'd been watching videos while I slept. His stitches were pretty solid, and I wondered if it was something else the lady from the sewing shop had given him.

By the time we arrived back in New Orleans I couldn't wait to get home and curl up in my bed with him. Of course, as we pulled up in front of my house, Lukas's car was already there, and I groaned.

"You knew he'd be here," Alex reminded gently. "We'll make him carry shit in."

I sighed. "I just want to lay on the futon with you, or in bed, and sleep for a week." My whole body ached, from sex and the run/fight with MaryAnn. "I probably need to work out more. Fighting takes more muscles than I use while hosting tours."

"I'd rather you not be fighting for your life."

"Same," I said to him, repeating what he'd given me before, with a little cheek.

He laughed. "Boring life filled with crafts ahead, got it."

I gaped at him. "Boring? What about crafting is boring?"

He got out of the car. Lukas and Sky were headed our way down the walk from the house. "I'm not sure I like the binding thing." He'd finished the entire thing during the drive, which was impressive since it was his first time. It also looked pretty damn perfect.

"Um, binding is part of quilting," I reminded him as I got out and hit the button to open the back.

"Yeah, maybe I can just do the machine quilting part?"

I rolled my eyes at him. "Just like I do all the seam stitching and cutting? The boring parts?"

"Yes, the boring parts," he agreed.

"I thought you wanted to be part of the magic?"

"I am!" He said. Lukas arrived and wrapped Alex in a hug tight enough to make him huff out a breath. "Unf. Not so tight, Lukas. I'm fine. And I am part of the magic," he told me. "I make pretty designs on the pieces you put together." He rubbed his hands together. "Can't wait to get the new machine set up. Do you have any quilt tops that need quilting?"

I actually had an entire bin of them. At least it would keep him busy for a while.

"You guys bought a ton," Sky said as she came around the back of the car to hug me too. "Glad you're okay. Though your face is still a little purple."

"Don't run into cars," I said. "Lesson learned."

She laughed. "So um, Lukas has something to tell you guys."

I narrowed my eyes at her. "Just Lukas?"

She nodded, her eyes huge as she gathered up a few bags of fabric supplies. Lukas came around the back of the car with Alex.

"I bought a house," Lukas said. He pointed down the street. "That one." Four down from where I lived, was a giant mansion of an old NOLA style house. The French Quarter was filled with huge homes with beautiful architecture. I knew for a fact that home had been up for sale for years. Sometimes someone would come in and buy it, only to have it listed again within six months.

Alex looked at me, seeing something on my face I'd only begun to think. "It's haunted, isn't it?" he asked me.

"There are stories," I admitted.

"Everything in New Orleans is haunted," Lukas said. "Plus, I have you two weirdos to scope things out for me. Going to put my new office on the first floor. It needs a lot of remodeling, but I've got ideas."

"New office?" I asked.

"I quit the force," Lukas said. "Getting my PI license."

Both Alex and I stared at him now, a bit shocked. Sky nodded like she was more than a little stunned too. Had he not discussed it with her at all?

"You've had a few busy days," Alex said. "We weren't gone that long."

"Yeah, about that…" Lukas began.

"Fuck," Alex muttered.

"I've got some details on your disappearance. Some people they think you were around. I plan on interviewing them."

"That's why you quit? Because of me?"

"Part of it," Lukas admitted. "There is other bullshit, but it's fine. This will give me more time."

"To look into what happened to me?" Alex clarified.

"And to remodel the house, and build my business portfolio. I already own three other buildings in the quarter. The one next to Simply Crafty is up for sale. I'm hoping to grab it at a discount. Maybe expand the shop."

I blinked at him. "Make Simply Crafty bigger?" I couldn't imagine the tiny shop having more space. What would I fill it with? Costumes? More artists? The shop next door had been empty for a while, had actually been an art studio. I wondered if I could set up classes in there. Would anyone be interested? Maybe I could do a community thing, look for teachers to do different types of arts, like sewing, candle making, or even music.

"Micah's got ideas too," Alex said reaching out take more stuff out of the car. "But I don't want you looking into my disappearance."

"You don't get to say what I do and don't do," Lukas said. He unveiled the sewing machine and studied it for a minute. "Fancy machine," he muttered.

"You don't get to say what I do and don't do," Alex echoed back at him.

They glared at each other, twin daggers of daring. I sighed and looked at Sky. "At least he didn't command us that we have to live in his haunted house with him." I took an armful of stuff and headed up the path toward the house. "I like my place."

"Has he asked you to move in yet?" I asked Sky.

"Not yet," Sky said. "Though I have to say it's big enough to fit a half dozen people. Never been in a house so big." She opened the door, holding it for me, and Jet greeted me with his normal leg rub. We began making a pile of the bags near the side window. It would take a bit of time to get it all sorted and put away.

Sky reached out and hugged me tight. "I was worried. Worried you'd be gone again."

"I don't seem to have control over that. But I have no plans to go anywhere. The whole crazy person after me is not a thing I want to repeat." I squeezed her tight.

"Heard you were badass." She grinned as she let me go. "Fighting back."

"My stick skills are on par. I mean she gave me a gun, but what do I know about guns? Sticks? Fabric and thread? Hot wax even, I know all about that. You think you know someone, right?"

"You haven't been a part of that group in a while," Sky reminded me. "Been too busy with the shop to run around the world."

"Makes me wonder if it was my fault," I admitted.

Sky took my face in her hands and smiled at me. "You know it's not."

"Alex tells me all the time I'm not the center of the universe."

"The universe probably not, but his? Sure. That boy traveled five hours to hang out with you and all your nerdiness. Serial killers aside, I think that's love." She ran her fingers through my hair, playing with it a little like she was fixing it, but there was little she could do to tidy up the small ponytail I had holding it back.

"He said he loves me."

"Yeah?"

"I told him I love him too."

"How'd that feel?" She wanted to know.

"Right."

"Good."

"What about you and Lukas?"

She huffed out a long sigh and went to start pulling things from bags. "Work in progress."

"But you're not giving up, right?"

"Of course not. Do you know how fine that man is? Sure he's got a few issues, but don't they all?"

"He quit the force."

"Yeah, butted heads with his sergeant. Had a feeling it was coming."

"Over Alex?"

"Yes, and no. Sounds like he was along for an arrest and the arrest went bad. At least Lukas wasn't hurt. But whatever happened turned everything upside down. He came home really upset and told me he'd handed in his badge. I spent the rest of the day looking up PI stuff for him and feeding him Oreos."

"Oreos do make things better," I agreed.

"Ben and Jerry's is better."

"Unless you're lactose intolerant like me."

"True. But at least you guys are home safe now. The house thing was a surprise. He asked me to tour it with him. Happened so fast I didn't even get to read cards on it."

"Uh oh."

"Right?" She shook her head, stacking some of the fabrics in separate piles based on type. "It needs work. Still has some water damage from Katrina."

"Wow. Did you do a card reading since?"

"Of course. The house is haunted, but it doesn't appear to be anything dangerous."

"Mhmm." A haunted house, a new job, and far too much time to focus on Alex. I had to admit I was a little worried about Lukas.

Alex and Lukas came in, carrying the new sewing machine. They set it down near the dining room table. I'd have to unbox it and find a good desk. It was then I noticed a stack of files on the table. "What's all that?" I asked Lukas as they headed toward the door.

"Tips on where Alex was," he said.

"In the month he was gone?" The stack was at least five inches thick. No way one man could go that many places in a month.

"The past year, since he got out of the military."

Alex paused too, looking at the pile. "I told you all about that."

"Mhmm," was all Lukas said.

Alex let out a long sigh, shared a look with me and headed back to the car. I wondered if there were things Lukas had found that Alex didn't remember. Would it help clarify things for Alex? Define what he saw?

There was also a miniature house on the table. It almost looked like a replica of mine. Tiny room, painted walls, and furniture built from wood.

"That's Lukas's new hobby. I ordered it for him to try. He spent the last few days working on it," Sky said. "I figure I'll order him a few more to keep him out of trouble."

Jet hissed and I frowned, looking down at my cat who had his back up and tail puffed up. He stared at one of the chairs in my tiny dining set. There was a white cat sitting on the chair, tail flicking like it didn't have a care in the world.

"Fuck," I grumbled.

"What?" Sky asked.

Alex returned with my old sewing machines and glanced at me. "What?"

I waved at the cat in the chair. He looked that way and his cheeks turned pink. "Sorry. That's sort of my fault."

"What?"

"She seemed lonely. And easily agitated. So I invited her along."

The words slowly processed. "You invited a ghost cat to come home with us?"

"Ghost cat?" Sky's eyes went huge, looking at the table and chairs like it would bite her.

"I thought Jet could use a friend."

Jet was not happy about the idea of a friend at that moment. "A ghost cat?"

"She's less likely to be agitated by us," Alex pointed out.

"But have cat wars with Jet?" He still had his back up and stood close enough to me to touch. "Maybe you can invite her to stay with Lukas. I hear he's got a new house that might already be haunted. Sounds like a great place for a ghost cat. Cats love him."

Alex leaned close to me for a kiss. "Sure. We'll work on that. Funny how you can see the cat now? Not just a shadow."

I blinked, realizing I had been seeing a lot in the past twenty-four hours. "Well fuck. This is going to make tours interesting."

"They always are," he said. He headed over to the table and began flipping through folders. "Wonder where he got all this."

"It might have answers."

"Or more questions." He sighed, and his eyes fell on the model. "That's cool."

"Apparently your brother's new hobby."

"Good. I'll buy him more to keep him busy," Alex said.

"Operation distract Lukas is on," Sky agreed, raising her hand for a high five. I had a feeling they weren't going to be as successful as they hoped. Lukas was nothing if not tenacious when he had a mystery to solve. He'd been investigating mine for two years.

Alex pulled me into a hug.

"What's this for?" I asked.

He let out a long slow breath. "Just happy to be home."

Jet hissed and dashed up the stairs to the loft. "You had to bring the ghost cat…"

LETTER FROM LISSA

Dear Reader,

Thank you so much for reading *Marked by Shadows* the sequel to *Stalked by Shadows!* This is the second mystery in the Simply Crafty Paranormal Mystery series. If you enjoyed this series check out my Kitsune Chronicles Series starting with Witchblood or my Haven investigations series beginning with Model Citizen.

Be sure to join my Facebook group for fun daily polls, writing snippets, and updates on new releases to this series and others. For a sneak peek at my work before it's published join my Patreon group. Patrons receive three new chapters a week and many other perks. For monthly updates on what's coming out and character shorts subscribe to my Newsletter. Also check out my website at LissaKasey.com for new information, visiting authors, and novel shorts.

If you enjoyed the book, please take a moment to leave a review! Reviews not only help readers determine if a book is for them, but also help a book show up in searches.

Thank you so much for being a reader!

Lissa

ABOUT THE AUTHOR

Lissa Kasey is more than just romance. She specializes in in-depth characters, detailed world building, and twisting plots to keep you clinging to the page. All stories have a side of romance, emotionally messed up protagonists and feature LGBTQA spectrum characters facing real world problems no matter how fictional the story.

Ascendance (Dominion 4)

Absolution (Dominion 5)

Haven Investigations Series:

Model Citizen (Haven Investigations 1)

Model Bodyguard (Haven Investigations 2)

Model Investigator (Haven Investigations 3)

Model Exposure (Haven Investigations 4)

Evolution Series:

Evolution: Genesis

Boy Next Door Series:

On the Right Track (1)

Unicorns and Rainbow Sprinkles (2)

Simply Crafty Paranormal Mystery Series:

Stalked by Shadows

Marked by Shadows

Made in the USA
Monee, IL
16 October 2020